T0117037

BIBLE HOAX

THE ULTIMATE TEST OF FAITH

Travis S. Colbert

iUniverse, Inc.
New York   Bloomington

Bible Hoax
The Ultimate Test of Faith

iUniverse books may be ordered through booksellers or by contacting:

iUniverse
1663 Liberty Drive
Bloomington, IN 47403
www.iuniverse.com
1-800-Authors (1-800-288-4677)

ISBN: 978-1-4401-6213-8 (pbk)
ISBN: 978-1-4401-6215-2 (cloth)
ISBN: 978-1-4401-6214-5 (ebook)

Printed in the United States of America

iUniverse rev. date: 9/10/09

INTRODUCTION

Hello. Welcome to the beginning of a great adventure that will make your soul want to venture. The heart of this novel didn't start when I wrote INTRODUCTION, it began with a child who pretty regularly was taken to Sunday church service, but didn't like one bit of it. You had to sit still, be quiet, it was just a bunch of adult people praising this "thing" that no one could see. There were a million other places that I would have rather been.

At the age of eleven, I experienced something that was meant to forever stick in my mind. Whenever someone would ask me if I believed in God or I would just happen to think about him myself, I always would announce that "yes I believe."

Deep in my heart, in the back of my thoughts, I knew that I didn't. I knew that I better say I believed in and loved God because grown-ups have told me all about hell and the stuff that God did to Old Testament era people, but I didn't love him, my feelings were totally indifferent. This way of thinking would carry on for the next twenty years; rarely did I let him into my life. I believed that there was a God, that wasn't the problem. I just didn't want to deal with him making my decisions, so I procrastinated about reading the Bible; I tried to negotiate with him on the few occasions that I did call his name. Belief in God is shown by allowing him to have the final say over your life; I couldn't give God that much control.

During this time, I got a family. A wife and two kids... and I'm not relying on God for nothing, but being the persistent father that he is, the Lord would talk to me through my children, out of the blue, every so often, one of my boys would ask me "why don't we go to church, Daddy?"

Slowly, seemingly out of nowhere, the Lord started honing my imagination through various daydreams which usually occurred as I drove to and from my job. Very exciting, in-depth, detailed thoughts about different situations began forming in my mind. I called them 'Mind Movies', and I would add new scenes and details onto these 'Movies' everyday. *I've never been a creative minded person, so suddenly being empowered with a deeper level of thinking was very intriguing and fun.*

One evening while driving home, He instantly put into my thoughts, "I can make a movie." At that moment my brain went from zero to sixty in one second. I had all of the major scenes played out in my head in minutes. *This marked the first time that I 100% believed that there is a God.*

"This is crazy, I ain't no Hollywood writer." I fought not to accept my new ability, I truly did, it was hard NOT to accept that this wasn't just dumb luck or my imagination, and most importantly, that this was not some ambitious quest created by me. *God doesn't always call the qualified, but he does always qualify the called. This is why my editor doesn't understand why I can't "spuce up" my author bio; the only qualification I have and need to write this book is God's anointment.*

I could truly feel the Lord's presence all around me, but as I accepted His destiny for my life, I still stopped him at the door and refused to accept his ticket into my heart, even as I begin to step up my spiritual questioning of the world.

In three plus years, I went on to pen three totally secular screenplays, having at times thought I was close to a breakthrough, but in the end there was no fruit for my labor. I had no idea these trials and tribulations were testing my faithfulness and grooming me for something so much bigger. *One of the worst lies many people have accepted about God is that he has left us here by ourselves. The world has made the terrible mistake of believing that after the biblical centuries were completed God stopped anointing people to carry out special purposes.*

There were so many times that I wanted to quit. There were so many failures but each time that I failed, he would put a new idea into my mind, a new way to assess my situation and rejuvenate me to keep going. When I was at my lowest point in believing that my writing career was meant to be, the Lord put the greatest, most daring idea into my mind to steer the disbelievers and the 'fence-riders' towards realizing the Bible's potential power for their life. *What's so head-scratching is I was still a 'fence-rider'.*

Out of nowhere, the Holy Spirit said to me, "People are always wondering if they should trust God, the real question is, can God trust you?" Then, I was asked, "What if the world was given scientific evidence that the Bible was a fake, what could happen?" *He knows that he can't get the attention of society as a whole through just using the Bible anymore; people think it's outdated, that it doesn't pertain to their life and times. He knows that a grave lack of faith in his Word is why his creations are enduring its current harsh times, so he's reaching for us our way! Through entertainment!*

More questions followed, "What internal truths would lose their fear of being revealed as my characters and the world around them must choose between believing their 'eyes' or faith? What role will society's culture play in people's decision-making, how could it effect their views and ultimately their choices? How will the lives' of the faithful evolve? And most importantly, how can all of this relate to and parallel the direction our world is heading in, so that we will reassess the priority that God has in each of our lives."

BIBLE HOAX... THE ULTIMATE TEST OF FAITH has been evolving ever since, I have been evolving ever since, starting months after I began writing this book, when I took Christ as my savior. I see it now, all of the pieces to my life's puzzle that started way back when I was eleven have come together and steered me to pen this book. As I wrote this novel before I got saved, its conclusion was built around doom and gloom, but when I came to Jesus and laid myself down, God showed me what this book was really to be about: love.

The Lord's spirit has crafted and shaped every page of this novel. His spirit has spoken so openly to me. Via entertainment, God is reaching out to the world like never before. That is the calling this novel has that possibly no other novel before it possesses, our Father allowed me to craft a modern day tale that will honor and glorify him, while at the same time not handicapping me by lessening the story's carnal entertainment value. So by the end of the book, after all of the blasphemy, killings, hatred, suspenseful plots, a brilliant and mysterious psychopath, and twisted love stories, lived out through my intertwining characters has thrilled your 'socks off': those who have not yet come to God will be inspired to reach for their Holy Bible and begin to forge the greatest relationship they'll ever share. *God loves us. I know the world doesn't want you to believe that, but he does… I just felt like telling you that.*

This book has six main characters, I tell this story through overlapping snippets of the moments that shape and propel their lives forward towards their unseen destiny, so pay close attention, the story moves fast.

Until now, there has never been a book or a movie focused totally on modern day people and their relationship with God that has captured the imagination of the general public. Congratulations! Don't think for a second that luck is responsible for you being one of the first to read God's exciting gift to us all. You are so blessed. Enjoy.

CHAPTER ONE

John 4:23 - Yet a time is coming and has now come when the TRUE worshipers will worship the Father in spirit and truth, for they are the kind of worshipers the Father SEEKS.

Thousands of years in the making has dwindled down to mere days, the time has come. Everything that humanity has built itself on is about to be shaken by two sentences from one ancient man, who planted a seed meant to destroy God's power here on earth by attacking humanity's belief in the Bible.

Who was this man? Was he someone who had seen Jesus but chose not to believe? Was he someone who had only heard of Jesus and through his finite mind couldn't comprehend the anointment of such a man? Or was he someone intimate with the Word itself, a lead participant who snuck out the truth for the world to see? The disbelievers won't care. Who he is will be of little consequence to them. Their only concern will be geared towards what he delivers.

Satan has helped to fill the world's 'bowl' with hatred, anger, greed, and mistrust, now the bowl is about to overflow. He has longed for the fruit of this day. His followers will number many.

They will follow him in spite of being given exact instructions on how and why not to follow him, but they choose not to listen. Their daily disobedience grooms them to accept this seed's pending devastation as enlightenment.

The serpent knows that he is going to lay claim to so many new lives. He knows that so many will come to him and will be indifferent about their choices. They do exactly what he tells them, yet they don't believe that he is even real and that he's their master. Their choices are about to drag everyone through hell on earth.

Time has made them complacent. Jesus has been at the right hand of the Father for so long that people have gone from believing, to believing that He isn't coming back, to believing that he doesn't exist at all. So many others believe that he does exist, yet they will not completely commit.

Time is also a liar. It has told them that they will always have it, so they've become procrastinators. All God does is love them, yet so many fear his path. He is a spirit; he put his himself into each one of them, so when you love someone completely and unconditionally as God does, because they are a part of you, you'll do anything to save your beloved, so he takes advantage of the opportunity afforded to him by the very one who meant to destroy him.

By squeezing their hearts' to see what comes out, mankind is stripped naked, exposed like Adam and Eve.

A new era of transparency is about to begin. God is anxious to see who will make a stand and be strong in him, just like he told everyone they should. Humanity's day to trust, have courage, and endure is here. It will bring about great days for Satan. But even greater days lie ahead for his creator.

This is the story of six individuals, who reside in an American city with the most unique name in the world; Anytown.

As each of the world's citizens does their walk through mankind's ultimate test of faith, this is their personal journey.

The calendar in Anytown reads late October, but the daily temperature lately has been anything but autumn-like.

Appearing as if they were sent down directly from Heaven, hot rays of sunlight shine brightly through the colorful murals stained on the long rectangular windows of this small countryside church. Joyous singing from the six member choir fills this small chapel, located just five miles outside of city limits, and seemingly the hearts and minds of its twenty seven member strong congregation as they stand and rejoice the Lord on this bright Sunday morning.

Amongst those in attendance, seated on the back row closest to the double exit doors, is once in a while church attendee, Ed Wilson, a well kept, slightly overweight man of European descent. He is accompanied by his wife, Sherry Wilson, their eleven year old son, Devin, and daughter, Mary, who is eight.

"This is boring, how much longer until we get out of here?" Devin, always a little sparkplug, whispers to his father, who gives no visible response to his son's impatience but fumes inside due to his disrespect.

As everyone continues to praise Heaven's name, Devin, visibly bored and angry, flops down in his seat and begins snatching wildly at his tie to loosen it.

Discreetly, Ed continues watch over his antics until the point where he can no longer hide his displeasure, which he conveys through a quick, but forceful kick to his son's shin and a spine tingling stare.

Inside the extremely modest two bedroom apartment that he shares with his grandmother and three cousins, Melvin Jenkins, awakens from his nightly somber in a pool of sweat caused by the unseasonably hot weather and their ancient air conditioning unit that blows out only a breeze of cool air.

There are two worn down beds inside he and his cousins' phone booth sized bedroom. Sixteen year old Melvin is the oldest; he shares a single size bed with his five-year-old boy cousin, Malik. The other bed is occupied by Malik's twin nine-year-old sisters, Rene and Rhonda.

He gently nudges Malik out of his deep sleep. "Little man, wake up." The girls hear his baritone voice rise from his scrawny chest; it causes them to slowly begin to stir.

In the kitchen, dressed in her faded and stained, but favorite ankle length nightgown, May, the children's grandmother, whose smooth facial features don't fit her advanced age, painfully stands over the only working burner on her decrepit stove, lively humming one of her favorite church melodies as she prepares everyone's breakfast: fried boloney.

May is not the type of person that would allow the dilapidated surroundings of the ghetto or a debilitating injury to her right leg and hip - suffered years ago during a workplace accident – to ever get her spirit down. Since long, long ago, she has let God and the Bible serve as her refuge from the adverse conditions that surround her home.

She turns and smiles when she hears the creaky door to the kids' room opening up. Melvin's short, slender frame, beneath his nappy overgrown head of hair, comes staggering out into the rest of the tiny apartment. He and his beloved grandmother (Me-ma as he likes to call her) exchange a warm glance, after which, he takes a step back to peek his head inside the bedroom. "Hurry up guys get dressed, Me-ma is almost finished making breakfast."

Outfitted in a nice pair of jeans, which by middle class standards wouldn't be considered that nice, Melvin sits down at the small kitchen table. His grandmother takes notice of his attire. "Hi Mel, I see you got your good clothes on again, sweetie."

He in a not so nice tone replies, "It shouldn't be a big surprise Me-ma, these are the only good ones I have."

Melvin didn't intend to hurt May's feelings, but he does. Her upbeat mood disappears along with the cheer on her face.

Her grandson senses her discomfort, so he walks up and

places his hand on her shoulder, kisses her softly upon her cheek, then, lovingly soothes her, "Do you know that everyday I wake up and I thank God for you more than I did the day before?" He continues to massage her heart as he lavishes praise upon her for taking him in after his father and mother abandoned him at the age of three. He gloats about how strong she is for also taking in her only daughter's three children, and never once taking out her life's frustrations on them, like so many others would if they had the extra responsibility of an irresponsible relative's children forced upon them.

"God rest your mother's soul... I know one day my son, your father, is going to get off those drugs and come see what a good man the Lord and myself have raised you to be." Riding in on a wave of pride, happiness returns to May.

Not wanting to dampen her mood again, Melvin throws her a fake grin and goes back to his seat, along the way he angrily thinks, "I hope that piece of garbage never comes back."

She almost slipped, but through past mistakes, May knows that it would be very painful to Melvin if he knew his father called and talked to her just days ago, but didn't want to speak with him. May tries to get Melvin's father to talk to his son the one or two times per year that she speaks with him. But he never does.

Dressed for school, the children come out of the bedroom making all kinds of racket, playing and poking one another, totally ignoring the small red roaches scrambling for their lives along the wall they playfully push one another up against.

Being the responsible man-child that he has been for eight years now, Melvin takes control of the situation by gently commanding the kids to calm down, keep their hands to themselves, and have a seat.

They all sit at the wobbly, hard plastic table that supports the gray cloth lying over it. Malik frowns harshly as he looks over and sees his grandmother lifting their breakfast from the frying pan. "Aw man, not fried boloney again."

Up in the hills overlooking the city, six foot seven, bronze chiseled, pro basketball megastar, Bryant 'Flight' Michaels, is playing host to a camera crew and thirty young boys and girls on the grounds of his thirty five acre estate.

The black man's dream and the white man's wish is in the mist of serious damage control. He is America's number one athlete-celebrity, and there is no public figure that cares more or has more financially on the line when it comes to public perception than 'Flight'. No platinum chains sprinkled with priceless diamonds here. You gotta go find one of those second tier sport stars if you want to see ridiculously baggy jeans being worn. Around here, there is no slanguage used that may possibly turn off white collar corporate money, however, in large part to his dynamic special powers on the basketball court and the rough neighborhood that he was born in, there is just enough street credibility for all of the hip-hoppers to love.

The disadvantaged children are having the time of their life at his beautiful home. Dressed in their swim trunks, several young kids run around in the grass enjoying a game of freeze tag, while a group of older boys attempt to show off their fancy moves on the outdoor, full-sized basketball court. The main attraction, however, is his Olympic sized pool and the see-through, forty foot, spiraling waterslide that empties into it. A gorgeous man-made rocky waterfall, complete with a grotto, provides the tropical backdrop for this piece of paradise.

The three man camera crew, led by the director, films the boys as they play ball. All of the children are required to wear the 'BRYANT MICHAELS LOVES THE KIDS' t-shirt that has been handed out to them. During an intense game, one of the sweaty boys begins to remove his shirt. "Hey kid, don't do that, if you're not in the pool, you need to keep your shirt on," barks Mr. Director.

Michaels walks over to the film crew and excitedly shakes hands with its leader. "Man, I know this story on me, showcasing the foundation I've set up to help these poor kids, is gonna do wonders for my image after all the crap I've been through lately."

The 'crap' he is referring to are the true confessions from his ex-wife confirming the longtime rumors of his various affairs during their marriage. Negativity like this does nothing for the image of America's most beloved and famous athlete, who has his many product endorsements tied to his Christian values and high morals.

The undersized director reassures him, "Oh yes Mr. Michaels, showing you out here having a good time, letting the public see these sad kids playing at your home, is going to help put all that garbage in your rear-view, get people back to talking positive about you."

An hour later, the two put the final touches on this afternoon of spin control by orchestrating a sit down interview, in front of the crowded pool, with a beautiful little girl on his lap, during which, Michaels raves about the money he gives to help the needy and the guiding force in his life; his unwavering faith in his Lord.

As a good looking, lovingly attentive, forties something, father and husband, David Gimmer, has it all. He is the senior executive director of operations at Positive Image Health Care Insurance, which is a small firm located deep inside the urban core of the city.

David, at this very moment, is seated in his Italian leather swivel chair, conducting his daily 'state of the business' meeting with his newly appointed V.P. of Operations man, Brandon Myers.

The *MTV Cribs* decor of his office screams, "I am the man in power and I want everyone to know it." He has the best leather sofa for his in-office waiting area, the enormous large screen television is there not just to entertain but to show power, the lush carpeting that only his office is furnished with, the personal soda machine, the gaudy gold trimmed glass trophy case with illuminating lights inside that shine down on all of his academic and professional accomplishments, and finally, the wall that used to be there before he had it knocked down in order to double the size of his work kingdom and comfortably accommodate all of these luxuries, serves notice to everyone just who the boss is.

In an office building where nothing is lavish, or top of the line, David's office is like a mansion in the middle of the projects. And that's just how he planned it; he loves the contrast.

During their meeting, Brandon Myers, a young up and comer in the health care business world can not keep from losing his focus on the task at hand as his eyes continually float above and behind David's head to the only prominent features on the light blue wall behind his boss. There alone hangs a gaudy four foot by four foot gold plated crucifix, and the equally large glass case enclosed snapshot of David's favorite hero, Bryant 'Flight' Michaels, flying through the air, dunking on some helpless victim of an opposing team. The hugeness of these ornaments looms over the room and continually snatches away Brandon's attention.

At the end of their productive hour long sit-down, both men are happy, they stand up and warmly shake hands. Brandon picks up the files lying at the corner of David's desk. "I think those are wonderful ideas, David. Those numbers really work, our low income customers will save money, while the plan will still allow us to turn a good profit."

David basks in the compliment. "Hey, I'm not going to run my firm like those greedy bloodsuckers at other health care corporations. The Lord did not put me here with these people for that."

The last part of that otherwise beautiful sentiment gives Brandon, who is half Mexican and half African-American, cause for pause, but he moves on.

"Come over here with me, Brandon…" David gets up and stands in front of his glass wall, which separates his office from the population, "Do you see all of those people, Brandon? Do you notice the common thread between them all?"

From the second Brandon walked in for his first day of work, he noticed that all of his co-workers were white. "Not really, David, tell me, what is the thread?"

"The thread is that all of them are beneath you. You are their boss, I give you the authority to have them do anything that you ask, and I bless you with complete control over them all."

"Wow! Thank you, David. I appreciate that."

"But always remember that just as they must yield to you. You must yield to me. I am the only one who has authority over you. This is like your Garden of Eden, Adam. You have power over everything that is before you; just don't mess with that tree in the middle...," David looks him in the eye, "I am the tree in the middle."

Brandon, a reliable Christian, is stunned by the strangeness of David's speech, "I'm going to do a great job for everyone, sir."

"I know that you will."

As his V.P. exits the room, with a pleased expression on his face, David thinks, "He seems like he'll be a pretty good boy for me. He doesn't seem like the type that would give me problems." David's thoughts bask in all of the contributions that he has made to the lives of those who are "beneath" him.

While he stands in front of his floor to ceiling length window looking down his 'nose' at his subordinates, David's thoughts flip through the multitude of times that his father would take he and his younger brother aside into a quiet room, then, fill their young impressionable minds' with propaganda, myths, and half-truths about America's brutal history in the "good 'ol days".

David resents so many things about his upbringing. The weight of his thoughts propels his body back to the comfort of his chair.

Brought on by self-doubt, his thoughts turn defensive against themselves, he puffs his chest out and says with valor, "I am nothing like them, I haven't been for a long time, God blessed me when he helped me climb out of my parent's darkness. Look at me; I am an angel for these people around here. My parents would have never done the things that I am doing."

"Mr. Gimmer… Mr. Gimmer, your wife is on line one, would you like for me to put her through?" His secretary's voice, through the intercom, redirects his focus.

"Could you tell her that I love her and I will call her back soon? I have another meeting to attend."

She does what her boss asks, but moments later she's back on the intercom. "She says it's very important, sir."

He picks up the phone. His wife, Sasha, has awful news. Their beloved fifteen-year-old daughter has been busted for skipping school. David can handle that, heck, his daughter is a focused, goal orientated, straight A student, "So she decided to be wild and crazy one day, so what sweetheart, it's not the end of the world."

"Honey, I didn't want to tell you this, but I know you'd be upset if you found out some other way. The girl that Gwen skipped school with isn't white, she's…"

Lessons taught long ago hijack the calm from David's mind and soul.

CHAPTER TWO

Melvin's world is a land where an academic minded young man will at some time or another be laughed at or ridiculed, because some of the natives feel he is somehow trying to be uppity or just plain wasting his time by caring about that "school shit". Negativity towards the school system runs rampant in Melvin's world, but my God is he smart.

We all know a Melvin. He is that kid in school that's not popular and doesn't have many friends. Melvin is that kid that we all make fun of and call names, then, we grow up and call him by a different name: boss.

Unfortunately born with two left feet and a measurable lack of hand-eye coordination, Melvin quickly figured out that athletics would not be his way out of poverty, so he puts all of his energy into navigating the long road to reach financial success, seeing how the street life is not a button that he would ever push.

The indifferent approach towards education by those around him has lead some weaker minded men to question whether they are doing the right thing by not jumping onto the fast track and "getting that paper" like the hood idols around them. The most supportive response a young scholastic mind is going to get on the 'block' is an unenthusiastic, "Oh that's good, little nigga, keep it up." People who take the slow track towards financial freedom aren't highly applauded in this land.

Undeterred, Melvin presses on, intelligently navigating the long route by outworking those in the system that he is supposed to fail against. When bragging to an ear that will actually be interested in his bragging, he doesn't hit them with a bunch of test score numbers, "I'm one of the smartest kids in the nation... period." It makes him feel so good about himself when someone from his neighborhood actually responds with real interest.

As he walks down the broken glass littered streets of his world, with his bookbag on his back, and his 'good' jeans covering his legs and bottom, Melvin Jenkins is definitely one of the proud men around here that's strong enough to be different.

With a look of disgust, he takes in a panoramic view of his neighborhood. "I'm so sick of living in this shit hole." Melvin turns his attention to the rotting project building across the street. He fantasizes that the huge 'storage camp' and the broken down playground next to it, where two men are beginning the process of openly selling drugs to an addict that approaches them, is a gigantic mansion with beautiful flowers and open grass surrounding it.

Snapping back from this brief escape brightens his words. "I'm a get my family out of here. I'm gonna make it. I know I will, it's just gonna take some time. Just stay focused."

Melvin has watched many of his male peers make the leap over to the fast money game, guys whose fathers, brothers, uncles, and cousins have been lost to the trappings of the street, guys who swore as children that they would never end up like those who preceded them. But they do. And Melvin, with great pride and focus pushes on, against this black hole stocked full of quickly fulfilled desires and lost futures. He knows that they are heavily influenced by the persuasive messages obtained through music and television - yes! - Melvin watches and listens to these same messages, but he does so with a healthy amount of enlightened scorn attached.

Me-ma has successfully schooled him against listening to the dangerous enticements the sensationalism of the media and his neighborhood teach. But as the musical intro goes, on one of the celebrity lives and homes shows that Melvin watches daily, "You ain't a thing if you ain't got no money/ women/ cars/ and rings!"

He takes a left at the corner, bringing him to within half a block of his high school, which serves as a highly recognized and accomplished academic retreat for the ghetto's brightest and most focused students.

From behind, the growing rumble vibrating out of a booming car stereo system heightens. The blacked out windows are the only thing that isn't shining like a diamond on this ride. The huge chrome rims and bright orange custom paint job, accented by sparkling flakes, scream out for the owner of this restored '68 Camaro, "Look at me, I'm different, I'm win'n, baby!"

Melvin wants to fully assess all of the car's attributes as it slowly rolls by, but this is the hood, he can't take the chance the car's occupants will mistake his staring at the car for staring at them.

Well ahead of him, the Camaro eases to a stop, alongside the curb right in front of Melvin's small high school on the big hill. He passes it as he gets to his destination and begins his long trek up the three separate flights of stairs that lead to the front door.

"Yo Mel, come holla at cha boy," shouts the driver.

He's apprehensive, the blacked-out window is only a fourth of the way down, and all he can see of the driver is the top of his navy blue New York Yankees baseball cap.

Melvin 'dumbs down', so he doesn't seem scared by the driver's attention, "Who dat is mane?"

Much to his relief, the driver lowers his window revealing his identity. It's Dane, a close neighborhood friend of his when they were younger. "Who dat is? Since when you start talkin' hood? Get cha silly ass over here, actin' like you don't know ya boy." Dane's huge grin reveals a mouth full of gold teeth covered by diamonds.

"What's up Dane, damn bro', you rollin' like that now?" Melvin asks with more than a hint of envy as he closes in.

"Yeah, I'm doin' my thang, makin' a little cake now. It's barely 7 o'clock, what you doing here so early?"

"I got this little project I got'a finish up. What you doin' up so early?"

"Hustlers don't sleep G, we move dem thangs all night," declares an unknown voice from the passenger's seat.

Once Melvin gets to the car, the old friends slap hands. Melvin, then, leans down to see who the passenger is that screamed out rule number one from the hustler's bible. The green fitted sports cap draped across his eyes doesn't conceal his identity at all, not when Melvin immediately notices the elongated lump of gunshot grazed skin that horizontally stretches across the left side of the passenger's neck.

He knows him, it's Stamp. To him, Stamp is that guy you're cool with because he's friends with your friend, but you don't particularly like him yourself. The three of them all went through junior high together.

"What's up Stamp, I ain't seen you for a minute."

His lanky body slouches in his reclined seat, his hat and freshly cornrowed hair presses against the headrest as he blows on a fresh cigar. A forty five caliber chrome handgun rests on his lap. "I know you ain't, that's cuz you don't ever come hang out on the cut with us, actin' all scary." There's obvious resentment in Stamp's words, in spite of his relaxed demeanor.

Just as Melvin is about to speak up and defend the distance he keeps, Dane chimes in, but it's hard to tell whether he's defending his old friend or being sarcastic. "You know Mel don't fool around like that, he's tryin' ta be somebody."

"Dawg, I've just been busy helpin' take care of my cousins and grandma an everything."

"If you really wanted ta help yo family, you'd get cha broke ass out here wit us, grind, and get some of this paper." Stamp testifies as he pulls a three inch wide stack of jacksons from the front pocket of his crisp blue jeans. Melvin takes a longggg look at his cash.

Lost in memories that never happened, Dane stares at the high school he never attended. Dane had the grades to attend this select school, but he chose to dropout. His motto was, "You can't be coo, sittin' up in schoo." School couldn't satisfy his cravings, Dane loves to be 'the man', and around here you ain't gonna be the man by going to school.

"Naw dawg, keep going to school, maybe that'll be the way you can get the hell up out of here," Dane says softly.

Stamp animatedly tells all doubters. "Man, fuck school, these honkies won't let us get out of the hood. They didn't put us here ta let us out, and since we can't leave, you might as well get money like a king by taxin' these peasants!"

Dane totally ignores Stamp's defiant proclamation, "Keep doin' ya thing, Mel. Yo, we out…," he and Melvin slap hands as each of them lean in for a light man hug, "aiight baby, I'll holla ya." Stamp returns the boom to the stereo as Dane pulls out into the street.

Now Melvin can get his stare. He watches the tricked-out ride guide away until it disappears behind a large building at the corner, before he starts back up the school's steps; doing so refocuses his mind to the big picture. "They're out here making money now, but prison or murdered, one of the two, if not both, is gonna happen…"

The enemy tries to take over his thoughts, "You working that minimum wage job ain't helpin' nothing," but it doesn't work, "I'm not going to let these streets kill me."

After Sunday morning church service, Ed Wilson and his family return to their isolated, aging, Victorian style farmhome on the outskirts of Anytown.

Ed's focus is entirely on Devin as the normal guy persona, exhibited in church, is completely missing as they walk inside and everyone takes the time to place their coats on the rack or inside the closet next to it. He is still furious with Devin for his behavior this morning.

Showing zero signs of emotion, he stays almost stride for stride right behind Devin, as his son walks through the living room and into the kitchen. "What are you doing, Dad?" Ed continues on like he's heard nothing. He has a plan, he always does.

Trying his best to ignore his father, Devin casually opens the refrigerator to find a bite to eat. From behind, Ed violently kicks the door shut, his ice cold, blank face never cracks.

Devin takes off! Fear fuels his sprint back through the living room. Sherry and Mary stay far out of the way as Devin races up the stairs towards the sanctuary of his bedroom. Although it has never been directed towards him, Devin has seen this type of crazy behavior from his father before.

Ed stalks behind his much smaller adolescent son, not trying to catch him, just staying close enough to antagonize the terror he knows his first born is feeling.

No stumbles. Devin makes a perfect, explosive leap to the top of the stairs, which sets him up to burst down the short hallway and into his room. His legs almost fly out from under him as his momentum is suddenly stopped upon grabbing hold of the doorknob. The young man gathers himself and puts his weight behind slamming the door shut. At the last moment, Ed wedges his open hand in the doorway preventing its closure. The door stops prematurely, as the sound of his father's crunching fingers ring in his ears. Ed screams out in pain.

The terrified boy retreats back to the farthest corner of the room. "Dad, I'm sorry, I'm so sorry! I didn't mean to." Huffing and puffing as he tries his damnedest to hold in the pain, Ed attempts, without success, to wiggle his fingers. Being overly demonstrative, his face shows his anger to Devin.

Lessons have to be learned, this is the first time Devin has had to crumble into the panicked, curled up 'ball' that he is in now.

Ed asks matter-of-factly, "What are you feeling right now, Devin?" He gets nose to nose with the shivering boy, "Devin, I have never hurt you, but if you ever disrespect our Lord again…," Ed screams, "in His fucking house!," then whispers, "I will be forced to do just that… Now, go wash your hands, I'll be calling you and Mary down for supper in a short while. Fuck my hand hurts!"

"Oh, o.k. Dad," Devin cautiously moves around Ed's hovering presence, then, darts into the bathroom across the hall.

The pain from Ed's swelling hand begins to kick up a notch, with every ounce of force in his body, he tries to wiggle his fingers again, but you wouldn't know it from his hand's response.

He heads back through the hall destined for the kitchen downstairs where his rail thin, subservient homemaker wife is already hard at work preparing his plate of food. Along the way, he passes Mary, who is on the way to her room, he gives her a quick pat on her backside.

Rounding the corner into the kitchen, Ed is pissed off about his hand, and upon seeing just the first one inch of Sherry's being, he redirects his anger into his favorite direction. This anger is built on knowing that he controls every faucet of his wife's life, it builds to its usual feverish pitch, just like it has, at some point, everyday and night for the past eleven years.

Ed routinely stands in front of her, with his fist raised, posed like he is about to give her the worst punch out of all of the thousands of punches he has brought into her life since the twenty eighth day after they met. He does this just to get a kick out of seeing her fear, to ingest another feeding of the high his total domination has over her. But today, for right now, Ed gives her a break. "Hurry up with my lunch, lard'o." He coldly demands while grabbing control of his 'throne', with his good hand, at the head of their old, square Oakwood table.

Ed's indentured servant speed-walks from the stove over to the table, making sure to carefully lay down his plate full of mashed potatoes, roast beef, green beans, and dinner rolls, which were all simmering in the oven while they spent the past hour and a half at church.

Sherry stands to the side of her husband's shoulder as she takes a napkin and tucks it neatly into his dark colored button-up shirt.

Excited by her close proximity, Ed harshly grabs Sherry by the waist just as she's about to walk away. He leans down and sniffs at her crotch. She fights to hold it together, she wants to cry out due to the weight that this life with Ed has placed onto every part of her being, but she knows that is not an option. Ever.

Ed stands; he slides his hand beneath her gray, polyester knee high skirt brutally squeezing upon her thigh on his way up. Sherry grinds her teeth as she braces for impact. Her mind recites what she always tells herself, "You're o.k, you're gonna be o.k, just hold still."

"You're not eating tonight, you're starting to get obese." This ridiculous remark is made as this monster gets off on abrasively squeezing and fingering his wife's desert vagina.

Sherry Madilyn Wilson has taken enough beatings to know that she better turn and look him right in the eye as he laughs at her; but not too much in the eye, because he doesn't like to be stared at, and she better not do too much wining either, that irritates Ed.

To endure his abuse, her deprived mind dreams of digging her nails deeply into ten spots on his face, and in one revenge laden show of strength, she rips away huge strips of his skin down to his neck. Oh, how Ed's three dry fingers would be dripping with her juices, if for once, she could enjoy seeing him flop around on the floor bleeding, him knowing, like she knows, that his entire life has been taken over, and there is nothing he can do to stop it.

Ed lets her go, he stands there, smirking at his prisoner. Wobbled, Sherry musters up a quick "just to please you" grin, only so she can move away without any further harassment. He knows that she hates it, but he loves to see her smile after absorbing one of his numerous forms of sexual torture.

He settles back down; free now to enjoy his meal alone, as always.

Upon his meal's completion, the tyrant dabs the corners of his mouth with the bottom of his napkin, then, pushes his empty plate an arms length away. No words need to be said, Sherry knows that's the signal, she rushes over and puts his dirty dish into the sink.

"Sherry, call the kids down for supper. And since you're not eating, you can begin washing the dishes early."

Maintaining his place at the head of the table as his quiet, stiff children take their seats and pick up their forks, Ed asks with surprising humanness, "What's the first thing you do before you begin eating, have you two forgotten?" They each hand over one of the two dinner rolls on their plate. "Thank you, now both of you, say it," he looks over at Sherry and gives her one of those looks.

In unison, his three servants recite. "The God of the home, as a show of thankfulness for him guiding us toward our salvation in Christ, shall always be given the first bite of life from all those he Lords over, before we are to nourish our own body."

He is pleased. Ed takes in a deep breath, slowly exhales, then, continues his daily, persistent brain washing over his family. "Very nice everyone, God is pleased, Jesus is pleased, and I, the gateway to Jesus, am pleased. You have moved yet another step away from life in hell."

"God bless you, Father." Sweet, little Mary says.

"God bless you, Mary. The Bible tells you that the only way to Heaven is through his son. Kids, you know that I have been chosen. I am Jesus' son. If you want to be spared from perishing on this evil, satanic land, you must always please me. Because pleasing me, pleases Jesus, which pleases God. I have been chosen to be the Lord of your life, until you die and move onto God's kingdom, then you will be worthy to walk with me and Jesus, beside our Father."

"Yes father," the kids say in unison.

Basking in his power, the almighty takes a bite from the roll Devin gave to him and declares, "Enjoy your food."

Ed is very impressed with his work, he thinks, "Great job, Ed. I am still amazed at how well all of this is going. They believe everything!"

CHAPTER THREE

Having switched into blue jeans and his favorite Bryant Michaels replica jersey, David presses the intercom button to enthusiastically divulge, "Diana, I won't be taking anymore calls this evening, I'm about to…"

"I know, I know, you've been talking about it all week, you have tickets to see your beloved 'Flight' Michaels tonight."

While trotting over to the closet to grab his thin leather jacket, with a child's excitement, David explains, "He's the greatest player the game of basketball has ever seen. There's nobody like him. Jordan, Kobe, and Lebron would have gotten schooled by this guy."

"Well I hope you have a great time tonight, sir."

"Thank you. When my daughter arrives just have her come right in please."

"I will definitely tell… oh, oh wait a minute, she's walking through the door right now."

"Great." David clicks off the intercom, his spirit lifts to even higher heights as he anticipates the sight of his cherished child.

"Hi, Daddy!" Gwen, whose body is just beginning to fully blossom into womanhood, comes into the room wearing a warm smile for her father, and sporting her authentic Bryant Michaels' NBA warm-up suit.

David cheerfully comes from around his desk to meet her in the middle of the room. She blesses him with a peck on the cheek. Gwen correctly reads the buzz upon her daddy's face. "Look at you; you're really pumped up about this game tonight, huh?"

"Heck yeah, this is our first time all season seeing his greatness in person, do you know how much money I had to spend on getting us the seats for this game?"

"It's going to be awesome. Ready ta go?"

He places his hand on her shoulder as they walk out together. A thought stops David, and therefore Gwen. "Tonight is all about having fun, so I'll wait till tomorrow morning to speak with you about this spook girl your mother told me you were caught skipping school with."

"Daddy, I..."

David interrupts, "Tomorrow sweetheart."

"Thanks for bringing me to the game tonight, Dane." Inside the stadium, strolling around the lower level's rapidly filling corridors is Dane, Melvin and Stamp, walking along together in a horizontal line.

Dane and Stamp are dressed to impress - 'hood rich' style. Their bodies are draped in all the latest ultra-expensive name brand hip-hop clothing, plus all of the above average priced jewelry that two mid-level project drug dealers could possibly buy.

As they move along, Dane fights to hold in his laughter as he checks out Melvin's attire. His eyes start at his dingy, worn out sneakers, on up to his color fading pair of jeans, finishing with the equally 'played out' matching shirt that Melvin always wears with it. "Hey dog, I'm a take you out and I'm gon' buy you some gear tomorrow," he snorts, "I can't take looking at this shit no more."

Stamp laughs loud and obnoxiously, while simultaneously pointing at Melvin's aged clothing, "Hell yeah, I'll throw in a hundred on it. Go buy this boy sum'thin please, somebody!" A twenties something, young white male, passing by follows Stamp's lead by giggling at Melvin's appearance. He sees him laughing, at that moment, a lasting impression is made in Melvin's mind.

Embarrassed and offended, Melvin fires back, "I'm not out here to impress people. Anyone can buy impressive clothes, I impress with my brain... Everyone can't say that, now can they?"

Stamp glares at Melvin, "What you tryin' to say? That we're stupid?"

He tries to conceal his fear, while quickly clearing up the meaning behind his words, "Hell naw, I ain't saying that, Stamp. It's just; I'm a get mine, when it's my time. I like nice things, but I work now, and the little bit of money I make goes to help my grandma," only half believing his own words, Melvin fights with the only advantage he has, "God is going to bless me with the things that I want, as long as I continue to serve him. Besides, I don't trip off the same things y'all do."

Dane is slightly offended by the last part of that statement, with his own pride he snaps back. "If by same thangs you mean, trippin' out seein' yo mom cry because you paid the light bill when she couldn't... Being able to go eat at a nice restaurant just like every other person that don't live in the hood do... Or maybe, it's the feeling of buying yourself something with money you worked for..."

Stamp 'sweeps' up for his homeboy. "And oh yes, Melvin, movin' coke is work, high stress high reward, America's most dangerous job. I got a better chance of going to the suburbs and doing some white boy's job than he has of surviving in mine."

Acknowledging the limited wisdom and truth in their words, Melvin nods his head as he concedes, "I can see ya point of view, but I know there's a different plan for me."

Dane disputes. "Screw that, I'm sick of waiting around for

God's better plan. The rich ball, while we fall. Now I see why they walk around so damn happy all the time, the whole world is different when you got money."

Stamp can't resist adding his 'two cents' again. "Hood money is what has you standing here right now. You out here chillin', havin' a good time, about to watch 'Flight' get his clown on tonight, I hope he dunks on somebody real bad!" Stamp emulates Michaels dunking and hanging on the rim, screaming, as he posterizes yet another opponent.

Dane, "That's real talk, Melvin. Sittin' there trying to live some goody goody lifestyle has done what for people like us? What, you waiting around for God to deliver blessings to you that may not happen for another fifteen, twenty years. Shit, living in our neighborhood, how do you know that you even have fifteen, twenty years? You better start living for right now, you can worry about God later. You missin' out on the good life, homey."

Outwardly, Melvin immediately dismisses his reasoning, but Dane's opinions attach to him.

Ten rolls back, just to the left of half court, David and Gwen excuse their way by people as they navigate past knees and feet to their seats.

"Halfcourt baby, we doin' it big!" Dane jubilantly proclaims as he and his two friends find their aisle and shuffle through to their seats.

Melvin's engine revs-up when he looks out onto the court and takes in a close-up view of Bryant Michaels leaping through the air during pregame lay-up drills. He taps Dane on the elbow, "Thanks again for bringing me to the game, bro. I'm glad you had that extra ticket. This is going to be crazy."

David looks over his left shoulder and sees gangsta clothing covering three young black threats heading his way. He frets, "Oh God no, I hope those criminals don't have seats behind us."

David's hopes abruptly deflate when Dane and the guys sit

directly behind him and Gwen. David puts his arm around his daughter's shoulders.

Curious, Gwen turns to see who's behind her. Stamp greets her eyes with a very flirtatious survey of her tanned, unblemished face, and her budding breasts.

David notices where Gwen's attention is focused; he also catches Stamp's obvious attraction to her. He gives Gwen a not so gentle squeeze to get her back in line. With hushed anger, Dad gives her crystal clear directions. "Don't turn around again, keep your eyes on the court."

The final buzzer blares throughout the arena. The final screams and yells from a raucous home crowd boom loudly. At the end of a hard fought victory for the home team, in which Bryant Michaels dominates, elated fans begin to fill the aisles of the sold out arena, merging onto the steps to leave the building.

During his normal ratings grabbing, on the court and still sweating, postgame interview, 'Flight' gives his standard rhythmic answers to the reporter's questions. "We still have some room to improve… that's a good team we beat tonight… I just prayed to God that we'd win… God was just on our side tonight."

Still riding the thrill, David and Gwen slowly inch their way along their aisle, "So what did you think Gwen, 'Flight' really had a great game didn't he?"

"Yeah, he was incredible, Dad." Feeling the heat from a set of stationary eyes, Gwen takes an innocent peek over at Stamp, then, quickly turns away.

Dane and Melvin are in front of Stamp as they all file out. Stamp taps Dane on the back, then, whispers into his ear, "That lil' freak keeps staring at me."

Dane looks her over. "Yeah, she's cute, too bad she's with her pops…" upon closer review, "I think she's a lil' young tho'."

Stamp doesn't respond, all he's thinking of is making his introduction to Gwen. He whispers to himself, "I don't care who she's with, I'm a holla."

David, with Gwen right behind, gets out onto the steps just

before the guys do. They pass by, Stamp seizes the opportunity. He reaches around both Dane and Melvin, to gently touch her hand, "What's up beautiful, what's ya name?"

David hears every word that is said to his precious little girl. He instantaneously whips his head around and shouts at the first brown colored skin that he sees; Melvin's. "Don't you dare speak to my daughter, you animal!" Everyone within a hundred feet stops to look around for the cause of all the commotion.

Feeling the pressure from an irate father bearing down on him, with a crackling voice, Melvin sets the record straight. "It wasn't me, I didn't say nothing!"

"I said it, bitch! What you wanna do about it?!" People congestion impedes Stamp's rush towards him.

When you grow up in an environment where many of your confrontations, even the small ones, are settled by violence, the world tells you there's no backing down, no apologies; even if you are in the wrong.

Their live interview stops. Bryant and the reporter spin around, looking for the source of the fracas up in the stands.

"I sure hope everything is alright up there." Michaels anxiously states.

Being a seasoned veteran of NBA sideline reporting, Mr. Interviewer knows that he should quickly get the attention back to the subject at hand. "Whatever it is, it seems that security is coming to handle it. So Bryant, besides yourself, what do you think was the biggest key to the team's success tonight?"

Melvin and Dane fight to hold Stamp back as the guards rush into the stands from the floor. Dane reasons with him. "Chill out man, I got some work on me. We can't be gettin' arrested." That information takes Stamp's temper down several notches.

David hurries Gwen away by the hand as the guys are quickly surrounded by four charged up security cops with billy clubs and pepper spray, out and primed for use.

On his way up the stairs, David turns back and makes eye contact with Stamp. He slowly mouths out, "Die nigger."

Stamp 'itches' to run up there and beat his head in, but he has bigger fish to fry right now.

"Officer, there was just a little misunderstanding, it was our fault, we're sorry. We don't want any trouble fellas." The calming effect of Melvin's polite, refined voice begins to put the officers at ease.

"O.k. guys, let's get it movin'. We're not going to have any problems go down on our property, so we'll just escort you gentlemen out to your car," says the lead officer.

Dane is in total compliance, "not a problem, sir."

The lead officer directs his attention towards Stamp, who is still huffing and puffing as he watches David and Gwen disappear into a sea of humanity, "Any issues with that from you?"

Dane and Melvin are on 'pins and needles' as everyone waits for Stamp's delayed answer, "Whatever dude."

Through his passenger's window, Stamp stares down the four security personnel who escorted them out of the arena. They stare back, snickering as they do. "Man I hate deez krackers. And that peckerwood gon' wait till he get to the top of the stairs, then say that shit."

"You know every time they get mad at us, even the ones that was cool with you before, gon' call you that," asserts Dane.

"Disrespect me like that, he lucky he ain't get shot."

From the backseat, defying the wisdom of not aggressively questioning someone with an attitude and who has just pulled out a handgun from underneath his seat, Melvin challenges Stamp. "Stamp, what did you except him to do? You disrespected him when you came on to his daughter right in front of him. Look at all these names you call them, you can be disrespectful and racist, but if they do it to you, you wanta kill 'em?"

Stamp is furious at Melvin's bravery, he halfway turns his way, he glares at Melvin through the corner of his eye, "What, you sidin' wit them now? Dane, why you bring this corny lil' bitch wit us? You actually believe ya white now, just because you try to be like 'em? They don't give a damn about you!"

"Just because I value my education, that doesn't mean I'm tryin' ta be white."

All alone in Dane's backseat, Melvin immediately feels trapped once Stamp's head and torso angrily snap around towards him. Lacking a good comeback, Stamp resorts to fear, "Bitch, you say one more word, Dane is gon have ta clean yo blood off the spot where your ass is now, say sum'thin else."

Dane passionately intervenes while steering his ride onto the city streets. "Ain't gonna be no black on black crime up in here! Chill out, the both of you startin' to get on my nerves."

CHAPTER FOUR

"Good game tonight, Max, God bless. Good game tonight, Leon, God bless. Good game, Will, God bless." Ricky Walters of the NBA's two time defending champions goes around to each of his teammate's locker and congratulates them on another victory.

The old saying opposites attract holds true when describing the relationship between good friends and locker room neighbors, Ricky Walters and Bryant Michaels.

Ricky Walters is white and very active in the church to which he is a member. He always wears cowboy boots, speaks with a bit of his grandpa's country twang, and loves his old Wrangler jeans. Ricky is far from being the star of the team, being the last man off the bench makes him more cheerleader than basketball player.

Ricky waits for some coaches and several media types to finish heaping their praise and repetitive questions upon Michaels before he gives his friend a victory hug. "Great game tonight, buddy. You carried us. You were the only one who seemed to be able to make a shot."

Their lockers are side by side, but it's easy to tell who the superstar is and who the guy is that's just happy to be here.

"Thanks Rick, I was doin' it for you, sorry I failed."

"Failed at what?"

Michaels enjoys a quick jab at his buddy, "Blowing them out, so that you could get into the game and actually have a good reason to shower before you go home."

"Oh you got jokes now."

Walters sits on his padded wooden stool, Michaels chills in his burgundy Italian leather recliner, as they relax and begin unraveling their taped up ankles.

Afforded a quiet moment, Bryant reminisces back to the first night he hung out with Mr. Ricky Walters.

What 'Flight' has never been aware of is, this night, this night that on the surface looks to him like so many other nights he's had that are full of partying, played a giant role in shaping his personal and spiritual life for years to come.

It's nearing the end of Michaels' junior year in high school; by now Bryant Micheals has been known as 'Flight' for four years, every since he easily dunked a basketball in seventh grade. His parent's are throwing him a party, full of family and friends, at a rented clubhouse, in honor of him being selected first team All-America for the second year in a roll.

Martha and Terrance Michaels could not be prouder of their son. They talk about his extreme athletic success to anyone that wants to listen; and everyone does. Once Terrance saw his son's grade school basketball prowess totally explode during his fifth grade season, he's trained him for this success every since.

Michaels' girlfriend, Stacy Stunning, walks into the party accompanied by her new friend, Ricky. They chat with Michaels' parents and a couple of his gawking uncles before she's able to make her way to the guest of honor, whom she can see is already beginning to enjoy the evening judging by the open bottle of champagne he is holding.

Stacy is visually perfect. Her beauty is as dynamic as her name. Flawless caramel skin from toe to head, beautiful hazel eyes, that are so stunning they almost draw attention away from her succulent lips below, and I won't even take you through the laundry list of details that describe her slender, but curvaceous body. She's just the type of 'eye candy' you would expect an athlete of Michaels' stature to enjoy. But there is more to Stacy Stunning than vanity, something much deeper and true.

"Hi baby… What up Rick, I didn't think you would show up."

"Thanks for inviting me, Bryant."

All day, since early that afternoon, Stacy has had a bad vibe about this evening. The slight wobble she detects from her boyfriend, after he loosely throws his head back and indulges in another drink, only heightens those feelings.

"Hey Ricky, you watch over my girl when I'm not around, so I got nothing but love for you, baby." Michaels knows that Ricky is no threat towards him and Stacy, so why not be the sophomore basketball player's friend and gain his loyalty.

Stacy finds it odd that Bryant has not reached down to deliver his normal tight hug and peck on her lips upon greeting her. "What's up babe? You lookin' good, as always." Bryant's words sound a bit forced and cold to her ears.

Some classmates of theirs' call Ricky over to their table, as he walks away, Stacy steps towards Michaels for that kiss. She's disturbed by the rigidness of his suddenly tense body. He gives her a brief peck on the cheek, after which, she notices him take a quick glance to his right.

Stacy stares right into her love's eyes, they always give him away. Her annoyance shows as her thoughts swirl and her eyes focus. "Why is he peeking over where all those girls are?"

"So what are you and Ricky gonna do tonight. Y'all gon chill at the house, do some Bible studying, go to a movie, what? Why you lookin' at me like that, what's wrong with you?" He asks, while his eyes 'dance' to avoid hers.

Her hurt soul wants to break her down into tears, but pride fights it back. She glares at two scantily dressed young women across the room, as they whisper and giggle to one another while 'rolling' their eyes at her. They provide the final piece to the puzzle, she has a good hunch about what's going on. Being the lady that she is, Ms. Stunning is not the type to star in some girl fight especially not with Bryant's family that's flown in from California, Kansas City, and Georgia, all in attendance. It fully dons on her as she looks around at all of his friends who have brought along an alarmingly high number of beautiful young women to the party; all of which are obviously way past high school age.

Her friends told her that this would happen. Her mother was also very honest with her. Vicky Stunning warned her daughter that there would be others. That 'Flight' was still very young, and very impulsive, so she shouldn't get too wrapped up into thinking that he is going to stay with her forever, or be faithful. Most importantly, Mom told her that there would be nights like this; nights that she could not bury her head in the sand.

Even after sharing all of the questionable details of Bryant's behavior with her mother, over an over again, Stacy would profess that her boyfriend loved her, that he was worthy of her heart.

Vicky knew that her daughter was searching for a reason to continue clinging onto her denial. "That's why I know you are just setting yourself up to have your heart broken, because you have more respect for yourself than that. God will send the right man into your life when you are ready, and honey, right now, you ain't ready. He'll bless you with a Christian man, who will live his life according to God's laws and not his own. And you know good and well that 'Flight' Michaels ain't livin' like that." Mom always ended with that sticky message before she would allow her baby out on a date with him.

Stacy and her parents always attended church, but she didn't turn her mind, body, and soul over to God until she and Ricky became friends and they begin reading and discussing the Word together each day. They set aside unbreakable time each day for their faith.

An angel spoke out of Ricky's mouth when he said to her,

"Do you know why so many men in prison turn to the Bible, and seem like they have really turned their life around while they're inside? Because that prisoner doesn't have the distractions that we have anymore, God is all he has to lean on. That prisoner can't dwell on material possessions, or what people think, they mean nothing; God is all he is left with. When a person is left with nothing, no family, no friends, no freedoms, suddenly they realize how important God is. They seek him, they'll live and think how he wants. But the sad thing is, for so many of them, that when they get out and return to this see it, trust it world, God gets pushed to the back burner once again, and they fall right back into what they came out of... You and I have to treat our faith like we're in prison."

Stacy would frequently lay that parable down onto Michaels' closed ears, in hopes that they would start to bond spiritually. But her newfound faith farther fueled Bryant's cheating, by allowing his conscience to o.k. his behavior, on account of him rarely being able to talk Stacy into fornication.

That night, Stacy breaks up with him right there on the spot. Her broken heart and fast getaway completely occupies her thoughts causing her to forget to tell Ricky that she is leaving.

Michaels is semi-crushed as he watches her go, he senses a deep seriousness in her tone and that has him a bit worried, but it's not enough to motivate him to go after her. He wants to reconcile their relationship, but his arrogance and self-centeredness, plus, the sermon that his meal ticket hungry, 'old school but tries to act new school' uncle, Gene, offers up prevents that from happening on this night.

Gene starts off by telling his nephew nothing that he didn't already know, all he does is reinforce the pampered lessons Michaels has been picking up on since the age of twelve, when a beautiful seventeen year old woman ended his virginity only because she wanted the "privilege" to tell others that she was the already well publicized basketball prodigy's first.

Gene reminds him. "There is no need to go chasin' her,

nephew. Don't worry about if Stacy and you are over, because your not. She ain't going nowhere. As long as she is your main one, women with men like you, learn to accept a few groupies along the way."

"I don't know unk, she seemed pretty serious this time. I don't think Stacy is the kind of girl that'll be cool wit that."

"Hey, you said she's saved, didn't you?"

"Yeah, that shit done messed my game all up, too."

"Well I'm a tell you how to take your game from messed up to stepped up! If she's saved, I'm sure that she wants you to be saved, so… get saved."

"Come on, Uncle Gene, ta tell you the truth, I really ain't ready to be living no Christian life. I wanta kick it for awhile. One day I'll do it, but not right now."

Uncle Gene is offended. "Man, you ain't gotta live it like how you think. I know you see your aunt Macy and ya cousin Eddie tryin' to live life all perfect an shit; and that's cool, I ain't knockin' that. God likes that, they good, solid Christians, but you see me, don't you?" Gene leans back and stretches his arms out horizontally, which lifts his tight button-up shirt over his plump and hairy belly.

Bryant giggles, "Yeah Uncle Gene, I see you."

Animated, "You see I don't live no goody goody life, baby. I still act just as crazy as I've ever been. I smoke, drink, chase titties around, lie if I need to, still cuss a mu'fucka out in a minute! Now quit laughin' young pup, I'm going somewhere wit this; my point is, I'm a Christian too!"

Now Bryant is really laughing hard, "Unk, you ain't no Christian, you wild as hell!"

Gene makes the devil smile. "True, I am. But that's the beauty of being a Christian that few people really know about. You can still do whatever you want, act as crazy as you always have, and still go to heaven."

Bryant slowly ends his laughter, "No you can't. You gotta live how God wants. That's what I've always heard."

"Not really… as soon as you say to Jesus Christ that you take him as your savior and you repent for your sins daily, you're saved, period. Read it in the Bible, that's straight from the Word of God."

Bryant's mind begins to ease, "For real?"

"That's scripture, baby! We live in New Testament times, now in Old Testament times, o' ya uncle be burnin' in hell cuz you had to do works or good deeds to go to heaven. But in our day and age - thank you Jesus! - all we gotta do is take him as our savior and ask for forgiveness when we screw up. That's it, works don't get you in."

Bryant never forgot what his uncle said that evening, in fact, that next morning he arose from his slumber and said to Jesus Christ that he takes him as his Lord.

And just like Uncle Gene predicted, the very next day, fractured self-respect and all, Stacy forgives her boyfriend amid all of his loving "I need your forgiveness" talk and her first ever bouquet of flowers. His sweet talk, her inexperience, and her strong teenage emotions towards Bryant was all too much to abandon at that time in her life.

Because of the emotional way women love, many will make heavy personal sacrifices, in hopes, that one day her special somebody will return the love, warmth, and faithfulness that she has brought into his life. But, in Stacy's case, there was just one factor going against her, for her deepest of prayers to ever be answered; Bryant never made the commitment to change. No matter how much Stacy prayed for it, God could not force change upon him.

Even though, she remained and their relationship progressed farther after this episode, seeds were planted, and their bond was never quite the same again.

Ricky snaps his fingers, bringing his friend back from his daydreams. "You're kinda quiet dude, what cha thinkin' about?"

Ricky knows exactly what Michaels was so deep in thought about, when, with a smirk, 'Flight' asks, "Why don't you come to the club with me tonight, just have a drink… It's been a long time since you've had a little sippy sip. Come on, just loosen up one time, don't worry, you'll still be a Christian in the morning."

Ricky picks up on Bryant's subtle references back to that night, a night that saw Ricky party wildly until the wee hours of the morning after Bryant told him a comforting lie about why Stacy left the party.

"Whether I have a drink or not has nothing to do with me being a Christian. I just don't want to be around people when they are in that type of environment."

"So you don't think that clubs are fun at all?"

"I didn't say that. They're a whole lot of fun."

'Flight' is baffled. "So why don't you go at least every once and awhile?"

"Because I'm trying to always honor God in the choices that I make, the places that I choose to go. I don't think that you'll give me much grief if I say that there isn't much God honoring going on in the nightclubs? Besides, since my one forgettable night years ago, that's the scene I've been trying to get you to back away from."

"Come on now, I don't go out as much as I used to…," Ricky stares at him blankly. Bryant burst out laughing, "O.k., o.k., well if I had someone special that was waiting for me at home, things would be different."

Ricky picks up on his underlying message, he chooses to casually move away from what he knows will become a touchy subject, so he offers, "Why don't you come to church with me tomorrow?"

Michaels hates when Ricky puts him on the spot about going to church, so like every other time that invitation is extended, his mind races to come up with an excuse. "Nuh, not tomorrow man, it's our off day, I don't feel like having to put up with all the attention, people mobbing me and everything. I'll go with you another day."

"That's funny… because you have no problem being mobbed when you're out gettin' funky in the clubs?"

Ricky's counter turns him defensive, "I don't want to attract attention away from the service. They should be there for God, not 'Flight', and let me say this… don't you ever say the word funky again."

With a frustrated smirk and chuckle, Ricky shakes his head. He's heard it all before. "I pray to God that you're not full of excuses on Judgment Day, like you are with me about Sundays."

"I won't need any excuses on Judgment Day. Just because I don't attend church, and I go to clubs, doesn't mean I don't care about my salvation. The most important thing I can do on this earth is to help other people, nobody in my position is as generous as me. I donate more money and have more charity events to generate more money than any other athlete or celebrity in the world. I do God's work everyday, so you can kiss my ass."

"So do you read the Bible?"

"No, I don't have to read the Bible to follow God."

Such ignorance doesn't even get him emotional, "Bryant Michaels, are you serious, were you just serious when you said what I know you just said?"

"Dead serious, so what."

"If you don't know God's Word, how can you know God, how can you follow him?"

Not wanting to answer such a revealing question, 'Flight' takes a detour. "What's been going on with you lately? You ain't never been like this, out of the blue, you've been questioning my faith a lot these last few weeks?"

Ricky gets a very distant look in his eyes, "I don't know, Bryant. My spirit has been stirred lately, concerning you, something is not right."

"Yeah, whatever…," Bryant doesn't really believe Christians when he hears them say that through their spirit they can feel this or sense that. It all sounds very fake to him, "just keep praying for me, Ricky, and let God worry about me."

"I will… You say that you pray, but how do you pray without knowing and speaking His Word to him?"

He laughs. "Goodness, would you stop, I don't need to speak God's Word to him, for what, it's the Bible, I think he already knows it."

"It's essential, Bryant. You are so gifted, you do very special things for kids and you send the right message out when you praise God publicly, but the way you live your life away from the cameras and microphones has to be your praise to God also. I remember that a certain lady we both know told you that."

"I don't care what you say, or what she says, y'all don't know my heart. I am saved; I pray every night to be forgiven for my sins."

"I have never said that you aren't saved-"

Just then, God reveals to Bryant's thoughts that he prays only when he needs to ease his conscience over some sin that he has every intention of doing again. Fearful, Bryant's mind quickly shifts, purposely leaving the truth behind. *He thinks that it's random chance when thoughts like this speak in his mind.*

Their heads' turn as they both see the team's under-paid, but overly flamboyant and purposely goofy, starting power forward, Mike Law, walking over with a big smile on his face, and his eyes fixed on Bryant. He chuckles as they slap 'five', "Ricky got you hemmed up again, don't he?"

'Flight' is thrilled by Mike's intervention, "Man, you know how he be doing me!"

Mike, "C'mon Rick, I know you over here trying to tell him not to hit da club up wit me tonight. Ain't you? I know you was."

"I ain't said na'thin about no stupid clubs."

"Good, then don't. God built man and woman to mingle and enjoy each other's company, so what better place could there be then where the clothes are small and the song is telling all the girls to throw that booty in reverse?! Believe me Rick, God understands."

Bolstered by Mike's like mind, Bryant's nodding head shows his solidarity with him.

"So the both of you are saying God is in support of the clubs? That he finds it acceptable for a man who has givin' his life to Jesus to spend his evening in a place where fornication, adultery, lies, drug abuse, and violence occur on a nightly basis? Is that what you are saying?"

Silence.

Very rarely does Mike not have a comeback, "Whatever dude, when do you ever stop talking about God? Can't you talk about anything else? Don't you get tired of that sometimes?"

"No."

"Whatever homeboy, hey, Flight? Holla at me before you leave."

Michaels is again left alone with Ricky, once Mike heads off towards the trainer's room.

"Bryant, I'm sorry, I'm not trying to be a dip, but something… O.k., I'll stop. I just love you, brother. You are my friend, so I will go until my last breath to make sure that we will walk and play together in heaven. Real friends aren't here just to lead you to some club."

That felt good, now Bryant remembers why he has kept Ricky as his good friend. "Thank you, bro. I appreciate the love, but I'm just fine, believe me."

Gwen and her lovely, career focused mother, Sasha - whom with good genes and some help from Anytown's top cosmetic surgeons has maintained her youthful appearance throughout these last few years of the forty seven she has existed - are seated at their circular marble dining table inside their spacious Mediterranean style upper middle class home. Gwen and Sasha are both enjoying a warm talk and a dieter's breakfast consisting of two eggs and one piece of lean bacon.

Sasha, adored in one of her many black business suits, is just as doting on her daughter as her husband is; when she allots the time for it.

In a bad mood and still wearing his pajamas, David stomps down from his bedroom and right to the coffee pot on the counter. Sasha is curious, "Honey, what are you doing, why are you not dressed for work?"

David gets his cup, then, joins them at the table. "I'm not going in; I don't think I can handle dealing with those people today."

"Dad just let it go, it wasn't a big deal."

His baby girl not being upset about what happened last night like he is, brings out all of David's racial paranoia. "Not a big deal, you don't ever let some spook put his hands on you! Oh, I forgot, maybe you'll just go ahead and have sex with one, seeing how you like to hang out with them now."

Sasha is furious that he would say such terrible things to their daughter. "David stop it, don't you dare talk to her like that!"

While she has only subtly spoken up against David's racism, Sasha does not share his closed opinions towards other races.

Gwen slams her fork down onto her glass plate, before running up to her room in tears.

David stares down at nothing, slowed by his own hurtful words. Just by looking at her spouse's face, Sasha knows that he already regrets what he said. She walks around the table to comfort him, but he ejects from her presence before she can get there.

Standing just outside of her bedroom, David can hear Gwen's sniffles. He timidly cracks open her closed door, "Honey, may I please come in and talk to you?"

Gwen does not answer, so he enters as she moves across the room from her desk to her bed. She lays face down, burying her head underneath one of her many decorative pillows.

David's tender voice asks that she sit up and hear him out. One of the three gigantic Bryant Michaels posters in the room hangs on the wall above and behind Gwen's head, as she slowly and reluctantly does so.

The posters contrast with an otherwise 'girly-girl' room, painted three different shades of pink and full of stuffed animals of all makes and sizes.

"I'm sorry about what I said, baby-"

"You are not sorry about what you said, you're just sorry that it hurt my feelings." Recently, David has grown more and more comfortable with his racist comments being spoken in front of his impressionable teenage daughter.

"Lately I've started to feel like I'm losing you to those animals. I've noticed you are starting to listen to their music, then, your mother tells me you ditched school with some black girlfriend of yours', and to top it all off, those pigs last night damn near tried to rape you."

"Rape me!? Why do you always assume the worst with them? Why do you hate different people so much?"

"I don't hate them, honey, I care about them. Your mother and I just think that you shouldn't mix with them on a close personal basis, because they'll bring you down. That's why we've been thinking about putting you into private school."

Gwen passionately protests. "No Dad, I wanta keep going to the school I'm at now."

"Well sweetie, then you better think long and hard about your actions lately, and keep those people at a distance." Gwen grunts and pouts as she feels the jaws of her father's supremacist attitude tighten and suffocate her open, tolerant world.

"I know you just think I'm just being narrow-minded, but watch how they act, the way they live, minorities never better themselves. I don't want you getting caught up in that."

"Dad, we see tons of successful black people everyday. Your favorite ballplayer of all time, the man that you think is damn near perfect, is black, remember?"

He snickers at her silliness, "Gwen, Bryant Michaels is one of those rare black people, like Oprah used to be. He's not like them, he's educated, he speaks well and lives his life the right way, because he is a man of God."

Smart-alecky, "Well my friend, Mia, the black girl that I skipped with, her BLACK father is the regional President for Pepsi Company and an ordained minister of a mostly white church. She's at the top of our class and is on pace to graduate at sixteen, and Dad, guess what, I even have a second black friend whose parents own and have built from the ground up their very own million dollar computer software business."

"That's awesome, Gwen. I'm not saying that there aren't any good blacks out there besides 'Flight', but just like with the Mexicans and Jews, there are just too many bad ones around to take the chance of getting too close."

"Doesn't the Bible say that all men are created equal, so shouldn't we love everyone, because God loves everyone?"

David's response is stacked on pride. "And that's what I do, that's why I love God. You know that I work in an all white company, right? But what color is the man right beneath me, who I have made the boss over this all white work crew? I chose a half-black, half-Hispanic man because God directed me that way, I could have chose anyone. I could go to any other health care firm and make triple the money I do now, but the Lord wants me to stay there and help poor minority people. It's my calling. So yes, I do love everyone; just like God said to do."

"So why do you talk so bad about them? You have minority friends, I've seen you talk with plenty of them even outside of work."

David chuckles at her naivety. "Just because I talk bad about them, doesn't mean that I don't care. And sweetie, I talk to Jews also, they work for me, so what. I'll say hello, chit-chat, I'm very polite to everyone. But they damn sure aren't my friends. Now your grandparents, they're racist, I'm not like them. They would have never done anything nice for other people. That's why God hates them."

Confused and frustrated by her father's justifications and the fact that she knows she can not change them, Gwen concedes.

CHAPTER FIVE

It is the middle of the night; all is quiet inside Ed Wilson's home. Wearing nothing but a pair of briefs and a dingy, old tee-shirt, he returns up the old, creaky wood stairs from the basement. The steps open directly into the kitchen.

No one is ever allowed down those steps; Ever. Sherry, nor the kids, would ever dream of defying his orders, but that is not enough reassurance for Ed's paranoia, so each and every time that he exits his private stratum he seals off the basement's door with three dead bolt locks that only he holds the keys for.

Ed ended his work downstairs a bit earlier than usual because his weary eyes were beginning to blur. But that's gone now, with each passing step, his sexual appetite energizes, perking up his tired body. As he walks and removes his shirt, his mind begins to lust for the same insane behavior it has enjoyed for the past two years.

"I almost feel sorry that Mary has to go through this. Having her life shattered before she even knows what life is about... however, it's kind of fun tho'. I wonder how far she'll fall into drugs or prostitution, God may bless her and she'll dig herself out of it early; but I doubt it…," out of his mouth comes a sinister chuckle, "she's going to be really screwed up."

The loud creaking wooden stairs, combined with the unpredictability of the man walking them, wakes everyone up. Just as it does every night that their 'savior' returns from the basement after doing whatever he does down there.

"Please God, make him go to her room first." Sherry knows that if he visits their daughter first, he'll be too tired to bother with her after he is finished.

Clutching her only friend, the only thing that she can talk to - her teddy bear - Mary pops up from her sleep. She shrivels into a ball, shaking feverishly, as she tries to fight back the tears and fears that her daddy sternly told her he doesn't like.

Through the pitch blackness of the night, Sherry judges the closeness of her husband's whereabouts by depth of sound as he slowly moves along the hardwood floor. She feels his presence growing close, just outside of their bedroom door, "Please God, no. Not tonight."

The monster passes, moving forth down the hallway. An unwelcome, vivid, and familiar daydream enters his thoughts. "No, I'm not going to do that. Don't think like that, that's evil." Ed pictures his entire family gathered together on the family room's sofa, stiff, paralyzed by fear, as he stands over them with a loaded pistol aimed at their heads'.

"Thank you, Father. Thank you," with clasped hands Sherry whispers.

Mary uses the same senses her mother does to gauge where Ed is. She knows now that her father is coming to see her. Between Mary's ears, the sounds of his footsteps trumpet. Then stop.

Her door slowly opens. A single sliver of moonlight shines into her room, spreading across her bed slowly. Mary speaks to the only listener she's had in her entire life, "Don't think about it, Teddy, don't think about it, God wants him to do this. Daddy does it because they love me." This sweet child utilizes her brain washed thoughts for comfort, but deep inside her eight-year-old soul, she knows that something is not right.

She peaks her head up. Ed stands in the doorway, smiling as he gently massages and squeezes his genitals through his briefs, "Sweetheart, time to wake up; it's snuggle time." Ed steps inside, closing the door behind him.

In the room next to his sister's, tonight, Devin isn't fortunate enough to sleep through what's going on, so he's angry. He's not angered by the deeds his father enjoys with his sister; he's pissed off because his peaceful night's rest was interrupted by that squeaking floor and the loud moans of his father's madness.

Ed Wilson rules over his family through a web of abuse that he has shaped and cultivated for many years. He makes sure that he and his version of God's love are their entire world. This is made possible by the one element that glues together his evil brilliance; the Bible.

Aided by lessons learned earlier on in life, Ed realized that if a master manipulator, like himself, took in an already deeply troubled young girl, then, ate away at the few crumbs of self-respect and dignity that hadn't already been destroyed; she, then, could be controlled to believe whatever and do whatever he wants. Even the most vile of ideas.

The ever increasing weight of Ed's onslaught has lead Sherry to 'bottom out'. Her mind is beginning to crack with hallucinations, delusional thoughts, sledge-hammering depression. Her hope and will to live is fading fast. And that's just what Ed has planned for all along.

At the beginning, Sherry really didn't believe any of her husband's gibberish about his extremely high place on Heaven's throne, but feeling like she had no choice, she went along with it. But Ed has repeated it so much, so relentlessly, that it's become all she can hear inside her head at times.

Ed enjoys plotting, then, playing evil games, just to torture Sherry's already brutalized mind. Over the past two years, Ed has developed a new way to torment and beat Sherry, without even touching her. But first, for the game to work he gives her a solid "just because" beating, then, from that point on, he is nice to her, he apologizes for what he did and does to her life. He asks her questions, strange questions like, "What goes through your mind as I'm beating you?" He talks to her like she's a human. Ed does this so convincingly that he gains her trust. Sherry dares to hope.

During these times, Ed really focuses his attention upon her. He asks and attentively listens to Sherry's answers from the multitude of questions that he asks her. Just when hope begins to shine a glimmer of light into Sherry's life, Ed turns out the lights. She's gotten comfortable, thinking good thoughts, hoping, and then, at the exact moment that Sherry cracks her first smile; an onslaught of two good sized fully charged male fists rain upon her head and body. He does this once or twice a year. Repeating the same pattern each time, building her up, just to purposely tear her down. After each time, it takes longer and longer for her trust to return, but Ed is patient. He waits.

He repetitiously drills into their heads' that they are worth nothing without him and that God will damn each of them to hell if they ever leave or don't follow his orders, this is the foundation of his role as 'the chosen one'.

He totally smothers and diminishes the size of his family's world. There is no freedom, no light for them to reach out to. Inside the four walls of their ancient Victorian home, lies their entire existence. They are never allowed out of it, except for Ed's carefully planned bimonthly visit to Sunday church service, but then it's right back into captivity they go.

Ed knew that doing all of these things would create the ripe soil he needed to grow and nurture his campaign. He said to himself long ago, in the hospital, as he smiled and looked into the eyes of his seconds old first child, "Devin, you are mine to control. Welcome my son, I will be your God."

The next morning, Sherry is up early in the kitchen preparing Ed's favorite breakfast combination: scrambled eggs, sausage links, and pancakes. At first glance, Sherry seems just like any other housewife as she stirs the batter for her husband's pancakes, but keep looking, you'll see a former child abuse victim, who was hooked on crystal meth by the fourth month after her eleventh birthday. Sherry has never experienced life without complete dysfunction.

Seemingly without cause, her nails brutally dig into her cheeks as she squeezes her palm against her mouth, blocking her screams. Out of nowhere, Sherry is engulfed by the throws of one of her many emotional breakdowns. In this one, as she rocks back and forth crazily, fighting back her roar, Sherry dreams of one day standing outside, alone, and letting her lungs and throat explode in one long soul-beaten yell.

Things have gotten that bad for Sherry, she can't even fantasize of escaping anymore. She's down to dreaming about just one good yell. The only real escape her sorrow has is through the tears that stream down her face, as her broken mind succumbs to the depression her horrible existence has cast.

Back to reality! She knows that Ed better not see or hear her weeping, that would be very costly. It's too good of an excuse to punch her around a little bit, just to give her something to really break down about.

Sherry's mind finishes its meaningless collapse, then, with schizophrenic precision shifts into her favorite part of the day. She hallucinates daily about defecating into the batter, or maybe urinating into it. Her fantasies feel so good, such a small measure of payback would be colossal in her mind, but she knows better; it would be too obvious, so she settles for his daily 'saliva cakes'. Her crazed soul giggles as she repeatedly sucks in her cheeks, building up as much saliva and mucus as possible, then, releasing it into the bowl to be stirred and cooked into his meal.

Having squeezed, to the last drop, all of the enjoyment out of the moment, Sherry's spirit and thoughts slip to a new low as she viciously chops up his eggs while they fry. "I hate Jesus' son, my Father. And I hate you for putting me here with him. I'm sorry, God, I know shouldn't, but I do. If I leave, I know I'll go to hell for betraying you, but I hate it here. Besides your house, Lord, I haven't been away from here in eleven years. I'm a caged animal, he won't let me go anywhere!"

She continues, mumbling to herself in an angry whisper. "I hate him, this house, this fucking kitchen that I'm always in; I wish I'd never had those stupid kids. Then he wouldn't have kept me. I would be free to be with some other man."

Stripping Devin and Mary's mother of her natural parental instinct is Ed's greatest demonic achievement. Even as newborns, Ed never let Sherry get close or bond to her children: no doting, no singing to or kissing on them, only feedings were allowed. Ed knew that if there was no bond, no empathy for the terrible things he puts the kids through, she would be less likely to try and escape the stronghold he has over them all.

Devin and Mary, also, are not allowed any together time. Even on the few occasions when they are allowed to venture out into their isolated backyard to play, it is never together, and it is always intensely watched.

Divide, and you will conquer, sums up Ed's thinking. He wants and receives indifference and abandonment coursing through each individual. He allows no one to hold lasting conversations; no one on one, no group, nothing, without his presence there. His nightmares that they will band together against him, then, bring down his kingdom won't allow it.

Ed allows no one to enjoy the only, even remotely, new item in their home; his bigscreen HD plasma television; except for the few programs, every so often, that his censorship deems appropriate. Ed watches television nightly after sentencing his family to bed. He is a big golf fan and he loves the dunks of 'Flight' Michaels, he tivo's them all. However, political debate shows are his favorite.

Sherry, Devin, and Mary know nothing about anything outside the walls that surround and squeeze them. Ed takes away every aspect of them living independent lives', so when the only voice that has been heard for the last eleven years says something, repetitively, it melts into them, until it breathes out of the very fabric of their being.

Breakfast is served. Sherry makes sure to check over the entire downstairs floor twice, making absolutely sure nothing is out of place or needs to be cleaned, before calling Edward down for breakfast. Her god better be pleased. "Ed, your breakfast is ready."

Panicked, her mind scatters in all directions, into every room of the house, fearing that maybe she left something out of place. Sherry loathes the meticulous inspections he routinely does. His footsteps close in.

"Is my syrup poured you fat whore?" She hurries over to the cabinet and snatches the bottle of strawberry syrup. Ed's servant has it poured over his pancakes before the 'chosen one' even enters the room.

With haste, Sherry moves back over to the countertop, and begins preparing the kid's meal. She sneaks a peak at Ed every time he takes a bite of his treasured cakes.

Her mind falls back into fantasy as she continuously peeks at her captor eating his meal; her dreams have come true, her saliva IS poisonous. With sick pleasure, Sherry's imagination watches as he takes that one magical bite which cuts off his air supply. Dopamine charges through her body as she intensely enjoys watching him flop around the hardwood floor, like a fish out of water, as he slowly, slowly suffocates and begs for her help.

"Um, um, that was delicious." His words partially snap Sherry back to reality.

Bear hugged by her crazed mind, Sherry forgets that Ed is not human, "Hey Ed, I was thinking that..."

His loud laughter interrupts her, as he dabs the corners of his mouth. "Thinking, you can't think, that's why your father and uncle raped you, because you're too stupid to think."

She awkwardly giggles. "That's true, but I was just wondering, maybe I could go out and get a job, you know, for just a few hours a week to help out. I'd love to help you, Ed?"

He pauses, then, frigidly turns towards her, showing her the same posturing that scared the daylights out of Devin. Sherry has seen this look on his face many times; she knows what's coming. She tries to back-pedal, "Oh God no, I'm sorry Ed, it was a stupid idea. I was just wanting to help my king, so I could prove that I'm a good wife. I'm sorry, please don't!"

Terror fills this battered woman from head to toe. She backs into a corner as he gets to his feet and slowly stalks towards her. "What are you saying Sherry, that I can't handle things around here anymore?"

She feels his deep, hot breathes hit her face, as he comes forth with the 'devil in his eyes'. "No Ed no, I know you are the god of my life, you don't need my help!"

With the precision of a striking Cobra, he snatches her by the throat, "You think I'm worthless like you are, don't you?" Ed spins her around, pins her arms behind her back, then, slams her forehead against the countertop, "Devin, Mary get down here right now, hurry up!"

"No Ed, please don't." Her blood, tears, and words fall helplessly.

"If you say one more word, I'll kill you."

The children rush down the stairs and into the kitchen. A sick excitement spreads like the plague through Devin's body when he sees his father's hold on his mother. He already knows what he's been called to do. Mary, who's as shy as can be, knows too, but she doesn't enjoy her mother's fate, or her part in it, with any of the zest that Devin does.

"Devin and Mary, your mother has broken God's laws. She wants to abandon her savior and therefore her salvation and join this Sodom and Gomorrah world, for this she must be punished."

Ed spins her back around to face her children. He puts her arms in a wrestling hold, above her head, so that they are pinned between his, exposing her tiny, frail midriff. He whispers into her ear, "Don't try to protect yourself; every time you raise your knees, I'm going to punch you."

"Please Ed, I'm so sorry." Her continued pleas fall on deaf ears.

Devin loves this. Ed's craziness is farther fueled by his son's eagerness. "Do it Devin, punish her for her sins." Sherry's first born runs across the room, bringing with him five hard knuckles that he buries into his mother's stomach. He delivers twice more to the same area. Ed reiterates, "Keep your knees down woman!" He pushes her to the ground. Devin's missile like feet and fists continue to pound away, beating her even as she curls around herself.

"Mary, your turn, get in there," Ed orders. Mary timidly strolls over to the action as Devin continues his work. She gets onto her knees and lightly hits her curled up mother twice on the thigh. "Harder Mary, the Lord has told my spirit that you must punish her or you will be punished."

Becoming sickened by the beating Devin is delivering, Mary gives her three solid hits on her back; just to please her daddy.

Finally Ed's content, "O.k. Devin, that's enough, stop, I said that's enough, I think she's gotten the message."

Devin is buzzing with adrenaline as he stands over his bleeding, battered mother.

Sherry's mouth is wide open for screaming, but no noise exits. Her pain is so great she can't cry or shout.

Father pats son on the back. "Thank you Dev, hopefully God will be forgiving and allow her to continue with us on our path."

Having just completed another day of school, from a nearby

bus stop, Melvin Jenkins boards a public bus that will take him to work another evening at his job well outside of the inner city.

Melvin enjoys the half-hour ride from his home to his job; it's peaceful, beautiful, and fills him with hope. No family, no school, no overcrowded apartment in an overcrowded, dangerous neighborhood; though he is still surrounded by many, it's one of the few moments he gets to be alone and relax. The ride also gives him motivation to keep working hard. His eyes stare out of the bus' windows everyday; they enjoy watching the tiny snippets of different lives go by. He sees meaning in being picked up in the torn down, frowning ghetto, then, dropped off in a stable, smiling part of town. This is the exact path he is determined to have his life go in.

Tuning out the surrounding strangers and the hip-hop music blasting into his ears from his headphones, Melvin gazes out of the window, in doubt about the present, "I've got'a get that health insurance bill paid up in a hurry… It's getting so hard to keep up with school and working so much," his uncertain future, "my grades are beginning to slip, I have to get them back up, so that I can get a scholarship," and the future of his family, "what are grandma and the kids going to do if I leave for college?"

Melvin steps off the sidewalk's concrete and onto the soft carpeting of the store where he is employed: Bobby's Kicks. The shoe store is currently empty. Only Faith Tillman, his fifties something co-worker, who is sitting on a stool behind the check-out counter, is around. Faith doesn't hear or see him enter. Her head is down; her mind is focused on the burgundy leather NIV Bible she is reading.

Faith puts her mark in place, then, closes the 'Good Book', as Melvin warmly greets her.

"I'm doing good, Mel, how are you doing?"

"O.k., have you been busy at all today?"

"Boy, I'll tell ya, it's been busy, busy, busy, until a few minutes ago. You just missed the rush."

Melvin makes a beeline towards the back room, so he can

switch out of his 'good' jeans and into his work uniform. While out of Faith's sight, he frets, "I sure hope we get busy again today. I know she's gonna start talking nonstop about God and Jesus, if we're just sitting around here with nothing to do," alarmed by his own honesty, Melvin immediately clears up any potential misunderstanding with our heavenly Father, "I mean, it's cool if she does, I don't care." A battle ensues in his conscience, "Yeah you do, no I don't."

Now in uniform, Melvin enters back out onto the floor with a clipboard in hand and begins checking stock in an aisle across the room from Faith. He likes his talkative co-worker, who also happens to be the senior minister at a local church, but he hopes by keeping busy and some extra distance between them, there will be less chance for his devotedly spiritual colleague to involve him in any deep religious conversation.

"How was school today, Mel?" Faith shouts across the room.

"It was o.k, I was a little tired towards the end tho'."

"I am so proud of you. You are a real man. I know God is going to reward you for being such a good, responsible person."

"Thank you." Melvin is working with his back to her, but he can feel her words and presence moving closer. "Aw man, she's coming over here."

Faith's heavy-set body, pale, but gorgeous face arrives, stopping right next to him. As always, Melvin's eyes are first drawn to the beautifully carved wooden crucifix, with its wooden Jesus, dangling from her gold necklace.

"Sweetie, you should have been at our amazing church service yesterday. You would have loved it. I think that the Holy Spirit really got through to some people."

Trying hard to camouflage his absence of interest, he replies, "Really, that's good."

"Why don't you come to our Saturday service this week, Mel?"

"Aw, I can't this week. I might come next week, tho'."

"Boy, you are always giving me some excuse."

"I'm going to go one of these times, don't worry… I've always wondered you're the head pastor at some huge church, right?"

"Yes, I am."

"So why do you work here?"

"I just like it, I get to meet different people, and hopefully, if they're interested, I'll invite them to our church. Many of our members, I've meet right here."

"So you don't have to work here for money?"

"No, money isn't a factor."

"Wow, that's crazy to me. If I'm working, I'm doing it for the money."

"Don't always base where you work around money. It can lead you to make some bad choices."

"That's easy to say when you don't come from my hood."

Faith moves on. "That's true. Oh my goodness, I gotta tell you about what happened to me earlier today."

The excitement in her voice draws Melvin in. He drops the clipboard down to his side and gives her his full attention, "What, what happened?"

"This guy, around my age, comes in looking for a good pair of casual shoes, right. So I'm helping him out, and he's asking me all these personal questions, then, he starts telling me about how good I look. You know, slow me, I finally started realizing, hey, he's hitting on me. So I politely tell him I'm not interested, but man, he just wouldn't give up. So he's like, 'is the reason you're not interested because I'm Hispanic?' I'm like no that has nothing to do with it. God will let me know when it's my time to have a man in my life and it won't matter what color or race he is, God will choose the right one for me…"

"Yup, that's right, He will."

"So after I said that, he shut up, got his shoes, and was gone. I tell women all the time, if some man is annoying you and you want him to shut up or go away, just start talking about the Lord… sadly, it works every time."

A young lady carrying her infant daughter enters the store, Faith turns on the charm, "Hello ma'am, I'll be right with you in a moment." She quickly finishes up her thoughts with Melvin, "Unsaved men looking for some booty leave you alone real quick when they find out you have Jesus in your life."

Faith's body walks away, but her words stay and have a profound effect on Melvin. He ponders, "That's kinda the same thing I do."

Flashes of all the different times individuals have or could have talked to him about faith reflect in his mind, but since he was outside of church, he ducked the conversation or the person altogether: Faith, his grandmother, the preachers on television that he always hastily turns away from, all have been 'shooed' away by him at one time or another.

The memories of these moments lead him to question his motivation for why he retreats every time the spiritual approaches. But just as he's beginning to elevate his internal truths to the forefront, he pushes them back down. His defenses go up. "I've talked about God with other people. I go to church all of the time and I pray… sometimes."

His thoughts ask him a key question, "But do you really believe?"

CHAPTER SIX

Ed throws a towel down at her, and says without a hint of caring emotion or sympathy, "Sherry, you have five minutes to have the table set and my children's food on it."

As her body recovers from the electrocution-like shocks of pain suffered from her beating, Sherry's brutalized soul cries out inside. "Lord, please end this; let them kill me, please."

At the far end of the countertop, Sherry's eyes catch a glance at what she sees as God's blessing, "Finally this will be over!" With what little ability remains in her body, she rises to her feet. Ed's staring suspiciously at her now; she prays that he didn't see what her eyes see.

He looks away, "Now!" She lunges for it, "Stick it through your neck," she says to herself. Sherry's hand races towards her ticket out of this horror. She has it clutched, but Ed stops her by the waist.

He squeezes her waist until the serrated knife falls from her hand. He snatches her in close to him. "No, my dear wife, I'm not letting you go that easy." Blood flies across the room and onto the far wall powered by the force of Ed's closed fisted backhand across her face.

From her seat at the table, staring at her bludgeoned mother floundering on the floor, Mary mindlessly rocks back and forth, trembling as she tightly clutches her teddy bear for comfort. Like a proud father, Ed extends his open hand, "Come here little girl, come sit on daddy's lap, come on sweetie." Mary's stomach is in knots as she methodically slithers down from her chair and over to her father.

"That's my girl." He lifts up her stiff body and places her on one of his knees. "You know everything I do for you… to you, is God's will. You wanta go to Heaven, don't you sweetie?" Mary nods yes as her daddy strokes her hair, "everything I do, God tells me to do it, right Devin?"

"That's right, Dad." Devin co-signs from his spot on the other side of the table, still charged up from the beat-down he just unleashed minutes ago upon his mother.

Devin, although emotionally poisoned, has never had to endure the physical abuse shared by the girls. Being the only other male, Ed permits him that luxury.

Ed stares a 'hole through Sherry' as she wipes her blood soaked face off in the sink. "The Lord was angry at your mother for wanting to go out into a world full of decadence and hate. Don't feel sorry for her, we did her a favor. The pain and anguish she would have received out there far outweigh this."

Fighting back tears as she quivers and wobbles her way over to the table, to serve the children their meal, Ed informs her. "Woman you have a lot of forgiveness to pray for tonight." Sherry's pummeled head nods her affirmation.

At the start of another Monday of ninth grade classes, Gwen is at her locker, which is along the wall of a high traffic hallway where students, of all races and creeds, are moving about in every direction. To keep from being bumped, Gwen darn near has to stand inside of her locker, as she searches through her assortment of schoolbooks for the one needed in her first hour class.

"Hey girlfriend!" Due to all of the traffic, Gwen hadn't even noticed that Mia, the African-American girl she skipped school with, has come over to say hi.

"Oh, hi Mia, where were you yesterday? I tried calling you over and over."

"I know, my parents had me in church all day."

"Wow, you had to go all day? Our church's services never last more than an hour."

"You're lucky, I'm all for going to church, but not all day. Five or six hours of God, in one day, is just too much."

"For real, I would have gone crazy too." Jenny Seever, Gwen's locker neighbor joins their conversation as she slams hers' shut.

Gwen. "I kinda like church and learning about the Bible, some of the stories are kind of interesting and we have a funny pastor."

Mia and Jenny glance at one another with a giggle, then, Mia flippantly disregards, "Whatever, church is boring. I can barely understand what the Bible is talking about. Don't get me wrong I love God, but all that junk puts me to sleep. You really like all that?"

Jenny heads off. "I'll talk to you guys later."

Not wanting to seem uncool, Gwen backpedals, "No, what I mean is, its o.k., but it's not like I'm all into it or nothing. I'm like you; I go because my parents make me... Hey, did the school call your mom and dad about us skipping, they sure called mine."

"Yeah, my mom was pretty mad, but she didn't go crazy. She just grounded me from my computer."

"Ugh, that sucks."

"Hey, do you wanna come to the sleep-over at my house this Friday, Shavon and Niesha are coming? I already asked my parents, they said it's cool."

A kaleidoscope of excuses zoom through Gwen's brain to cover up the only answer she knows her father will give, "Uh, um, my parents are really protective, they don't like me staying over other people's houses."

Bewildered, Mia laughs, "What are you talking about? You just spent the night over Janey's last month?"

Saved by the bell! The warning alarm sounds indicating to the students that there is one minute remaining until classes begin. Gwen snatches her book down from the shelf. "Hey, we'll talk about it later; I have to get to class, bye." She quickly merges into the 'Autobahn' of speed walking students racing to their class before the final buzzer sounds.

Her quick departure leaves Mia standing all alone. "Oh, oh o.k., see ya," Mia's words float away, never reaching their intended destination.

His bedroom is the size of a middle class man's entire home. The walls are totally covered with mirrors, which makes the room look like the size of a small town. His specially made bed is the size of two king sized beds put together. Black satin sheets cover it, him, a statuesque Spanish 'mamacita', whose naked body is sandwiched, snuggled, between an exotic Brazilian, and a caramel skinned, voluptuous African American hottie. Ladies and gentlemen, welcome to Bryant Michaels' world away from the cameras.

It is the middle of the night, the girls are all asleep, tired by the pleasures of a marathon sex session with America's most sought after bachelor. However, between all of that female and money brought beauty, lays one wide awake superstar.

Bryant Michaels is in the middle of doing what he often does after sex with members of his ever increasing harem of groupies; he's fantasizing, longing for the love of his ex-wife, Stacy. He enjoys these random women, he enjoys the Hollywood starlets that he chooses to date for a couple of months before moving onto the next 'it' diva, he delights in the envy that others feel for him because he is one of the few that has access to these opportunities, but when it's all said and done, the measure of all these women still fall short of her; Stacy Stunning.

He raises his head and a shoulder up slightly to have a look at tonight's chosen. He thinks, "Ugh, I would never marry any of these whores or have babies with them. They're just as beautiful as Stacy, but they're nothing compared to her."

Stacy loved this man. After Michaels jumped straight from high school to professional basketball, she was right by his side supporting him; continually trying to help him become a better man. She tried to make him see that Jesus needed to be the foundation that would keep him grounded as the overwhelming sea of money, fame, and women tried to sweep him away; all three succeeded. But that's not due to the fact that he didn't listen, he knew what she was telling him was the truth, he just didn't care enough. He WANTED to be sweep away by the indulgences within his reach. He wanted the lifestyle she spoke down upon, but at the same time, he wanted the support and stability of having a good God fearing wife at home.

On her way out the door, for the last time, after many half-hearted exits that she always returned from, Stacy was stopped by a conniving, desperate man, who once again convinced her that he would change. She really thought this would be the time that he actually meant what he said, seeing that he was serious enough to propose to her, and the fact that he defied everyone's advice, including hers', by not having her sign a prenuptial. He told her that's how she could believe that he would not cheat or lie to her ever again, but most importantly to Stacy, he once again pledged that he would fulfill the promise he made to her about strengthening his relationship with God. It was all a lie.

Well before marriage, Bryant and Stacy began talking about having children, but a part of God's spirit always told her to wait. She was very observant when it came to Bryant and how he operated. She picked up on how all of his baby talk would increase after he would be caught doing something, with someone, he shouldn't have been with. The Holy Spirit always told her a child would be just another way Bryant would keep a hold over her, so guided by her spirit and not her flesh, she time and time again declined when the subject of pregnancy would come up.

Finally, after four years of swimming in the same pool as other married to rich men wives, Stacy gave up. Her faith in Christ strengthened as her marriage weakened, she came to realize that she could not be happy with or commit herself to a man who had no discipline and did not love the Lord first and foremost. She realized that she made the same mistake so many other men and women make; she allowed her emotions to choose her mate instead of allowing God to choose him.

Stacy knew that she was committing a sin by dissolving her marriage, but she prayed for forgiveness and went through with it anyway. When she filed for divorce, then, and only then, did Michaels take all of her talk of leaving him seriously. Finally, the reality that he cheated and neglected away his truest chance for happiness slapped him across the face.

Since the day he signed those divorce papers, Bryant has never totally trusted if a woman is one hundred percent there for him or fifty percent there for the fame and the money. But with Stacy he knew, and he blew it. Too consumed with looking through life's rear-view mirror, his days have only grown more unsettled since.

Everyday he wants so desperately to pick up his phone and beg her back, and promise her that he's changed. But he's played all those cards. When she started speaking to him without any of the emotion that a painful breakup brings, that's when he knew that it was totally over.

He still calls her every so often just to talk and see how she's doing, but hearing her speak about how happy she is with her God filled life, and hearing nothing from her about missing their relationship is more than he can bear.

He can't take it any longer. Michaels scrambles out of the bed. The commotion causes the sleeping beauties to stir briefly. He snatches the phone from its golden nightstand. His Brazilian toy quietly mumbles, "Where are you going, baby?"

"Go back to sleep, I'll be right back." He mutters as he

marches his way into the biggest, grandest master bathroom one could ever imagine.

He stabs seven numbers on the phone and waits. "Wake up man, I need to talk to you for a minute."

With a raspy voice, Ricky asks, "Bryant, what the heck are you calling me for at this hour?"

"Bro, I'm sorry for waking you, but how's Stacy been doing?"

"She's doing fine."

"Good, good, hey, I need a flavor. I know you don't like to get into the middle of things between me and her, but buddy, please, I need you to help me out just this once."

"Bryant, I love you, but if you're going to ask me to play Cupid for the two of you, I can't."

Michaels' patience wears quickly; his frustration loudly bubbles to the surface as he embarks on a rant. "I'm so damn sick of the both of you treating me like I'm the devil, like I'm not worthy of forgiveness. All she ever stresses is the negative about me. The things I've done with my money has saved and changed more lives than any priest or anybody else who is like you or her. Do either of you give me any credit for that? All she wanted was a half million dollars when we split up, out of the generosity of my giving heart, I gave her fifteen million! Fifteen million! Do I get credit for that?! Why doesn't my good weigh as heavily with the two of you as my bad?"

Two of the heart-broken divorcee's lady friends peek their heads' inside the door, "Bryant, is everything o.k?"

He covers up the mouthpiece, while shooing them away. "Yeah go on, I'm cool."

Ricky is fully awake and stirred up now. Out of character, his voice and emotions rise. "We do recognize and respect what you've done for her and others, the both of us love you for that, but you wanta talk real? You really wanta know why she won't be with you again, even without all the countless women that you can't seem to ever stop fornicating with?"

"Oh please, O' Perfect One, do tell me."

"The reason is, instead of giving yourself to Christ, so that he can lead your life and your marriage, you believe that you can buy or good deed your way where you need to be."

"That's a lie. No, I don't."

"Yes, you do. You know how I know… because you told me."

"You have gone straight crazy. When in the hell have I ever told you that?"

"You're always so quick to bring up your list of charitable achievements anytime that you feel defensive, plus, when you got drafted, you told me, while you were drunk, that you wanted to be America's highest paid endorser, and you thought that playing the "God card" would help to get you there."

Bryant's slightly humbled, yet still defiant, "I told you that?"

"Yes, you did. The good deeds you do should be effortless, without thought of what's in return; it shouldn't be done to score points with God or Stacy."

"O.K., so I do some good things for my own selfish gain, so what! Other people benefit along with me, everybody wins, what's wrong with that?"

"The problem is, is that you're fake…," he knows that calling Bryant a fake will farther anger him, so he gives him no time to respond, "the Bible says, 'if a man gives all he possesses to the poor, but doesn't do it out of love; that man has gained nothing'. Bryant, you do what you do for yourself; you're a fake!"

"I don't care what the Bible says, I ain't fake!"

"You're right, you don't care what the Bible says, because you have never read it."

"If you were here right now, I'd punch you right in your holier than thou face."

Ricky calms himself to change the conversation's flow, "Bryant, it's so simple. Just humble yourself and let him in. You're fighting a battle inside, I feel it in my soul, I know it. Just accept Him, then, you won't need to rattle off some grocery list of things that you know God or Stacy will like."

An all-out arms flailing, spit flying, fury erupts from inside of Michaels. "To hell with you, you just think you're so perfect because you walk around babbling to everyone about how great a Christian you are!"

They descend into a shouting match, "I've watched and listened to you over the years, all you do is fit Him into little convenience spots whenever it serves your selfish needs to use His name."

Michaels sarcastically yells as he paces in a large circle from one end of the room to the other. "Hey Ricky, your right, you know everything. Only you, God, and Jesus have that power. You must be so proud. I'm surprised that they didn't mention you in the Bible."

"How can you be sure that I'm not mentioned in the Bible, you've never opened it!"

"Suck off!"

"I bet you sit there in your palace, looking around at all those things that money has brought for you, thinking that it's all you need. That this is as good as life gets."

The Lord blesses Bryant, he reminds him, "You just thought that like a hour ago." A feeling flashes through Bryant, but another overpowers it.

"Just because I may not be the most spiritual person in the world, like you are, you perfect asshole! That doesn't mean I don't love God. Besides, even if I didn't, does that mean you should just give up on me? It's just like any other problem in a person's life; it gets fixed when you're ready. When you came to God, it was something that pulled you in because it was your time, not because someone else decided it was your time; so fuck off!"

The truthfulness of Bryant's words, up until that last bit, calms Ricky's emotions and his voice. "Bryant, my spirit is reaching out to yours'. I'm not trying to be mean when I say these things to you, but I see such a great Christian man in you, and something deep inside my soul, every time that I'm around you now, screams out for me to help you."

Bryant barks, "Ricky, I am great. I don't need or want any of your help. Almost every facet of my life is great, so I don't care about your visions, dreams, or whatever you call them. Ain't nothing bad happening to me, unless you count the attitudes I have to put up with from you and Stacy."

"Bryant, communication between you and God is being blocked by the choices you are making with your life."

That feeling returns. Bryant's spirit breaks down his flesh. The levy breaks and the tears come rushing out, he fights to control his heaving chest quietly, while the eerie calm makes Ricky wonder until Bryant's shivering voice removes doubt. "I don't do drugs; ever, I barely drink, I don't gamble, I try very hard to be loving to everyone, why isn't that enough? Why am I made to feel like shit even when I'm doing so much right!"

Ricky isn't given a chance to answer. Bryant's index finger brings an abrupt end to their verbal sparring.

'Flight' takes time to regain his cool, before walking out of the bathroom to re-medicate himself in the pleasures of his flock. As he walks across his vast bedroom floor, with forced confidence, he thinks, "I know I'm going to Heaven. I'm a good person, Ricky doesn't know shit."

A thought speaks, "yeah he does."

"Thank you, God bless you."

God's child, Faith Jylin Tillman, is farther saddened, due to another tally mark she is forced to slash on the left side of her notepad, which is divided into two columns marked: nothing and blessed back.

She is leaving her last check-out aisle after a day of shopping in the upscale commercial corridor of town, as she's done all day, she's also been doing research for her upcoming book, "Why Are Christians Embarrassed About Their Faith In God?"

So far on her yearlong long quest to gauge the public's pulse, she and her faithful employees have randomly surveyed close to three thousand of their fellow townsmen, and only two hundred and thirty eight, "Thank you, and God bless you too," or like sentiments, have been tallied. Many of them were given by people that know they are of the church. As one of Anytown's leading religious leaders, Faith isn't surprised by the staggering numbers.

The lack of Godly responses moves her to want to reverse what's behind those numbers.

Words have power. Words create action. Spoken words are always heard, always taken seriously, and always carry consequence; good or bad.

The Creator hears their words, their prayers, but He also sees their actions. He doesn't understand why they won't appreciate that a piece of him lives inside of them. They just won't rely on the power that they have at their access, so they are fooled into being weak.

He despises how they base their lives off of their physical world, and then claim their love for him. He's saddened that so many have cut him out of their life completely.

Their words and actions, so often, differ so greatly, but he loves them anyway. Anything that has a part of him, he can't help but to love it, he can't help but to hope for it.

The Father aches to end man's confusion, this 'faith-straddling' concerning him, before Peter sounds the trumpets. Their unfaithfulness has opened up an opportunity.

He sees that they have gotten too comfortable with asking and receiving his forgiveness without, in return, giving Him their faith. He's always wanted them to see their hearts' completely revealed, hidden by nothing.

Their words have created action. With God, there is never 'promotion' without first passing the faithfulness test. Through His love, through His grace, humanity begins its ultimate test of faith.

CHAPTER SEVEN

"Is it true, is it true?" Everyone is gossiping about the sudden rumors that have begun to surface surrounding a team of American archeologists on a dig in Jerusalem. Media leaks have outlined a sketchy unsubstantiated story that supposedly, sixty years ago, American archeologists unearthed an ancient writing that strongly implies that the Bible is not the Word of God. No one believes it, but it does make for some interesting and passionate talk.

Wally Richards sets everything into motion. An elderly nephew of the dig team's lead member, Wally, tells the press that sixty years ago, his uncle, John Richards, arrived unexpectedly at his home. Wally speaks about how John was acting strangely, kind of nervous, as he told him about finding the well preserved scroll and the potential devastation it could bring to the world. "The world will fill with disbelief, it will become evil," John was said to have told his nephew.

While at his home, John made him promise not to reveal this information until he and his team, "Talk to some people."

John also told him. "If you don't hear from me again, if anything happens to me, don't you even think of saying a word about this; tell no one. I don't know how far this could go."

Wally has no hard evidence, just his elderly memories. This makes it easy for the government to dismiss his story as the ramblings of a senile old man. But his account, coupled with the suddenly courteous nature of the veiled plane crash that killed the men and their entire families two years after John showed up at Wally's door, along with his claims of running from the U.S. government for the last sixty years, because he fears for his life, makes this a sensationally dynamic story.

Panicked believers, spanning all religions, are outraged that these lies are being spread. "It's terrible, the importance of God's Word has been diminishing in society as it is, but I never thought that evil could go this far. When people start making up things like this that really shows you where this world is headed.

"This just goes to show you what a truly sick world we live in today. Scripture by scripture the Word of God is being taken away from the foundation of society, and now these atheists have even went so far as to try and erase God's Word altogether…," so spoke a passionate Baptist leader on CNN's most highly rated evening news show.

Even with no evidence put forth, the story is a hot topic on talk shows and around office water coolers, all because of one question that no one will admit to thinking.

People fight not to ask themselves that one question, but it burrows relentlessly, "what if it… No! No! Shut up!"

Their mind's mouth can only hold it back for so long, before it must speak. They fight to resist all thoughts and new ideas that support what they've just been given. No one wants to infuriate God, and therefore, risk their eternal rest by entertaining such blasphemy in their mind, but the "what if's?" and the possibilities that come with it keep coming in wave after wave.

Behind the scenes, in the shadows, the largest newspaper organization in the world, the *New York Daily Enquirer*, is applying the 'full court press' to an investigation that will change the world forever.

Inside Ed's immaculately kept living room, the ruler lords

over his loyal subjects as he positions himself at the edge of his worn out, color faded, gray cloth recliner. Sherry and the kids sit Indian style on the wooden floor forming a half oval around and beneath him, as he reads Bible verses that are twisted and misconstrued to support his mission. Everything to the contrary was previously blacked out with a marker.

Ed's book closes to end another session of his omniscient Bible study. In a dire tone, he speaks to his family. "We must keep ourselves pure and unsoiled by this devil's playground that we live in, if we don't, we will be become just like them, one of the walking dead...," Ed glares at his wife with a message in his eyes, "just like Sherry was before God directed me to put my loving hand on her life and give her a home, and take off of the drugs that were destroying her."

"No Dad, I don't want to burn in hell." Devin blurts out, frightened by his father's dark predictions.

"That is why we must remain hidden, so evil can not reach us, because it is spreading." Ed gets a far away look in his eyes as he shuts his Bible, "I was watching television earlier today and a cold feeling covered my body... I saw Satan."

He's prodded their curiosity to its hilt. They randomly blurt, "What? How? You saw the devil? Where?"

"I saw the Antichrist; there is not one, but many of them. They were trying to poison God's only remaining Earth angels."

"What did they say?" Sherry cringes, fearing she's about to be kicked, as Ed darts out of his seat. He steps right between her and Devin on his way to the 65" screen. With curious, attentive ears, Ed's congregation spins around. Ignited by a few button pushes, they all watch and listen to a recorded news report outlining Wally Richards' claims.

At its conclusion, they all are speechless, nothing but their rapid breathing can be heard. The Wilson family looks at one another in fear and awe, as if one of them could explain how such ludicrous words could ever be spoken.

The worry they see on Ed's face frightens them. "They hate the

Bible so much that they're trying to erase its entire existence. The demons know if they erase its existence, they erase God and Jesus."

Introspection from Sherry, "Ed is right, he has been right all along. Forgive me Father for ever doubting him." Now, for the first time in years, Sherry's mind wholeheartedly accepts that her life with Ed is God's will, that this is her destiny, that he is the one who will lead her to the Kingdom. This puts her mind at ease. Now it will be easier for her to weather the showers of fists that muddy her life.

Leaning all of the way back in his recliner, Ed looks up at the ceiling, as if he were speaking directly to Heaven, and mumbles prophetic words, "Our time here is almost up."

Weeks pass, other countries have long since put the tabloid-like Bible Hoax story to rest, but in this country, the sensationalism of the story keeps it alive much longer. The *New York Daily Enquirer* ups the fervor when it announces that they have taken Wally into their protective custody "just for precaution." But after a few more weeks in hot rotation, with no real facts coming forth, the heated emotions and conversations surrounding Wally's story begin to fade. Publicly the story is dying, weeks pass without any new information coming forth.

Inside the White House, our first term President is about to be blind-sided by some history erasing news.

"Do not shower, do not get dressed, right now ma'am." Still in her pajamas, barely having been awake long enough to wipe the sleep from her eyes, President Nicole Cecilia Thames, America's first female commander, has been told by her secretary that the chief of staff, Jon Wilhelm, has requested a Level Three emergency meeting in the Oval Office.

Through their photograph, taken on the bank of a nearby lake while on a family fishing trip, Thames looks into the eyes of her husband and daughter as her mind scrambles, "What in the hell has happened?"

She speculates whether it was the Koreans, or maybe the Muslims, "No China wouldn't do it, would they?" A Level Three meeting is reserved exclusively for only eminent continental calamities.

President Thames may be diminutive in stature, and big in beauty, but after a rocky first few months in office, due to her detractors persistent claims that she would not be able to handle her job when the going got tough, which only heightened when her husband and daughter died in a boating accident one month before the election, America's third youngest President ever has gained almost everyone's respect.

As Thames walks the long hallway from her bedroom to the pristine double doors of her Presidential office, her nerves begin to rattle. She feels the history, the gravity of the position that she holds. She thinks about the many, but few men, she shares this bond with, all of the men whose legacy is forever etched in history. President Thames usually is overwhelmed with pride as she steps through the hallway and passes the framed pictures of all the former United States Presidents lining the right side wall, but it is not pride that she feels today; its fear. Knowing full well all of the madness that is out in the world, Thames' fear is that she is about to face a situation that none of these great men ever had to endure.

The President takes a deep breath before opening the doors. Upon entrance, she is immediately unnerved by the tension weighing down the air. Her entire staff is in attendance, including the heads of the FBI, the CIA, and the Department of Homeland Security.

As is her protocol, they all stand shoulder to shoulder, on the left side of the room, in a line leading all the way to her desk at the back of the room. Judging from the eerie silence that loudly engulfs her office, along with the many devastated faces around her and, in many cases, the tears that fill those eyes, President Thames is too frightened to farther speculate about what has happened.

She is the President, and she has a job to do, Thames must show strength in the face of whatever is about to come next. Her bouncing brunette shoulder length hair taps her sculpted shoulders with every step, her hazel eyes stare straight ahead, her jaw clenches together two smallish, but fluffy red lips, as she slowly passes by each of her employees.

Closest to her desk are the three men that she knows will have all of the answers. Being the leaders for America's most powerful intelligence communities, you are taught to always look your general in the eye, but none of them can as Thames stops directly in front of each man on her way to her seat. Right then, the commander in chief gets a hunch that this is something that 'we' have done.

She takes a second to get situated in her chair, then, on a churning stomach, through the deafening quiet of a room full of people, she asks, in a voice much stronger than how she truly feels, "Alright Mr. Middlebrook, give it to me straight, don't beat around the bush."

The head of the CIA, Frank Middlebrook, gingerly steps forward out of the line and stands directly on top of the eagle's head. It takes a few moments for him to force the words out, but then, "Mrs. President, as the director of the CIA…"

"Look up please," Thames instucts.

"I've had to make some very tough decisions, and sometimes I inherited decisions made by my predecessors that I must continue to follow through on."

"Point blank, Frank."

"Mrs. President, it's true, it's all true, the Bible is a fake. I, I, we think that it may not be God's Word given to man. We're fairly sure it was all made up."

A professed spiritual woman much of her adult life, those words rip at Thames' heart. She stands up, her knuckles press brutally against her oak top desk as she leans forward. She asks in an angry whisper, "What in heavens name are you telling me? You said this Wally Richards thing was all a lie, that it was all fantasy, Frank!"

"I know, I'm sorry, I lied to you, but ma'am, it goes much deeper. That's only the beginning."

Late last night, the *New York Daily Enquirer* informed the CIA and the FBI that they know the entire tale, including their part in it, and most damaging of all, they have proof!

The FBI and CIA worked out a deal with the *Enquirer* not to run the story until the next day's paper, which would give the President time to gather herself and think about how she wants to address the country, but by late morning, just hours after the President is first told, anonymous sources open the floodgates by leaking it and many of its sinister details to the networks. Within minutes a worldwide media blitz, like none ever seen before, converges upon our great country.

All across the world, everything stops: work, play, and everything in between. People 'glue' themselves to televisions, radios, the Internet, whatever news source they have at their disposal. They all stop to watch the media talk about the impossible.

"Hello, I'm Stan Bather, we interrupt your regularly scheduled program to bring you breaking news out of Washington D.C. and New York City. It is being reported that tomorrow the *New York Daily Enquirer* will run a story that confirms previous rumors that there is a definitive writing that strongly brings into question the authenticity of the Holy Bible.

"Tomorrow, the *Enquirer* says it will outline compelling evidence that they say may prove the Bible is merely the works of imaginative writers who wanted to create a power higher than humanity. But that is only the beginning, we go now to Lucy Goldstein, in Washington, to give us the details of a government cover-up, like none other in the history of our world. A cover-up that has spanned decades and killed many… Lucy."

The award winning, veteran field reporter and her camera crew are set up directly across the street from the White House, which provides the perfect background for the biggest story ever.

"Thank you, Stan, as everyone can see I am just outside of the White House, where today or tomorrow our President will address the country, the world in fact, about not only the proof the *New York Daily Enquirer* says it uncovered about the government's knowledge that…," her voice slows for emphasis, "some sixty years ago, in Jerusalem, American archeologists unearthed an compelling ancient scroll. According to the Enquirer, the scroll's wording clearly implies that the Bible came from the imagination of man. It is said to imply that the entire story was passed down and added to as generation's lived and died. We will get more into those details later, first, we must start some sixty years ago, with five now historic men, where this incomprehensible saga first begin. Lies, unbelievable threats, and a by whatever means necessary desire to make certain this story would never see the light of day, only partly describes the decades long cover-up efforts by our country's top intelligence agencies."

Narrated by a man's deep, but sultry voice, the nation's most watched television network begins a shocking documentary style report. "Weeks ago a firestorm of controversy was set off when this man, Wally Richards…," previous footage is shown of Wally, sitting in his wheelchair, surrounded by media, at his news conference inside the bedroom of his nursing home, "told reporters that his uncle, John Richards, one of the top archeologist of his time, and his four man dig team, while on an Israeli and American funded excursion for ancient artifacts at a site that had previously been partially excavated, stumbled upon a well preserved writing that the American team removed and slipped back into our country.

"We may never know what these men initially saw in the document to make them hide it from their Israeli counterparts and risk everything by taking it, but once back into America the team decoded the writing. Shortly after, they debated about whom to share their history changing find with.

"As a team, the archeologists decided to let the FBI in on their secret. For them, this is where things began to go horribly wrong. After taking possession of the writing, the FBI took the team and their immediate families and flew them to one of the government's most secretive, closed off locations in the world; Area 51. There they were told that no one could ever find out about their discovery. The families were told that the world would be better off if the very fabric of what holds civilization together were never brought into question, so the men, their wives' and kids', were abruptly and without choice placed into a witness protection-like program. Each family was moved to a separate location, given new identities, and purposely made to live in fear and constant threat by their own government."

The narrator continues, "The men were told to never tell anyone about what was going on. They were told their homes would be bugged forever. The limited locales that they were allowed to go would be watched and listened to at all times, and worst of all, they were told if there was ever a time the government felt someone would reveal this secret, that all of the men, not just the one who violated their rules, would be brought up on charges of international theft, tried by a secret grand jury, be found guilty, and imprisoned until the day he died.

"From the very beginning, they all were told that soon no one would know they are still alive, the families were denied contact with anyone the FBI didn't deem necessary. 'No mistakes, no slip ups' was the slogan, and it was constantly drilled into their collective heads'. By separating and isolating the men, but at the same time keeping them linked, by keeping them accountable for not only their own lives', but also the fate of their comrades and their loved ones, the FBI felt they were in total control of the situation.

The operation, dubbed 'Sky Preservation', was so covert, so secretive; it gained its own department, which was kept buried deep inside the CIA, once the agency took over total control in the years that followed. Only a handful of top agents, even within the CIA, knew of this department. Let me end with a freshly released statement from the *Daily Enquirer*, they want to make it perfectly clear, that no United States President, to their knowledge, was ever clued in to any of this, in any way, shape, or fashion."

Just hours before the world finds out, President Nicole Thames continues to be briefed.

"Jon, pour me a glass of vodka please." The President's

foundation is wobbled, she can't quite wrap her mind around the incredible story that Frank is telling her.

The CIA's director eloquently understates. "Mrs. President, I know this is a lot to take in all at one time…"

"No shit, Frank, really." Mr. Middlebrook has no idea how much, because just like many people across the world, Thames' mind has already had brief flashes of "what if?"

"Frank, are you absolutely positively sure this isn't a mistake or some kind of trick?"

"No, Mrs. President, we strongly, strongly believe that this is not a fake."

The nation's chief circles around her desk. First she looks at Julian Pierce, her longtime confidant and the U.S. treasurer, Thames can't wait to get to her, but first she starts at the back of the line. One by one, she gazes into the faces' of her employees and shares their immense pain and disbelief through warm hugs.

This warm moment stretches into an hour. Their pain is as intense as the loss of a child. Emotions pour out of everyone inside that office. Thames looks around the room at all of the despair, and her jaw tightens as a renewed strength courses through her body. She returns to her desk. The leaders of the three intelligence agencies are told to stay, along with Chief of Staff, Jon Wilhelm, everyone else is asked to leave.

"So where is this writing, was it destroyed?" She questions, as she dries her eyes with the back of her hand.

Fidgeting, Frank adjusts his tie just before he gladly steps aside and allows the FBI director, James Beck, to step forward to speak. "Mrs. President, it has always been close to you, and to every President before you."

Thames' eyes search around the room like it is suddenly going to appear, "Where?"

The FBI's director continues. "The agencies thought that the safest, most secure place to keep it would be right under everyone's nose. Mrs. President, it is buried underneath you."

Thames' brain is on overload. "You're telling me the document that could change the entire world is right here, beneath the White House?"

"No one knows that it's here. We told the newspaper that for the good of the world, we destroyed it."

"So what real proof do they have that this scroll ever existed?"

"Without the FBI and CIA's knowledge, one of the archeologists shot a video of it before our men got to him. The paper found the disk beneath the cement driveway of the house next door to Wally Richard's old home. Little did any of us know, but it's been there all this time."

"Please tell me that the media doesn't know everything about what you gentlemen have told me today, they don't know about the agencies whisking these men and their families away to hide them, do they?"

Beck's eyes drift, "If they hadn't found that disk we could have wiggled out of this."

The President's mind begins separating her personal emotions from that of a world leader, "So the Enquirer knows we took hold of the writing, that we took these men and their families, placed them in secret locales, and kept them silent as a means to protect citizens worldwide from this catastrophic news…"

Mr. Beck knows what his boss is trying to do, "Madam, stop please."

Thames doesn't hear Beck's request as her mind and mouth are in hyper-drive formulating a positive spin to feed the media. The President's voice and gestures grow more animated as she continues, "In time, we can make the media understand, and get them on our side. Things were done and decisions were made for the good of the world, to uphold the foundation of society. If we orchestrate this carefully, slowly the American people will come to understand, then, the rest of the world will follow, then…"

Frank jumps back in when he shouts, "Mrs. President, I don't think that's going to work!" Startled by Frank's aggressive tone, Thames abruptly stops.

Calmly, in a hushed voice, Frank informs her. "Nicole,

everything was going fine, but everyday there was this dark cloud hanging over the department's head. Former director Weldon was never comfortable with that."

A chill runs down Thames' spine, "What are you saying, Frank?"

Slowly. "Mr. Weldon made things feel… comfortable."

"Entire families?"

"Yes." Thames says nothing, she just takes it all in.

"But it goes deeper than that."

"What in the devil do you mean, how could it?"

Frank gets very calm. "They were paranoid, Mrs. President. Mr. Weldon was very paranoid that a leak, just like this, may get out, even though their watch over the families was relentless."

"What did he do?"

"He disposed of friends, cousins, uncles, nieces, grandparents, at different moments; opportunities were taken to end their lives. Staged car crashes, kidnappings, undetectable poisonings, so-called random shootings…," with sorrow, he slowly shakes his head from east to west, "he missed only one."

"Wally Richards?"

"Yes, Wally Richards. We've tried for decades to get him, but he fled the country long ago, he must have kept switching his name and kept getting new aliases. I'm sorry, we tried our best to eliminate him once he popped back up and started running his mouth to the press, but that damn Enquirer hid him. If we'd have really pressured them about it, it would have just added credibility to his story."

"What have we done?" Her mind tries, but it can't begin to take in the ramifications of everything she has been told today, "What am I going to say to the world?"

James Beck, "I know that this isn't much consolation, but you do have some time. The Enquirer assured us that they wouldn't run the story until tomorrow."

CHAPTER EIGHT

It feels so intense in every part of them. They feel it in their brains', their souls'; their bodies' feel its effects. Having their plasma televisions and do everything phones and computers tell them that the greatest teachings on life, by the highest of high powers, has all been a fake - races the imaginations of them all.

Powerful thoughts speed through minds' across the world, doubts overpower faith, "The American government wouldn't go to the lengths that they did, if there wasn't some truth to all of this."

An overwhelmingly boorish feeling of complete loss rampages through the lives of many. Blue-collar citizens on up to scholars pick over the Bible with a fine tooth comb, especially the books of the New Testament. They search for anything written that may lead to some hint that something like this would be coming.

Some hide. Others pray! Some others, they pray and hide.

Murder, anarchy, and rape, all spread like the wind, in the days following the reports, the well measured and cornered confessions by the government, and the video footage that backs it all up.

Panicked fear is unleashed across the earth with the speed and strength of ten nuclear warheads; billions fear that this may be the end of the world.

Minds' snap. Fear, anger, and hysteria fuel devilish rampages throughout the world's streets. Senseless killings occur by the dozens every hour in our country alone. Across America, Marshall Law is quickly enacted in an attempt to calm the violence.

This is nothing like past riots. From the wealthy suburbs to the inner cities, branches of the military are called in to take back the streets from the hooligans who are setting fires, looting businesses, and shooting people at random. These bandits span all social and economical classes.

Many people feel that they can do whatever they want now. Societal rules don't apply; souls feel no need to restrain themselves anymore. No Bible, no God, no God, no Heaven, no Heaven, no hell; there is no reward, no consequence at the end, so why should they care?

Across seas, militias are forced to shoot and kill hundreds of civilians across Europe alone.

A level of worldwide chaos is reached unlike ever before. Many of America's friendliest nations immediately turn into its enemies. They call America the land of Satan's angels. Nuclear powered countries threaten to drop their bombs on our continent, if we don't take back and rescind all that has been told.

The White House is blocked off within a two mile radius to protect itself against its protesters. Citizens of every nationality, every faith, every belief, join together in solidarity, Klansmen stand by the side of men with skin colors they have always hated, it doesn't matter, more serious issues are at hand. Angered that their mind would dare think such blasphemy, many individuals focus their emotions towards the government.

Protesters by the hundreds of thousands fill the streets of Washington daily. Voices scream through hateful words and picket signs, "You're all lairs, you'll burn in hell for this, Thames. The government is trying to end the world. They want to send us all to hell, God is coming to exact his revenge!"

"I think if maybe there wasn't some true to this...," an outspoken interviewee is quoted in the Tuesday edition of the

U.S.A Today newspaper, "and I'm not saying that there is, but I think, maybe God would have given us some clue that this would be coming. I'm not sure what to think." The thoughts of subtle doubters influence many of those who listen. People begin to weigh the Word of God against man's own reasoning.

He knows them. He knows their habits, their patterns, their weaknesses, and their strengths; He made them. He told them that He would allow trials and tribulations to pass through their lives' so that they could have the chance to ascend to a higher, glorious life by walking out their faith in Him. But he continues to see so much untapped greatness in so many of his creations because they won't totally trust him.

God sees that they were coming to accept the wrongs of the world, and that which they don't accept; they look in the wrong places for change.

Our Lord sees that he has been losing them to themselves. Things have gotten so bad, that hundreds of millions of them don't believe that he exist at all, billions more do believe He exist, but don't trust him to lead their lives. For too long, they've relied on each other and their possessions for their happiness. They put their money, time, hopes, and their faith, in a system of daily life that their intellects have created. All of which diminishes God's power in their life.

If this were a political election race; God's once large lead over the devil has dwindled down close to a deficit. The enemy has made their world so eye appealing, so carefree, so self-reliant, that they have put God's guidance and his opinion in their back pocket only to be pulled out in a pinch.

A strange phenomenon is also occurring; as distrust spreads throughout the population churches across the world are seeing their buildings fill to capacity, not just on Sundays, but each day. Complete strangers to the Lord, people who never or barely ever attended church before band together and celebrate His name with an emotional passion a thousand times greater than they ever did before.

God chooses to look down at the world with fresh eyes, He's anxious to see who will dig deep, who will grow, who will learn. He looks down upon them with such great belief, such great hope, such love… but He knows them.

In what will become a time of immense madness, full of great deception, yet rampant with hidden blessings and miracles, the Lord's goal is to see who'll seek comfort and direction from the only one who can provide it.

As time moves forth, the chaos subsides. People's initial burst of violent emotion dies, order is gradually restored to a livable level. Anger and shock starts to move out, as personal denials move in. But for those who are faithful; little changes. They continue to rely on their faith and prayers for their strength and answers; but for all others, a very clear pattern is beginning to take shape.

Everywhere people go nothing else is talked about or thought of. Society is bombarded with twenty four hours a day, seven days a week coverage of the "Bible Hoax."

All forms of public entertainment ceased, immediately, once the big news hit, but several months later, the return of sports and other venues of entertainment signals that the routine of daily life is officially returning to society.

Ricky and Bryant Michaels are out early, seated near the mid-court emblem of their home arena, going through their pre-game leg stretches for the game later tonight. This is everyone's first game back. Throughout the entire arena there is a silent, eerie uneasiness worn by everyone as the crowd slowly makes its way in. There are no faces painted with the team's colors, no jeers towards the players on the opposing team as they warm up, just a sense of everyone going through the motions, trying to work their way back to normalcy.

Bryant, "Look at where I'm at, Ricky," full of humility, he stares up at the team's championship banners hanging down from the ceiling, "look at everything I've accomplished in my life. I come from nothing, and I'm here. I can remember praying to God when I was a kid to make me the best player in the world, and He did it. I was chosen for this very moment."

"Yes, He definitely made you the best player ever, you have so much to thank him for, there's no doubt about that, but..."

'Flight' is immediately angered. "I'm serious, Ricky, don't start with that nonsense. I got a lot on my mind, just like everyone else does, right now."

"Bryant, all I was going to tell you was to be careful because there are forces out there working hard to pull you down."

"There is nothing that can pull me down. You know what? The guys on the team always ask me why I'm friends with you..."

"Well, I hope that you tell them 'because Christians are the best friends that a person could ever have?"

"Anyway... we're nothing alike, but I love you like a brother, and you still constantly disrespect and doubt me. Do you do this to your family members, do you hassle them like you hassle me?"

"No, something in my spirit..."

"See, there you go again with your premonitions about some bad thing happening to me. I know that you don't think that he is, but God is the most important thing in my life. All of this bullshit being spread around just reaffirms what I already know."

"That's good, Bryant."

You would think that Ricky agreeing with him would be to his liking, but 'Flight' gets more defensive. "I help bring God's children home to him. Since all of this crap has begun, I've gone to church several times just so people would see me and follow my lead. I've been telling the world to keep the faith, and drown out all of these ridiculous lies, because I know the Bible is real." Bryant peeks around, hoping no one has noticed that his voice has gotten a bit out of control.

"Bryant, why are you getting so angry? I'm not attacking you, I've said all that needs to be said."

"Hey, and I've been spending more time at home and not going out with this chick or that chick. I think God wants me to slow my life down, right now, you know?"

Ricky grunts out during toe touches, "See, now you're talking like a man that'll sacrifice himself for God. He always replaces what you sacrifice for him with something even greater...," optimistic energy comes out in his words, "hey, have you been praying more?"

Bryant sins. "Oh yeah, I do everyday."

"That's awesome, that really is."

"Oh my goodness, finally a compliment from you...," they share a laugh, "I just can't fathom that anyone would ever believe any of the garbage that has come out recently, look at the violent way some people reacted, they went crazy."

Frightfully, Ricky looks his friend right in the eyes, "I feel sad for so many people, because the evil that harvest inside of them, will try to infect the lives' of others. You can already see it happening."

"You really think so?"

"I pray that I'm wrong."

Bryant's eyes dance as he leans forward to lengthen his left hamstring, "Yeah, me too. But you know the experts have been running a lot of tests on the videos, and every time, they say that the video looks very authentic."

"So what are you saying, Bryant?"

"I'm not saying anything. I'm with you. I don't believe it either. I'm just telling you their facts, what they said."

"You're a child of God, Bryant, whatever they might say shouldn't effect you, make sure you don't start believing man's words over your faith in God."

"Bro' you don't have to tell me that. No one will ever make me believe the Bible is a fake. I guarantee you, watch, pretty soon they'll come back and say that it was all false, that this whole story was just a big mistake."

"It doesn't matter to me whether they do or don't. True

Christians worldwide, like me and you, know that the Bible is real."

"That's right, baby." They slap hands after they rise to their feet.

One after another they head towards the sideline to pick from a rack full of basketballs to begin shooting warm-up shots.

Bryant proclaims, "People are going to feel so stupid when the real truth comes out," while simultaneously, mixed feelings about that very possibility develop further.

David is in the mist of one of his favorite parts of the day, he and Sasha promised themselves twenty one years ago, right before they were married, to always spend at least twenty minutes before sleep, each night, lying in bed snuggling with each other, talking and sharing, so that their love would remain emotionally connected.

"David, I am so happy to be back at work now. We've been shut down for weeks. Things got so scary with all of the violence and looting that went on. I thought it was never going to end."

"I knew all of that would happen. I knew all of the blacks and the wet-backs would take advantage of the opportunity and do what they do best; rob and kill."

Sasha gives him a weird look accompanied by a "I can't believe you just said that" snicker. "Uh, sweetheart you act like white people weren't out there doing the same things they were. In fact, when I watched coverage of the rioting on television, excuse me if I'm wrong, but it wasn't blacks or Mexicans that I saw shooting people or burning down mansions out in Beverly Hills."

With nothing better to counter with, "That's just the networks trying to make all of them not seem as barbaric as they really are."

"David, that's ridiculous. When are you going to stop believing that crap? White people are just as screwed up as black people when it comes to this and everything else."

David remains light-hearted, "Wow, I see that my beautiful wife may be the person fueling our daughter's recent actions."

"David, you're still hanging onto that?... But I do feel the same way as her. You've just never known it because I just let you spout your little redneck hatred and make your close-minded observations, but I have never thought like you. But we can talk about that later, right now, sweetheart, I wanta ask you something that I hope doesn't upset you. It's just a question, and it definitely doesn't mean that I feel this way, o.k.?"

She has just glossed over it like it was nothing, but David's mind is 'spinning.' "A, what is it, honey?"

She takes hold of his hand for comfort. "Since all of this, you know, fake Bible stuff began... has there ever been a second where you thought about the possibility that it might be true?"

David snatches his hand away, then, wiggles himself back a few inches. "I can't believe you. You actually are starting to doubt our Savior's existence. Jesus died for you, and you're willing to throw Him away, because the media, a piece of paper, and some scientists say so?"

"No honey, I'm just saying that I'm human. I just thought about it for a second, that's all."

"The only good thing that my parents ever did for me and my brother was to take us to church every Sunday, so that we could have a relationship with God. I came into His house and He saved me. That was real, a supreme being that exist did that for me! So if you want, go ahead and perish in hell by believing their lies, but I'm damn sure not coming with you." David flips over, away from her, upon completion.

"Sweetie, all I was saying-"

"I don't want to talk anymore, just go to sleep, Sasha."

For the rest of the night the room is silent. Sasha soon falls asleep, but David can't. He lays there, his body is still, but his mind is active, "What if... There'd be a lot less to worry about... Stop it, shut up, that's just the devil talking," David doesn't want to admit why he got angry with her, these are not new thoughts for him, he just can't bring himself to admit it, not even to his wife.

He dwells on what she said about her feelings towards other races. He's shocked by her stance.

The questions going through their minds' are the same ones people across the globe are experiencing. Those people just aren't built like Sasha. They'll murder, they'll steal, they'll hate, but with their mouths', no one outside of an atheist will openly admit their "what ifs" for fear that openly expressing doubt about the Creator's existence may bring upon great vengeance, if they're wrong. But slowly, no matter how hard they try to deny it, their character rises. *Of course, the atheist was the first to go. Then came those who are just totally indifferent, they just flat-out have never thought about their life and God together, so they just go with the flow. Next to cross were millions of the Young - teenagers to those in their thirties - personal contact with God in this generation was made wicked by the preceding generation and their lackadaisical Godly approach to raising their children; yet they are the loudest of the Young's critics, when it is they who have trained them to trust the 'Media God'.*

He just stares at it, he examines the image's every detail; the bright light coming out from behind his back, the angels around Him. Melvin takes notice of the similarities they share. How both of their noses' are wide, how both of their lips are full, but not to full, their woolly hair, and the bronze complexion of their skin.

Never before has Melvin looked so closely at the majestic black portrait of Jesus that hangs over his grandmother's bed. He lies horizontally across her mattress staring at this man. The man that his grandmother always said he needs to talk with before he decides to 'lean' on one of us. "Don't go to your friends, go to God," she says.

Tears begin their flow, Melvin can't stop his stare. The 'Bible

Hoax' has intensified his fights and struggles with his doubts concerning his spiritual devotion.

Melvin has been watching television almost nonstop lately; he's kept constant tabs on all of the talk show debates and discussions that have been raging nonstop. He listens to their differing opinions: some soothe him, some anger him, and others make him afraid. He ponders the opinions of those people who are bold enough to not have their face blurred out to say, "We knew it all along. The scroll just confirms what science and common sense have told us all. People just needed something to feel lesser to. This was just ancient man's way to control people."

An hour is packed into two seconds, a powerful out of body experience begins as this conflicted young man gains a glimpse of what Jesus went through during his crucifixion. He becomes totally immersed in the moment; he is Jesus. For a blink of time, HE died on that cross.

Melvin feels the pain of being beaten to near death, his skin being torn to shreds. He feels the stakes being driven through the tendons, muscles and bones of his waists and ankles.

He feels Jesus' pain, and with the same free will that he had, Melvin looks down at the very people crucifying him, murdering him, and he can find no reason why they are worthy to die for. He snaps back!, instantly knowing he has experienced a life changing moment.

Youth counselor for his church up until six months ago when his hours at work began to interfere with his duties, the pastor and the church's deacons would sometimes get on him about picking up his intensity, and getting more enthusiastic about the work he does inside of the church, but he gave a decent effort to the children Hat he mentored.

His feelings begin to dig. "The biggest reason I liked going to church was because I got to sing a solo each week." Singing has always been the favorite of his many talents, "Church just gave me a place to go, I felt wanted there."

Melvin exposes everything and hides nothing, "I just talked

it. I just went through the motions. Real Christians don't have doubts, I always have. I think I was just trying to be the man Me-Ma expected me to be…," his thoughts turn to the ideas that outside influences have let in, "this was just a way to control us." He thinks about all the evidence and doubts that his eyes and ears have been fed, "everyone else sees it, too."

Melvin's mind races through recalls of all of the previous instances his thoughts tried to reveal the 'truth' to him. "I knew, I always knew. I wanted Him to be real, but deep down I always doubted if He was. I always told myself that was just the devil trying to make me think something that wasn't true, but in reality, it was the truth speaking to me. I'm just like that dude on television yesterday, I just talked myself into feeling that I believed, because that what has been drilled into me."

As he gains total comfort in everything that his words have released, something totally unexpected takes his focus away.

It's his grandmother's commotion as she crawls up on the bed with her cherished son. His mind was so focused, he didn't hear her and the kids come in after their trip to the welfare office to collect their food tickets. Despite May's disabilities, she long ago made a promise to God that she would always rely on his Holy Spirit to give her the strength to proudly walk her way down to collect her aid, no matter how bad the pain or neighborhood.

May greets him with a tight hug. "Have you been crying sweetie?" She asks through controlled, but huffing breathes, "Your eyes are kinda red, baby?"

He doesn't need to answer: the portrait of Jesus, Melvin facing His picture, all that's going on in the world, plus the faith she knows he has in God; May puts it all together.

"Beautiful isn't He?"

Melvin casually replies. "Yeah, he is."

"Those tears come from your heart, son, they come from your acceptance of God in your life." May's words and facial expression turn cold as she looks back up at her Savior, "Those people are going to burn for what they are trying to do to the Bible and God's name. I feel so sorry for anybody who believes their lies."

He has heard enough, Melvin kisses her on the cheek, then, rolls off of the bed. "Me-Ma, I have ta get to work. I'll see you later tonight."

Melvin could have stayed and talked. He does have to work; but he had time to talk and listen. Old habits die hard.

Full of energy and confidence, young Mr. Jenkins walks in, "Hi Faith, how ya doin' today?"

"I'm doin' great. Our good Lord has blessed me with yet another day… another day ta work with you is always a blessing."

Melvin turns playfully coy. "Stop it, you're gon make me blush."

Like always, he walks straight into the shoe store's back room to switch clothing. Any other similar day, when they are not busy and they have a moment to talk, Melvin would try to avoid having any type of spiritual conversation with Faith, but today is different. He seeks it.

Immediately upon exiting the back room, Melvin sits down on the small stool beside the check-out counter, next to Faith. "You seem to be in a really good mood today, Faith. I figured you'd be a little down because of all the stuff people continue to say about the Bible."

"Why should I be? I know God, I know Jesus, and I know the Bible is real. So all of this garbage they're coming up with doesn't affect me… No, I take that back. I hate the fact that the lies being fed to everyone are going to destroy the lives of a lot of impressionable people out there. Look at how many got killed when all of this crap was made public. They killed each other left and right, because they lost all hope."

"I watch the news everyday, they said more people are going to church now than ever before."

"Yeah, church attendance skyrocketed after nine eleven also, but it didn't last. Many people are just emotionally into their salvation right now, we'll see if their heart is really in it."

Her words bring him comfort, "They just in there cuz' they scared, huh?"

"We'll see, all I know is, I just have to keep my mind clear of this nonsense, that's the most important thing that I can do. Somehow, someway, this is all in God's plan for us."

"I know, I feel the same way, but I'm just saying, with all of the talk and the proof they have, that doesn't make you kinda… you know."

Faith knows exactly what Melvin's hinting at, it's the same kind of hints that other people have been subtlety dropping. She gently takes hold of his hands, "Don't you let them start putting doubts into your head, Mel. Don't you form your opinion from what they tell you, you are a Christian, so at times your faith is going to be tried, and this is a big one, but you rely on the strength of your faith. Rely on what you know, not what you see."

"Oh no, I'm cool, I know the Bible is real."

"Amen, don't you ever doubt that."

"You know, people are really trippin' off this stuff tho'. On my way in, I was listening to some talk radio, and some preacher was going back and forth with some lifelong atheist guy. The preacher asked him, 'so if there is no God, no supreme spirit, then what power is it that saves lives when they are in horrible, no way out situations? Luck, as you want to believe? No, it's God's grace."

Melvin does not like the emotion behind Faith's passionate response. "That's right, it's God's grace that does that," he can feel the sureness behind each of her words, "He blesses us with miracles to remind everyone that His power is the mightiest of all. He has the final say. We just choose to ignore or minimize his blessings by calling them something else; like luck. But that preacher shouldn't even waste his time debating about God with some disbeliever."

"Yeah, I know, but this atheist guy said that Jesus was just the lead character in a well conceived, well intended plot to keep society reined in. He was saying like 'show me some visual, tangible proof concerning any of the events written of in the Bible… they can't.' He thinks there might be other documents buried that just haven't been found yet."

"For one, there is tangible, physical proof of some things spoken of in the Bible…"

"What? Are you sure?"

"Yes, I'm sure. I wonder if this guy has ever thought about the reason why there aren't a bunch of books that speaks of Jesus and His works…," with a message in her staring eyes and stern voice, Faith probes, "Do you want to know why there aren't a bunch of other books, Mel?"

The entrance of a customer brings Melvin relief. "Finally somebody comes in this place, so she can shut up for a minute." Melvin hurries to the customer like he's the finish line of a race. "Hello sir, how may I help-"

"Oh dude, my trip, wrong door." The heavily tattooed and pierced 'skaterdude' walks out and immediately turns left to the door right beside theirs'.

"Shit, he was looking for the sports shop."

Faith does not waste time getting back to the topic at hand. "You wanna know, don't you?"

He drifts back over coolly, in no hurry, "If you want to tell me that's fine, go ahead."

"The same reason why Mr. Atheist doubts the Word of God is the same reason that I know it's real. The Bible contains all the reporting of Jesus' work that any of us will ever need. God wants it to be faith that brings you to him, if there was an abundant of different books, pictures, and bones, then, we wouldn't need faith, would we? He doesn't want the same sight that you use to watch television, and the same ears that people use to reason you into believing deception, to bring you to him. His written Word, the Holy Bible, is sufficient. You can't start doubting God because of their evidence; keep your faith in God's evidence."

Melvin fills with rage. "O.K., whatever, I was just telling you what the guy said, so just shut the hell up about it. You're pissing me off."

The air between them goes dead silent and still. She has never once heard her friend speak with such language and tone. But Faith fears not. She steps closer to his face. "You listen to me, and know that what I am telling you is the truth. I'm not sure exactly what this Bible Hoax stuff is all about, but it can't be what you think, it can't be what any of them think. Just because you can not physically see our Lord, like you can physically see that stupid video, don't doubt that He and his angels are not all around us. God needs your faith, sweetie. Look beyond your eyes, don't be like them!"

Melvin looks away to hide the dubious smirk forming on his lips. Faith's soft hand guides his attention back to her. "I understand that it can be hard to believe in God, when the world all around you is going away from Him, it feels normal, because that's what everyone else is doing. But Melvin, faith dares your soul to believe beyond what your eyes can see. Everything that God promises in the Bible is real, you have the power to turn it into physical things. Faith is not something that you can't see, but you gotta search."

She knows that he could care less about what she is telling him, but Faith hopes that she's planted a seed that will blossom later. He has totally shut her and the truth out. And Faith knows it. But still she loves and believes in him.

"We certainly owe an apology to the American people. Their government was put in the worst possible position any country, any decision maker, has or will ever be involved with. In hindsight, some terrible and unfortunate choices were made by some overwhelmed men. Choices were made that none of us would ever want to be graded on if we were in their same position." So contends the White House spokesperson, through a statement issued to the press.

The Thames administration has completed a one hundred

and eighty degree turn. The intelligence agencies have gone from totally dismissing the Bible story, to now, that the 'truth' and all of their predecessors corrupt and murderous behavior that followed is out there for all to hear and judge, to thoroughly backing it. The world's outcry has forced the government to fiercely back the validity of the video. Their hope is to gain some sympathy for why America's leaders, leaders that have always prided themselves on their high morals in regards to humanity, would choose the murderous course that it did.

Even with world renowned scientists, in and outside of the U.S., co-signing for the authenticity of the disk, there are many, especially outside of our country who still say that the United Sates is manufacturing this entire thing, so that it, the world's greatest power, will somehow profit by stripping away all religion. International tensions rise to new heights with each passing day.

While still partaking of American money and aid, nations who have always supported our government, through public and private dialogue, begin to show signs of descent.

President Thames lays out the details of her counterattack to her staff. "We need everyone, especially the Arab countries, to believe us, to know that this situation is not something we wanted or created. Once the rest of the world sees them soften their stance, they will all rush to be the first ones back to our side. If the Arabs don't believe us, they'll continue to create propaganda against us…," a lifelong non-drinker, Thames stops her speech for a brief sip of vodka, "If we give the world concrete proof that what they've been told is real, that this is not something we chose to have happen, the resentment will subside much more quickly," she breaks again for a longer sip, "it's time to play our ace."

CHAPTER NINE

She's locked herself inside her bedroom. She paces the small floor like a bull behind its starting shoot. May is having the worse day of her life. She can't control her mind, she can't make it stop repeating itself, she prays but her troubles remain, leading her into panic, "Satan is trying to steal me from my Father. He's trying to destroy me!"

May drops to her knees, only the palms of her hands come between her head and the floor, she wishes she were at the feet of Jesus. Through excited breath and slightly slurred speech, May battles her demons with the only shield that will not break, "above all, taking the shield of faith, ye shall be able to quench all the fiery darts of the wicked!"

Her mind soon works itself into a craze, illusions creep in. She thinks she spots a black figure peeking up over her shoulder. May turns to face it, but it's gone. A whisper is heard in her head. "God doesn't love you, because you don't love him."

May's hobbled body burst through the door, immediately, the kids feel her frenzy as she enters the rest of the apartment, "Children get over here, now!" She sits down, with her arms outstretched, east and west, across the dining table, "Hurry up and sit down, we must pray."

The twins ask, "Grandma what's wrong… What happened?"

She doesn't even hear them, she shouts, "Put on the mo army of God, that ye may be able to run against God!" Scribbled scriptures blur her words.

Weeks have come and gone since Melvin tearfully laid on May's bed. Having just returned home from another evening of work, Melvin reaches for the doorknob. Being that he's a novice, he almost forgets to un-cock the forty five caliber handgun concealed in his waistband, before entering his grandmother's home.

His fear of random violence, in this new day and age, suddenly barreling his way has caused him to make some drastic decisions, so Dane, having plenty to share, loaned him one of his weapons of mass destruction.

Melvin can't make out her words, but from outside of the apartment, he can hear that his Me-ma, who never raises her voice, is shouting. Fearing a break-in, he holds the gun behind his back as he rushes in. Upon entrance, for Melvin, that panic ends, as a new one begins.

May, and Melvin's cousins, are seated at their small, round, dining room table holding hands in a circle around the Holy Bible that lays in the middle of them all. May feverishly chants a prayer of forgiveness for her doubting the Bible's existence. She is oblivious to his presence, as her everything is submersed into her disjointed prayer. As May puts extra emphasis on key words, she squeezes and jerks on the hand of Malik and Rene, the two children her hands are connected to. Her passion and emotions build to a higher uncontrolled pitch with each passing word.

With his back to his big cousin, Malik's frightened eyes turn around, they cry out to Melvin. To Malik, he whispers, "What the hell is going on with her." Malik shrugs his shoulders.

Melvin sees the anguish and fear on the faces' of the beautiful twins. Tears stream down the girls' blood rushed cheeks as they squeeze their eyes shut and grit their teeth to keep from crying out.

With the same hand that has just tucked his gun into the back of his jeans, cautiously, he places that hand on May's rigid shoulders. "Me-ma, Me-ma, calm down please, you're scaring the kids."

Like a hypnotist, whom has just snapped his fingers, May jumps as she rushes out of her state. Her teary bloodshot eyes pop open as she instantly releases the hands of the children. The relieved siblings loudly release their frightened bottled up tension.

May's one track focus blinds her to the ordeal she has put her young grandchildren through. She desperately clutches her hands around Melvin's forearm, her fingernails dig across his flesh, as she tries to pull him down into a seat, "Come pray with us, Melvin, pray with me that these evil lies will stop poisoning our mind." She is certain that the God fearing man she has so proudly raised will want to mix his spiritual energy with hers'.

Melvin softly and lovingly speaks to her, while he coolly loosens her grip on his arm. "Me-ma, let me get you something to drink. I want you to calm down." His thoughts, "She's fighting what she knows is the truth, and it's freaking her out."

As soon as Melvin turns towards the sink, his eyes see something that sends feelings of agitation coursing through him; it's the family's insurance bill lying on the counter. From where he stands, just a few feet away, he can see the big, bold printed words on the previously opened bill: DUE TO A FAILURE TO TIMELY PAY YOUR PREMIUM, YOUR INSURANCE HAS BEEN CANCELED. The weight of so much responsibility and Melvin's sense of failure to handle it becomes fuel for the dwindling light inside him.

He stomps over to the refrigerator, grabs the handle and angrily flings the door open, causing it to slam against the cabinets to its right. He knew that nothing was in there, but his anger guided him to see the sad sight again. Only a few condiments, one slice of old bread, and a bare bone that is poking out of its aluminum foil wrapping are present.

At that moment, for the first time in his life, thoughts concerning all of the roaches and the musty scent inside of their home, which is due to the unkept world surrounding it, not to mention the empty refrigerator, all join up to anger him. The eyes to his soul view his home differently. Melvin's sixteen year old face hardens, the frustrations of living in this environment finally has gotten to him, just like it has so many others. His heart rate heightens as he stares at the emptiness of their uninhabited icebox, and parallels it to the quality of their lives.

The focus of the siblings' fear shifts from their grandmother to the man-child that has helped raise them, once Melvin smashes the refrigerator's door shut. Malik boldly screams out, "Why are you slamming stuff around, Mel?"

Malik's cousin moves over to the sink and turns the knob for the cold water; nothing. With more than just a hint of annoyance in his tone, Melvin asks, "What happened to the water, Me-ma?"

She doesn't even acknowledge his question. Resuming her desperate pleading, May extends her hands and arms out to him. "Please son, come pray to our Father with me. Come honor the Lord that I have raised you to serve your entire life."

Frightfully calm, he responds. "No thanks, Me-ma. I'm a bit more concerned about getting a fucking glass of water from this piece of shit sink!" His vexation has boiled over, he's sick of hearing her babble about some God that doesn't exist, "We live in a house full of kids and we don't even have water to give them, what the hell are we going to eat tonight?!" He snaps, Melvin tugs and jerks on the sink's knobs like a madman, "What happened to the damn water! I'm sick of living like some filthy rat, what did I do to deserve living like this!"

His cousins huddle together, frightened and shocked at the sight of the man they've always looked up to totally losing control.

A knowingness covers May's face, her bugged out eyes look past the crazed antics of his physical and into his soul. Her schizophrenic emotions settle, allowing for a heart-broken calmness to control her craze. "Kids, y'all go in ya bedroom, lock the door." Without a moment of hesitation, the little ones rush off.

May knows exactly what's going on here, what's behind her beloved child's outburst. Providing him zero comfort in any form, May waits patiently as his emotions lead him into a tearful breakdown, his heaving torso drapes the countertop. May senses a dark aura surrounding her grandson.

Barely audible words spill out of his slobbering mouth, "I'm so sick of living like this. We don't have na'thin... na'thin Me-ma. If God was real and he loved us so much, why would he keep us here?"

"You're just like the rest of 'em, aren't you? All of the blessings God has given to you... and you're turning away from Him now when He needs you the most!"

Melvin laughs while gathering himself. "Are you serious, blessings, what blessings? Look around Me-ma, open your eyes, ain't no blessings around us!"

"You believe their lies, all this blasphemy that you've been fed. I can't believe you'd turn your back on our Savior, and believe people. I raised you in the church, to love God, and this is what you do, turn away from your faith?"

She has read him completely, he knows it, but he is done cowering, done pretending. His grandmother's challenge to his newly excavated freedom, coupled, with a new, bitter outlook towards his life, brings a demonic confidence out of Melvin. "How can I turn my back on something that I never believed in, something that doesn't even exist, Grandma? You need to be more worried about us getting some money, so we can get out of this shitty apartment, than you do worshipping some myth."

Silence fills the air. Melvin's eyes lock onto hers', his face carries a temper reserved only for ones' most hated enemy. His adrenaline flows like never before. It feels so good to let it all out, he doesn't want to stop. "You know what, I'm relieved. I feel unburdened now that I know there definitely is no higher power than us, that I no longer have to play this game of tug of war for my soul. I tried to let God in, it didn't work, and there is a good reason it didn't work… BECAUSE THERE IS NO GOD!"

He points at the Bible on the table, "So, I don't give a damn about that book, Jesus, and most of all, God. We have nothing! Since you don't seem to realize this, I'm going to tell you… we're beneath the bottom of the barrel, Me-ma. We've wasted our lives away waiting on Him, or them, or whatever. So, you tell me, what has faith in God ever done for us? Did God heal your leg like you asked him? Did he get your family out of this shithole like you asked? Where's the fruit of your faithfulness, Me-ma? I really wanta know, where the hell is it?"

Absent of the pain in her leg, with the swiftness of a woman half her age, May flies out of her seat and gets right up into his face. All Melvin has time to see and react to is the blur of five fingernails coming for his eyes. He catches her wrists, but moments too late, the long nail on his grandmother's left middle finger deeply scratches him diagonally along the right side of his neck, unleashing a decent flow of blood down his chest.

She answers his verbal rage with her own passionate outburst. "Get out, don't you ever again bring Satan into this house. You are not my child, you are not God's child, you are his child, leave, don't…," everything instantly changes.

May clutches her left breast, the left side of her face stiffens.

"Grandma, Me-ma, what's wrong?" In a blink, panicked love for his loved one replaces his boiling, hellish anger. Melvin puts his forearms under her armpits to soften the blow as she crumbles down onto their cold, bare floor.

May's zigzag thinking suddenly remembers that her preoccupied mind had been forgetting to remind her to take her diabetes and blood thinning medications.

With little strength remaining, May tries to push Melvin away. She knows her time is critical and she doesn't want her last 'ticks' to be in the arms of someone who has turned his back to the Lord. The loving grandson she has always known has returned, but it matters not to her.

Dying inside, Melvin bravely puts on a good poker face to help keep his cherished grandmother calm as he, on bent knees, cradles the back of her head as he lays it across his thighs. For him, everything is in slow motion, he goes into a surreal state that reduces him to mindlessly mutter, "Me-ma don't, Me-ma don't."

He places his palm over her heart. With only a few precious bits of life force left inside her body, May aggressively pushes his hand away, but it keeps coming back. It has to, he can't let her go.

Her voice grows weaker, breaking apart her words. "Don't touch me. I will not spend my last moments touched by you."

Melvin can't hear her. Absent of conscience thought, he chants the Lord's Prayer to her. He knows that was her favorite, since he was a child she would recite that scripture to him.

"Let me go, let me go, Melvin." Although she fights, her heart squeezes like a vice, sapping her strength, preventing her from rolling out of his cradled arms. Over and over again, Melvin pulls the one relative that cared for him and loved him back into his life. While May is only able to feel the darkness and pain that these horrible last moments of her relationship with her grandson have brought, his mind races through snapshots of a lifetime filled with loving memories created by his sweet Me-ma.

May's fight draws closer to its conclusion. Melvin feels it, he transfers every bit of his love for her into his embrace; he won't let her go, he can't. Her breathes shorten. Her saucer sized eyes close slowly like an electric garage. He feels the last bit of this life leave what has belonged to God, ever since she was fourteen years old.

The children rush out of their room screaming hysterically. They all clasp some piece - waist, leg, hand - any piece, just to feel warmth from the woman that nurtured and kept them safe when no one else would.

Crying out through heavy sobs for the return of Heaven's newest angel, Melvin screams at the top of his lungs. "Help us somebody, help us!"

"Yes, I'm sure that's what I want. I'll still make all of the appearances for my foundation, but I need you to cancel that four hundred thousand dollar check I donated this month." While being chauffeured down the highway, surrounded by the 'Melvin' part of town, from the passenger's compartment of his limousine, over the phone, Bryant Michaels tells his accountant what his next assignment is.

America's number one current athlete stares blankly as the identical, impoverished conditions and homes he grew up in, whiz blindly by his dark tinted windows and his heart. His conscience speaks, "I can still get those poor children the same amount of money. I'll just put together more events, more fund raisers. I'll use the strength of my name, and let others use the strength of their money." His behind kissing accountant fully agrees right before his boss clicks off the phone and clicks on the thirteen inch television monitor that has just flipped out from the purple velvet lining of the limo's door panel.

'Flight' immediately flips to his favorite sports network, which is in the mist of showcasing highlights from the Monday night football game that was played last evening. His eyes watch the screen, but his thoughts carry his mind far away. "Man, I really tried. I wanted to live that life, but damn, like Uncle Gene was saying, 'that ain't what life is about'. It's about fully enjoying this world if you're lucky enough to get the chance, like I am. Ain't nothing wrong with life being carefree, that's what's fun. The Bible holds you back from that… but I've done many wonderful things for people, and I will continue to do that, just not with my money.

Arrogance fills him, "I have touched the lives of so many, so many children. If God would have been real I know He would have let me into heaven, just on the strength of that." Out of the blue, panic assumes control over his feelings. Bryant suddenly fears that which he considers fantasy, causing him to do something he has not done in quite awhile. His knees fall to the floor, his eyes close tight, his palms slap together to form one fist, the backsides of his thumbs rests against his forehead. "God, if you are there, I'm sorry, I repent. I'm repenting for what I believe. I'm bearing my sins to you, so if I'm wrong dear God, you still must bless me with your forgiveness. That's your Word, you must..." He passionately says "you must" at least ten times, before he can move on.

Feeling sufficient that he has covered all his bases, thoughts once again shift, a tremendous smile brought on by ungodly thoughts loosens his hands along with the rest of his tense physique. "Man wrote the Bible, everyone knows that. So why isn't it within reason to think that man probably embellished a bit, to say the least? That's what people do, it's natural, people have always loved a good heroic story. They meant well, but its just fake...," 'Flight' laughs, "making up all of these dramatic, magical stories; that sounds just like something man would do." He finds such comfort here.

Next comes memories of himself, years ago, as he told Ricky about his future plans, "I'm free to do whatever I want now, without worry or consequence, but I've gotta be smart about it. So many people still believe. There is so much milk left in this cow. I can still make a gang of money working this God angle."

That thought sparks an action from him that will impact people across the world.

It's not bad. The leather is a wee-bit worn in a couple of spots and there are a few dings mainly along the doors and hood, but its o.k.

It's not a bad choice to quickly pick off of a local used car lot, just fifteen minutes ago, after you were dropped off by your chauffeured limousine.

The ten-year-old white Ford blends in with all of the other cars it passes, making its new owner very pleased.

He hasn't been in a car with this level of quality since he was in high school. He feels awkward riding around like this. There are no hi-tech gadgets to play with, there is no superiority felt riding down the street in this, no one peers inside its windows to discern whom the driver is. "This is perfect."

He picks up his cellphone and speaks through its speaker. "Are you down there yet? Do you have the camera ready? Good, I'll be there in about five minutes. Be ready."

Bryant 'Flight' Michaels insatiable thirst for public adulation and increased wealth has driven him to 'jump off of the cliff', as he steers down suburbia's side streets; while hidden behind this car and dark, oversized sunglasses. His mind delights, buzzed by fantasies about how great his stature across the world is about to become.

The adrenaline of the moment causes Bryant's heart to race like he sprinting down court for a game winning breakaway dunk.

He arrives at his mark, inside Anytown's bustling downtown shopping district. Bryant parks curbside in the busiest of crowd sections. He steps out, his eyes search. Sorting through the masses of bodies, he spots his young female accomplice, who is standing across the street alongside an open air ice cream stand. "Good, she's right where she is supposed to be." He nods to her, she nods back.

"Is that Bryant Michaels, Mommy?" A male youngster questions as he and his loving provider, who is occupied by her cellphone conversation, walk by.

He ditches his eyewear. He knows that he must act now or never, 'Flight' glances over at his aid, his eyes are gleefully met by a small hand-held camcorder in front of her face.

Showtime!

His arms shoot his hands straight up into the hot blue sky. Ten fingers and two palms gyrate feverishly. His resounding and shocking shouts freeze feet and turn heads on all within his voice's range. "Thank you Jesus for the blood! You are real, dear Father!

Bring shame to those who do not believe in the glory of your name...," like a starving man dropping to his knees from the ravages of extreme hunger, Bryant falls upon the pavement, "I believe in you, Father... I choose you and not the world, Father! Is there anyone here who loves you the way that I do?"

Those in attendance are stunned. People can not believe what they are seeing. One of America's heroes, one of their personal heroes, the man that they have scheduled moments of their life around so that he may fill their eyes and their emotions with exhilaration, is down on his knees right before their very eyes and he is praising God and outwardly backing the very God and Christ that many of them privately doubt even exist.

His antics renew their belief.

The adrenaline of the moment has them. The spirit of the moment works its way into their bodies, arrogance steps aside, they fear God!

They rush to his side. Usually, they shove and push in their angst to be next to him, but they file in nicely. This is bigger than them. Within thirty seconds, nine nations are represented in the rejoicing, praising, thanksgiving, and repentance, openly spoken by the growing thousand or so in attendance.

'Flight' rises back to his feet. His extreme height helps his sinful eyes search above the crowd, he spots the thumbs up. "Good, she's getting it all on film."

'Flight' is starting to feel the love from the swelling crowd. The idol worshipping awes him. Those who are truly praising God, he does not feel. 'Flight' feels powerful, as he looks into the faces' of various people around him, he thinks, "Wow, look at them, this is beautiful. Man this is almost like some big cult worship or something. They're almost making me want to believe in God again."

The scene becomes a spiritual revival that stretches on for close to three hours, all of which is successful recorded by an 'anonymous' citizen that just happened to have a camera handy.

People can't control their fervor, especially once all of the news vans and its storytellers arrive at the location to illuminate the story for the entire world to see.

They go home feeling good about the Lord, confident in their love and faith in God. The Holy Spirit fires through them; but for how long? What happens two hours from now, when the passion of the situation has died down and they are free to return to their life's normal routine, will the spirit remain?

Jackpot! Bryant gets exactly what he wanted out of his big theater duet. The media coverage and its resulting publicity is nonstop. Every newscast, every conversation starts with Bryant's shocking "breakdown for faith", as it is dubbed. For the doubters, his actions salute the part in them that does not want to give up on God. His over-the-top display of faith makes them feel comfortable to celebrate God in the open.

He touches America. Everyone wants to be like 'Flight'. In a runaway victory, up to the second polls have him ranked as America's most beloved and recognizable person.

Bryant's introspection about what he's done surmises the amount of REAL wealth he has in his life, "My endorsements deals are about to at least triple. But it's not all for me, look at how many people I'm saving, so what if I don't believe it myself. If they wanna believe they're getting closer to God, great, they feel better and reward me for inspiring them, what's wrong with that? Everyone benefits. Man, it's almost a shame that God ain't real," he sighs sadly while internally basking in his glory, "I really do have the power to bring people to him."

Ricky is torn apart. He couldn't tell you which emotion is stronger, joy; which he feels watching the footage of his friend's open devotion for their Lord and Savior, or shame; for being a condemning, brow-beating pessimist Christian, who prayed for his friend to reach this high point, but never believed he would; so he pushed and pushed, instead of allowing the Lord to handle it, as he so often requested of Him. "Man, I was so sure God had spoken to me through my spirit about the danger Bryant was in. I was so wrong."

Ricky and Stacy watch the news coverage together from the living room of her home. "Look at him, Stacy. Testifying and breaking down in front of the world for the glory of God. Boy, oh boy, do I owe him a big apology."

Stacy seems confused. "Why do you say that?"

"I owe him and I owe God one too, because our dear Lord was working on him, while I continuously doubted them both. As I mistakenly felt some bad spirit surrounding him, Bryant put his life in God's hands, but I didn't see it, because I was too busy judging him."

Stacy Stunning says nothing discouraging, but something inside of her isn't so confident in this 'new' Bryant Michaels.

Months pass by, it's late in the season now and after a great start, the reigning two-time champions have tumbled mightily, having lost eighteen of their last twenty games. The deluge of fan and media scrutiny has intensified tenfold, so the players all decide to arrive at the arena three hours early for some much needed extra practice time, before tonight's crucial game. Only one beat writer and his two man camera crew await their extremely early arrival.

None of the men present has any idea that they are about to play a key role in a societal changing, major news frenzy.

Inside of the locker room, Ricky Walters sits comfortably on his cold, polished wood stool dressed and ready to sweat. He is in the mist of his daily pre-practice routine of whipping out his Bible for a quick spiritual feeding.

Various players and team staff members mill about, playing around or talking on their cell-phones, while a select few gawk over the beautiful women on the pages of some triple x magazine. Bryant Michaels was one of them, until he seen Ricky break out the gospel. The sight of Ricky enjoying 'his best friend' brings about a dark ire inside of the superstar.

These last few months have been a mixed bag for 'Flight', and he can't stand it any longer. He didn't plan for or even look at the 'breakdown for faith' situation from this end, before he did it. Bryant has leapt from top athlete celebrity status to the totally intrusive movie star icon status, but his star power is not that of some Hollywood bad boy, it is that of a saint. Even though all of his financially targeted motives have been reached, he still can't take much more of this. Unbeknownst to him, his blessing to himself has become God's canvas.

Lately, he can feel some distance growing between himself and the rest of the team. He goes to the clubs now, no woman will accept him. He has gone on eight different occasions and has received the same fate each time, they look at him with such reverence, in such glory and high standing, they won't even think of touching him sexually.

His frustration leads to desperation. He acts crazy in his nightlife, fighting to let the ladies see that he is not this angel that they have cast him to be. Drugs, fights, being overly profane and rude, making the money constantly 'rain'; he involves himself in them all, but he receives none of the responses he aches for. None of the scantily clad hips and breasts he seeks accepts him in this way. Their actions say to him, "Your like God to me."

He can't stand this posturing any longer. All of the interviews submersed in religious discussions, having to constantly put on his mask of faith, which steers time and attention away his mask of vanity, has gotten to be too much. "No one wants to talk about me, or basketball, anymore. All they want me to talk about is God this, Jesus that."

Ricky Walters is the face of Bryant's frustrations. Demons motivate Michaels to nonchalantly stroll back over to his locker. From atop the million dollar chair, that neighbors and dwarfs the ten dollar stool, 'Flight' enjoys a disdainful stare into the side of his best friend's inattentive eyes.

He desperately wants to annoy Ricky, who has been slowly alienated by his teammates, even though no one has clearly stated why; but Ricky has a hunch. Bryant hasn't uttered one word to him in a week. For the life of him, Ricky just can't understand why such a faithful and active Christian, who now parades his devote and active Christianity as a beacon for the entire world to follow, would distance himself from such a like-minded soul.

Michaels aches to enjoy the pain on Ricky's face when he rubs his fallen God's face in it. His eyes snarl at the book inside Ricky's cupped hands, he travels back to when he felt he needed to avoid Ricky when IT was around. Bryant fears IT no more.

From behind Ricky's shoulder, 'Flight' lets out short spurts of laughter just loud enough that Ricky will hopefully hear him, but his teammates won't. His frustration over the situation he has created and an inordinate lack of humility capitalize and seize the moment. This is his chance to knock Ricky down from his God-fearing pedestal.

He is positive that Ricky, deep down in his heart, knows that everything the world has been told and shown is true. "Ricky is just in denial, I can break him." Bryant is sure that only one finger of faith is all that is keeping Ricky from falling away from his beliefs, his mind tells him "that if I can just pluck that finger off, then Ricky will fall and abandon his imaginary idols. Boy, I bet he feels real stupid right now. He won't admit it because he's stubborn, but he knows he's been lied to, just like the rest of us were." Bryant wants so badly for him to feel the same way he does, that his mind distorts reality.

The spirit flourishing inside of him would love to get some payback for all of the times Ricky or Stacy even dared to say a word about who should be leading his life. He thinks about how their words ate at his conscience, which in turn, made him debate the path that his life was on, which in turn, made him debate what his uncle said all of those years ago.

Across the gigantic room, completely away from the rest of the team, head coach, Lance Peterson, ends the on camera portion of an emotional interview, in which, he deflects the blame for his team's slow finish away from its franchise player. However, off camera, Coach Peterson wants to vent, he wants to tell the truth to somebody, anybody. And since they follow the team all over the country, plus the convenience of them being right there, he feels safe in choosing - Channel 9 - the team's trusted local camera crew to bounce his frustration off of.

Coach and crew step into his office, he asks that the camera and the sound boom be left behind, so he can leave his politically correct assessments outside with them.

They sit. Lance offers up a drink to everyone. "You guys see it, we've been losing the close ones because of Flight's poor shot selection at the end of games. I don't know what's come over him. It's like he's a different player this season, for someone who believes so strongly in the Lord, it's strange that he's become really selfish. He's not being a leader at all."

Back at the lockers, Ricky is not oblivious to Michaels' taunting presence coming over his shoulder. He blocks out his silent ridicule and continues strengthening his faith through the Holy Bible.

Mitch Law, the team's leading rebounder, whose play has also deteriorated mightily, sees Michaels glancing down at the Bible, and then staring chillingly at Ricky. Intrigued, Mitch's attention attaches to the situation. Michaels' eyes suddenly look directly into Mitch's. Through a wink, his eyes try to tell Mitch's eyes that the time has come; it's time to stop the pretending. Demons tell 'Flight' to "go for it, and do it big!"

He leans over Ricky's shoulder, the room quiets, basketball players become fans as Mitch quietly tips off the other guys to what their leader is curiously doing.

A condescending whisper, from Bryant, farther dims the room's quieting noise level, as it echoes inside Ricky's ear, "Hey buddy, what cha readin' there? I was just wondering, me and the other guys were taking bets. Who do you think would win in a supreme, no holds barred, winner take all, battle for the universe? Huh?"

Bryant waits for him to bite. He doesn't, so he goes on, "God or Zeus?" 'Flight' puts the 'cherry on top' with a demeaning follow up giggle.

The athletes inside that room can't believe that Bryant is

talking this way about God. Their thoughts are critical of him, even though most of them aren't totally shocked that he feels this way, everyone is completely surprised by his bold arrogance.

Ricky Walters is not one to be belittled or intimidated by Bryant or anyone else. He slams the Bible shut, then, smiles over his shoulder back to his neighbor. "Well, well, well, look who's turned the light on in the closet. You really had me fooled. But I should have known you were just hiding with the door open. So, when are you going to come clean to the public and stop this ridiculous circus act you've been performing for so long?"

"The day will come, but not too soon."

"The devil really has you, doesn't he?"

Ricky is surprised by the honesty of his hushed response. "No, Ricky, reality has me... I'm just giving the public what they want. It makes them feel better about themselves."

"Bryant?"

"What?"

"You know God still loves you, don't you? Don't force him to love you all the way to hell."

Those words bring fear to the listener's ears. "Just shut up with that crap, Ricky. Him loving me is like a young girl's teddy bear loving her. You of all people should be happy; my act, as you call it, which it is, brings people to the God that you say is real. There are people out there getting, quote unquote, saved, because of me. You owe me more appreciation than I'm being shown...," his smug face laughs, "but I'm a let you in on something. They still don't believe, Ricky. I can see it in people's actions, in what they say, and how they say it. They want to believe, but at the same time... they know that they shouldn't, they're faking just as much as I am."

"You may be right, that's what's so sad."

"We know that scroll and everything written on it is real, so why should we be forced to keep living a lie?"

"I hope that your heart and mind changes, Bryant. I decree, in Jesus' name, that the demons that bind you will exit your heart and mind..."

"Man, I don't need you performing some meaningless ritual for me, so move that hocus-pocus demon stuff on down the road. Ain't nobody buying it over here."

"You have it all figured out, huh?"

His response comes with great arrogance. "I believe I do. I'm going to do what I do, for awhile longer, it won't be long before some other celebrity cracks and openly admits what we all know. Once that happens, I'll gauge the public's response to it, if it's favorable, I'll come in behind 'em, act real deep for 'em, then wrap this nonsense up." 'Flight' leans in closer to his target and viciously spouts, "I love the humility I feel from you right now. You know He's dead, Rick… and I love that I know you know it. I'm just soaking it all in."

With pity in his expression, Ricky simply shakes his head and sighs at Michaels' assessment. He, then, looks at the faces' of the men with them in that locker room, but they won't look back. "I'm all alone."

"I'm a tell you the truth…," Michaels leans back in his 'throne' and throws his hands into the air, then, with childish joy, he spins himself around, "it feels unbelievably good to have all that spiritual weight off of my shoulders!…", his feet halt his spin, Bryant's eyes confidently return to Ricky, "I was so tired of trying to live up to His impossible standards. That whole God thing always did seem absurd. I knew there had to be a reason why I always doubted there was some no shape, no age, colorless being hovering above our heads', changing and creating life with a stroke of his magic, invisible wand."

Admitting aloud what had been 'bottled up' for weeks on in, especially to Ricky, the man that he now speculates secretly fueled he and Stacy's breakup, wildly energizes him. Michaels lets out a loud cowboy cry, "Hee haw!," in honor of the large cowboy hat Ricky wore in this morning.

Bryant 'Flight' Michaels has never felt this level of power; ever! The man has felt as many different levels of it as anyone in the world, but none have equaled the exhilarating high now occupying his body. "I tried, Ricky. I really did. I gave God the benefit of the doubt for a long time, but we can't help but to look at it from both sides."

Everyone is frozen, they don't know what he will do next, but they can't wait to see.

Ricky glances around the room, "You guys are going to give up on faith for man's evidence. All you guys have done is look at faith through sight, and sight can't recognize faith! You men are playing yourselves."

'Flight' takes in nothing that he says. He reaches down and puts on Ricky's dark brown, ten gallon hat and walks to the middle of the room, and like a king he announces, "Let it out people, its o.k, God is gone! You don't have to hold onto this lie any longer. Ricky, its party time baby, get out here with the rest of us and have some fun!" Trying to farther antagonize, Bryant extends his open arms and hands while dancing some silly little hip grinding dance.

He knows their shocked; he loves it! 'Flight' knows that everyone inside that room either loves him or fears him, so he's not worried, he can finally be free with his brothers. "The boogeyman is not coming back. You don't have to fake it any longer…" With tremendous volume and confidence, he urges his listeners to release the anxiety that every person in that room, except for one feels, "say it with me, I'm free, I won't go to hell!"

His target audience only responds with nervous smiles, they look for signs about how to respond from each other. Michaels grows a bit agitated by the continued sedateness that is over them. He knows they're at the edge of the pool, but they're scared to fall in and wash away the greatest fantasy ever told. 'Flight' gives them that shove.

Like a great comedian reeling in his audience after some super edgy joke that didn't go over well, "Come on now, tell the truth people, it really wasn't the go to Heaven thing you were most concerned about was it? It was the fear of burning in hell, of having Satan as your landlord! That's the piece to the puzzle that we cared most about. Y'all got'a give me that one!"

What he is saying, they battle not to like, but they see his confidence in it, they see that he was not struck down by lightning or turned into salt, or put into the belly of a whale. No, he is standing there, smiling, o.k. just like them.

Their bodies begin to loosen. The pleasure and ease of mind in thinking that they are not going to hell and won't endure torture and sadness, the scale of which, no living person could ever fathom, is too much for any of them any longer to hold back acknowledging.

Their eyes try to remain neutral, but Bryant sees his likeness in them. He puts it all on the line.

Les Wakken, the team's starting power forward, and the second most popular guy on the team, is the one randomly chosen. Bryant's smiling, arrogant physical shell approaches him with his hand out to the side, stretched out chest high, "You feel me, big Les?"

A few seconds feels like minutes. Everyone readies for Les' response. "Yeah, I feel you, 'Flight'." They, aggressively, slap hands and their chests unite with a bump. Their agreement calms many other nerves.

Les' remaining doubts about his decision clears away once Mitch, over to his left, breaks down to his knees, and through joyous fake tears proclaims, "Thank you John Richards, thank you! Now I don't have ta feel that irritating guilt itching at me when I cheat on my wife with her cousin anymore, thank you!" Like a slow clap that builds, the room's laughter builds to an explosion.

Bryant's 'windows' scope around; they are pleased with what they see. White, black, European, Jewish, Catholic, Baptist -Bryant's openness is rewarded by the number of souls that accompany him into the abyss, "Be honest, y'all… We only cared about heaven, because we feared hell. If there wasn't no hell, I wouldn't have gave a damn about Heaven, shit, I'm fine with it just being over when I die. No this way or that way, just over." Their bond of commonality deepens.

Looking at the same picture, Ricky looks around and sees an entirely different scene than Bryant. He sees men, ex-friends, that he has sat and prayed with, had passionate discussions about faith with, men he has heard pledge their devotion to God, time and time again, over the course of years, men that he had seen just days ago standing with Bryant, in front of the camera, confessing their love for Jesus Christ. Now he watches those same men rejoicing the Bible's 'extinction' and dancing on God's 'grave'.

Ricky addresses one and all. "Boy, it didn't take long did it? As soon as the tiniest shred of what looks like real evidence appears against God, you people show your heart...," he glares at Bryant in disgust, "and y'all takin' comfort in your decision because he says so? I guess I should look on the bright side, at least now, I won't have to listen to anymore meaningless babble about the love and faith you guys still have in our Father."

Thoughts waver, but the spirit influencing Bryant Michaels' and his words soothes them. It speaks through 'Flight'. "The only father you or any of us have is the one that had sex with your mother and created you. Give it up Ricky, there is hardcore proof that the whole God, in seven days, Jesus on a cross story, was just a beautifully crafted, creative fable. There are no aliens, and there is no God; there's just us... that's it."

Les chimes back in. "Come on Ricky, this is just like way back in ancient times, when the Greeks believed that their Gods were real. We're just the modern day version of the same thing." Les enjoys a deep exhale, those words have been on his chest and mind for so long. Heads nod and mouths mutter, strongly, in agreement.

"Hey guys, check this out!" One of the team's trainers turns up the volume on the clubhouse's monster screen television.

A special news conference by President Thames has begun from the White House Rose Garden. The leader of the free world reads a prepared statement. "Just today, through farther investigations by the beleaguered CIA, knowledge was gained that proves the biblical scroll was not destroyed, as we were told, but in fact, with no previous knowledge by any President's administration, had been buried beneath the White House almost the entire time. Once it is dug up, which is beginning at this moment, and extensive tests are concluded, we all will finally have more definitive answers. Thank you."

Ricky is disgusted by his President. "Definitive answers, don't tell people those are definitive answers. Man, the devil is slick."

Energized by new information that reinforces what they have already come to accept, the guys 'hoot and holler' like a pack of overly sugared kids on a playground.

"Well Rickster, how much more proof do you need? You know it's going to come back authentic, baby! The government is screwed up, but I don't think they're even capable of inventing ancient writings," touts an ultra-confident Michaels.

Ricky watches with sadness as their high sweeps away their minds'. He knows that this life has them boxed in, that they are drowning and don't even know it. His voice abruptly stops their laughter, "My faith is not added to, or subtracted by, any so-called evidence by any country or any person. That's why it is called faith, and all of you will perish for your lack of it; if you don't change. You guys need to think about what you're doing before it's too late, but until that day, I'll still pray for your souls' because God loves you, and so do I."

With complete surface seriousness, Bryant replies. "Damn Ricky... that's deep."

One isolated crackle is heard, setting off a chain reaction that echoes off the room's walls. Ricky's strength grows stronger as he yells over the roar, "And all you must do is look into the sky, look BEYOND your eyes, and beg Jesus to forgive you."

"Turn the faucet off on all that bullshit. It's eating you up now that you can't feel that you're better than us, isn't it?"

"Why do you think that?" Ricky retorts with great resolution, "I am better than you, FLIGHT! From what I can see, I'm better than each and every one of you."

The giggles and laughter settle again. Some are shocked,

some are curious, some are angry, but all want to know why a quiet, non-arrogant, believer would say such a boastful, arrogant thing.

Bryant. "Boy, Ricky, all this time I've known you, you've really hid your large ego well. I thought God's people aren't supposed to speak with arrogance."

"If you knew anything about the Bible, you'd know it's called holy boldness, and the reason that I can say what I said is the Bible tells me that 'greater is the spirit in me than the one whose spirit is of the world.' I am of God's spirit, and you all are of the world's spirit, so yes…," the boldness and sureness of his voice expands, "I am greater than all of you combined; praise God, hallelujah!"

They mock his assertion; they run around the room hysterically, flopping around on each other, heading towards exhaustion due to their chest heaving, nonstop gaiety. The fear is gone, it's dead in them.

Undeterred, Ricky asks 'THE' question, but being so drunk off of their newfound freedoms, the guys drown it with more laughter. "What are you going to do when Jesus returns and you have to answer for your lack of faith?" And with that, Ricky is done defending, done debating.

CHAPTER TEN

Any other day, David Gimmer would begin this new morning as he has every other morning for decades, first he would sit down at his dining room table and read the metropolitan section of Anytown's newspaper, but this is no average morning. David goes right for the *Across America* section. With complete concentration, he reads every article related to yesterday's shocking news from the White House. Across the table from him, his wife, Sasha, enjoys the Fashion and Arts portion, as always.

David reads while feasting on his customary breakfast consisting of four strips of bacon, two scrambled eggs, and a biscuit with gravy, which is all capped off by a huge blood pumping mug of coffee.

Sasha refolds her paper, then, goes to the counter to retrieve another cup of caffeine. Her mind tingles as it replays snapshots of the new Dior and Prada dresses some of Hollywood's top starlets were photographed in a few nights back at the Oscars. "Honey, I've been thinking, maybe it's time for you to quit with the charity cases and see what the big corporations have to offer. You've done your good deeds by working for less money to help the poor, now I think it's time to focus on the financial rewards of your position. We make decent money now, but think of all the things even more money will allow us to have."

David is two steps ahead of her. He has been debating a great deal lately about making that very leap; yet, the other side of him continually craves the feeling of superiority and praise heaped upon him for all of his perceived nobility that only his current job position can bring.

Whenever someone asks David what he does for a living, he's always sure, with subtle arrogance, to make them aware that, "I could be making way more money, at a bigger firm, but I feel that helping the less fortunate is God's calling for me. I could easily be making three, four hundred grand a year. It's not about money for me." The pats on his back are priceless.

Besides, Sasha is a 'big wig' at one of the most sought after, up and coming, advertising and marketing firms in the region, so they are far from just living average.

He tells his spouse. "I may do that one day, but not right now. They have just found the writings that could change the course of history and the future; we have bigger worries to focus on." She says nothing, Sasha 'turns' up her nose and with the strutting glide of a runway model she moves her scalpel enhanced physique into the entertainment room to watch one of the morning talk shows on their recently installed eighty one inch plasma 'movie screen'.

Minutes later, she yells out, "I can not believe he just said that, David come here, look!"

His section of paper slips off of the table's corner, as he rushes in, and takes a seat next to her on their ostrich skin sofa.

David enters and the television screen is black. "What's going on?"

"Just watch."

Captioned words from an ongoing conversation scroll across the bottom of the screen to help clear up any muddled ones that can't clearly be heard. David is stunned by what he hears, "He couldn't have said that, I don't believe it."

"David, you know his voice as well as anybody, yes, that was 'Flight'."

By early afternoon, most of America will have listened to, or heard about, Bryant's locker room omissions concerning his real thoughts and feelings towards God's existence, how he's been faking all of his publicized faith, and his personal relief that the Bible is a 'fake'. Yes, his teammates joined in on it too, but 'Flight' is the star, his is the name that opens ears and gets mouths talking.

The sound was unintentionally recorded by the local camera crew in attendance at the arena. Accidentally and unbeknownst to everyone, the crew forgot to turn off their equipment before they went into coach Peterson's office to listen to his rant. And just that easily, history is made.

The same man, whom on the streets of Anytown and to the public paraded himself to be a pillar for godly faith, has now become the first public figure to 'come out of the closet' and say exactly where his belief lies.

Sasha is comforted by what she hears. David is incensed by it. In his eyes, Bryant has gone too far this time. A large part of the reason David loves 'Flight' is his devotion to Christ. He has made excuses for and forgiven his sports hero's every public indiscretion, but not this time, he has gone TOO far. "His black ass is just like the rest of them. He believes all of the lies that are being spread around!"

Even though many brief moments of doubt have seeped into David's head, he has tired greatly to hold on. Since he and Sasha's bedtime talk, David has renewed his biblical reading and he has been watching more of his evangelical tapes.

Sasha has been attentive of her husband's renewed actions. She senses that he is weakening, in spite of his words, in spite of his actions. "His heart isn't in it."

She correctly detects an ongoing battle inside of his mind, for his words and for his actions. "On one hand, he watches a show or two and reads the Bible, for a minute, on the other; he doesn't go to church much anymore, he makes up lame excuses that before never would have stopped him. "He used to sometimes speak about God's direction for our life during 'cuddle time', now that has ceased. I see him, when he thinks that I don't. He reads the Bible, but questions everything it says, it bores him until he nods off or closes the book to turn on the television. I bet ya, doubts about the validity of God's Word greet him each time he steps towards that book."

Like others, David listens to public opinion, outwardly he denounces thoughts that support the 'Bible hoax', but his mind replays their ideas, their opinions, and their beliefs. Seeds are blossoming inside him, much to Sasha's delight.

She loves that David's hero is the first star to be caught expressing his true feelings. She knows that so many have been thinking it, now they have a lead voice to stand behind. Sasha can't wait to get to work and gauge the responses of her co-workers.

After another brief racist outburst by David, Sasha turns the television off, so that she may 'tiptoe' a general question to him, but it's really his own personal views she's pecking at. "Wow, what a news week. Do you think that Bryant's comments will help change peoples' minds if the writing is found to be authentic?"

Once again, David adamantly defends God's existence, but concurrently, a few more doubts trickle through the cracks.

Across office cubicles, in parking lots, breakfast, lunch, and dinner, wherever two or more people stop to hold a discussion, Bryant's comments are discussed.

Sasha gets to work and discovers that no one feels as she feels, they all crucify him, so she plays along with the majority, for now; but Sasha has a hunch that all is not as it seems.

Twenty nine thousand square feet of elegance, yet it feels like a shoebox. The opinions of the world can bring much fame and fortune, but its weight can become more than one can bear once intense negative personal coverage dominates the airwaves. Bryant 'Flight' Michaels now knows both sides of the ledger.

Nonstop coverage surrounding all of his antics weighs extensively on his head, so much so he has taken a leave of absent from the sport he loves.

The last few days, since his 'caught on camera' revelations, have tightened and condensed everything his mind sees, "They don't love me anymore, the whole world hates me." Just today, his employee that he paid to 'accidentally' record his theatrics has sold her story to the tabloids.

He sits for hours in his bedroom, alone, watching the public's opinions through his television. They speak so strongly against all of his lies, his lack of faith, and his phoniness.

He's so angry at himself for talking so loosely. Having lived in the spotlight for so long, he knows better. He can't stop himself from replaying everything that he said and felt as he cursed God's name, and how he reveled in it.

As the hours pass, Bryant's hurt sinks him into despair. He knows that there will be no more shining moments of stardom, no more good favor with the media and public, "My life will be filled with plagues now." His so-called friends haven't called, all of his endorsements, status, and the worth of his name is disintegrating across every television screen across the world.

All of this imprisons him, he is left all alone. Bryant 'Flight' Michaels is scared, the loneliness humbles and moves him to speak with God. From atop his bed's mattress, sitting up on his knees, Bryant thrust his head down onto his bedsheet. "Heavenly Father, I come to you in prayer through your precious son Jesus Christ… Father, I am sorry. I apologize for my horrific sins. Everyone is turning their backs' on me, Lord, you are all I have. I don't think that I ever truly believed the words that I said against you anyway, I was just speaking out of some kind of hurt or something, dear Lord… I promise that if you get me out of this, I will start reading the Bible and learning your Word. If you do this for me, I won't only publicly praise you, but I will praise you when I am all alone, like I am now."

Days later. "For every dark day, a brighter one always lies ahead," Bryant's smiling lips say to his ears, as he happily exits the double doors of his mansion for the first time in over a week.

All across their follow the leader, follow your eyes world, a growing sense of relief spreads as the initial shocked and angry reactions towards Bryant's comments wane. They think, "Why do we scorn him?" They come to realize that their scorn brings them no advantage. They love to crucify their fallen stars, but it clicks that their silent thoughts have gained a voice, "This is a good thing," minds' turn to say.

Now that the masses have heard someone, especially someone of such great prominence, finally say the same things that have been ducking in and out of their own thoughts, many feel secure enough, free enough, to openly voice their similar choices of belief. As public opinion over the last three days has turned, so has the media's all-important slant towards the story.

The words written and spoken about him have softened. Now that they see the tide turning, celebrity friends return and come to his defense by opening up with their own personal testimonies, "I, myself, battled with many of the same thoughts that Bryant said. I think it's just human nature to doubt. I think that all he did was voice what many of us have been thinking, he just got caught doing it." Hearing Hollywood's support brings upon a tsunami-sized wave of acceptance to society's ears.

Media attention turns to a new villain in the whole 'Bryant Michaels compares and equals the only living God to a mythical figure, caught on camera scandal'. With communication to the world only being a few clicks away, some guy in Nowheres, Montana directs his ten fingers to blog about Ricky and how Christians always think they're better than everyone else, "When you're a Christian you're supposed to love everyone, correct? Did any of you hear this so-called Christian's arrogance, how he tried to make all of these men, who were just voicing their freedom of speech by the way, feel like they were beneath him?"

News articles, talk show debates, and internet chat rooms jump aboard and turn the focus of the entire incident to the true statement made by Ricky. By blasting him, they've found an effective avenue in which to medicate themselves from having to deal with their own faith choices and decisions.

"How dare he be so smug and arrogant, while at the same time spouting off about how faithful he is to God…," writes opinion columnist Jason Jack of the Chicago Chronicles, "Christians just want us to lose out on living life, because deep inside, they know that's what they're doing under the mythical master they serve."

Political talk show host, Mark Billingley, receives an arousing ovation from the studio audience after he speaks his heart, alongside other panelists on his hit show, "Since I was a little boy, I've noticed how arrogant some Christians can be, they're always telling us how to live, what to think, when in fact, half of them are hypocrites. And I definitely think Ricky Walters fits that mold."

Like dominoes they fall. The hiding is over. Forbidden thoughts and words that have never before in history been spoken against God's Word fly around freely. People have openly lost their fear of the unimaginable. The faithless take great delight in the number of Christians that slowly trickle out from hiding behind the faith that they never truly had.

A powerful shadow invisibly darkens the world, created by the people for the people, and it looms larger by the minute. Everyday thousands more leave their souls' open for the enemy to step in. Even the truly faithful are touched, their flesh also falls under attack.

An unspoken about epidemic spreads out upon the world's doubters, caused by their words and their heart, which is thoroughly explained in the book they've abandoned.

They exchange to each other, so imaginatively, how they will hold hedonistic, wild parties to celebrate their release from all biblical rule. They boast of dancing in the streets upon 'official' word of the Bible's 'death'. In them, the Word of God loses all credibility as constant nurturing of what their senses has told them breeds great pride.

Their minds' don't fight anymore, total comfort and ease settles into their thinking. So many believe everything that is said against God's Word, and doubt anything said in favor of it. Their thoughts are contagious, their words infectious, this 'Pied Piper' society allows the enemy to swallow them. It's becoming more and more cool and normal for people not to believe in the Bible. They've been givin' an out, a seemingly legitimate out; and they are gone!

Although the doubters have compartments of their life that they live according to the way God would have it, worry-free sinful joys grab their minds' focus when they are awake, while dreams of the worst and most personal kind invade their sleep. HD quality nightmares, with the entire storyline centered on one thousand earthly years in hell, interrupts their peaceful rest.

They experience different episodes of the tortures Satan has waiting for them. If their fear is being stuffed inside a tight box, still alive, with a rat whose appetite is never quenched; they 'live' it. If a person's worst fear is drowning or suffocating; they dream it. In this future, they never die, they endure its horror; but never the completion of death.

They jolt from their bumpy slumbers, sweaty, shaken, have just witnessed their possible future. They brush these dreams off, the faithless think that it bears them no relevance. They think that it's just their mind's way of deprogramming all that has been built into it. They wrongly reason, "I'm just going through 'hell shakes', it's nothing."

After fighting it back for so long, David has given in, he joins the pack. In the mist of a chilly fall night, atop the deck of their home's enclosed patio, he opens up to his wife as they lounge closely together in their steaming, bubble filled jacuzzi, sipping champagne. "Even now, it's kind of scary to admit, but deep down, I was always curious to why year after year I would attend church routinely, but I still hadn't felt his presence within me. I think I fooled myself into thinking that I felt Him, because I felt that I should."

The formerly double-minded big boss feels liberated, "If there was a heaven, I don't think that I would have gone being the way that I was."

Sasha couldn't be happier that David feels the same way as she. "It's good to let it go, honey, it's time. It's not like we chose for this to happen?"

"I know, but it still kinda bothers me that I was being fake for all of this time."

"You were a fake because this whole thing was a fake. It's not your fault, if you would have went around and asked a thousand people if Jesus were to come back, would they go to heaven, most of them would say yes. But within that number there are people that have never opened a Bible, followed, or cared about God's will for their life."

David is captivated, his new beliefs are bolstered by Sasha's support, "They would, wouldn't they? I never thought of it like that."

"I know that I'm right. From our birth, we were taught that we must believe in these ghosts, or we would burn in hell. Look at society, David, everyday people talk about how evil and full of decadence this world has become, if it was filled with so many truly saved people, like everyone claims to be, than it wouldn't be this way. Most people didn't love God, they believed that there was a God, but they didn't want to live their life following the rules he imposed. All of this stupid fear that Christians drilled into everyone's head, they just used it to control us."

Strengthened by Sasha's resolve, David confidently responds as he reaches his hand out of the hot tub's water to pour another glass of wine. "I understand what my guy, Bryant Michaels, was talking about now. All that abracadabra, He's here, you just can't see Him garbage was so stupid, isn't it? How in the hell did we fall for that crap?" As they continue relaxing in their hot tub, David and Sasha are almost too shy to look at each other, due to their embarrassment from being 'duped' into following a fairy tale.

"David, we were made to feel guilty and ashamed for the life that we've built. We are the Gods of our own life; we don't have to be ashamed of how we live. Hallelujah to us." The loving couple's champagne glasses ding together.

CHAPTER ELEVEN

Three months after the announcement of the scroll's existence and Michaels' recorded confessions come the results. An animated Stan Bather leads off the Wednesday evening news with a breaking report. "The results relating to the authenticity of the 'Bible Hoax' scroll, which undoubtedly is the greatest historical find ever known to man, if it is found to be true... a piece of ancient paper that has caused a tidal wave of emotion and varying opinion from everyone, in every country across the globe, we are told the results will be announced, at this time, next week. We will be right there bringing you the best coverage in the business, for an event, which is sure to be the biggest, most watched event in history."

Previously, four diverse countries were voted on by the United Nations council to conduct their own individual tests, which were all overseen by inspectors for the U.N.

One, the United States, of course; two, China, which used its ever increasing economic-fueled political clout to gain its place, once Russia and France backed China, that decision became easy. Three, Israel, for all of its obvious reasons; and four, the United States government, surprisingly to those outside of the administration, had no issues with a hard-line Muslim state like Iran being the fourth choice. Once America was assured that all tests would be intensely monitored to guard against any foul play, they were all set to go.

As with nine eleven and slavery, the world can only resist the urge to become desensitized, and therefore, make light of a horrific societal cataclysm for so long. So why would the demise of God and the Bible be any different? "Hey, did you watch Friday night's comedy sketch about God's incest with Jesus? I felt kinda bad for laughing about it, but it was so funny."

So called innocent humor minimizes and desensitizes the importance and deep pains of such historic matters, deep pains that are meant to be learned from. All the different forms of media join in, casting doubts with their slyly suggestive articles and programming.

Comedians, talk shows, 'Joe Blow' off the street, for weeks everyone had a joke to tell; well not anymore. Once the day of the verdict is set, nerves tighten, stress builds, many of the same individuals that have been rejoicing the Bible's demise, suddenly are worried that they may be wrong, that they may have chose their alliance too soon.

"What if the tests come back to show that what was written isn't from that time? Will God forgive me?" Fears like these sweep across the minds' of the faithless. The very people that have 'spit' on Jesus' life, the Bible's teachings; now that doubt has crept into their head have doubled back. The jokes stop, comedians and late night talk show hosts are quickly and heavily criticized by the same public that yuck'd it with them up for weeks.

Late into the evening, practically walking on air, Sasha floats into her home. She shouts, "David, David are you here?"

"I'm upstairs, sweetie. Where have you been, it's late, I was getting worried?"

Sasha throws her business belongings and her purse down on

the living room's stretch sofa, "Hurry up, come down here. You are not going to believe this. I've got incredible news to tell you!" David comes speed-walking down, Sasha waits at the bottom, bouncing around like an excited five-year-old.

"My goodness did we win the lottery or something!"

Sasha's 'fire' is doused somewhat by what has accompanied David down those steps, "I thought we threw away that fairytale…," she viciously asks, "why do you have that?"

What she's referring to is the miniature sized Old Testament inside David's right hand. "I went out to the book store and brought another one. You would not believe how long the line was. By the time I got up there, all they had were these, the New Testament Bibles was long gone." He holds it up to show her.

It's been weeks since she's had to deal with seeing David with that book. It frightens her. It concerns her that his feelings may be changing. Totally side-tracked now, she delves farther. "David, I know the reason why you're wasting time reading that stupid thing. Don't worry, honey, I know the tests are going to come back in our favor…," she laughs, "you're just panicking, so you're trying to cover your ass because of all those things you've been saying lately, but it's o.k., it's all true. The Bible was completely made up, you'll see. Everyone else knows it, you've just gotten scared. Poor baby."

David's defense sounds like he's trying more to convince himself than he is his wife. "I was just playing around when I said those things about God and my faith. Every since I was a kid I've been a devoted religious man. I was just joking around. I don't care what the results are, I'll always love God."

Sasha laughs.

David is insulted. Centered in his heart, anger rockets through his being, his fists ball tightly, "I do love him, so you better shut da fu…" David takes a breath, "I don't wanna hear another word about me and my faith. I mean it."

David quickly reflects; the height that his anger reached alarms him.

A third voice breaks into their two-way conversation, "Oh chill the hell out, Dad! I seem to remember when I was a child, you would get so annoyed with me for loving my make believe friend, Angel. So why is it o.k. for you to have an imaginary friend, Daddy?" Leaning against the hallway railing at the top of the stairs, Gwen surprises them with her presence.

Gwen's faith has become such an unfortunate story, but an all too familiar one. Like so many teenagers and young adults, the importance of Gwen's spirituality has been lessened by a pop culture that rarely ever portrays God as being of any real importance, also by the like-minded friends that she chooses to hang around, and the parents who aren't faith-based so they don't show their kids any differently. Sitting on top of all of that is the crowning reason - they haven't been given great reasons to think that God is cool. All of these 'winds' blowing in the same direction reduce her fear that she is going in the wrong direction.

Before the 'Bible Hoax', Gwen was like so many others, she'd whisper to herself, "Man, I'm going to really get into my salvation when I'm older, but right now I just wanna have fun. It's not like I'm a bad person, I love everyone. I just don't want to have to think about God every time I do something."

Now, she has completely given in, she conforms to the world around her, "I don't wanna stand out and be the only one who still believes. I don't wanna look stupid. There has to be a good reason why everyone else thinks this way."

Sasha couldn't be more pleased that their daughter has intervened and is backing her up. She and Gwen both laugh at David. "Yeah sweetheart, what's the difference?"

David turns the talk back to its original direction. "So why did you call me down here anyway?"

Sasha's focus and energy instantly reignites. "Oh my gosh, yes! You two are never going to believe who I met today, who I am now working with?!" David nor Gwen say a word, Sasha doesn't give them time. She answers her own question in a singing, childish manner, as she swings her hips and shoulders from side to side, "I had lunch with Bryant Michaels!, I had lunch with Bryant Michaels!"

David looks at Gwen, Gwen looks at David, starry-eyed, they both look at Sasha. ""Are you serious, Mom? How did that happen?" Gwen rushes down the stairs' expensive carpeting.

David drops the Bible. It is he, who has now turned gitty, "No freakin' way, sit down and tell me everything that happened!"

The three move the conversation over to the sofa.

"I told you guys, a while back, about the huge campaign I've begun working on for Casserly Motors, right?"

"Yes, yes!" Her audience shouts.

"Well, I'll give you one guess who their new pitchman is?"

Their jaws' 'almost hits the floor'. Thoughts of grandeur instantly fill David's mind as he envisions himself rubbing shoulders and becoming friends with his hero.

"If you guys calm down, I'll tell you exactly what happened."

Their introduction happens inside the plush business offices of the top selling car dealership. Sasha has already been there for an hour, she and her intern assistant have been setting up their storyboards and going over every detail of her verbal presentation.

Ten minutes after their preparations are complete, Michaels, his agent, and Mr. Casserly all walk in together. Sasha was told she'd be working with a celebrity, but she had no idea it would one on the scale of 'Flight' Michaels. "This is Sasha Gimmer, she is the brilliant exec that will be handling our advertisement campaign… Mrs. Gimmer, I'll venture to say this man needs no introduction," Mr. Casserly gleefully remarks.

Sasha turns on the charm. "Oh my goodness, hello Mr. Michaels, it is so very nice to meet you. And please, call me Sasha, not Mrs. Gimmer." Unlike the rest of her family, Sasha has never shown much interest or enthusiasm towards 'Flight' Michaels, she's never been much of a sports fan or been swept away by any of the hoopla that surrounds him, but he's an American icon, it's a different story when you're face to face.

The wings on the 'butterflies' inside Sasha's stomach flap rapidly, she realizes that a marketing campaign starring America's top icon could translate into a mountainous career leap for her.

"Look at you, you're blushing. You look nervous, please don't be, I'm no one special." Michaels has always had a way with words; false humility can be a great cover for arrogance.

She has to remind herself to keep focused, but that's not easily done. The man has an alluring presence surrounding him. What woman would not be impressed by the medium caramel, smooth skin that covers the chiseled sculpture of a towering super athletic physique, inside a light gray tailor made Italian suit. His perfect facial features, charm, money, and fame, does not hurt either.

"You are such a humble man, my husband has always liked that about you. I think he's probably your number one fan."

"Well, tell your husband that I definitely appreciate that, thank you."

"I'm very excited to work with you and Mr. Casserly on what I'm sure will be a very successful and lucrative partnership."

Time to get down to business; everyone has a seat near the front of the long mahogany business table. "Well Sasha, I see that you came prepared this morning. Please, show me what you have for me." Michaels says, while fishing deeply into her eyes.

To her, show me what you have, means stand up and start the presentation. To him, show me what you have, means stand up and start the presentation, so I can check out your curves that are titillatingly concealed beneath your form-fitting knee high skirt. 'Flight' listens attentively to her lengthy presentation during the moments he isn't fantasizing about what she'll be like once he gets her into bed.

"That was really good, Sasha. I really like your concepts for the commercials. However, I have a couple of different ideas I would like to bounce off of you for the print ads, if you would be interested in hearing about them over an early lunch."

Seated beside his boss, Michaels' agent gives him a subtle "I know what you're up to" kick to the ankle. He's seen his most valued employer work his charms on enough women before to know what that invitation likely means.

'Flight' can't help himself. With Sasha being married, that makes her forbidden, sinful fruit; he has a fetish for that. Plus, beautiful older women are in vogue right now in his choice-making for his conquests.

It's just Michaels and her, walking through the dealership's long corridor of business offices, side by side; no words. Perfect for Sasha, she soaks in the moment of momentarily feeling like she is the most important girl, walking with the most important man, as all eyes are on them. The surrounding attention literally makes her high.

Yes, David has always made her feel important, but this is different. This is royalty, American dream important; rich and famous important. This is "I don't care what his color is, I want him" important. Sasha is seduced by the same mirages so many women, with men of his distinction, fall for.

Michaels kindly declines autograph requests as they stroll through the glass enclosed showroom on a beeline towards his silver 'two thousand and next year' Bentley and the chauffeur that waits.

Thirty five minutes later. "So tell me Bryant, what's been the worst moment of your wonderful life, so far?" Having talked the entire drive, Sasha feels comfortable enough to get personal as they settle in for their luncheon in a secluded and private corner of Anytown's most exclusive restaurant.

"I don't know, it was probably when my...," he knows better than that, he almost slipped up. 'Prince Charming' was about to say that his ex-wife, Stacy, leaving him was his worst moment ever, but rule number one hundred and something in the fictional player handbook clearly states that when you are trying to remove the pants from a woman, you must never bring up another lady's name unless it will somehow serve and assist your own selfish goals. So when you're trying to seduce a married woman, especially one that isn't necessarily unhappy in her marriage, bringing up how infidelity broke up your happy home, is a severe violation to the rules. He goes to his backup answer. "I guess I'd have to say that my worst moment never happened, I got lucky."

"What'll you mean?"

"You know, all of the hoopla with me being caught talking about how God never existed and all that crap?"

Sasha laughs. "That was crazy. At first, my husband was so mad at you for saying that, he was about to pull his hair out."

"Yeah, that whole situation was scary, especially when everyone got on their pedestals and threw stones at me for speaking my mind."

"They did, but everyone quickly came around to see the good, or should I say the great thing that you did for all of us? You got everyone to open up about their feelings and tell the truth."

"Yeah, I guess I did, huh? Thankfully it all worked out. The media really helped out a lot as they got off of my back. They challenged people to look within themselves and not paint me as the bad guy."

"And I just loved the way they really took it to that arrogant asshole, Ricky Whateverhisname."

"Right, I tried to make him see the light, but he's just stuck on what he believes."

"My husband used to hide behind his so-called faith, just like that guy does. I remember when we were younger he was always going around quoting different biblical scriptures to people; but then pick and choose which ones he would follow. I kept my mouth shut, but even back then I knew he was simply going through the motions. He just claimed to be born again because his parents forced God on him, and he had to go through a bunch of crazy shit with them...," Sasha's thoughts drift to her twenty plus years of compiled memories concerning the maliciousness of her husband's racist beliefs, "he talked and acted a good game, but he damn sure didn't have the heart of a Christian. But like everyone else, he finally came around."

"Great, that's awesome."

"He pretended to be full of the Holy Spirit, but he found out that he was just full of shit." They both get a long laugh out of that one.

"He was mad at you, for awhile, but he didn't open up and be honest with himself until he really sat and thought about the truths you said. Now he BELIEVES IN YOU again."

Her praise brings about a big smile, "That's great, Sasha, be sure to tell him I said thank you for the support. I'm just wondering… did you ever, even for a little while, believe?"

"I used to believe that there was a God. But I can't say that I ever believed IN God. The Bible, to me, always just sounded like a really cool fantasy novel, you know, it'd make a great Oscar winning movie. It has all of the elements, a bunch of magicians, magical lands, lessons to learn from, heroes to root for, and best of all a master villain to hate. It was always hard for me to believe the incredible stories that are told in that book, there was never enough tangible proof for me to really believe that strongly, tho'. I always kept my doubts."

Her testimony brings him added comfort, his eyes talk to her body. Their like spirits bond quickly. The lion's eyes and lips turn seductive, Bryant plays coy, he ekes out a boyish giggle. "O.K. Sasha, so are you getting a little nervous now that the results are almost here?"

"Not at all, I know what that scroll says is real."

The first thing David wants to know upon Sasha's completion of her version of events is, "While you guys were talking, you didn't tell him the exact words that I said about him when I was mad, did you? Please tell me you didn't?"

"Yeah David, I casually mentioned to him that you called him a rich, no good nigger, whose no different than the rest of the no good niggers," Sasha sarcastically states.

David breathes a sigh of relief, "Good, you didn't."

"So when are you going to see him again, Mom?"

Sasha's voice turns sheepish, "Soon, we're going to meet up again in a few days. You know, just to figure out our next steps."

The story Sasha told to her loving family was the truth, she just left out a few precious details. Like how she and Michaels started off casually flirting across the lunch table with one another, which then turned into heavy flirting as the distance between the two narrowed to nothing by dessert, which then, progressed into hot and heavy petting in the back of Michaels' black windowed Bentley on the return trip to the car lot.

David took Sasha's, "We're going to meet up in a few days" comment to mean, meet up to discuss business in an office. They may discuss business, but it will be after they've sex'd each other to exhaustion in the hotel that one of Michaels' assistants will check them into; just as he did tonight. False names of course.

"Hey do you think during your next meeting that you can arrange for me and Gwen to meet him?"

"A… honey, um… maybe, I'll see what I can do." Sasha has no sense of remorse for the Commandment she has broken.

The day is here!

Though many people's words and actions say differently, even with this much on the line: their present, their futures'; most of them can't break free from the mental and physical darkness this world holds over them. On the surface, they deny it even to themselves, but deep down; they want the Hoax to be true!

All of the bets are placed; literally. Vegas has been taking them for weeks now. The little countdown clock, that has been running for days, winds down in the right bottom corner of every television channel.

Eyes close, hands grasp tightly, and during these last possible moments before all of the build up ends, when their minds are no longer able to hold back the truth concerning what it wants; they pray. The faithless pray in confusion, "Please let the Bible be fake… please be true… be real, please be real! But in case it's not, I repent for my sins, Lord."

The truly faithful, most of them, they don't even watch the proceedings, why should they? Their beliefs and the course their lives' are on, is not going to change no matter what the verdict is.

The clock hits zero, the United Nations spokesperson steps to the podium and calmly announces the words so many had been waiting to hear, "With 99.9% accuracy; the scroll is authentic, it does date back to biblical times, futhermore, it dates to within a one hundred year radius of when Jesus supposedly walked the earth."

The worry is over. For so many, they have been given an answer that is good enough. They have been granted their sense's explanation; their reasoning is validated.

The United States and China do publicly acknowledge that, yes, the conclusions from their tests fully back up the spokesperson's words. Iran and Isreal allow their silence to speak for them.

The stress is gone; a day of crippling delight begins. They're delighted by the news, but crippled by its gravity. Billions take time to sit back and reflect on a day that Alzheimer's couldn't cause them to forget.

By western nightfall, after everyone has taken a few hours to digest the day's events, its party time! People eat, drink, and be merry, while still dropping priceless one liners like, "We still have mixed feelings about things… whether it was myth or real, God and the Bible will always have a special place in my heart."

Across the globe, countless numbers fill the streets of nations in celebration. No more worrying, no more 'riding the fence', within days, half of those who stood by the Word throughout this whole ordeal begin entertaining dangerous words and thoughts. "Facts are facts, we all heard them. We can't change what is, I don't know what I'm going to think from now on."

Thames' goal of gaining support from the Middle East seems bleak at best, those countries aren't so quickly convinced by anything American led. The sentiment shared by the crowds of millions protesting America on the streets of Islamic nations is much harsher. "I don't care what any scientist says. This is just another attempt by the Americans and the rest of the Zionist devils to totally submerge us into their material driven world. To go as far to disgrace God by creating this meaningless writing shows you that they are willing to walk through hell to accomplish their goals of destroying us. Death to America!"

Even the government of Israel, who has long been America's most subsidized country and closest of friends, has to squash anti-American riots and walk a fine line between the politics of money and the politics of their peoples' heritage and faith being turned into a fable.

Weeks later, after much deliberation, and to everyone's surprise, our most hated foe in the region releases a statement filled with encouraging words that resonate throughout the White House on several different levels. "We have gathered and listened to all of our brother's (Iran) evidence, and they do look fairly similar to the Americans. So if the Americans, and the rest of the world, would like to go jumping to conclusions about their God, this is their choice. But the factualness of Mohammed's life is not to be discussed, demeaned, or debated."

The good news the White House has longed for has come. Now that one hard-line Islamic state acknowledges that this is not some sham put together by the West, the rest of them may accept that the writing is legitimate, which would hopefully lead to the rest of the 'dominoes' falling into place for Thames, who is under tremendous pressure to end a war that no other President has been able to end.

As the jovial temperament and total disrespect for everything Holy, picks back up tenfold, regrettable for the world, the leader of its most prosperous superpower gets in on the act.

Riding the wave of optimism during the 'chill' those few encouraging Islamic words provided, President Thames speaks at a pep rally like atmosphere abroad the Navy's top battleship.

Making her way through countless handshakes and smiles, Thames gives short answers to a few questions shouted at her by the smothering press. "Mrs. President, should we have hope that this may help to bring our troops home?"

"That's not up to us."

"Madam President, to end this war do you think it's necessary to discuss the Bible Hoax with leaders of the Islamic countries?"

She smiles and says in passing, "No, but it would be nice if they'd let go of that silly Mohammed junk, that would make it easier for us to come together." That three second blunder by our ex-deeply religious President turns real hope into no hope.

To end a war that has totally crippled their country, our nemesis would like to take a softer stance against Thames' lapse of judgment, but that option vanishes once the backlash of her inflammatory remarks spread.

Many Muslims have had the same doubts and 'what ifs' that fill Western minds', but living in a world and a culture where the word - change - is rarely a verb, most Muslims have been much slower to openly accept any western talk of God being some mirage.

Israel, for one of the few times, on any issue concerning the United States, sides with their neighbors, when their Prime Minister delivers a short, but powerful 'backhand slap' to the White House. "Though we have never seen eye to eye with hard line Islam, they should have the right not to have their beliefs ridiculed by ANY country. President Thames owes them a huge apology."

Syria, Iran, and many of the Islamic terrorist groups that operate against the United States, seize upon this opportunity to farther crank up their propaganda machine. The top leader for a cell whose organization has been helping to fight against America throughout the war speaks to his legion of followers via the internet. "The Americans invented these lies to destroy Islam. That is what this is all about. They will even sacrifice their own Bible and Christianity to disgrace and spit upon the Quron.

They know if they erase our religion, they'll erase us. That is why we must fight them to the end!"

In response, protesters fill the streets of every Arab nation, and for the first time, and with great furor, tens of thousands of American Muslims converge upon the steps of state capitols across America's major cities.

Law enforcement fights to control its temper as the crowds grow larger and angrier each passing day.

"Is that guy wearing a bomb?... there's a person with a bomb?... run somebody's got a bomb!" Words of hysteria rip through the crowd on the fourth day of Detroit's protest at jet-like speed. The police are besieged by stampeding 'walls' of extremely frightened people. Law enforcement is overwhelmed, on one hand, they're frantically searching for a potential suicide bomber, on the other, they must simultaneously control the crowd of panicked citizens that would run through fire to get away from there.

In the mist of the chaos, one officer feels a tug on his hostler. Seconds later, a shot is fired, no one knows exactly where the loud bang comes from, the level of pandemonium rises for the protesters and the disjointed officers, who begin firing indiscriminately. After the screaming, shooting, and pandemonium clears; twelve people are left dead, but everyone, there and abroad is affected.

As the next light of day erases the night, local and federal law enforcement is fearful the Detroit situation will spill over into other cities. And so is their chief boss.

A whisper, "I hate those sand monkeys."

President Thames peeks around at the Secretary of Defense and the Director for Homeland Security, hoping neither of them heard her politically and racially insensitive candor, as they all re-watch the previous day's mayhem unfold on a closed circuit television inside the belly of Air Force One.

While sipping on this morning's second glass of vodka, Thames contemplates as she stares blankly at the screen, "Infidels...," she snorts, "they're the only devils on this planet." Something ugly has begun to spread out from the pit of Nicole Thames. It's changing her down to the very depth of her character.

Thames, no different from any other Christian who didn't hold onto their faith, has successfully made the adjustment away from God. Her caring, fair actions, that voters have come to expect, are absent now. All that is left are insecurities, anger, intolerance, and vodka.

"You tell them that I don't want any quick triggers out there, but if a few messages need to be sent today; than do it." Through a phone call, those words, and its underlying message, are given to the FBI's director, so he may spread them to police chief's across the country.

"Let them shoot those motherfuckers, I don't care... Screw those countries and their murderous, dead religion... I don't like it, but if they get out of hand again, the police have to do what they have to do... hey, if they don't like our country, they can go back to their sand and camels." So much anger and hate is shared and accepted, by so many, across this country. Not since the days of town lynchings has so much violence been openly o.k.'d against fellow citizens of what should be our racially and religiously tolerant society.

Over the next few days, everyone is braced for battle, but none comes. The 'death to America' call was not answered by America's Muslims. In the days that follow, the protesters come; the crowds remain large, but subdued. The American Arab leaders convince their brethren to turn their efforts towards diplomacy and an apology while calling for calm in the streets. But here and abroad, the simmering anger and hate remains.

After the raging fire gets back under control, President Thames finally gives a public apology for the comments she made. She acts her way through seemingly heartfelt, award level performances, in several speeches, aimed at massaging every Arab person she offended. Total disaster averted - this time.

─────── CHAPTER TWELVE ───────

The sight of Dane, Stamp, and two of their homeboys, 'posted up' against Dane's ghetto fabulous Camaro, smoking weed while chatting up two local, half-dressed, teenage girls, along the curb of a rundown city park; looks like the typical scene from a thug turned rapper's video. But this is real, this is their day, and this is also the perfect spot for their three underage workers to slyly sell cocaine - soft and hard - along the park's edges to customers that walk or drive by.

You take away the drug dealers, the addict that comes by every fifteen seconds, the cops that infrequently cruise by knowing full well what's going on and who's doing it, and the disgusting fact that there is not one father to be seen, enjoying time with his son or daughter, inside the ghetto's square recreational yard; erase all that, then, you'd see the beauty of the innocent children running around, playing and climbing, and the mothers whose minds' fought through the fear of bringing their children out to play in an environment, where today could possibly become another day that bullets fly within mere feet of what should be their sanctuary.

"Yo, I holla at yo phat ass later, girl," Stamp disrespectfully contends to one of the two well-built, young women. As the girls walk away from the four rims of chrome bling that initially lead them over to the guys, there is a great chance that the boys will indulge in a few testosterone minutes talking about what they would do to them in bed, but as fate would have it, not today.

"Hey cuz, I wonder how ya boy Melvin is taking that Bible myth shit."

Stamp's query stops Dane's mind from entering lust mode. "Aw I bet my dudes' all jacked up. Dog, think of all the time he wasted up in church. Him and his family used to go to church two, three times a week, then, be up in there for four or five hours every Sunday."

In the back of Dane's conscience, crumbled up into a small ball, rests another part of him that says, "I got time, even if I'm wrong. I'll come to God right before I die."

Stamp chuckles. "I don't know about him, but I'd be looking for a refund."

That suggestion amps Dane, "That's real, it'd be tight if the government gave church people back a whole lot of money for all of their wasted time and money that they gave those crooked ass people."

"Hell yeah, dem krackers in the government pushed God on us all the time." Stamp begins to mimic 'the man', "God don't want you to smoke, God don't want you to kill, God don't want you ta get no booty if you ain't married-"

Dane breaks down laughing at that last one, as the rest of the crew nods their affirmation. Then one speaks, momentarily silencing everyone, "Nigga, da government didn't start that stuff, it's in the Bible."

Dane breaks in, "Hey pimp, say the government says if you put in at least a thousand hours of church, then you could collect fifty grand for all the time you wasted. Black people everywhere would be lying ta get that money, knowing damn well they ain't been in there ten hours." Mass laughter ensues.

Stamp 'fires', "Oh yes we would, and white people be tryin' ta find ways to screw us out of our money. They way greedier than we are, they already got money, but they still lie to get more…" from the corner of his ever alert eyes, "hey mane, ain't that cha boy coming down the block over there?"

Dane looks to his left, he sees Melvin cutting across the playground focused solely on reaching the 'crew' as he quickly dodges little kids along the way.

Stamp. "Damn Dane, ya man looks pissed."

"Hey dog, be ready, pull ya shit out."

The men all do as they are commanded, "What, you don't trust homey?" Stamp asks.

"Man, I don't trust no mu'fuckin' body these days."

One of the guys speaks up, "Dude, how many years this nigga gon wear dem jeans."

Dane remembers, "Shit, I never did take his ass shopping."

Melvin has made a firm decision that he is suffering his last days in those "raggedy ass jeans." He's not going into this blind. He knows that this decision may cost him his life, but he is willing to take that chance, "But that's o.k., me dying now is not such a big deal anyway, that must have been why I got into God, because I was afraid to go to hell."

He accepts the truth his eyes have set before him, this way of thinking frees his mind to relax and not be so restricted towards his choices in life. A dangerous hardness is settling into Melvin's character.

Sudden recollection hits Stamp with such surprise, he flinches wildly upon its remembrance. "Aw shit, I forgot to tell y'all, dudes' grandmama died. Show my man some love when he gets here."

Dane's expression reveals a pinch of sorrow and concern for Melvin just as he arrives. All of the young men greet him very respectfully, offering their condolences followed by quick man-hugs. A man's loved one that has passed allows for one of the few circumstances that these battle-torn, prideful souls feel it's o.k. to show weakness or sympathy towards others. "I appreciate that, fellas. Dane, Stamp, can I holla at y'all for a minute?"

The three separate from the pack. Melvin pauses a moment, as he takes in a deep breath, "I'm just gonna come right out and ask y'all straight up… If you can, do you think one of y'all could front me a couple of hundred dollars and show me how to play this game." As he asks his favor, Melvin looks a lot more at Dane, than he does Stamp.

Dane looks around, pretending to be puzzled, Stamp just smiles. Dane knows exactly what Melvin means, but he doesn't want to believe it. "What game?"

"Come on dog, you know what I'm talking about. I need ta make some fast money. Since my Me-ma was their guardian, the state took my little cousins and put them in foster care. I gotta get 'em back for her. I got nowhere to live, those krackers even tried to take me into foster care, but I said ta hell with that, so I ran. I hate dem fucking people; I wish I could kill everyone of them!"

Dane's flesh celebrates, but something in the pit of his stomach hates this proposal. "Where you been sleepin' at, dog?"

"I just been sleeping on the street lately, wherever, whenever…," now they both know he's serious. Melvin lays out his plan, "I make some money, set up a business so I can go straight… by then, in a year when I turn eighteen, I can go get custody of my cousins."

"What kind of business do you wanta set up?"

"I don't know, I haven't thought that far ahead…," he chuckles, "I always thought that I would have a few more years before I needed to worry about that."

"Damn man, you want him to fill out a questionnaire, too?" Stamp intervenes to stop the potential of Melvin changing his mind. He understands and sympathizes with his struggle. He lived a mostly abandoned life in his early-teenage years. "I feel you, dog. Make that money for ya family, baby. That's what I've been telling you to do all along." He embraces Melvin, who tries to play it cool, but tingles inside. He knows that he's almost in.

Dane, "I feel you, I do, but I ain't sure you're built for this, homey. For right now, just keep workin' at that shoe store you at."

"I'm no longer employed there, cuz my peckerwood boss caved in to the system, so he let me go because they're looking for me."

Dane is pissed because he already knows the answer to his next question, "You dropped out of school, too?"

"Nigga, fuck school! You was right Stamp, dem honkies ain't gon let us out this mu'fucka. So I'm ready to ball, baby! You feel me?!" Stamp vigorously nods his approval.

No one made Melvin quit or 'chased' him from his job, he has simply decided that he'd rather be the hare instead of the tortoise in his lust for the financial prosperity he's never had. The merchandise on all of the 'bling bling' shows that he's watched over the years have blossomed in importance. He wants their gratifications right now.

Dane. "Well why don't you go with the foster people, just for awhile, so you can keep working?"

Stamp, who has grown annoyed with his co-hustler's apprehension, practically takes the words right from Melvin's mouth as he was about to humbly challenge Dane. "How you gonna tell another man to do something that you know good and damn well you wouldn't do?"

Reluctantly, Dane gives up the fight. "For the last time, are you sure? A lot of bad things can happen to you when you living off of these streets. This is your same neighborhood, but you going into a different world, dog."

No words, Melvin coldly stares through his friend's eyes, silently telling him that he's ready and willing for whatever.

"Come on in then, welcome to the click." Dane says with a cautious smile and much less opposition. Melvin and Stamp bump fists, right before Dane gives his new 'runner' a real hug.

Inside his luxurious office, David has just settled in for his monthly consumer status meeting with his V.P., Brandon Meyers, and the head of the collections department, Sandy. David has reviewed the files she brought in earlier, and he is not happy. "Well well, big surprise, we still have a lot of lucky consumers that don't seem to realize how lucky they are to have life insurance at such a greatly reduced cost."

Sandy defends the company's clients. "Yes David, but if you look at most of their files again, you'll see that most of them have been with us for a long time. They get behind on their payments, but eventually, they always catch up."

"Sandy, do you know how many jobs we can eliminate from your department if we get rid of some of these people. I have been researching, and I think there are about one hundred and forty cases we should drop. The economy is slowing a ton, so we'll improve our profit margin, if we scrape away some of this scum off the bottom of our shoes."

Brandon stores the scum comment away and moves on, vigorously joining the fight to save these families. "I've done that same research, David, and our savings would barely be over minimum. Our reputation is built on serving this community, we can't take minimum over their lives. We are the only option most of the families have around here."

"If they don't keep up on their monthlies, I don't give a damn what they're options are without us. They can go back to welfare for all I care. I've already slashed about two or three deadbeats over the last month or so, and there will be more accounts to come. These people sponge off of enough charities in their lives'...," he holds up, then, lets the large stack of files, or should I say families, slam down onto his desk, "we're not in business to become another one."

Brandon questions. "David, what is going on with you? Since before either of us were born, this company was run very successfully, because the community always felt that we were fair and understanding to their unique needs and circumstances...," aided by the name tabs that stick out from the body of the files, Brandon rapidly thumbs through and finds the one he wants, "here's an account where there is a single, hard working mother of five, who has been off of work because she has been battling breast cancer. She has only been getting behind the last six months since she suffered a relapse. These are the people that you want to leave behind?"

David takes the outstretched file from Brandon. He does not appreciate having his authority challenged by any of his underlings, and especially not by Brandon. The boss calmly and at leisure scans through it. He speaks to himself, "Oh yes, nice one." David has thought up another jewel to try and slide past Brandon.

He likes to get in little jabs, since he can't throw knockout punches, "Come on Brandon, she has fifteen and seventeen year old sons. Are you tryin' ta jive me into thinking that one, if not both, of those homeboys ain't out in the streets getting his hustle on, to bring home some bling, baby? They probably have money, they're just too busy buying jewelry and telephones with all their cash, dog."

Brandon gets the underlying message in each one of David's suddenly slang words. Being a truly faithful Christian, Brandon's thoughts concerning his boss always reminded positive, they always worked out of love, but this is the final tug that fully removes his blinders concerning the type of man David is.

Like a piece of bologna between two slices of bread, Sandy feels trapped in the middle of an awkward moment. "Sandy, would you please leave the room so that David and I may talk privately?" Say no more, Sandy snatches up the stack of files from the desk and walks out; but she would have loved to run.

Maintaining the correct spirit keeps Brandon calm. "David, I don't appreciate…"

The savvy veteran steals his thunder, "I'm sorry, Brandon, I know what you're going to say, I was just trying to be funny, you know, break the tension. I went too far, I really apologize."

David's unexpected, but calculated apology throws Brandon off course. "Should I still tell him off or let it go?" He goes middle of the road by sternly telling him. "This is the first and last time that I'm buying that excuse."

David puts his hands in praying position against the middle of his chest, then, gives him a condescending bow, as Brandon stands up.

Just as Mr. Myers strides outside the threshold of his boss' door, David re-cements his power. "Tell Sandy that I want a copy of every cancellation letter that she sends out, starting with the one you just showed me. Thanks buddy."

Even though he hears him, Brandon doesn't show it. He wants to spin around and tell him where to shove it, but he does not. Instead he says a quick prayer, in Jesus' name, for God to help change David's heart.

"That should remind that boy of just who runs this show." The guiding spirit inside of David is very satisfied.

"I know girl, white people be gettin' on my nerves too. Half of dem walk around like they better than everybody else."

Unbeknownst to the four black girls reveling in their prejudices, at the table behind theirs', the only white person within a three table radius, Gwen, is about to sit her body and lunch tray down next to her good friend, Mia.

Mia feels as awkward and uncomfortable with this situation as Gwen will in a moment. She wants to tap one of the offending girls on the shoulder and scream in her face to "shut the bleep up", but being that she chooses to be a follower at this time, and not a leader, she does not want to deal with the "what, are you selling out, why you kissing her butt" remarks that may come from her own race. So Mia allows the snickering and snide comments to continue, as do the other teens that witness Gwen and this conversation about to converge.

Offending girl, "At the beginning of school yesterday I was standing behind some stupid white girl, and I guess she had just washed her hair because it was still wet. Girl, I'm telling y'all, that shit is true…" Gwen's presence is finally noticed from the corner of another girl's eye, who is seated at the table with the rambling one. She tries to nonchalantly tap her friend on her thigh, but the girl is too caught up in her story to even take notice, "white girls do smell like wet dogs when their hair is wet."

Curious because no one is laughing with her, the offending girl looks around and quickly spots Gwen's stiff 'shell' sitting behind her. "Aw, my bad girl, you know I was just playing around. I didn't really mean none of that stuff. I was just talkin' silly, you know I love you." She follows her forced apology with an equally awkward hug.

"Oh, I know… I'm not tripping," says Gwen, who is very much 'tripping'.

Mia seriously, but not too seriously, because she still chooses to tow the racial line, speaks up. "Now you know that was wrong of you. One of them say something like that about us, you'd be going off." Mia follows up her announcement with a telling grin and giggle, just to let the crowd know she is still on their side.

Racist talk like this is on the increase in these new days. Even with the other races being full of people they will continue to like, they become cynical towards that race as a whole.

They believe that they are moving along fabulously without It and Them. They see their friends, or their loved ones, or their co-workers gaining confidence and comfort in what they believe, and it infects their thinking. It's become the norm. People say things, in ways, that they don't even know influences others, things like, "Damn, it's crazy how EVERYBODY is cool with the Bible being KNOWN as a fake." Untrue generalizations like this make people think that they'd be nuts not to take safety in the greater number.

Television ratings for shows that glorify and/or make fun of the Lord's death reach new heights every week. Songs of every genre that totally disrespect or rejoice in the freedom that God and Jesus not being real has given them, are just beginning to hit the airwaves, and because of the raw subject matter, they instantly gain huge listening audiences.

All of man's witty one-liners are printed onto bumper stickers, little suggestions like, "Honk, if you were born right the first time!" Heaven's demise has become a national sensation in the media. So many shows, covering tons of different angles, have become must-see tv. The 'Bible Hoax' is big business, and everybody wants their slice.

"We are free to live life how we see fit without having to look over our shoulders because of the fear God gave us. This rules! I'm so thankful that John Richards freed us. He freed the world. John Richards still lives, John rocks forever!" And with that nationally televised impromptu interview with a drunken reveler on Times Square New Year's Eve, America's love affair and hero worship of the man "who dared to show the world the truth" begins. Hollywood jumps right into the frenzy when it announces that the movie chronicling John Richards' life has just signed a top A-list actor to play his part.

A poll taken by the *New York Daily Enquirer*, the same newspaper that first released the story about the Bible, spreads across the world and through the thoughts of all non-believers and doubters, giving them reason for another pause. The question: If you could make God real, therefore, bringing a return of all the Heaven or hell pressure to live up to His will and standards, or, keep things the way they are; which would you choose?

The first and natural reaction from most of them is, "Of course I would make Him real, I didn't want this to happen, I'm just going with it," but then, they begin to really think.

One of the effects to His not being around is the luxury of not having any fear to be totally and completely honest about the spiritual path he or she was on. Now that the doubters have taken off the veil, they can be entirely candid about what was REALLY in their heart. "I do like life better without the fear of damnation. I only have to live up to my own standards now."

No way would they trade in their 'sinless' life to bring

God back; they say. They're free to cheat, steal, break marital commandments, lie, envy, and be just as greedy as they want to be; without guilt, or having to justify and reason away their wrongs to God and themselves. An added bonus they believe is not having to spend time praying, and no more repenting. All of that is stacked under the very best, the most comforting detail; the piece of mind in knowing that there will be no Judgment Day, that this existence is all there is, that when they die, that's it, their soul will die with their body, and that is just fine with them. No more having to question what voices and ideas they chose to listen to, no pressure to get to Heaven and avoid the tortures of hell; all of this makes the question easy to answer.

Society is reaping the effects of its slow movement away from the Bible's love. This movement has been generations in the making. Everyday that passes the faithless walk farther away from God's love and his unlimited abilities to help them.

The physical erasure of God has begun. Churches begin to be demolished for economic progress. Most are empty now that hundreds of millions have no use for them. Businesses and new homes replace these once sacred lands. A few are earmarked to be left for the faithful, while others are saved to be kept as historical landmarks for future generations to walk through and gawk at like dinosaurs in a museum.

An ex-pastor of a local ex-church sets up a once a month revival where people can come to talk and reflect about all of the good values and morals the myth of God and the Bible brought to their life. Values like: having pity on those less fortunate, love for your fellow man, and most of all, respecting the life of your fellow man by not killing him, even if he has wronged you; that is the essential reason that spurred the ex-pastor to organize this day. Because after taking a brief dive in numbers, murders, senseless "because he looked at me the wrong way or I was just sick of being married to her" killings are on the rise.

Months pass, attendance at these revivals remain small, few have any interest in spending time at them. That is until one of Hollywood's top starlets shows up, closely followed by the paparazzi's shuttering cameras. Her attendance leads another member of Tinseltown's 'it crowd' to attend, suddenly the stature and 'coolness' of these functions suddenly explodes.

'A Day For Reflection' becomes an attendance blockbuster, the revivals quickly become the sheik place to be seen.

Hollywood's biggest writers are in discussions to begin penning a series of movies that will chronicle the Bible's fascinating and inspiring stories.

CHAPTER THIRTEEN

Through the dark, Ed, alone like always in the middle of the night, is watching news coverage on *CNN*. "Look at all of them gunning each other down, not giving a damn about their brothers and sisters, it's so sad...," he quietly laughs, "and somehow they still don't believe that demons truly exist."

Today's 'who got murdered' coverage ends, as the programming turns to the Reflection Revivals. Ed continues his snickering at how stupid and foolish they all are. "Look at them; they're eating everything their eyes have fed them... They have no idea what they are doing to themselves." Ed has no doubt, whatsoever, they are being duped and that the Most High God does exist.

Bored of their silliness, Ed takes a stroll down memory lane. He reflects about all he's gained through his manipulation of the Bible and God. His mind loses focus of all the celebrities parading by the click cameras and he drifts into daydreaming about what he is going to tell God on Judgment Day. "Lord, everything I've done, I've done to help the world, to benefit someone other than myself..." This diabolical maniac pauses his thoughts, to really ponder his words, "haven't I made the ultimate sacrifice, Lord?

I know, Father, thank you, you're welcome. Yes, I would love to enter your kingdom."

Ed's eyes catch something that's flashed across the screen, momentarily returning his concentration to the A-lister celebrity that is being interviewed by some overly enthusiastic twenties something show host.

He shakes his head, in pity, for all of the lost souls out in the world. "Jesus, I can't believe that they would ever believe that you did not die for them… what a shame."

Ed's thoughts shift gears again. He feels a sense of accomplishment as he thinks about the power the fear of God has helped him to attain. It has given him a lifelong rape and drug victim wife, whom through much assistance from various verses in the Bible that he has brilliantly twisted just right, he was able to easily pry away from the shelter she'd been resting and strengthening her broken mind and body at.

He basks in his righteousness that justifies him to keep his family locked inside their home, not to hide them from 'Sodom and Gomorrah' as he claims to them, but to insure that his doings inside never get revealed; at least not until he is ready.

He's proud of his self-molded religious explanations for his loathsome behavior with his daughter, and how she, because of his "God loves for us to do this" lies, doesn't even know its wrong. He marvels in his divine "I am your ticket to heaven" status that he has over his family's life. But dearest to Ed's egotistical heart is the brains that it took to pull all of this off for so long.

But all is not good, at times, he feels it slipping away. It's not slipping away, but like many people who are power crazed, paranoia sets in that it might be. "What if they start to believe that the Bible is a fake? They'll try to leave before I am ready." Frenzied 'could happens' streak across Ed's unbalanced brain. He knows he needs a new angle to scramble into the heads' of his flock.

The next day, after the kids finish their breakfast, Ed reveals his new helper in his paranoid fight to remain in control.

"What's that Daddy?" Mary questions, as everyone gathers around.

"This is a newspaper, it tells you all about the evil that's going around snatching souls across the world." He puts the paper on the middle of the dining room table so everyone can see. As he does with the Bible, Ed blacked out any and everything that does not suit his purpose.

He reads the important points from a selected article to his family. "A new report that came out yesterday shows that the overall murder rate in every single major city has tripled, and in some areas quadrupled in the time..." Ed marks out the next few words, seeing that it says, "since the Bible was definitely found to be fake."

Ed senses new fear taking root inside of them. He looks each of his followers in the eye. "Satan's children are out there killing all those who put God before themselves. People just like us are being slaughtered. I have never told any of you this, but I am not the only son of Jesus, there are but a few of us left, and every since Satan's lies tried and failed to erase the Word of God, they have stepped up their killings of us and our families. That is why you must never leave this house without my protection."

He reads to his audience other articles on murders that have been reported: a woman carjacked, then, shot to death, a baby accidentally shot in a drive-by, the serial killer who has just murdered his twentieth victim in the last five months. He made sure to save this one for last; the guy who fell asleep at the wheel and crashed head-on into a family of four killing them all, "But through the power of Satan, the driver mysteriously manages to walk away with only scrapes and bruises. I'm sure those were God fearing Christians that the devil had him kill."

Ed reads to them one of the opinion articles concerning and reasoning away the Bible's factualness. "Don't you hear their words, Devin, Mary, Sherry? This is Satan trying to destroy God, and if you don't follow and do exactly what I say, he will cast you all down to hell with him. That's his entire purpose for all of this happening."

Score another successful manipulation for Ed. He had no idea that giving his family a visual device from which they can see the evil that he has constantly preached into their brains would be this effective. The kids are so moved that they embrace their abusive father with a thank you hug. Sherry is allowed to show her gratitude by praying at and kissing Ed's bare feet.

Soft rock songs from the radio discreetly provide the background for the lively conversation between Gwen's sleepover pals, Randi and Tina.

Gwen is in quiet mode, sitting on her bedroom floor as Tina sits atop the mattress behind her, tightly braiding a second French braid into her friend's brownish blonde hair. Randi 'bounces' around the room, meddling with the various belongings that sit atop Gwen's shelves, all the while, still managing to remain the focus of the conversation. "Oh my God, did you guys see Christie Banning today holding hands with Durrell?"

"Durrell is hot." Attests Tina.

"Yeah, but I never pictured her to be the type that would go out with a black guy. They make such a cute couple, tho." Randi reports.

Tina brings the hostess into the conversation, "Would you ever go out with a black guy, or say even a Latino guy? Because do you know who Armando Perez is? He's cute, and I heard that he likes you."

"Armando is hot, too. Yeah girl, would you?" Randi eagerly piles on.

"Fuck no!"

Her friends are shocked by how strong and ugly her answer is. Tina leans around, so that Gwen can see her face, and in a bit of a 'ghetto girl' voice asks, "Damn girl, what's up wit dat?"

An uncomfortable giggle comes from Randi. "I think I'd

probably date a black guy, Latino guy, whoever, if it wasn't for my parents."

Tina enthusiastically chimes in, "Your parents are the worst hypocrites I have ever seen."

Randi feeds off of her friend's honesty and voices something that she wishes she could say to her Mom and Dad. "I know, I'm like, hello your lifelong best friends are black, so how can you dumb asses even think the way that you do?"

Tina replies. "They're all jacked up. But my parents, they'd be cool with it. My dad used to date a black chick, a couple of them a matter of fact. My parents love any and everybody...," she giggles, "they're so crazy, they're still trying to believe in God, too."

David got to the door late, but his paranoid ear has heard enough of Tina's interracial love-speech. It burns him up to hear anyone equating a loving person to a person that still believes, because he knows that isn't the person he is. He ends his undetected eavesdropping by taking his 'burning' ear off of Gwen's door and startling them all as their privacy barrier burst wide open.

"Dad, what are you doing? Can't you knock?"

"I need to speak with you out here in the hallway, right now, young lady!"

Gwen's pals know all about her racist father, so they are not completely shocked by his timely break-in.

After shooting Tina an evil glance on the way out, David slams the door shut. Hateful words fight to be the first out of his undisciplined mouth. "I'm tired of this crap with you, Gwen. If your friends wanta date coons and spics I don't care. But you..."

"Dad, don't worry. I'd never date niggers." Briefly, it scares her to say that word in front of her father, but then, she likes it; it feels good. That word has always represented the side of her father she hated, the great barrier that always stayed between them, but now, they stand together on the same side. Gwen has been saying that word many, many times in her thoughts, as Satan's curse of hate withers her mind.

David's 'brakes' are instantly applied. "What did you say?"

"I said I'd never date a nigger." Gwen smiles and gives her father a hug, in one dual attempt to show him that she's both serious and comfortable with her feelings. "I'm done defending them. I see what you've been talking about now. Don't worry, Dad, I hate all minorities."

You would think this would be a triumphant moment of fruition for David. You'd think he would revel in her newfound abhorrence, and give his daughter a "welcome to the club" celebratory hug, but he doesn't, his body freezes as his mind races. He puts an awkward hand on her shoulder, then, meekly questions, "Ah… a… when did you start feeling like this, honey?"

"I'll gladly tell you all about it later, if you let me go back to my friends. Come on, Dad, you're embarrassing me."

"Yeah, sure honey, I'll just-"

"Thank you, Daddy…," she opens the door and leaves her still stunned father standing on the other side, "love you." Gwen shuts the door and causally regains her place beneath Tina.

Randi, "So did he start going all spastic on you with all of his racial crap?"

"I don't think its crap anymore. I understand how he feels."

"So what are you, like prejudice all of a sudden? I'm not prejudice, and you have more black friends than me," defensively, Tina attests to her.

"Obviously you haven't noticed that I don't hang out with any of them now. They're always trying to make us feel bad about how we treat them unfairly, when at the same time they are more racist than us." Gwen proceeds to tell them about the cafeteria incident.

Randi, "That was so mean for those girls to say that, but Gwen, you shouldn't hate everyone because of what a couple of idiots said."

They try over and over again to bring her back, but Gwen won't listen to anything negative spoken against her hatred.

Gwen assumes, as her friends speak, "I bet Mia talks the same way about me that the rest of them do, when I'm not around."

With Sasha out shopping somewhere - everywhere - in his bedroom, David lays, alone, on his back, staring up at the blades of his slowly rotating ceiling fan. He didn't just hear his daughter's hateful words, he's coming to the realization that he felt them; deeply. And he never thought it would feel like this, knowing that he has now successfully passed down his family's legacy of intolerance, to yet another generation, unsettles him.

"Stupid niggers, those dirty wet-backs, I hate those greedy Jews…" David's mind alternates between his childhood full of his mother's racial putdowns and his visualizations of Gwen all grown up, angrily screaming her grandmother's same detestable words.

Small pieces of self-doubt towards his feelings and way of speaking about others, for the first time seriously in his life, occupy his thoughts. He paused for a moment back when Sasha told him that she never saw race the way he thought she did, but he quickly brushed that aside. His mind won't let go this time. He questions the intolerant views that were taught to him, the same ones he hid behind his good deeds.

Gwen's voice attached to those familiar words, hits him down to his core, and the truths they bring up make David very unsettled; they frighten him, because the blame keeps coming back upon him.

Suddenly, he recalls the hip-hop gear wearing young man that walked by him in the neighborhood grocery store parking lot the other day. David remembers tightening up as he went by, scared that this man may rob him. This assumption was based solely off of his sagging clothes, dark-brown skin, and David's persistently refined negative view of black men. David recalls his surprise as his quick opinion of this man fought to remain, once he watched this 'hip-hopper' open and close the car door for the young lady that was with him. David was so impressed with his chivalry. "That's how I have always treated Sasha, I would have never thought someone like him would do that," he thought at the time. Now he questions, "am I just like my parents?"

David conjures up the different conclusions he draws when a black or Hispanic person commits a crime, as opposed to a Caucasian assailant. When it's the minorities doing the crime, he faults the entire race, but when a face that looks like his does wrong, his judgments scold only that individual.

Freshly unleashed, his inner-man probes for a deeper understanding; this in turn frees him to receive a great blessing.

Mr. Gimmer is no longer in control of his thoughts. His eyes lose conscience focus of the ceiling fan, as everything that comprises him goes to another place; another life and time.

It is he who is being taken from his land, like cattle he is stuffed onto a boat along with hundreds of other men with blonde hair and blue eyes. Once onto their captor's stolen land, tan and black strangers take control of him and harshly guide his every moment. They treat him worse than an abused animal, all because of the only crime he is guilty of; being one of God's creations that is blessed with white skin.

Over and over again, David feels the sting of a rawhide whip slicing through the skin of his shirtless back. He feels the daily despair of a life where no choice is his own, the hopelessness of looking into the blue eyes of his children and knowing that this same fate of ownership, of being told and made to feel like they are less than human, will engross their entire life and soul as it has his. He stares into the eyes of his black 'owner', wishing he could kill this one man, this symbol of hate that has taken every ounce of happiness and independence from his being. But he knows this isn't even a remote option, so instead, his damaged mind tells his feet to run away from this pain.

David flees his enslavers, only to be hunted down by them and denied freedom and a decent life yet again. Now he must watch as these men discipline him by raping his wife and almost beating the pulse out of his children; all because he ran towards equality, all because he wanted a life of freedom and choices.

He fast forwards to modern day. Surrounded only by his Hispanic and African-American classmates, he feels awkward and belittled, as they sit in class and learn through their history books about Black America's brutality of his ancestors.

Tears rise up from his soul, as his torso rises from his bed, David's eyes are wide open, but he cannot see the closet door that is directly in his line of sight. The moment still has total control over him, as he walks by a group of Hispanic men, who, for kicks, devalue his life by shouting the one detestable word that they know will remind him of the subhuman, heartless way "his kind" was treated in the past.

His enlightenment comes to a screeching halt. The demons inside of David fight relentlessly to regain their stronghold. His mind suddenly shuts down and shields itself against this invasion of renewed thinking and higher understanding.

The devil speaks to his heart. "This is what they want me to do. They want to trick me into thinking that they are just like us, that they're not beneath me." David wipes away the liquid running down his cheeks, and does what any upper class, executive business man would do, when they are faced with a life changing moment that they are not ready to accept; he calls up his golf buddies and they go play a round.

She wants to, but she does not look. Her instincts stop her for the moment. She thinks about his strength, how he is so aggressive; it excites her! It brings her the moistness that Ed's harsh, dry fingers have never delivered to her. Her eyes cannot avoid getting in on all of this sexual arousal much longer; they have to look.

There he is, standing there, another man, another penis. Unlike her husband, she knows that a thirteen year old boy will not be as nearly concerned about beating her, once he is allowed inside of her body. Glimpses of some of the past sexual brutality her husband has inflicted on her and how she's forced to watch the delight in Ed's twistedly horny eyes flash through her mind. "No, he'll just want sex."

Sadly, Sherry has reached the same utterly despicable level that Ed reached long ago. Yes, Ed's treatment of her is the main reason why her beaten, lonely thoughts have sunk to these depths; but ultimately it's her choice that has caused her to slip this far. Most extremely battered victims don't sink down this low, but unfortunately for Sherry, this adds another horrendous chapter to the horror story that is her life.

Melvin inches down the crowded aisle happily knowing, "This is the last time I'll ever have to ride one of these." He hops off the bottom step of that metro bus, and onto the sidewalk's cracked pavement, feeling oh so good about his life. He's dressed 'fresh ta def', his one pair of good jeans were put in the dumpster weeks ago. Now a sixty five dollar white t-shirt, covered up by a thick, black, five hundred dollar leather jacket, that would have touched the top of his gray and black ninety five dollar, top of the line, name brand jeans, if they weren't sagging down on top of his two hundred and fifty five dollar white on white sneakers; adorns his frame. And he has many more color coordinated outfits like this at home.

Melvin crosses a busy intersection to begin a short jaunt along another sidewalk that leads to the home of his former place of employment; Bobby's Kicks. Along the way his darkened soul changes his perceptions. "Look at all of these stuck-up white people. I bet they got a big laugh out of seeing me when I was poor." Walking on this familiar pavement feels good, it felt good before, but this is different for him. His ego tells him that the fine linens that so crisply drape his frame will show these strangers that walk and drive by him that he has money to, just like them.

Like so many others out there, racism is an easy slope to tumble down when things have gone against you, when the rage inside of you is not satisfied by just hating the ambulance personnel that did not arrive at your home until forty five minutes after your frantic 911 call to save your already deceased grandmother, or the all-white (so he perceives it to be) social service system that took away the only family members that you have left. No! Young Melvin's dark feelings will not compartmentalize any longer; except for one beautiful Caucasian woman, he hates them all.

To Melvin, Faith isn't like them, she's different. He can't wait for her eyes to feast upon him, for her to see that he is o.k., for her to see that he is caring for himself, for her to see his ninety five dollar jeans, instead of the bummy gear that he always wore.

O' beautiful Faitthh?" Sweet and soft, he announces his presence by singing it, just like he sometimes did in the past when he needed a favor from her.

"Oh my goodness, Melvin! You wait right there, don't you move." She finishes helping her customer find the right fit, then, hurries over to greet him with a huge hug after guiding the patron to her co-worker at the register. "It is so good to see you? I've missed you so much, how have you been?" She says while continuing her tight squeeze.

Melvin thinks. "How have I been? Can't she tell by the way I look?" He answers, "I'm doing alright, just trying to survive out here since my grandmother died."

As they move over to a nearby bench, in front of the store's only window, Faith takes hold of his hand and gently strokes the back of it. "Oh my goodness, sweetie, I've been praying for you every since you called and told me about it. I know how much you loved her, but be happy that she'll be at peace in heaven, just try to focus on that…," Melvin's eyes roll away from her, "I remember you telling me how deep her faith was in our Lord, so you know she's in a beautiful place now. So have you heard from those precious cousins of yours'?"

Melvin's emotions rise angrily, "I have no idea how they're doing, your guess is as good as mine. Since I won't come in and be a slave for the state, and I'm not eighteen yet, they won't tell me where they are or let me talk to them."

"Oh honey, I am so sorry for you. God is going to bring those kids back to you, you'll see."

Melvin doesn't disrespect her by laughing at that ridiculous notion like he wants to. He simply turns away.

He does not have to say it, Faith feels it. She knows that he still believes all of the lies.

"So where are you staying, where ya workin'?"

Melvin partially lies. "I've been staying with one of my boys since everything went down. I'm just been doing a couple of odd jobs here and there for his dad."

"You know if there is ever anything I can help you with, you know you can call me day or night." Faith's voice breaks down, hurting for her friend.

Touched by her emotions, Melvin reassures her. "Faith, don't cry. I'm o.k., I really appreciate how much you care about me. Don't worry, my life is going good now, look…," he pulls out a super thick stack of twenties, "I'm making great money. (Laughs) I'm not in those same dirty clothes you used to see me in all the time. I've got my life together. I'm the last person you need to cry over."

A burst of tears roll down to her cheeks and land on her forced smile to her friend. Faith has some really good ideas where that much money may have come from, but she knows it's pointless to say anything against his new way of life, at least in here, right now.

Now that God and all of the morals and values that go along with his presence have been 'stoned to death', many of the faithless are left without any balance inside their conscience, so it's improbable that Faith can tell a man holding a six thousand dollar stack of cash anything against how he got it.

"I love you with all of my heart, Melvin, and I know you don't want to hear this, but Jesus and God love you way more than I do…," he sighs, then, stares down at the ground. With one loving finger placed upon his chin, Faith softly raises his head and turns it back to her, "and yes Melvin, they are real. Please keep them somewhere in your thoughts. Because I know they can heal you, and I'm going to do my part by praying away these beliefs you have taken inside of you. Please, don't lose hope, Melvin."

"It's hilarious that you would say that God is going to heal me. Answer this for me… why didn't God heal my grandmother of her poverty. She was a hard working, good, and faithful follower of him, what did she get for it? He let her get seriously injured at work, which took away her livelihood and left us broke. For all of her faith, she got so little in return. The Bible says that a believer will have prosperity in all areas of their life, including financially, I looked da shit up! He left her broke and trapped in da hood, so where the fuck was her prosperity?"

Faith's spirit is greatly moved, "Oh Melvin, that's simply not true. God gave her beautiful grandchildren that she could delight in; did she ever allow her surroundings to distract her from raising you and your cousins to be respectful, intelligent, God loving people?"

"No."

"She was God's gift to you, her love through God saved you all… she never yelled at you, did she? She was always really upbeat and supportive, right?"

Melvin fights to suck in his tears, "Yeah she was."

Faith voice softens, as revelation lands on her tongue. "Her spirit was God's. Every time, you hugged her, you hugged God. When you spoke to her, Melvin, you were talking to God, through her flesh. She was the blessing put in your life to form you into a great man. She gave you everything that money couldn't buy. All you had to do was continue to be patient. My beautiful boy, you were the brilliant A student, goal oriented son meant to fulfill God's promise of financial prosperity for her; it was you."

He has never looked at his life through this picture. He yearns to crumble down to the floor, weep and scream for the memories of an opportunity he'll never get, but the inner man that controls him is strong; so in the eyes of his shrinking heart that's weakness, which is no longer allowed to be a part of his character.

"Don't give up on God, Melvin."

He then says the worst words to her that he could ever speak, "I have no hope, Faith."

She tries to keep her breakdown quiet, "Don't ever say that, please. There is hope if you'll just look the other way."

Melvin turns his head and looks the other way. Faith brings his attention back to her with the touch of her soft palm across his cheek.

"Will you do me one favor? If you care one tiny bit for me, please do this, I mean it. You always put me off, now I'm begging you."

"What? Do what?" He answers, while discreetly wiping his eyes.

"Come listen to me preach at my church this Sunday."

His shoulders lump, he sighs and giggles all at the same time, "Come on Faith, why you gotta ask me to do that?"

"Please Melvin, just one time… please."

Moments pass. "Alright, I'll do it. I think I'll be able to withstand one last time inside one of those."

"God is going to give me revelations that are going to change your beliefs, Melvin."

With a soft kiss to her cheek, Melvin holds up his right hand, and with a smirk confirms, "I'll be there… I swear to God."

That evening, Faith does exactly what she told Melvin she would do. And God does exactly what he told her he would do. "Glory to God, it's 11:59. I better get to sleep. Thank you so much for what you have given me this evening, Father. All praise your name, Jesus. This is everything that they need to hear. Sunday, through you, Father, I am going to change so many lives back towards you. Lord, I bless you."

Faith has been at her small office desk inside of what used to be her sixth bedroom, before it was converted into her room for prayer and for business.

She shuts down her office, brushes her teeth, disrobes, and enters the bed. To free herself from worry, she begins to talk out of faith, to God, to bless Melvin, "You are such a great man.

I thank God that he has already spoken into your life, which brought you back to him. I thank him that you will be free from all of the world's lies. I pray this into existence through my savior Jesus Christ." Faith's soul lifts greatly knowing that she does not have fret, she has put the responsibility of her wants into the accepting hands of the Lord.

WHAM! Suddenly, an intrusive idea causes her defenses to rise. The 'what ifs' have gotten through, the devil's suggestions try to speak their way into her life, so that he may find a path into her heart.

Faith knows that she must react immediately. She knows that she can't sit there and listen to Satan plead his case.

Faith flips over onto her stomach, supported by her elbows; she buries her forehead into her palms. She counters the enemy's press with the only defense that can defeat him; worship through the Word of God. "Father God, in the name of Jesus Christ, I pray; And they overcame him by the blood of the Lamb, and by the word of their testimony, and they loved not their lives unto the death... Trust in the Lord with all your heart, and lean not on your own understanding-" Faith repeats that saving scripture three more times, until the 'what ifs' are cast out. Now she's free to lay her untroubled mind down to rest.

—— CHAPTER FOURTEEN ——

Inside of the ghetto fabulous living room of the apartment that Dane now shares with his new roommate, Melvin relaxes on the same identical sofa that David and Sasha have in their home. He and Dane, who is 'sunk' into the matching recliner on the other side of the room, watch their favorite television show, 'Celebrity Bling'. Both keep guns at their side; never knowing when it may become a much wanted commodity. Their eyes stare at the high resolution screen with great envy.

Dane, "Homie, we keep ballin' like we doin' now, we gon' be up at that level. Buying that fly shit like them."

"Hell yeah, I'm a get one of them iced-out Rolexes that white boy got on, right there."

"I know, I like that Lambo too."

"Imagine pulling up to the club and hopping out that whip. People'd be fallin' out seeing a local D-boy doing it that big. That's unprecedented pimpin' 'round here."

"That's real talk right there."

"Hell yeah, I'm a go rent one this weekend, yeah, I'm a do it, I'm a rent one," his tone saddens, "hopefully I'll have enough money left over to buy the good champagne in the club." Melvin hopes his underlying message got through to his boss.

Dane picks up on the displeasure in Melvin's words, but right now, he's only concerned with what his mind had never considered, "I can't believe you thought of that shit before me. Renting it, I only thought of buying one! All this time I could have been stuntin' rides like that through the hood. I'm a get one, too!"

The show goes to commercial break, causing Dane's focus to detour. He turns and addresses his roommate. "Yo playa, I think it's about time we start talkin' promotion for you, G. I ain't gonna lie, I was scared shitless that you was gon' screw up at first, you know, with you going through your family crisis, but you proved me wrong. You serious boy, you stay on your 'grizzly' daily, so I gotta reward that."

"Thanks baby, I appreciate that," is what Melvin's mouth tells Dane, but what he would really like to tell his boss is, "it's about time, homeboy, because I was really tired of being your stupid little mule. I'm the one out here makin' runs to Texas, South Carolina, and Florida. I'm taking all of the risks, so you can get our coke for cheap, while you and Stamp take the majority of the profit... Naw, those days are over, so the next words out of your mouth better massage me really, really nicely, or you're going to have a problem, roommate!"

Melvin loves Dane, in his own way, he really does. He appreciates that he took him in when he could have left him out, and he has also come around to liking Stamp - well enough.

Before Dane can tell him his plans, he gets a call on one of the three cellphones he carries around everywhere with him. He bolts off into his bedroom, chatting up one of his lady friends.

Melvin's eyes wait for the show to return to their theater sized television, but his real concerns are somewhere else. For a split second, he fantasizes about putting his gun to the back of Dane's head and demanding, "I want it. You are the only one who knows how to contact our big supplier." He tries to shake the thought, but various versions keep coming back.

"Naw, I wouldn't do that to my boy." Lately, Melvin has had to block out other flashes of evil scenarios his greed and jealousy has envisioned towards others. "I'd never kill my homeboy." He says while twirling his .45 caliber handgun on his index finger. "You gotta have some kind of honor in this game… this dude better come back in here talkin' right, tho'."

Right on cue, the door opens. Dane strides back into the room and flops back into his seat, to the left of Melvin. "As I was about to tell you, baby. You ain't no runner. I think you're a leader. I want you to come sit next to me and Stamp and run this street game with us."

"That's what's up! That's what I'm talkin' 'bout, boy! I appreciate this dog." The friends share a hand slap. Immediately, Melvin's feelings towards Dane flip; it's all love. He wants to reward Dane's promotion of him, "Lately I've thought up some new ideas that I think could have us makin' money out of control," Melvin excitedly states.

"I know homie, you've probably thought up the same ideas I have, but we need to chill for a minute. There's enough money out here for our whole squad. We could get bigger, but if we get too big, the cops gon' shut us down or some other thugs gon' come gunnin' for us. We in a good zone, right here. We need to just chill and enjoy where we at. Shit, we already making crazy money, why do something stupid." Content with his stance, Dane slouches back into the padding of his seat and returns his attention to the mansions and jewelry, "We good right where we're at… Nigga, I'm about to drive a Lambo."

Unknown to Dane, angry eyes stare intensely at the side of his face, Melvin does not care about the long term wisdom in his boss' words, his thinking is all about right now. He contemplates, "The hell with that, there's a lot mo' money to get. How you gon' be kingpin if you scared to go get every dime you can? I want it all!"

What has happened to Melvin? Why has his life done such a complete reversal? He was so positive, so focused on living a fruitful, clean life. He swore that he wouldn't let the streets get him; but here he is, and this was not how his plan was supposed to go. His intentions were to allow himself to be sidetracked, for awhile, by making a few thousand dollars off the destruction of those in his community, then, he was to jump back onto the mainstream track by usage of the great intellect that he processes, enabling him to 'flip' his ill-gotten money into sound business investments or college, which would then allow himself and his cousins to live out a comfortable life just like he always planned. He only intended to sell drugs for a short time. But like so many others, once the money starts rolling in, all well-conceived go straight plans get crumbled up and thrown away. In eerie similarity, he's beginning to sound like the addicts that he helps to destroy. "O.K, o.k., just a couple of more times then I'm goin' ta stop. I just need to do this just a little more that's all, then, I'm done. I'm serious this time, I'm done."

It started in Asia, and affected Europe soon after, it's been building for quite some time. Since its forthcoming influence on America was not greatly reported on and taken seriously by Americans; its effects hit them all at once.

Markets slide down steep slopes on Wall Street, consumer confidence plummets. Greed runs rampant through corporate America as company assets become grab-bags for CEO's who see that their boat is taking on water.

This new economic landscape causes the faithless and the powerless Christians to live under constant dread each moment. The media pounds home the facts and possibilities of another deep recession landing on their shores. Most of the things said about the economy are negative and reeks of people's fear of lack and poverty.

The darkness is race-less, it is religion-less, and it does not care about economic status, all that it wants is for them to fail.

Confident belief in the Lord's existence takes another blow as the country's economy slows. Just as faith and confidence in walking a Godly life can be built up and nurtured, so can one's reliance on man's economic system. Satan most powerful weapon - fear - is on full blast.

Their fear births worry, worry causes frustration, frustration leads them to restlessness, and restlessness introduces them to lack of patience, patience's lack steers them towards anger.

They believe the illusions contained within the enemy's reality is just how life is supposed to go.

Excluding Ed and his family, via various reasons and circumstances, in-house and abroad, they are all in attendance. The faithful, those that waver, those who live in denial; they all are set to hear her.

Today is the day of the Lord.

One is here because he was invited by tonight's speaker. Another is here, along with his family, because something in his spirit moved him this way. Two have come together, just to add another brick to their fortress of faith. While another two watch from home.

"And why, again, did you have to drag us to this pointless and ridiculous place?" His body tenses, David's bludgeoning eyes look for a bobbing face that is about to angrily turn and confront Sasha about her overheard sacrilegious words, as he, and his wife and daughter walk through the crowded corridors towards the aisle that contains their seat.

To David's relief, no one turns, "Sasha, come on, I know that you don't want to be here, but you don't have to be disrespectful to everyone that still believes."

"She and I are free from this place and all of its fairytales, Dad. We thought you were too."

"Gwen, I just wanted to come for the heck of it. Don't you know there are still many good lessons and values that the church and the Bible holds."

"Hey homey, thanks for agreeing to come here with me. My homegirl damn near put a gun to my head to get me here, so I figured why suffer alone?"

Dane, "Wow, thanks a lot, Mel," they share in a laugh, "I didn't have na'thin else to do. Plus, it can't hurt to hear some of this stuff, naw mean?"

"Yo, I can't quit tripping off of how big this church is. Faith gotta be making some serious bread if she's the pastor of this piece."

"You ain't lying, there has to be close to ten thousand seats in this place," answers Dane, as his eyes, like Melvin's, take in the sight of the hundreds filling the upper rafters of the oval shaped megachurch, while they themselves arrive at their floor level seats; tenth row back, middle aisle.

Melvin delights that there is only ten minutes remaining until she is set to begin and there are still many thousands of seats left to be filled. The sad sight reinforces belief.

He and Dane sit quietly. Being seated in the Lord's house after such a prolonged absence suddenly brings about ideas of change inside of Dane's heart. It has him questioning if he'll get out of the dope game before the inevitable downfall crushes his life, and if he does get out; how would he make a living?

The oppressor sees sparks of questioning flickering in Dane's soul, so he halts them with self-doubt and condemnation. "Man nobody is going to hire an uneducated, junior high dropout like me... I know white people gon be looking down their noses' because of where I'm from and what I've done... I'm trapped in the game now, I mind as well just ride this on out."

Guilt, a sense of remorse, a burning desire to place another X on his scorecard; all of the above combined to make Bryant Michaels flip to Anytown's community channel to watch something spiritual this morning. "Flight' knows that at this time of the day on Sunday there is always something "churchy" on. This, and going to a couple of the Reflection Revivals, is his promised payback to God for what he did for him.

Bryant counts on this spiritual act to make up for his backsliding from the other things that he told God he would do. "Alright, I'll give this one full hour, then, I gotta get going. If there is a God, he can't say that I didn't try to keep my word."

Ed has everyone literally locked away in their rooms, so that he may watch. He is fascinated by the 'Bible Hoax'. "Society's evolution is so predictable."

He enjoys listening to preachers of the Word speak the gospel to their depleting congregations.

After a small, but powerful choir sings a few praise songs, Faith steps up to the podium under the cover of a loud applause and begins telling them what God told her.

"Good afternoon, everyone. God bless you. I am so happy all of you chose to be here today...," with a sad grimace and a slow shake of her head, "it's so sad that the master deceiver has gotten to so many of our loved ones and friends, thereby preventing them from joining us in worship."

Amen's and praise Jesus', by a few boisterous believers, echo through the ears of the thousands in attendance. "As I look out at you all this morning, I am saddened by what I see. There used to not be an empty seat in this church, now I look out and see at least five thousand empty souls... I mean chairs," joy and brightness quickly spark the tenor in Faith's voice, "but that's o.k., because we're here, and we gonna set 'em straight this afternoon and uplift our Christian hearts' and minds' as I hope to make you and everyone within the sound of my voice understand what is really going on in this once majestic, Heaven on earth, land we live on.

"Early this week, I was putting the finishing touches on today's sermon that I am about to share with you all. And I was contemplating what my title should be, how could I describe and encompass my entire lesson into just a few words. Then, a few days ago, Thursday, to be exact, it came to me soon after the Lord kissed me upon my cheek and I opened my eyes to begin another day. He told me the title should be *The Ultimate Test of*

Faith." She pauses to allow the truth to settle into their minds' after repeating those five powerful words once more.

"That's what each and everyday of living in this physical world, in this day and time, has become; *The Ultimate Test of Faith*. We're surrounded and influenced by all these distractions that we, as a society, have created for ourselves. Folks, we are under attack like no other generation has ever been. This generation, young, old, white, black, and everyone in between, is being tested and tried to a greater degree than any other people this planet has ever seen. Never in the world's history has the human race had so many diversions trying to take our focus off of God. With every two steps forward we take in our worldly advances, we take three steps backward spiritually."

"It's so sad that we've found out that it's not just the people who've never believed in God that have abandoned him, it's also the carnal Christians… people that took Jesus as their savior, but continued to live as the world would have them to live; those are the ones who have totally failed this test.

Bryant 'Flight' Michaels is still; numbed by her words and the personal truth that is hitting him.

"God wants all of you, he doesn't like to share. They're allowing their flesh to misguide them due to overvaluing its value. They won't pay attention to the Bible, but they're sure attentive of their bills, cars, jobs, college, girls, boys, clothes, children, wife, husband… ancient scrolls! Don't we see that if your spiritual health doesn't matter to you more than ANY of those other factors, that means that you are of the world. Yes, you are. And who is prince of the world… And we wonder why we see so much of Satan everywhere we look." The true believers and the 'sometimesies' break into a wild cheer. The rest just stay uncomfortably quiet.

Faith allows them ample time to rejoice in the power of the truth. Big smile, "I saw y'all faces', y'all looking at me like you're shocked…" Faith goes into the voice of some lady acting like she's speaking to someone else, "Did the pastor just say that we overvalue our children? The pastor doesn't love the babies? How is she gonna preach to me about God's love and she doesn't love the most precious gift of all?

"No, that is not what I'm saying. I love these precious children as much as anyone, that's why I'm telling y'all, (dramatic pause) stop trying to show love for your kids by just shaping their physical world, instead of properly leading them into God's open arms by shaping their spirituality. Through your spirituality, lean on God to help you shape their physical world for all of the success that you want them to eventually have.

"We'll send our kids to the best schools, work overtime to provide them with the best clothing for those best schools, show and lovingly nurture them through many of life's lessons, so that they may go out into the world and build a successful life… That's what good parents do, but too many of us never show them how to have spiritual success. And without you setting them up for spiritual success in life, you are totally handcuffing any chance they have for ultimate success."

"Some of us try to rely solely on churches to do it, but do we spend time at home, together, building a bond through our Lord and Savior? Why not? Maybe because we're trying to build great boys and girls by the fluctuating standards set by this world? That leaves us open for attacks by Satan, who tries to gain control of you by fooling your mind to put all of your eggs in the wrong basket. That's exactly what is going on across the world today; people's eggs are in the wrong basket.

Faith holds up her black covered Bible for all to see, "It's all right here in this book; in the Word of God. But God won't force you to come to this book, he'll chase you, oh yes, he chases each and every one of us, that's Him chasing you when your conscience tells you to trust in him, but instead you do what you want to do. He could make all of us do right, but He won't. He loves us enough to allow us to choose our own destiny."

"This is all a test. And as you all can see, just look at the empty seat next to you, too many people are getting an F. We are way too immersed in the world that we can see instead of the world that we can't.

The audience speaks.

"Folks, everyone, please...," Faith moves from behind the red velvet draped podium, she wants them all to see and feel her strength, as she speaks matter of factly, "I say this, and I'll put my life on it," her voice moves up to a much more emotional octave, propelling she to deliver some of times' most stirring words, "and when I say I put my life on this, I mean send my God fearing, God obeying, love for what He sent His only begotten son down to this Earth to give his life, so that my sinful soul could somehow be blessed enough to join them in Heaven, Yes!, send me to hell if I am wrong!"

God's spirit entrances most, "This world would not be anywhere close to greeting Jesus' return if it were run by agape love, which is the love of God, like he designed for it to be.

"Read my lips; we can't go on much longer living in a world driven by our sight, our emotions, and our will, it goes against everything that God will support. If we put as much time, thought, faith, and money into real love, which is all God is... this world would change. Oh yes, it will change, right along with our fate because, for the first time, modern man would allow the spiritual world to again lead his physical world.

"When are we going to get serious about our seriousness towards our devotion to our Creator, when are we going to quit doing just a little bit and calling it a lot?

"Don't you Christians understand who you are? You are the righteousness of God, you didn't earn it. You became the righteousness of God the day that you took the Lord Jesus Christ as your savior; so don't you think that the least you could do to show God your love for what he has done for you would be to stop doing a little and calling it a lot? Doing a lot isn't just going to church every now and then, a lot ain't settling for being a good person by worldly standards, to substitute for not getting your thoughts and your eyes in line with the gospel, a lot ain't you being the same person, years and years later, after you say you've accepted the blood of Christ, but you still live by the same decision-making that you had before you got saved."

Hearts' fill with emotional energy, the faithful want to openly rejoice, but Faith won't give them time, she has more, "The Lord ain't playin' around with us no more, his Word demands that there be a change in the hierarchy that guides our lives' or there will be no life, everybody in here knows that we've been heading that way for a long time, so don't act surprised that I said it…"

A crowd of heads' nod in agreement.

"Our favorite thing to say and confess to doing is putting our children number one in our life, that's a problem Christians, too many people love their children more than they love God, when actually them having a world tomorrow in which to give to their kids, depends on parents, of today, loving God above all else. He can not be second to anybody or anything. See it's easy for us to love our children, and our mother, and our husband or girlfriend, because we can see them. That's the difference right there, we don't even have to get all deep and philosophical with it, we can see, and we can touch, and we can control our husbands, children, and etc, so for many people that makes it easier to love them over God," Faith gets sarcastic, "who man only supposedly seen some two thousand odd years ago."

"We put God on our life's back burner, far too much. We take His importance too lightly, we procrastinate with him, but if we reverse that and bring him back to being the head for our body, the Lord will reward us. And when I say reward, I mean reward us heavily. It's told in the Bible! Don't think for a second that our Father doesn't want us to continue to live, hear me when I say this!

"We are the ones pushing and bringing about the end of time, it's not God's choice for this to happen; not yet. HE DOES NOT WANT THIS WORLD TO END! But he can't go on supporting a world that does not support him. He can't go on supporting a world that has more demons in power, controlling things, than his followers; earth's conquerors. God loves life, He wants us to have life, the very purpose of the Bible, is to make us understand how to sustain life through God. The way this world is and the way we think, then, live; this is not a sustaining type of lifestyle.

"When people look out at the world and all of its problems, far too much we just see the physical, the see and touch side of what is happening, we don't view it from the spiritual, because too many of us don't think that there is a spiritual. That's why so many people ran away from the spiritual when this so-called 'Bible Hoax' junk came about.

"Let's talk about God, the way that he really is. Yes! He will let this world suffer and crumble, not because he doesn't love us, but because that is the path of the freewill that we chose. And he will not impose his will on us, even if it means our death. All of you Christians will agree that the clashes societies are having today is putting us on a collision course with extinction, right? Not many will deny that. Well, it's also forcing God's hand. HE HAS TO BEAT US TO IT."

"Follow me on this… his Word tells you about the rapture in Revelations, it speaks about what the people will go through, what they not only will see, but also hear. The Word of God is always true and accurate, so that means there must still be people around who haven't been annihilated by a nuclear bomb, correct? HE WILL BEAT US TO IT! Revelations tells us that Jesus' return will end life on this planet, so if man and his bombs are about to end it… which do you think has to happen first?"

"They are correct when you hear people say that man will destroy himself, but it won't be because of bombs he's dropped, but it will be because his lack of obedience to God. How much longer do y'all think that God is going to tolerate us living life with him in the background, and Satan everywhere you look?!"

"But do you know what's beautiful? What's beautiful is that we don't even have to go there. If we would just truly change; stop the pretending, stop the excuses, stop the half-hearted effort and most of all, stop the procrastinating. Get your eyes off of this world and open them to this book!" When Faith's right hand raises God's glorious instruction manual towards the heavens, the four walls of the auditorium vibrate against the audience's united, standing and screaming, eruption of emotional faith!

The applause travels on for minutes.

The time calms her voice. "This is what I don't understand about people. You know all of this mayhem in our lives' has already been predicted, you see the loss of our reliance upon the Word and what happens because of it, as it was predicted; and we still never change our course. When are we ever going to learn? When are we ever going to stop being our own God by trying to do things our way? Lying about where you are with the seriousness of your faith and dedication to the Most High, scared to question it because of the answer the mirror might give to you, too darn arrogant and full of pride to be critical of yourself."

She stares out at them pitifully, everyone feels her truth. "Look at how bad we have allowed our lives' and this planet to get. We bleed nature, which is what keeps us alive, destroy it because we only think about the moment, and not the future. And God told us not to do this, when he said 'replenish the world.' We live in an age where Joe Blow off of the street could possibly build a bomb that could end tens of thousands of lives instantly. And we all know that is just the small end of that scale!

"Pick up any history book, the beings who were created to be earth's master, the beings created in God's likeness, with all of the brilliance he placed in our minds', still haven't learned to change. We still haven't worked back to him... Every generation, repeats the same cycle, and every time, with every new generation, the cycle gets more deadly and massive.

"And still we don't change. We're standing at the bottom of the hill, but somehow we ignore that ten ton boulder steamrolling down it. We've paid a huge price spiritually for all of our earthly advances, now we have to get it back by moving forward."

"It's hard to humble yourself in this world by somehow

allowing an unseen being to guide you; be honest, isn't it? I'll tell you what I think is the reason why so many in today's day fail to achieve spiritual triumph. It's because we don't see it being of any real importance to the success of the people surrounding us, who we wish to be like. Too often, the success that everyone covets, we don't see God being a necessary ingredient for that success.

"The loss of our spiritually has become a socially contagious epidemic! We envy successful business people, so we think that being great in school is the main tool we'll need to be successful like them. We see all of the celebrity type people, and the crazy, extravagant lives' they lead, and we darn sure don't see most of them relying on God to get them where they are. This thinking is shaped greatly by television and the internet, which then gets us to sharing, repeating, and spreading the wrong thoughts and ideas amongst one another, because the shaping of the way we view society's envied few is geared upon materialism and what THEY did to get where they are at. Oh!, I know I'm right about it."

"Television producers have found out that you, as a middle class or impoverished follower, use these shows as an escape to visualize your life being the same as theirs', so they fill your eyes with as much of it as they can.

"People at the head of all these different media outlets are very smart people, they know your dreams and your wishes. They know that you dream of seeing yourself on those 300' yachts, you can almost feel yourself behind the wheel of that half million dollar car, they know that you want your home to be as big as this guy's or that star.

"What they don't focus on is the fact that you should go to God first, so that what you get will be blessed, then it will last and never leave you."

"And you know what's crazy, what's truly crazy? Satan has got us so twisted that now we think that people who do have financial success AND openly serve God; we think that they're all crooks! If you make money from serving man's businesses or man's carnal entertainments that's fine, but if you get financial reward by influencing others to strengthen their relationship with God, just like the Bible tells Christians they are to do, then you sir are probably a crook.

"Don't get me wrong, there are people using God for nothing but their financial gain, but I'm talking about the good men - God men and women - who deliver a spiritual blessing by having their ministries on television, or like this used to be, leaders of a church with thousands of members for a wide audience to learn from, or maybe just the everyday citizens out there who live a life full of faith and are monetarily successful. But what does the devil tell the faithless, 'They're all phony, look at how much money they getting, you can't make that much money and still be working for the Lord'.

"One of the best tactics that Satan uses to twist our minds' against proper thinking is through character defamation. Think about it, every time that you see a minister, pastor, or priest, portrayed on television, do they not always have a negative stigma attached to them? They're portrayed as crooks, pimps, and child molesters. You have to understand that this distorts people's reality, because when they continue on with their life after watching this, subtlety they begin to associate crooks, pimps and child molesters with religion and spirituality.

"America stereotypes Christians much the same way it often does African-Americans, the Jewish, and women. While the devil just sits back on his throne and laughs...," Faith looks directly into the television's camera, strong in stance, "y'all can take me off of the air for saying it, but it can no longer be denied; Satan, the devil, Diablo, whatever you wanna call him, he is winning more than he is losing at a greater rate than ever before in history. And in my opinion, told through my spirit, our Father won't tolerate this much longer."

"We gotta start being careful about what we watch and read. You watch Ms. Celebrity finish showing you all of her goodies, 'oh I just thank God for my home and my diamonds, I am truly blessed', but the other ninety nine point nine percent of the time all she talked about was herself and her possessions. When you see her, you don't see a representative of God. You see a representative of the world.

"And you just sit there wastin' your day away, eating it up. They may have stepped on, stole from, gave up their bodies, lied to, or killed to get where they are, but people don't care. All that matters is, they have money, you see success in that person, they can afford the fun that your eyes want, and God is not needed in that equation!"

"Oh dear carnal Christians, you say that you're gonna be different, that you gon' praise and worship God if He blesses you with their good fortune, but riddle me this, when you daydream and you picture all of the exciting activities and ways that you'll spend your newfound days, how much do you daydream about praising God, how much daydreaming do you do about spending your day reading and listening to deepen your understanding of His Word, so you can successfully maintain God's will for your life even with all of this newfound materialism surrounding you? Is your way of serving the Creator going to be just giving away gobs of your new money, or are you taking time away from your buddies, and shopping, and partying, to, in the mist of all your wealth and the freedoms that come with it, take the time to really worship and learn what He wants you to do with your blessings? How much time is spent daydreaming about that part of your new life? Think about that."

"Don't we understand that God WANTS you to have financial prosperity? He just wants you to get it through serving Him. Instead of trying to go directly to financial happiness, martial happiness, or personal happiness, true success is as simple as A, B, C. You start at A, which is God first, work your life through him, and then you reach B, through him he'll take you to happiness, in all aspects of your life, not just financially, that's when you'll organically float to C, which is happiness and completeness greater than you ever desired.

"That's why we see these celebrities acting crazy and out of control, because they keep on skipping A and B.

"We can't just stick our toe in the water, when it comes to our faith, because you still wanta have the flexibility to jump back into the world and do what they do, whenever you feel like it. This is why it's called a Christian walk, everyone. Your spiritual life, your Christianity, is an ongoing development. When you walk you aren't still, there's movement, correct? Don't even bother to get into this, if you're not willing to do the walking! Too many people sit around thinking that they're safe because they say they took the Savior Jesus Christ into their life, they think that's all they have to do.

"Let's go to first John 1:6 - 'If we claim to have fellowship with him, (that's what you're doing when you take Christ as your savior) yet walk in the darkness (that's what you're doing by thinking and walking the same as you were before) we LIE and do not live by the truth'. That tells me, that when you really haven't changed your heart, you really haven't come to God.

"This is why our Father says in his Word, John 4:23 - 'Yet a time is coming and has now come when the true worshipers will worship the Father in spirit and truth for THEY are the kind of worshipers the Father seeks'. If the Bible says the Father seeks TRUE worshipers that must mean that there are false or fake worshipers masquerading around also? Which one are you?"

"You're a Christian, don't do a little bit of Christian stuff, then turn your back to God's will every time temptation confronts you, that's showing God where your heart truly lies. What do you think that it meant when you took Jesus as your Lord and Savior? That means that YOUR ways no longer exist, it means that you signed the dotted line stating that you will live God's way, all day, everyday, not just when it is convenient or doesn't trouble you. Look at our world today, that's why so many Christians have left God. Man dug up some temptation, a couple of people started saying that it was true, and soon billions more latched onto it. Faith in God is shown by what you resist, by your obedience, and when push came to shove carnal Christians and the others resisted nothing. When Christians continue to live and think like the world, you're open to fall victim to its whims.

"We are Christians! We are Christians! God has given us power over everything, but many of us don't live like it. Don't rely solely on what your mouth said, because you may get burned! Turn to Matthew 7:21. Just so you know that this is no joke, let me give you a scripture from Jesus, so we can end any wavering you might still have. 'Not everyone who says to me, Lord, Lord, shall enter the kingdom of heaven, but he who DOES THE WILL of my Father in heaven'.

"And Jesus tells us how he will judge those who do not DO the will of God, drop down to verse 23 - 'And then I will declare to them, I never knew you; depart from me, you who practice lawlessness'. Do I really need to tell you that lawlessness to God is you going against his Word? And by practice he means your everyday walk?

Faith's voice slows, "Why do so many of us think that we're losing something by submitting to Him? What are you losing, your see-sawing attitude towards loving people, your lack of discipline, the loss of indifference towards your rightful place in the eyes of our Father, fun? Yeah, I'll admit that one! You do lose a bit of that wild, don't give a blank fun attitude, let's not get all super-spiritual and think that you don't; but look at everything that you get in return for your minimal sacrifice. You get eternal life, and the right, I SAID THE RIGHT, to live this life in abundance, to the full, until it overflows! God will give you life grander and more glorious than you have ever imagined; if you'll just try to pass this ultimate test of faith." Faith waits for the wild applause to taper.

"It's hard to not believe that your will shouldn't control your life sometimes, isn't it? For many people their brains' are so arrogant, so conditioned to the world, that it becomes extremely difficult to put any trust in something that they can not see or touch. That's why we have so many people today that have fallen victim to believing all of this nonsense about the Bible."

Melvin burns inside, as he witnesses Dane hanging onto every word and staring so attentively at Faith.

"Your faith and worship has to be like a forcefield that you wrap around yourself to seal out the barrage of temptation that comes at you daily."

"For the last couple of years now, I've been working on this book I have titled, 'Why Are Christians Embarrassed About Our Faith In God?' In it, the premise of my book is just that, just what the title says. Let's go back, take these last few years away, part of what I talk about is, had anyone noticed how openly expressing your love for God had gotten to be something that was almost taboo? I'm looking for a show of hands here, be honest, long before you got saved, when you were out there just floating in the wind, didn't you get kind of nervous and feel a bit awkward when some Christian would start talking about God and all of his powers?"

Over one thousand brave hands rise. Melvin sees himself in that question. His emotions rise again, when he sees that Dane's right hand is one of the thousand.

David's joy wants to push his hand skyward, but he allows Sasha's scornful eye to keep it down by his side.

"Folks, let's really think about this for a moment, look at all these hands around you. If that right there doesn't show you the power that this life we've build has and how we need to stay centered on God, and not doing what the world tells us is cool, nothing will. Evil influence can be so powerful that it can make you feel almost corny or foolish for talking and rejoicing about the very one who created you, and the only one that can save you. All of you can converse or gossip about your friends, about sports, children, who is sleeping with whom, what this celebrity or that celebrity did; but as soon as you start openly testifying about the love that the Lord has brought to your life - watch! - people gonna start dropping out of the convo, their voice will dim, they'll avoid looking you in the eye all of a sudden, they'll try to steer the conversation away to a different topic, or my favorite one, they'll get defensive and say to you, 'oh so now that you're saved, you think that your holier than thou, huh'?

"They're afraid of the new person that you are! And I can understand that, they ain't livin' the life that you are. But my question to you is, Mr. or Mrs. Christian, why are you afraid of the person you are? Why are you so quiet? Why do you not speak and praise your savior's name, like the Bible says you must? I don't know about y'all, but as crazy as people have gotten these days, it makes me want to shout His name louder and with more confidence than I ever have!" Thousands loudly agree.

After a few quiet moments to gather herself, Faith's hushed voice returns, "I don't know about y'all, but feeling awkward, uncomfortable, more at ease in talking about all these worldly subjects than God and this Bible…," she nods her head while biting her bottom lip, "that ain't the way I'm a represent my God, the one who makes it possible for me to rest in peace instead of suffocating in hell!"

"Remember this: we are all on this earth for one reason, and one reason only, to GLORIFY GOD! Period. And God is love. You can't get around it; you can't put religion in front of it. There is but one living God! So whatever religion you lay your faith on, remember who God is; God is love. Jesus Christ, Mohammed, Buddha, whomever, your savior is nothing if he ain't about unconditional love for others.

"Look at the war. When Christians and Muslims begin to think and react out of love, everything else will take care of itself, God will make the pieces just fall in place. He really will! This concept is really hard for people who don't know God to really believe… that love changes things. That you and your interests can make some concessions on the behave of another party to show your love to God, then trust, BECAUSE OF LOVE, that party will embrace your love, then because of your God given love that was given to them, they, being now filled with love, return twice as much love back to you, and you give more love right back, so that cycle repeats over and over again, which does nothing but build more love. And pretty soon you see the economy shooting up, you see wars ending, because countries are making concessions to one another. Our country is willing to give, their country is willing to give, now we're working out our differences together with love and respect for our fellow man. No matter whom they are! And God will bless us with abundance, because we love!" The eruption vibrates through Sasha's, Gwen's, and Melvin's chest, as David and Dane along with thousands of others stand and cheer.

Ricky feels alone, like he's in a small classroom with Faith, and she is telling him the greatest story ever. Thousands of others, like Stacy, who is right beside him, inside of Anytown's landmark church, feel the Holy Spirit teeming through their body.

Faith shifts gears.

"Folks, we gotta quit thinking that constant stagnation is a trait of someone who is on a fruitful path to heaven. If I may be allowed to step away from the Bible and into my own hypotheses, for a moment... on Judgment Day, I believe that you will be graded on one crucial element to your life; it tells the entire story of how much God's will became your will. I think that you'll be judged on if the people in your life and the people you had an influence on knew that you were a born again Christian; not because you told them, but because, you lived it, you shared it, and you loved them the way God told you to love.

"Let's remember Christians, God is always doing something for your life, in your life, so that it will benefit others. So if others aren't influenced by your walk of faith, how can God judge your life to be a success? Don't confuse a walk of faith with just being a nice person, or a caring parent, or someone who has done some nice things for others. Sure, those are all acts that God wants from you, but God wants your heart first, then the acts will follow, acts without faith are just acts. God wants us to be people of constant faith, ever-growing, developing Christians."

"We have got to get out of this casual attitude towards our relationship with Him. On the streets, it is a disgusting shame to end my pleasant interactions with people, by telling them God bless you, and I hear nothing in return. If you ain't even comfortable enough to tell someone God bless you, how in the world do you think that you are going to pass Judgment Day? When you have to face the Lord and explain to Him why He should let you in, but you couldn't speak His name in the face of others, you get nervous or annoyed when someone tries to enlighten you about the power of His name."

"Everyone, the time has come for us to end our casualness, our procrastination. You see what it has done to so many other people. The clock is ticking towards zero. We gotta get focused back on His love, and honoring it, by staying focused on his Word. There's no getting around it! Not if we want this life to continue on. Read the book of Revelations, read about how the world will be in the last days; it looks really familiar, doesn't it? Well guess what? If we turn away from all the perversion that goes against God, He CAN'T come back. The rapture can't happen in a world overrun with agape love! But it sure can in a world like this. WE MUST GIVE HIM OUR FULL ATTENTION!!!"

"The Lord knows that he could make things so much easier on us, if he would just show us modern day people his physical body. He knows that would make our ability to believe so much easier. But the Word says to 'trust that I am with you'. Why do you keep choosing not to, then saying that you love God, then, only lean on him in a crisis... do your daily choices mostly oppose his Word? Don't ask God to come into your life and be the head, however, when decision time comes you still call all the shots. But you're saved, so that's o.k.; right?"

Faith's eyes lock onto Melvin's. "It's up to you to renew your mind. Stop that God don't love me stuff, the question and test is; do YOU love him? Will you break away from the norm or are you going to drown in it like so many others you see today?

"If you don't believe AND live the way God would have you to live, if you believe that the Bible is just some fantasy novel, if you don't have faith that this book holds the keys to the ONLY real success this life has to offer, then I suggest that you refocus and reassess the priorities and thinking that governs your life, before it is too late. This book is absolute. You may not like everything written in it, and neither do I, but it doesn't matter. The Lord has never asked our opinion. If you're going to follow God's path, and never meet your death, then, you must adjust to Him, don't expect Him to adjust to you. Don't even waste your time trying to bend his rules and provisions. What, what you gonna tell Him on Judgement Day, 'Oh I know that you said to love, but my daddy always taught me to hate other races, yeah, I felt you tugging on me all those times you provided me with chances to open my heart and change my destiny, but heritage, or bad experiences, or what others think held me back'. Is that what you're gonna tell Him? Or is it, 'the society we live in was just too powerful for little old me to overcome, I was too weak to break away from its influence!"

Finally, reluctantly, the 'wheels begin to spin' for those in attendance, who have set their mind away from God.

In a planned attack to switch the focus of their minds', Faith's palms bang out a short rhythmic beat onto the podium, "All right, I'm done playing around with y'all, do you want to get to heaven?" The audience answers with a thunderous applause, "Well, for all of you untrusting ones out there, the Lord has anointed me with the directions, I'm serious, this is not a joke. This will work for anyone! There are steps to this, so listen closely."

"First, you go home from here, don't go nowhere else, go home, while God's energy is still firing in your brain. Now on the way there the devil, like never before, is going to try and talk you away from what you're about to do. Notice I said away, because that is where the devil always tries to steer your attention, but no matter what, don't do it! You get home, and in the first room that you come into, drop onto your knees and tell Jesus that you want him to come in and transform your life. With that, you and God have accepted the responsibility to change your life, physically, mentally, emotionally, and spiritually.

"Now you are saved, congratulations! But be careful, being saved means little without born again thinking and actions; this is your job, not God's. And to be born again you must empty out all of the internal garbage you've stockpiled over the years leading up to this. You have now chosen life, so you can be totally open with yourself, so dig through all of those layers of pride, denials, and wrong thinking, that you and other various people and situations have filled your head with; throw them away! You are no longer homeless; you live in a kingdom now, so don't dig back into that garbage can and pull that trash out ever again!"

"Your life is transforming, now everything is a possibility for you. But this is where so many people get lost, but you won't because you know what to look for. Christians get lost when the emotions of the moment are gone and the temptation returns to challenge your decision.

"You MUST take some time away from some of your 'per-saved' activities - which Satan just loved for you to engage in - to make time for praying, and reading, worshipping, and meditating. I guarantee you, that old deceptive devil will try every trick to convince you that you don't need to do these things, but you must! Resisting these traps and involving our time and mind in things that draw you into his presence honors God, which brings more blessings to your life. Folks, this is where you might be made or lost, this stage is where life or death may be decided. But you're locked into it, so you resist Satan as he tries to tempt you to continue being the same 'ol person you walked away from. And because you resist his attack, another wave of Satan will come at you through people, or through your feelings and emotions, and what your eyes see, because Satan will NEVER stop trying. So don't you ever stop resisting him.

"You can get to Heaven!, stop believing for another second that you can't, that it's just too hard, that you have time to get serious about your faith later. Stop listening to a world that tells you God isn't cool, that God isn't necessary to have a successful life. God is the coolest and most necessary friend you will ever have in your life!"

Faith does not allow anyone to know just how much her next words mean personally, "God's children, listen to me, we've all thought it, if even for a second, from the strongest to the weakest Christian, but you better forget about it; the Bible is not fiction. God is real and He is here, right now.   HE WANTS YOUR ATTENTION!"

CHAPTER FIFTEEN

Feeling spiritually electrified, joyous and confident shouts of praise echo all around them, out of the various mouths of those in the dispersing crowd, as the parking lot fills with believers walking out from the church to their cars.

Melvin fights ardently to shake it all off - the soul searching, the information that he didn't know but now does, Faith's voice; his conditioned mind doesn't welcome their presence. He pops his knuckles, he does little bunny hops as he moves along, desperately trying to relieve his body and mind from the tight shell it has been held in for the past hour and a half. He looks over at his friend walking beside him; annoyance and anger enter the soul of Me-ma's grandson due to what he sees. Melvin's thoughts, "He's acting just like them...," he can easily ascertain that Dane is deep in thought, and Melvin has a good guess what it's about.

He doesn't like that his friend's soul has been touched, it makes him uncomfortable. With an overabundance of enthusiasm, meant to break apart whatever is burrowing into Dane's thoughts, Melvin asks, "Hey homey, do you wanta head over to those lil' honeys' house we met at the club last night, or you wanta check the spots and see how business is pop'n?"

Dane does not return his zeal, "I think I just wanta go home."

Melvin's heart starts to race, fear pumps through it. He knows why Dane wants to go home. He knows what he will do, once he is there.

As Melvin looks away, from the corner of his eye, thirty yards away to his right, crossing the parking lot in horizontal unison with him, Dane spots a familiar face. And that familiar face spots his.

Both beings are full of the Holy Spirit, their eyes lock onto the others. Dane and David exchange a warm, but awkward smile. For differing reasons, each smile is a breakthrough for each man.

Melvin continues to stew quietly until they reach the flip up doors of his fire red, rented, Lamborghini. They enter. "Man, what the fuck is your problem! I'm trying to kick it wit my dog and you over there bullshittin'."

It works. Melvin's vile language takes Dane away from his self-revelations, "Watch ya mouth, why you comin' at me like that?"

Melvin inches out into the line of exiting cars. "Cuz man, I know that your head is over there swimming with all that nonsense my girl had to say-"

"So you really think that it is all nonsense…," he asks, half tough and half thirsting for knowledge, "you really think she's got it all wrong?"

"Man, I love Faith, but she's just a person who is set in her ways. She's been a believer for so long that she just can't break the habit. She's just scared to believe the real truth. God, himself, could tell her that he is not real and she wouldn't believe it…," Melvin seizes the light given by Dane's slight giggle, "come on bro, people like you and me, we're the strong ones, because we can see through, over and under, this myth. Don't let some emotional, but meaningless, sermon make you start believing that God is anything more than fantasy."

Dane follows the leader, "I feel you, dog…," his thoughts and concerns retreat back into the pack, "yeah, let's go see what these broads is talking 'bout."

The corners of Melvin's smile darn near touch the bottom of his eyes, "That's what I'm talkin' about, that's what's up." They speed out onto the freeway's onramp and disappear into traffic. Melvin can't control his smile.

As they all do, Melvin disregards the enviable downfall. His thoughts rejoice his perceived success. "I'm a get rich. I'm talkin' rich people rich, I'm going above hood. When I was being all Godly, I was dead broke, I didn't have na'thin. Now look at me, I have everything." He drifts into picturing Scarface seated beside him, instead of Dane. As Melvin's idol stares at his next in line, he does so with great pride. In him, Scarface sees the same go all out approach to the drug game that took him to the so called top.

Melvin is totally enamored with the celebrityism of what he does. The fast money, women, toys, the perverted and misguided respect others show, the money. Oh yes, when confronted he'll throw up the usual "I was forced to enter the game because of my situation" excuse; and many times that does play a real role with people that share his reality, but a lot of it, if they're honest, is the lust for the drug game's celebrity benefits.

Melvin, "Yo Dane, that movie Scarface is still my favorite dopeboy flick. How long has that movie been out sixty, seventy, something years?"

A lackluster answer comes back, "What, oh, I don't know, maybe longer." Dane doesn't want to talk about movies. His zone isn't with his friend, he displays it with his turned head endlessly facing his window. Since they are not heading home, Melvin doesn't crash Dane's solitude, he goes back to his Tony Montana daydreams.

They don't snuggle like they used to. She no longer gazes into his eyes as he says sweet things to her. All of her answers to his questions have shortened into one or two annoyed words. When she is around him more than a few seconds, her mind drifts, "He is so boring. He would have the money to take me on exciting trips and buy me super-expensive things all of the time, but he's too worried about being Mr. Goodguy." Through her senses, even their spacious home now feels smaller.

Having been raised to be a materialistic, high maintenance woman, Sasha, has always been very hard to please. But David did it, things were never perfect for her, especially where money was concerned, but he always did enough to keep her content.

Why would a woman, in what seems to be a happy marriage, take the chance of throwing it all away? Was it the sex?

Sasha built up all of these fantasies of what it would be like sleeping with 'Flight' Michaels, but the reality did not reach the heights of her fantasies. Michaels didn't touch her, kiss, or caress her body from head to toe like David did for her, he was just in it for himself. He did not give a damn if she was fulfilled or not, he sexed her on three separate occasions, got bored with his conquest, and told her it was over. Bryant. "I think that we should just keep things professional between us, besides you have a family, it sounds like you have a great husband too, you don't want to mess that up, do you?" Plus, to her great surprise, Michaels' anatomy didn't quite measure up to the superior length that she so eagerly anticipated.

With that all said, she still wants to continue jeopardizing her marriage to a man, whom despite all his other faults, when it came to loving her, was one of the good ones.

Like a gently squeezed lemon, lust, hate, anger, indifference to what's right or wrong, greed, and a lack of patience, all combine to slowly drain the good from the world. It has never been something that's overwhelmed them all at once, but even on the sunniest of days, the light is dimming inside and outside of the afflicted. Gwen Gimmer is no exception.

What was once a 'cup is half-full' mind-set towards blacks and other minorities has gone completely empty. Gone are all of her, "everyone should be judged on their own merit" views, one ill-timed, demeaning, overheard, diss session, allowed hate to seep in and erase all of that. It waited for one tiny opening to present itself, then, entered her soul. Once inside, it immediately began to shrink the openness of her heart.

Now everything about them she dislikes. Everything she dislikes stays on her mind, burrowing farther and farther. She interprets their looks, their behaviors, totally different now. "They do kinda look like monkeys, the only thing that separates them are their huge lips."

Gwen snickers to herself about the same stereotypical features her father always did, while eyeballing a female black classmate across the room, "Look at her, they are nothing like us. They don't walk or talk like I do." Gwen used to champion those same variants as beautiful characteristics that made everyone unique.

Her scorn turns to the Mexican boy seated directly in front of her, "when is America going to get rid of these filthy spics? Why are we being forced to learn their language, just because they want to cross our border to scrub our toilets and mow our lawns? I think that they would make better slaves than niggers did."

Gwen feeds off of knowing that she gets better grades than every minority person at her school, then, she remembers Mia, the school's highest graded out pupil; the sophomore who should still be an eighth grader. Her new problem with all whom are different leads her to quickly develop intensely jealous, bitter feelings towards Mia. "I hate her. She was probably given those grades, probably because of some affirmative rights law." RIINNGG! The loud bell that ends Gwen's fifth hour class and all of her racist daydreaming alarms her body causing it to jerk.

She finds a lane in the quick moving sea of students. Gwen has a long walk back to her locker to get books for her last class of the day. Along the way, all of the race mingling between students hurts her eyes and angers her heart. She wishes she could scream her racial slurs at the pants sagging, 'G'd up', black male walking a few people ahead of her.

His sagging pants catch their exit at an intersecting hallway, from that opposite direction, Mia, guides onto Gwen's 'freeway'.

Camouflaged by the mass of bodies around her, Gwen realizes that Mia does not realize that she is anywhere around. "I've gotta get closer to that bitch," Gwen thinks. She squeezes between others, steps around two more, all the while remaining inconspicuous to her target. Now, there is no one between them, she creeps up just behind her.

She sniffs at Mia's hair. It has a scent. Gwen's mind scrambles to find something negative to associate the smell with, so this time, she can be the one to think up some derogatory putdown about her race to go along with it.

Everything is ready. Their lean steaks are cooked to everyone's known specifications, the mashed potatoes, broccoli, and dinner rolls are hot and ready for demolition. David smiles as he puts the finishing touches on his brilliantly planned, intimate reconnection dinner with his two favorite girls.

Gwen mostly stays to herself lately, cooped up in her room. When she does venture out, she has nothing to say at all or she says it with a bad, snapping attitude. His wife, their relationship, lately, can be summed up in one word; distance. He plans on changing all of that tonight.

David has been watching and reading all of the frightening reports, he's well aware of the breathtaking rate of decay for marriages since the 'Bible Hoax' began. He sees how divorce is up fifteen percent, over the fifty percent that it used to be.

All mention of God has been removed from the wording that unites man and woman. People no longer feel bound by so-called outdated biblical marriage values; David looks at these numbers as a wake-up call, it energizes him. There is no way he is about to allow his marriage to add to their statistics. His mind is made up, this is the night that all of the chaos in his home ends.

Yesterday's sermon by Faith has renewed David's spirit, he has taken so much knowledge away from hearing her truth. He has begun the process of retaining those truths in his life.

Although he is not quite ready to erase all that he has come to believe, he admits to himself that all along he was just a hearer of the Bible.

The evening has been playing itself out inside his head since the moment he thought of this beautiful, surprise family dinner. First, to break the ice, he will greet each of them at the door with a bouquet of flowers. That gesture will create a few cracks in the brick wall that separates everyone, setting the mood for a jovial dinnertime conversation, just like the ones they have enjoyed so many times before. After dinner, he will whisper to his sexy wife to go up into their bedroom and slip into the new lingerie that he has laid out for her, while he has a heart to heart talk with their daughter about her racist ideology, and more importantly, his own. After setting things straight with her, he will return to their bedroom, which he'd previously transformed into a haven set for romance, there he will see Sasha lying on their rose petal covered bed, just like he directed her to in the arousing note he left for her just inside the door on their bedroom floor.

From then on, he'll have her right where he wants her, he hasn't even touched her yet, but her body will be alive like he has. Once her anticipation reaches its boiling point for him to make passionate love to her, he'll stop, David isn't through making love to her mind just yet! He'll get down on one knee, take her left hand into his, then, he'll read to her the heartfelt poem that he took the entire day off from work to spend writing.

Over the years, David has done many romantic gestures for his wife, but never has he written a poem for her. After listening to his heart, she'll be moved to tears, and want to sit and talk out their problems, OR her sex drive will rise to a new, never seen before level and she'll demand it, right then; either direction is just fine with him.

After that is over, as they lay in bed atop their sweaty sheets, he will reveal the two grand prizes he has in store for her. First, he will take off her wedding ring and slip on the new ten times as expensive diamond flooded 'jaw dropper' she's been begging years for him to buy. Then, for the grand finale, David will announce that he is searching for a far more lucrative position, than his current one, at the second leading health care insurance firm in the country. He knows exactly what that will mean to Sasha, her every materialistic desire may soon be fulfilled.

IT'S SHOWTIME! Passing by the large bay window in the front room, after having just fluffed the pillows on the living room sofa, David is lucky enough to catch sight of Sasha's Mercedes pulling into the driveway. In a nervous frenzy, he does a final quick check to make sure everything is in place. He hears two car doors slam shut, his nerves really begin to swirl as he waits just inside the door with a bouquet inside each fist.

"Surprise my beautiful ladies, this is for you… and this is for you." He follows up his thoughtful gesture with a kiss upon the cheek to each of his loves' as they step inside.

The guests of honor are unmoved, Gwen stomps by him and heads straight upstairs. "Thanks dad." She unenthusiastically says halfway up.

Sasha enters and immediately begins griping about everything. "Geez, just walk upstairs to your room like always Gwen, I'm so sick of you. You're becoming such a little bitch!"

"Thanks Mom, I hate you too!"

"Good… the freaking traffic was horrible coming home. Have you gotten the mail yet? Why the hell are you giving us flowers?"

He's speechless; they have never spoken to one another like that before. David hurts, "It's spreading…," as he feels the weight of the discontent shared between his wife and their child.

His angered spouse slams her files and laptop down onto the sofa, loose papers litter the cushions and floor area below it. At least she doesn't throw down his flowers, they're laid on the glass coffee table, but still, she is clearly not focused at all on his sentiment.

She spills her tired frame onto the cushions, beside the mess she has created, while doing so, she wildly scratches at her scalp turning her neatly cropped updo into 'bedhead'.

"People drive so stupid these days. I'm getting so sick and tired of that job, I think I'm going to start looking around for another firm."

"Doesn't she smell the aroma from the food? Should I say something about the way she talked at Gwen? She didn't even look me in the eye or say thank you for what I've done." Thoughts 'tornado' through David's mind as he fights to uphold a positive spirit.

He crouches down in front of Sasha's feet and begins unbuckling the straps attached to her three inch high-heels. She pulls her foot away with a huff. "Don't, I'll do it myself."

His smile remains, inside he fights to conceal his disappointment and pain to her, as his plan quickly begins to detour, "O.k., well I'm going upstairs to talk with Gwen for a moment, then, I'll come back and we can eat the great dinner that I've prepared, or if you'd like, I'll relax you by massaging your feet for you?" He waits for her reply, his hopes are high, Sasha loves to have her feet massaged.

"Don't worry about it, David. I'm fine." She coldly barks while turning away from him, and towards the television. She watches, not because she particularly wants to see anything, but to create a distractive buffer between her and the man she took her vows with.

His smile has departed. David battles to keep his eyes dry. All his fantasies about how this night would go have already been erased. His marriage is in deep trouble and he knows it. Even in the worst of times, they were always able to reconnect through something: torrid sex, laughter, talking, a romantic night, a massage. Sasha isn't interested in any of them. She won't even make the effort. He wants to say something, anything that would close the distance of separation between them, but he chooses to walk away. For right now, it would hurt too much to get shot down again.

Leaving her, places him nose to door with his daughter's bedroom. David takes a moment to clear away his hurt feelings concerning Sasha, so as not to carry any baggage into his talk with their offspring. He puts on his best fake smile, then, slowly opens her closed sanctuary. "Gwen, may I come in for a second?"

"I don't give a shit, Dad, what the fuck do you want?" Despite the cursing that he has never before heard flow so freely out of her mouth, David remains upbeat.

Gwen is on her bed, lying on her back, reading a book that her skyward arms and hands hold suspended over her head.

While simultaneously taking a seat next to her and easing into the conversation, David notices that all of her posters of 'Flight' have been taken off of the walls, and that they lay ripped and crumbled up inside the small wastebasket next to her closet door. "How have you been feeling lately, honey? It's been quite awhile since we've talked."

"I'm feeling fine, why?" She never takes her eye concentration away from the book, but she does crack a quick smile.

David's hopes once again rise, returning the energy to his voice, "So, is that a pretty good book you're reading there?"

Electric, "Oh my God, Dad, this is so good. There is a lot of stuff in here I bet you didn't even know about."

Now he is genuinely curious. "So tell me about it. What's going on?"

Using her thumb as a page marker, Gwen closes the text and excitedly sits up to show him the cover. David is mortified, speechless at the sight of its simple, yet powerful photo. The picture shows a hooded clansman, in the middle of some barren field at night, surrounded by dozens of burning wooden crucifixes that fill the space for the rest of the cover. "It teaches our people about our true heritage through the eyes of the Klan. I never really knew why we should have hatred towards the Jews for all their lies and greed until I started reading this. I thought it was mainly all about the spooks."

Sorrow fills his eyes. Like a person taking their last breathes, in seconds, his mind replays a lifetime's worth of memories, all of which center around his hate filled words and actions that are accountable for shaping this very moment.

Gwen is baffled. "What's wrong, Dad? Why are you crying?"

David knows her situation is dire. He knows he needs to end this cycle now, before she falls any deeper. He takes one of her hand's inside of his, while feverishly stoking her forearm with his other palm. "I am so sorry I have done this to you, Gwen. Forgive me, I going to make things right."

"What are you talking about?"

"Sweetie, all of this hatred you're feeling, is plain wrong. This connection you feel with others that also race hate is wrong. I've been wrong my entire life, hate and negativity toward blacks, or whomever, is so evil. It's just what the devil wants us to do and I am so sorry that I was your role model for this hateful way of thinking. You're letting the world shape you just like I did."

With defiance written across her face, Gwen vehemently fires back, while snatching her hand away. "Really, why don't you tell them that? They complain about how they're treated when they hate and say prejudice things about us just as much."

"You should behave the right way because you know its right. The wrong that someone else does shouldn't affect how you think and speak. Hate is nothing but an emotion that will handcuff your entire life until you get rid of it."

At this stage, change doesn't have a chance. Gwen loves her anger, she thinks that it empowers her.

Gwen's harsh attitude chameleons into one of compliance, "Sure dad, you're probably right. I'm really going to sit and think about everything you've said today, o.k.?" Like every teenager, she knows the quickest way to get a parent out of your room is to submit to whatever they are in there for you to submit to.

David gives her a warm loving hug. On the other side of that hug, Gwen rolls her eyes as she fakes returning the affection of his embrace.

"I really want you to think about what I have said, honey."

"I will, Dad. But I'm curious, what made you stop hating nig...," Gwen catches herself, before she blows her cover, "what made you stop hating African-Americans."

"A few weeks ago, my parents died."

"Oh, I'm sorry to hear that. I don't mean to be insensitive, but you didn't really care for them anyway, did you?"

"I despised my mother for the abuse that she dealt out to me and my brother, and I hated my father for sitting back and allowing it to happen. I had never gotten over that. But yesterday, I threw that hatred away-"

"Why because you liked the way that lady preached?" Gwen's sensitivity towards her father is gone.

"It's not the way she preached, it's what she preached. She preached the truth." Hearing himself not stutter such bold, unworldly words increases his spiritual strength, "I think that I fully believe that the Bible is real. I realize that my hatred of my parents had been part of the reason why I'd held onto my anger towards others. For the first time in my life, I'm thinking outside of the box that they created, and now I'm free to see life for what it really is. I did little acts to make myself feel like I wasn't like them, but my true self always bubbled to the surface."

Gwen is intrigued by the grandparents that she hadn't seen or talked to since she was barely two years old. "I wish that you would have at least let me see them every now and then."

"My parents were vile people... but I must forgive them anyway and hold no grudge against them."

Gwen's eyes homicidally peer at her father, as she devilishly threatens him, "Mom is not going to like, one bit, all this God talk that you are doing...," her voice darkens to the point that it sounds as if someone else has taken it over, "I know why you're talking this way."

David feels the evil surrounding her, "You're right, and I'm not ashamed to admit it. Everything I'm telling you is the truth, Gwen, now I'm experiencing the openness and the equality that you used to treat others with. Before, I was teaching you, when I should have been letting you teach me."

Her mood and tone reverses again. "That's great, Dad, but I'm getting kind of tired, so if you really don't mind…"

David picks up on the hint. "O.K. honey, I'm going, but please remember what I said, and most importantly, remember how you used to think and feel. That's the right way, not this…," he points at her book, "holding onto all of that anger and hate won't do you any good, it'll just eat away at you. Trust me, I know."

Big smile, "Thanks Daddy."

He kisses her on the cheek, then, begins walking away. Gwen thinks of something really 'cute' to say on his way out. "Dad, at least tell me that you still have a little bit of hate for the Jews, come on, we're German?"

David turns around wearing a half alarmed smile that conveys his disbelieve in what he's just heard. "I don't hate anyone, Gwen. I've been freed from that sickness." Hearing himself announce his freedom from bondage uplifts his soul.

"I was just kidding, Dad." Gwen's smile follows him until he leaves the room, "Screw that…," she reopens her book and resumes feeding her angry soul, "I hate them all, I don't care what he says."

David feels a buzz - a triumph - that lightens the heaviness in his heart. Even with all of the unhappiness in his home, there is a joy growing inside of him.

The focus of his mind stays with the victory that he thinks he's accomplished with Gwen, that is, until he's halfway down the stairs and the return of the chill he's been receiving from his ex-loving wife hits him. He tries to suppress the worry and desperation as they return to his thoughts. "Just be patient with her. It'll work out."

He reenters her area with the right frame of mind. He didn't need her huffs and disgusted expression, when she sees him return into the room, to know this is not going to be easy. Not quite ready to 'stick his hand back into the fire', he walks past her and into the kitchen. For no reason, he opens the refrigerator and looks inside. "If only I knew what was wrong, I could push the right buttons to make everything right. What's most frustrating is she won't tell me what the problem is."

He closes the icebox and leans against the countertop with crossed arms, "Do I not please her sexually anymore? What did I do or say that made her so mad at me? What did I do?" As he asks himself these questions and many more, his mind tries to calculate the time when things between them begin to change. Something clicks. He recalls that it was around the time her work with 'Flight' Michaels and the car dealership began.

It suddenly hits him, he's got it! Now he understands her behavior, his hopes for a reconciliation climb. "This is her biggest, highest profile campaign ever. The pressure on her has got to be enormous. She's been wining and dining only at the best places, I'm sure her firm has been spending big money to keep Michaels happy...," David thinks he has it all figured it out, a sense of relief gratifies his thoughts, "Sasha loves those kinds of things. She's probably mad at me because we're not exciting like that."

His illusions overflow with images of his wife falling into his longing arms after he tells her the big news, "When I tell her about the new job I'm seeking, and the ring I brought her, I know that will help get us back on track." But in the back of his thoughts, the Spirit inside of him hints, "That's what it takes for her to love you?"

Confident, he re-enters the room and sits right next to his mate's rigid 'shell'. He can't wait to end this madness, he begins, "Sweetie, I've done something important that I know is going to make you very, very happy," but she does it again, his psyche takes another punch when her curiosity nor anything else, is not peaked, in the least, by his come chase the answer statement. His heart falls off of the cliff. Inches apart, but there might as well be a country between them; she won't even look at him. He's seen this lack of caring and indifference enough in the last few weeks to last him a lifetime.

What the Spirit previously spoke to him, speaks again, and this time he listens. Suddenly he no longer is motivated to tell her what he's done. The reality surrounding the type of person Sasha is, smacks David right in the face, and he is not going to excuse it this time. "I am so sick of this crap. Money is the only way I can get back the woman that is supposed to love me for better or worse? What kind of marriage do I have if that's all that matters? There's more to her story than what she is telling me, there has to be?"

David has no idea where his 'nose' is leading him, but it goes outside of the norm and finds light there, "Maybe she's been having an affair?" A chill runs down his spine. He wants to ignore this first gut feeling that he may be on to something, because he's afraid of where it may lead, but he can't stop now. His mind digs, once again, he thinks back to when her behavior begin to change.

"Why is it that every time I mentioned to her about setting up a meeting for me with 'Flight', she avoided the conversation or she got angry?" David thinks back to various incidents, and the three nights, over the span of two weeks, that his wife did not come home until the wee hours of the morning.

Sasha's probing husband reminisces about the attitudes, the wall she would put up as soon as he asked about her whereabouts on those occasions, how she would retract like her skin touched a hot stove as soon as he would try to be affectionate with her on those days.

David's sharp movement away from the cerebral and into action, as he wildly digs into his back pocket grabbing for his team schedule that he carries everywhere with him, jolts Sasha. She feels his intensity, she has no idea what he's onto, but instinct tells her that it isn't good. Its power is enough to bring her out of her isolation, as she tries to keep her eyes focused on the television and not on him. Sasha tries to mask her panic with mere curiosity, "What are you doing, Davie, what are you looking for?"

He whips out the schedule, and with bloodhound precision, scans over the small lettering and numbers, he says aloud. "No... Two of those nights were home games for the team, the other was an open night before a road trip...," mumbles, "this can't be true." A huge part of him wants to chalk it up to coincidence, deep inside though; he knows that it's much more.

"What are you doing, baby?" Her 'caught' conscience, sweetly, but nervously, asks as her eyes are drawn like magnets to David's small, but powerful piece of evidence.

He doesn't need for her to say another word, he knows he has the answer. He just looks into Sasha's heart, through her panicked eyes and nervous body language, to tell him what he needs to know. Finally the reason for all of his heartache has been found.

Anger should immediately overwhelm any other emotion that may want to surface, but he is one of the few cases, in this kind of case, where is doesn't. The opposite happens. Sarcastically, he slyly giggles while staring at the face responsible for his broken vows. "Six foot seven, athletic, rich, and famous; heck, if I were a woman, I'd have probably screwed him to, I can't blame you... Oh shoot, well, I guess that I can, seeing how you're a married woman!"

She's speechless. She knows that she better come up with something. Her thoughts scramble for suitable words, only stuttered words come out.

David's laugh to keep from crying stance crumbles under hurt's weight. He breaks down, burying his weeping eyes inside of his open palms. The "how in the hell could she do this" feelings build, now anger suddenly bulldozes everything in its way as it steamrolls to the forefront.

Screaming, "Why'd you do it, Sasha, why did you do this to

our marriage? Was it just for sex, because he's rich, what are you going to run off with him?"

As Sasha stares at David's chin, she lies, "I haven't done anything, what are you talking about?" David doesn't have to be a college student majoring in body and eye speech to know that she is lying, that every husband's worst fear; he is now living.

His breathing heightens into intense short spurts, his body shakes as veins pop out from everywhere. The man she said her vows to yells out, "You're a fuckin' liar, stop lying to me!"

David stares 'a hole' through the crown of her bent head. Breathing like a bull readying for attack, he ponders about the twisted pleasure one slap would bring to him, the satisfaction he would enjoy for the pain she has forced in his life.

Two minutes ago, Sasha did not give a damn about her dilapidated marriage. Now she is thinking of what strings she can pull with David and her fear that those strings might not work. Her "me me me" mind strategies, "I've gotta turn some blame back onto him. How can I blame Bryant also? Oh my God, he's not going to take me back because I slept with a black man."

David Gimmer has never thought about hitting a woman before now. Not in high school when his, then, girlfriend went psycho and her nails slashed away a fair amount of the skin on his neck, all because he didn't want to be with her any longer. Nor did he think about it when his anger and resentment would return against his mother, as he tried to make sense out of why she would make young David watch as she molested his younger brother.

Maybe it's those past events that are fueling him not to miss out on another opportunity. Satan encourages his anger, "Do it, she deserves it. Think about everything you did for her. She destroyed your marriage to have sex with the man you idolized. Get her back, punish her for screwing that nigger!"

David's arms, fist, and torso tighten, preparing for launch. Sasha's survival instincts detect an eerie second of complete silence, her bent down head snaps up, then, back with the rest of her body, as her reflexes ready for defense.

And just like that; the beautiful happens. His anger vanishes, humility grows, the darkness inside his soul is cast down as he realizes what he is about to do. His weary soul can take no more, it cries for help.

For most people, it's a journey of discovery, trials, and errors that finally ends with them 'crossing over'. David is no different. What had been kept out for all of those years that he was just going through the motions, his mind fully allows in. The heart of the Savior finally beats inside of David, it instantly overwhelms his hurt feelings and emotions by renewing his mind.

This saved man's eyes are wide open, but he sees nothing. The closure of his hate and all of its worldly justifications has brought him an inner peace, which has freed him to truly accept God into his life. The Light that only some have real knowledge of electrifies his body, while simultaneously bringing calm to it.

As this all transpires, David and Sasha are not aware that their daughter has been listening from the top of the stairs. She's heard everything. Gwen is crushed, her whole world feels like it is tumbling down on top of her.

She tip-toes back into her room, covering her mouth, so that her sobs will go undetected. She wilts down onto her bedroom floor, and for the next hour she lays there crying, wanting things not to be the way that she's heard them. Her oppressor allows her time to hurt, so that her anger can build, then, he will bring his onslaught of hateful blame into her misguided mind. "That filthy spook broke up their marriage, and all my dad does is call on Jesus instead of doing something about it? I promise I will find a way to repay 'Flight' for what he has done to my family!"

Later that night, as Sasha would describe to David. "You really don't remember? You flinched towards me, I thought that you were going to hit me, but instead, you fell to the carpet on your knees and you just started crying. You just stayed there rocking back and forth. Oh yeah, and you kept whispering…

and whispering… 'thank you Jesus, thank you for saving me'. I don't mean to change the subject, honey, but if you'll forgive me, I will never cheat again. I was wrong, but you should shoulder some of the blame, you weren't doing enough to keep me happy. We both were wrong, we can start over."

David has but one question for her, as he stands next to their home's front door with a suitcase inside of each palm, "Sasha, I'm not at this point because you committed adultery. I can forgive that. I need to know only one thing from you, are you willing to honestly and wholeheartedly open your mind to understanding the challenges that are before us?"

"What do you mean?"

"I mean the Bible is real, and so is God. Is there any chance at all that you will ever even think about accepting that?"

"What do you mean?"

"Stop your stalling, yes or no."

A long pause ensues as Sasha thinks. On one hand, the enemy tells her to lie, "Just tell him what he wants to hear," because he would love to keep David with an ungodly woman, to increase his chances of one day 'turning' him.

On the other hand, the enemy is strong within her, he will have her do no more cowering to any believer, so she informs him, "David, I don't see the reason why what I believe should make a difference in our marriage. If you want to believe in this myth, fine, but don't hold it against me because I've moved past that."

He sits a bag down, then, cracks the door open. David repeats his question, "So you won't open your mind towards gaining an understanding about God and what is really going on in this world?"

She smirks. Her head drops, shaking from side to side as her mouth ekes out a snicker. With a smile upon her lips, her head rises, "David, I'm sorry, but you can't ask that of me, or be mad at the fact that I don't believe in what we've all found not to be real."

"Goodbye, Sasha."

"Why don't you be honest about why you're leaving? We both know that it's because I slept with a black man, or a nigger, as you like to call them."

"That's the old me, Sasha. I actually have you to thank, God used you to help me break out of those chains. I'm finally a new man who is not weighted down by that way of thinking."

She laughs. "O' really, look at you, now you're all holier than thou, huh? You seriously expect me to believe that you've changed in what, the last two, three hours?"

"Believe whatever you want. I know where I stand."

"So what are you saying, do you want a divorce?"

"No, I am not saying that. I'm not sure what I should do right now?" He and his two suitcases exit their home. From the open doorway, Sasha cries out for his return.

CHAPTER SIXTEEN

If the brilliant side of Ed's forever calculating brain could have kept the other side of his cerebrum from jumping off track, the man could have been a great lawyer or a doctor, maybe even a minister, but due in large part to parental negligence during his developmental years, his life was set up for destruction. Unfortunately for humanity, Ed has never altered the course they set. His life, his world, is one that evil brilliance has created.

Devin's demeanor has changed, so has Sherry's, Ed's suspicions have been building concerning both. Amongst other things, he's taken notice of all the quick eye contacts exchanged between them. Suspicions speak, "They have never done that before, they'd never even look at one another. Why do Sherry's nerves tighten up when Devin is around all of a sudden? No, it couldn't be; they wouldn't!"

Ed harkens back to the childhood crimes imposed upon him. "Of course, that's it! Wow! I never expected all of this dysfunction to turn down this road. This is very intriguing."

At first, from his isolated basement perch, Ed starts out to do what he always does. He's very upset that something has gone on under his watch that he did not o.k., so he heads off to find

Sherry and bruise up any unbruised part of his wife's body that his fists haven't gotten to yet, but then, he stops; evil brilliance steps in.

This was something that he finally missed, something he didn't preplan for, "If I play my cards right, I can use this to my advantage." In minutes, his brilliant mind works out most of the details.

"Devin is getting older and stronger, pretty soon if I don't do something, he's going to want to get out of here, and I won't be able to stop him. I need to form a deeper bond with my son, become his friend; trap him."

Ed thinks back to how genius a move it was to distance and isolate his family, so that no bonds were formed, "If I do this correctly it should work."

That evening, in the living room, Ed has a one on one sit-down talk with his boy over an ice cold beer. He even goes as far as to allow Devin to sit in his cherished recliner, as he settles next to him in a chair that he's pulled away from the kitchen table.

Big grin, "Hey son, anytime that you wanta grab a brew out of the fridge, ask me and I'll give you one."

Cautiously excited, "Cool, thanks Dad."

Ed whispers. "Hey…," Ed leans in towards Devin, which he reciprocates, "I'm even going to allow you to stay up later into the evening, so you can watch a little t.v. with me."

"Are you serious, Dad?!" You'd think it was Christmas.

"Hey, I know what's going on between you and Sherry. No, no, son, don't run away, sit back down, I'm cool with it! Really I am. It feels good, doesn't it?"

Unsure of what to expect next, Devin slightly nods in agreement.

"Do you know why I've always liked you the most? It's because, next to me, you're the smartest and the strongest. Let me see you flex those biceps; wow, look at you! I am King Ed and you are Prince Devin. Welcome to the throne, my son, I want you to share it with me, just remember… there is only one king."

Both are thrilled. Ed's trap is working. He knew just what an uneducated, inexperienced, horny, thirteen year old boy would love to hear.

"Just don't touch Mary, she's mine." Devin's young mind is already dreaming up ways to enjoy his new power and freedom.

This move will not fool Devin forever, Ed knows that, he hopes for another two to three years, if he's lucky, and that's just fine. "I'll be ready to go to Heaven by that point. I can't wait to see the world marvel at what I've done."

That thought comforts and motivates Ed's madness each day.

Goodbye Sasha and all you other groupies; he's done. He has said those very words something like a million times in the past, but he's mature now, he can look you right in the eyes and stand behind his words now; they have his heart behind them. There are no more new doors to be opened in that lifestyle, he's done it all and he's content to never go back. He watches his teammates, other players around the league five to ten years his senior, he sees that they're still participating in the same old juvenile behaviors by living their life without any true commitment to the woman that they love. He does not want to end up like them. Bryant 'Flight' Michaels dares to be different now.

He knows that if he can get his sincerity across to her, if he can make her feel the realness in his heart, so she knows that this time he's coming with more than words, then, "Maybe she'll take me back." Michaels' mouth says maybe, but that's just him trying not to be too confident, too early. Deep down he believes this will work; the timing is ripe. "It's now or never."

His mind is clear; his priorities are in line. His energy is 'gassed' up, he can't keep from thinking about the new life he and Stacy will share, about the new life; or lives, they will create together. "Plus, I know that she'll love the fact that I really do believe in God now!" Faith's electrifying sermon has Bryant riding the wave; he's excited about his life again.

A private detective has followed Stacy's every move for over a week now. Money well spent, Michaels is delighted to be informed that there is no one he doesn't already know or needs to worry about in her life. "Great, she doesn't have a boyfriend. The coast is clear, I'm going for it!"

Two days later, on a crisp Saturday evening, just after the shadow of night has totally removed all bright signs of day, he makes his move.

With his confidence high, he softly knocks twice on the door of Stacy's immaculate countryside, ranch style home, which sits atop a small hill surrounded by several acres of open grass on each side.

He's learned that dazzling her with large bouquets of flowers or expensive gifts does not work, material things mean nothing to her without substance leading the way. If he's going to win her back, it's going to come from what's inside of him.

After a long wait, she opens the door. Stacy is slightly shaken from the surprise of seeing her ex-husband in front of her. "Bryant, hi, what are you doing here?"

She's more beautiful and elegant than ever before. She's captivating. Wearing nothing but a long velvet robe, her wet, silky, but wavy, jet black hair glistens, the woman has on no make-up, but her flawless face would dazzle the cover of any magazine. Just being this close to her again overwhelms Bryant. He loses his 'cool', his smooth words have left his mouth.

Hearing her call him Bryant warms his heart, like Ricky, she has never once called him 'Flight'. Money, fame, all of the women in the world, can not bring him the happiness he feels at this moment. Michaels wants this reunion to succeed with every fiber of his body. He's ready to be everything he was supposed to be, before they signed the divorce papers. He bites his top lip, he squints his face to hold back the tears, as he gently sways from east to west. The intensity inside his soul overcomes him.

Concerned for his well-being, Stacy asks, "Are you alright, is something wrong? Come here." She takes his hand and leads him into her home. The baby-soft touch of her lotioned hand and the emotions of their past connection tempt Bryant into wrapping his arms around her, but he can't afford the risk of rushing her. "Come over here and sit down."

He can't take his eyes off of her, he stops her right before they get to the sofa.

"Yes, Bryant."

He has to do it! He can't wait another second without feeling her touch. "Not to aggressive," he over-thinks to himself. Being that he's an entire foot taller than her, Michaels leans down and puts all of his love, all of the pain he's felt since the day she walked out of his life, into a soft, non-intrusive hug. And sure enough, she hugs him back!

No words are exchanged, they just enjoy the moment of swaying in each other's arms for what is maybe ten seconds, but to Bryant feels like much longer. Her tender touch speaks for her feelings. It tells him that maybe, possibly, she's willing to give him another chance and it definitely spoke the three words he has missed hearing from her for so long, "I miss you." It's almost like when they were young teenagers after their first kiss again, they both giggle due to awkward butterflies upon separating.

He directs himself, "Take it slow."

Bryant and Stacy relax and chat the entire night through. There's no bitterness, no spite, no pressure to do anything. Just two people very slowly trying to find their way back to one another. Stacy sees the changes in him; the maturity, how he's much more humble now, the complete openness in his words. He's not just saying things that she wants to hear. He didn't come in and run down reasons from A to Z why she should take him back. He just let things flow, and she likes that.

As the night disappears, and the sun rises to another partly cloudy day, Michaels 'unglues' himself from the sofa and thoughtfully offers to end their conversation, so that she may get some rest. Genuinely reluctant, she accepts.

They slowly walk to the door, hand in hand, neither one of

them is in any hurry to get there. He steps out onto the wooden porch, she stands just inside next to the door, Ms. Stunning's shy head coyly leans against it. Adolescent goosebumps and butterflies fill Stacy's body, it feels good, once again, she's smitten by him. Stacy's infatuation with this 'new' man prompts the question, "If you could, if you don't mind, I'd love for you to come back this evening, so that we could talk a little more."

"I'd love to do that, around what time would be comfortable for you." Michaels softly replies.

"It'll probably be around nine or so. I'm going to get some sleep, then, around three, me and my new girlfriend, Faith, we're going to meet up at our church to do some cleaning. Hey, why don't you..." She stops right there.

Michaels' high hopes immediately know they are in danger of a crash landing, but he's prepared. The entire night, they had been so wrapped up in talking about themselves as they reconnected, that talk about the biggest anything ever, and which side of the fence 'Flight' was now on, never came up.

She detects nervousness and fear in his suddenly shifting eyes. "Hey, Stace, about that, um, I've really been reading the Bible a lot every single day and I've been listening to this minister, Faith Tillman, preach the Word-"

Big smile, "Oh, that's probably the same Faith that I'm talking about."

"Probably."

Stacy's expression turns serious, "Is that the truth, Bryant?"

"Yes, it is."

"So after everything that has come out about you through the media, and me knowing how you used to be, you're telling me that you are different now? You completely believe that the Word of God is real?"

The good inside of him doesn't want to lie, but the controlling faction that dwells inside pushes him to sin, "Yes, I do." The enemy will stop at nothing or exclude using anyone to bring Stacy down.

A carnal-set mind would call it her gut feeling, but those who know God know that the Holy Spirit placed these feelings inside of her. It gives her revelation about his heart, "He isn't being totally truthful."

"Bryant, I just think that we need to take things very slowly, let's be sure that there is something new between us." A lack of faith and devotion to our Lord and Savior is non-negotiable if you want to share your life with Stacy Stunning, she's been down this road, and heard all of this talk from Bryant before. Her past screams out for caution, and her love for God and him agrees.

This is a serious blow to Bryant's ego. He hears the doubt in her voice, and he knows that it's because she does not believe him. He feels like he's back in the starting block and that does not sit well with him. 'Flight' is sick of not being believed. The sweet and caring Bryant that Stacy had been talking to all night, suddenly disappears, in steps a bitter man in his place, "You know what, Stacy? I'm not going to sit around waiting for you to pass judgment on me. I don't know why I love you so much anyway, I should hate you after the cold-hearted way that you keep treating me. You don't doubt anybody but me."

Her warm feelings dissolve, "The Lord says to judge a tree by the fruit that it bears. So if I've already seen rotten fruit fall off your tree, you think I'm going to automatically bite the next piece that falls?"

Screaming, "I got into God for you! I been reading that boring ass book for you! I listen to preaching for you! But it's never good enough, is it? I do all of this, but you still wanta make me fuckin' wait for you!"

"Bryant, please, just go. Get off of my property!"

The door slams, as he shouts into it. "Your property, your property, whose hard work and talent is responsible for buying YOUR property? Answer that, you holy bitch!"

He never worried about her motives, she was the only woman he completely trusted to never want him for his money.

Bryant knows that he possibly had her back, and now she's gone – again.

Receiving a small taste of the joys a second chance with her would have given him, knowing that, more than likely, this is the last chance he'll ever get with her, deteriorates his spirit.

The devil has manipulated him into putting his entire life's worth into being with her, so that now she's gone, he can 'bury' him.

To make big, big money moving drugs, you have got to make major connections that can supply you with large volumes quickly, not the around the corner ounces and halves that any hustler worth his scale can make decent money off of.

Dane's operation has evolved into this realm, and he alone is the street pharmacist that holds the connections to the people who hold these colossal amounts. All 'King Dane' has to do is have the money and help arrange for the cocaine to get from point A to B. His hands never touch anything.

This is his set. Stamp and now Melvin are the lieutenants, for Dane the General. The lieutenants are in charge of the guys on the corner, in the crack houses. They supply them, put them in the right spots, and it's their responsibility to make sure Dane ALWAYS gets his share of the money. "If your cut of the money comes up short, that's your problem, deal with it. But I never get shorted, I always get paid first." That is Dane's number one, two, and three rule.

When everything goes right, which it always does, the lieutenants give the guys on the front line their cut, the rest comes back to Dane, who then divides it on a fifty, fifty split between the three of them. He gets fifty percent, Melvin and Stamp split the other fifty.

Melvin loves this life. He now wonders why he didn't do this sooner. The money is crazy, he gets props around the neighborhood for being reckless enough with his future to endanger it by dealing drugs. He does whatever he wants to do all day, except for the few hours per that he spends distributing the city's purest cocaine out to his corner men, and the time he spends collecting all of the money from his workers.

The man is ghetto royalty, when he cruises by the little kids playing on the streets, they look up at his brand new Hummer H7 truck, or whatever car he's in that day, and their impressionable minds aspire and wish. "I wanta have what he has one day. He's different, he's rich, he's not broke like us."

The women love him; he's no longer the nerdy, broke, bookworm that they used to see him as. To his benefit, television, music, and movies have glorified men like him in these women's eyes. He has a new confidence, before he would never even fathom speaking to the most sought after girl that all of the guys wanted, now, he considers it HER honor if he stops to talk.

The attention, the women, the freedoms money can buy, Melvin is being seduced by them all. All of Melvin's plans for making this a brief career choice have vanished. Like most dealers, the money blinds him. It even blinds his concerns towards his fostered cousins. Excuses relax his conscience. "It's not my fault that I don't know where they're at. I'm sure they're doing o.k. I'm a go out and look for them, pretty soon. That's real talk. It's not like I can go to child services and demand that they come with me. I gotta just chill and wait, I'll get 'em back."

Just when life could not be going any better, Melvin gets a rude awakening, a hard hitting reminder about what line of work he is really in.

One of the crack houses that are under his domain was robbed. The masked assailants caught his men off guard, tied them up, and then stole twenty thousand dollars worth of product and cash that he is responsible for, which means that is twenty thousand dollars that must come out of his pockets.

The three 'heads' meet up for dinner, at their usual ultra fancy restaurant on the high end of town, to hold an urgent business meeting to discuss their new problem. They love to venture out of the hood to eat at places like this; it gives these boys from the hood that 'Tony Montana' feel that they all envy.

"That's fowl niggas hit us up like that, but I knew it was comin', that's how this game is." Dane matter-of-factly states while buttering his complementary dinner rolls.

Melvin is extremely offended by his leader's sedateness. "That's how this game goes...," Melvin catches himself, he almost forgot that he is in a public place, so he lowers his voice, "that's all you have to say? They disrespect our whole click like we ain't shit, and that's all you have to say? Well since you ain't trippin' about twenty grand being stolen from us, I guess you won't mind if I don't pay you back, huh?"

Melvin was definitely not expecting the answer he receives, "I'm not worried about it, Mel, you don't have to pay me back."

Stamp draws some conclusions based on Dane's tame answer, body language and tone. He slouches back against the comfort of his padded chair. "I gotta ask, Dane, and I'm sorry for testin' your nuts like this, but are you not concerned because you're scared of getting into some gangsta shit?"

Dane sarcastically quizzes. "What do you want me to say? We don't know who did it, they had ski masks on. Do you just wanna go around killing everybody until we kill the right ones?"

Melvin jumps back in. "You damn right. We let them get away, we might as well shut down, cuz' thugs gon be running up in our spots everyday if they think we ain't gonna do na'thin. I ain't scared, I'm ready ta blast!"

Stamp provides key information. "My man Cortez thinks he may know who did it."

Frightened, but masked by a cool exterior, Dane quickly asks, "Does he think he knows, or does he know he knows?"

"I told him to put a percentile on it, he said he was sixty percent sure."

"Sixty percent is good enough for me. Whoever did this is dying." Melvin in no uncertain terms attests.

Dane tightly runs his palms down his face as he ponders. "So is that really what you wanta do, Mel? That's where your head is at now, you wanta start killing people? If we do that, it's the beginning of the end for us. Nobody is watching us. We're flying under the radar, baby. If we bring that kind of attention to ourselves, we'll be the brightest light on their radar. We can't make money with that kind of heat on us. We start banging, we either going to jail or somebody's gon kill us eventually. Haven't you ever noticed that when thugs start shootin', it's always towards the end of their story? Is that what you want, for this to be your end?"

The waitress brings each of their lavish meals out to the table, cutting Melvin off before he responses to Dane's cautious testimony. She makes sure everything is comfortable for her patrons before leaving.

Upon her exit, Stamp reveals a new plan. "Dane is right."

Melvin is mortified. "Are you serious, bruh?"

"I am. We should chill and hope this is a one time thing…," Melvin huffs and shakes his head in disapproval, but Stamp continues on, "but we should also prepare like it's not. We need to put some boys near each end of our corners that we have a house on, they can just act like they chilling, servin' a little bit, but they really our lookouts. If somebody runs up in one of the houses again, our soldiers fold in right behind them, blastin'!"

Dane, immediately, o.k.'s the plan, not because of its potential violence, but because it buys time.

It takes a bit of coaxing for Melvin to sign off, but begrudgingly he does.

Coming to a resolution frees them to get down to the business of filling their bellies, while doing so, Dane has some introspection concerning the course that Melvin's life has taken. Dane thinks about how this brilliant young man has gone from totally distancing himself from this dead end occupation, to where he sits at this very moment; wholeheartedly embracing it and all of its trappings. He thinks about how Melvin used to speak about God, how he used to be different from them. "I think that he would actually kill somebody."

Mulling over Melvin's destructive path causes Dane's thoughts to turn inward, "Am I going to get myself out of this, is this all I'm meant to be? I need help… I got'a go to God." His thoughts turn, "You just trippin', he's not even real. What are you going to do, you're trapped in this life, anyway. You see that no one else believes the Bible is real, why would you? You're going to look stupid."

Deep into the belly of the night, Dane returns home from another evening of setting up 'death deals' with all of the various people he conducts his business through.

You'd think that a man who has just made thirty thousand dollars within the last two hours would be on top of the world, but all he could think about during this entire time was Faith's truth and his see-sawing thoughts about leaving the game.

Having been raised in a deeply religious home, until the crack cocaine epidemic swept through and killed the morals and values contained within his family, Dane was taught right. He was taught that the Bible is the only resource that he should ever completely trust. Now years and years later, the foundation that was laid during those former lessons of a Godly upbringing have resurfaced in his mind.

Dane's soul has awaken from its rest, and its ever increasing cries have brought him to the point he can no longer ignore them.

With Melvin still out somewhere, Dane has the apartment to himself. Onto his back, he flops onto the sofa. The challenges his mind is experiencing pause his body, while freeing strongholds. He questions, heavily, not only the damage being done to his life, but also the damage he is doing to the lives of those around him by selling drugs. Never before has his conscience wanted to be so truthfully critical of the life's choices he has made. "I'm helping to destroy people for money."

Before, to excuse away his responsibility, Dane would inform his conscience that he's not making them use drugs, "If they don't get it from me, they'll get it from someone else."

His heart opens up to care about the crippling effect the

business of crack cocaine has on the lives of individual people and families; the very men, women, and children, he lives shoulder to shoulder beside.

New awareness helps him see the same picture differently. He's beginning to see his neighbors for the people they are, which is more than just a potential customer whose life is o.k. to harmfully alter, as long as it will put more money inside of his pockets.

Dane's thoughts travel back to an hour ago, when he drove up to the neighborhood park, the sight where so many of his dealings have taken place. It was basically empty, he remembers sitting and thinking about all of the idolizing young kids that flock around him when he shows up, how he basks in the admiration their downtrodden eyes show to him. They look at him like he is a star. When they see him, they see hope.

Memories replay the conversation, through his mind's snapshots of Zane that transpired as he waited for Stamp to deliver today's duffel bag full of money. Zane, a ten-year-old boy, whose mother's house sits on Walsh Street, which happens to be the most lucrative strip under Dane's domain, is out walking alone, aimlessly, down these crossfiring streets.

"He's such a cute little kid. He looks even younger that his ten years." Dane calls him over.

"What up, young buck? It's damn near two in the morning, what's you doing out here this late? You got school in the morning."

"Man, fuck school. Nigga, I ain't been a week. I'm just out chilling like you."

Ten years old.

"Where ya moms at?"

Dane knows his mother, she's one of his best customers. "She out high, somewhere. I ain't sure where at."

Those words etch into Dane's mind. The gravity of what this innocent child is telling him weights on him like a ton. Dane hurts for him. He solemnly asks, "You ain't got nowhere ta go?"

"I can go back in the house and sit there, but it's hot. We ain't got no air-conditioning and da t.v. ain't working…

Hey dawg, do you think that you could let me hustle for you. I need to get paid."

Thoughts, "This boy wants to sell drugs at ten-years-old, he's just a baby."

"You don't wanna do this, bro."

Excitement spreads across the boy's face, "Yeah right, I want everything you have. You fuckin' rich, dawg. Look at yo ride. I wanna come up too."

"I can't do that, bruh. You too young."

The ten-year-old Zane comes out in his demonstratively sad, teary eyed response.

Dane reaches into his pocket and hands him a wad of cash. "Hey, you my little homeboy tho', anytime you need some money just ask me. I got you."

He can't believe it! Zane is overjoyed. "Thanks dawg!"

"Put that money in your pocket, don't be running around tellin' everybody you got it. You know how these dudes are around here."

"I know I'll put it away. Thanks, Dane."

"I'll holla at you, later. Go on, I got some business here I gotta take care of." Heavy in thought, Dane watches him disappear into the night.

Dane rises up from the sofa, alarm tingles his body, "What am I doing with my life?"

Satan has had enough, he brings his own ideas into Dane's thoughts, "You told Lacy that she could come over, you better call her before she falls asleep." The devil knows that Lacy can be a very alluring and distracting woman.

Dane brushes his tricks aside, the Holy Spirit has him working on something. What was cool and acceptable for so long saddens him. "What am I doing to these kids? Those little dudes' are going to grow up and be just like me."

Dane's evolution takes his memories to past scenes concerning the dozens of cracked out bodies that he's laughed at upon seeing or hearing them perform some disgusting act. "They're women with kids, babies. I've thought nothing about fathers who've taken everything from their home and sold it, so he could come see me. These men could be changing these streets, instead of lying down on them. I'm killing them, and myself, all for greed, while I sit up here thinking that I'm the shit... I'm so lost out here, God, please help me."

That last sentence releases power that Dane has always had, but never utilized before. Tears create streams as they travel down his cheeks, then onto his chin and neck. He reaches into the large front pocket of his baggy jeans to pull out a cash wad containing only Benjamin Franklins', totaling close to seven grand. The sight of such ill-gotten riches repulses him as the eyes to his soul look beyond its surface.

Dane no longer plays the blame game when he looks at his life. It's not his environment, or the government, or the 'fiends', or his family's mistakes, who are the cause of his trapped body and mind, no, Dane looks within to find the blame for the direction of his life.

Determined, he quickly gets off of the sofa, knowing exactly where he's going. The devil, frightened by his new strength and changed thinking, fights him every step of the way.

"Just do it later... I can just sell for a little longer, than I promise I'll stop... I have no education, no skills... I'm going to fail, I can't walk away from all this money."

Unsure, but undeterred, Dane walks with faith into his bedroom and begins searching through all of his possessions, "I can't find it," but he won't give up. Finally, his sight catches just one corner of it, beneath some old DVD movies inside a box in the corner of his closet. His right hand reaches. Its sight, its touch; that long forgotten book brings another avalanche of emotion to his heart and eyes.

He sits atop his bed, humbled by the book's presence. Satan's steady stream of fearful thoughts and ideas pause his decision-making.   Dane's imagination thinks badly of the born again Dane that he may become, "Man, how am I supposed to act around my friends? I can't suddenly talk and act different around people? Nobody else believes this book is real. I'm just being soft right now, it'll go away."

He wonders how the ladies will perceive him. "What, am I going to talk all nerdy and shit now?"

He pictures Stamp, Melvin, and the rest of his friends, standing before this new man; the thought causes him to giggle, "Man, they gonna be clownin' on me."

He knows that he shouldn't, but he does it anyway, Dane places the Bible beneath his bed, walks away, and calls up Lacy.

Physically, the faithless don't feel the devil, they don't believe the faithful who tell them that his presence is real and it has increased. He has engulfed them, the mountainous foundation of suggestions and circumstances that he has laid in the past, that they have come to accept, nurture and spread amongst one another, has set the stage for the world they exist in now.

The Bible told them that there are ways that seem right to a man, but in the end will lead to his death; but that has been ignored. The clues are all around them, the error of their ways loom larger with each passing moment, but they are too blinded by the norm to see it. So it is no surprise that so many of them don't dig any deeper or look any higher.

—— CHAPTER SEVENTEEN ——

Months continue to pass by, and society's non-belief level continues to soar. Questionable and harmful behaviors occur fearlessly, without hesitation, and without thought.

The slow downswing in the economy is beginning to take its toll on them. Worry is everywhere; they spend much of their day talking and thinking about it. They watch as its broadcast into their homes, they read all about it on their computers, they see it when they get their bank statements; its effect is there when they go to buy groceries.

So many people allow worry's weight to damage their mind, to the point, that their every thought is dipped in fear. Many of them face that the world in which they've put their trust in is the culprit for their concerns, afraid, they reach out for help.

National statistics show that after a drop, propelled by the positive tests on the scroll, church attendance is up 15% over last year. Most people polled cite the economy as the catalyst for their return to God's house of worship. People cite, as motivation, the prosperity of Christians across the land, who are remaining abundantly successful in spite of these hard times.

"It's absolutely beautiful that our brethren are returning to the house of the Lord. When times are tough, like they are now, we usually see a spike in parishioners walk through our doors," Faith is quoted as saying. Similar to everyplace else across the world, believers at Anytown's largest nondenominational church share their pastor's joy in witnessing so many past and new church members return to worship. But what they don't see is something that will become clear in the months ahead. It can be summed up in one word: motive.

Most of the faithless that have returned to church are still faithless. Their motivation for worship is not to serve God, they are not interested in any of his promises except for those pertaining to their financial prosperity. On bent knees, they pray to keep their possessions or to acquire new ones; that is all. They are not there for service, to be a guiding light for others; they are not there for thanksgiving.

God tests their motives by bringing nothing to pass for those with wrongly motivated hearts'. The faithless go for months and see no results, frustration builds, and everyone's motivations are brought to the forefront.

A few catch onto the error of their ways and change their motivation towards truly serving God. They realize by serving his will and not fretting about money, they in return will be blessed with prosperity in every facet of their life.

They try to tell the world of the blessings that are happening in their lives', due to their change of heart. But the faithless just won't stop pretending, they would rather listen to the wrongly motivated, "Man, I tried and I tried to have faith in God. I actually convinced myself that maybe he does exist, so I've been going to church, praying, every Sunday, for like four months now, and ain't seen a lick of results. My house is about to get foreclosed on, I'm hiding my cars at different places every night, so the snatch-man won't take them, I've even paid tithes a few times and ain't got nothing back from Zeus... I mean God. If he's real like the Bible says he is, isn't he supposed to help people like me? So where is he at?!"

As the faithless leave God's house possibly for the last time, their hearts' and minds' turn colder than ever before. Their experience solidifies their previous stance.

Ricky's recorded comments are still fuel for the faithless. A clear line is becoming very visible all across the land as the disbelievers are growing desperately annoyed and angry with the believers. As with race and differing religions, their hatred stems from those who are different than they. Devilish influenced minds' think, "Why won't they just give up? They still think that they're better than us, because they choose to hold onto a lie. All of us see the truth for what it is; why won't they?" The distance widens between the two factions.

The 'Neverending War' continues on, however, it's rarely front page news anymore, unless there is a high casualty day for our American troops.

Tensions between our country and the rest of the world remain high. Washington has been watching the situation between Israel and its Islamic neighbors very closely. For thousands of years, Israel's relations with its neighbors has been strained to say the least, and while Israel continues to take aid from the United States, the easing of those strained relationships is cause for great torment inside the American government.

President Thames has grown deathly tired of Israel's standoffish position towards her beloved country, and she is not about to tolerate it any longer. In her office, she lays out her feeling to the Secretary of Defense, "Those Jews finally got their shit together with the Muslims, now they wanna turn against us, to unite with them…," her tone turns sinister, "they think that because I am a woman they can run over me, they think they'll get away with this. That's the wrong way to think when they're dealing with this President." Thames' demon and alcohol oppressed mind uses her gender as a new crutch for her increasingly devious mind-set.

In her State of the Union Address, Thames delivers a resonating ultimatum to Israel. "If the cooperation between Israel and the United States does not improve, expeditiously, I may be forced to go before Congress and ask for a reduction in the amount of aid that we send to them. I will not allow the disrespect and ingratitude they have shown us, since all of this has begun, to continue any longer. Over the past months, Israel has sided against us on many of the same issues that we have always seen eye to eye on. This has occurred only because America had the guts and took the responsibility to tell the world the truth. This decision I am making has nothing at all to do with Israel's relationships with any Islamic country. It has only to do with our ties, ties that I thought they treasured just as we do."

With renewed intensity, the worldwide protests begin again. Thames doesn't care, she lied to the American people and to the world. This is about power. This has everything to do with Israel's relations with its neighboring countries, and if she has any say so about it, Thames is not about to allow their strengthening bond with Islam to continue, but if it does, she is going to make sure it comes at a heavy price.

"President Thames does not want peace in the Middle East! As soon as ourselves and the Muslims begin to put aside our differences and come together, she wants to punish us!" A rabbi at a rally in Washington voices the opinion held by most outside of the States.

Through her eyes, Thames does not see any positives in Israel being 'buddy buddy' with Islamic nations, and she is beginning to convert those in Congress to her way of thinking. Alcohol tainted thoughts fill her paranoid reasoning, the intensity of which consumes her more than the day before. "If their battles and religious differences get settled, and we're pushed away, they might reel in other countries to their side. We've given Israel so many weapons, they could allow the Muslims or even terrorists to use them against us. We've shared so many technological and security secrets with them, what if they share those details with these countries?" She spreads her fears to those in Congress, and they agree.

Israel's bond with even the strictest Islamic nations tightens, when, as a group, Iran, Iraq, and Syria offer to supply their new friends with any amount of aid that is lost through American sanctions.

Tensions and fear of an apocalyptic war skyrockets when Israel, the birthplace of so much biblical history, informs our country that, "The world will respond swiftly to any new aggression towards us or any other Middle Eastern country, be it political or militarily. America, its troops, and their desecration of the holy land, must leave immediately, or there will be grave consequences!"

It's been over for two months now, but Bryant Michaels is still trying to take his mind off of a horrible season, in which, his team not only didn't win its third consecutive title, they didn't even made the playoffs, and he received the brunt of the blame.

'Flight' relaxes, in an attempt to bury his worries, by taking a vacation to the South of France with his new girlfriend.

From inside the pocket of his plaid shorts, he feels the vibrating buzz of his cellular phone. He drops his fishing pole down onto the marble floor of his rented multimillion dollar yacht.

It's his agent and he has horrible news. "Hey 'Flight', I hate to tell you this, but Ricky was in a horrific traffic accident. His car was basically crushed around him. About an hour ago, he was life-flighted to the hospital; it's pretty bad, 'Flight'. I'm sorry buddy. I'll make all of the arrangements to get you a private plane so you can get back here as quickly-"

A hateful satisfaction shines on Bryant's face, "I'm not going anywhere, just keep me posted," he hangs up, then, props his feet back up onto the yacht's rail and throws his pole back out into the calm, clear blue waters of the sea.

From the other side of the deck, lying out topless, working on her tan, his newest toy asks, "Who was that honey?"

He pauses. "No one important."

After being informed of the accident, eight full days and

nights pass before Ricky Walters' former best friend returns home. As Bryant requested, his agent has kept him abreast of all the happenings concerning Ricky, and 'Flight' could not be more pleased with all that he has heard. He happily makes a trip to the hospital, to see his old buddy, his first priority as soon as his chartered G4 jet touches down.

Turning down autograph requests as he makes his path to Ricky's private room, he can't help but beam. He gets to room 816, while right outside of his door, jitters begin to form due to his excitement and joy towards seeing the new Ricky.

'Flight' quietly opens the entry. The first thing that greets his eyes wipes his despicable smile right off of his face.

The love of his life, the woman whose heart and companionship he was so close to regaining, is leaning over Ricky's bed, showering him with pecks of loving kisses, while gently stroking his short hair.

From across the large room, with their backs' to him, they don't even know he's entered. "I love you, sweetheart...," Stacy touts, "God has been so truly good to us."

Michaels is silently jolted, but internally, his raging emotions scream louder and louder by the second. He remembers the feel of her soft hands as he watches her caress Ricky's face. He remembers the feel of her succulent lips as they gently kiss his ex-best friend over and over again. To see another man, especially one whom he personally was so close to, receiving the affection he misses so much, is more than he can bear. 'Flight' can hold his silence no longer.

He breaks up their tender one on one time with a pained, sinister snicker as he shuts the door behind himself. Stacy's head whips around, "Bryant, hi, we didn't know you were here."

He fights to talk calmly as he walks towards them. "I knew it all along. I tried to tell myself, 'no it can't be', but I knew it. I just gotta know Stacy, Ricky, how much of my marriage consisted of you two screwing behind my back?"

Stacy looks at him like "how dare you". "I can't believe you said that. You were the cheater, not me. You are out of your mind."

A wide eyed, demented gaze dons, "Funny you'd say that, because right now… yes, I think that I might be."

As he walks around Stacy's body, which from Michael's angle, along with the bedsheets, helps to shield the lower half of Ricky's physique, the secret of Michaels' enthusiasm for coming to see his old friend is revealed. Due to injuries suffered in the accident, Ricky has lost both legs up to his knees.

Michaels sits down in a chair on the opposite side of the bed from Stacy. Raging jealous emotions inflate his body once he catches notice of the diamond ring on Stacy's ring finger.

Ricky sets the record straight, "Bryant… Stacy and I only begin seeing each other a couple of weeks after this season ended. As you can see, we're getting married, but we never-"

"You're a liar, like I'm going to believe anything that you say."

Stacy, sternly, takes up for her man. "The only liar in this room is you."

Michaels claps his hands and rocks back and forth, chuckling hysterically, while pointing at Ricky's missing legs. "Look at him, Stacy. What kind of life can you have with this? Even after it all, you idiots still praise God and worship that stupid book. Ricky is God's number one follower, the loving, caring God that you two always preached into my ear wouldn't do this to his main homey, now would he?" He pauses for a moment, before he continues, "You wanta know why God did this to Ricky…," Michaels shouts, "because there is no God, never was!"

Realizing that he is entirely too loud, Michaels' eyes flash over to the door, that he hopes has contained his volume.

Stacy has a look about her that speaks of killing Bryant for the unforgettable, blasphemous words he's said about the two most important beings in her life. "Well well well, my spirit was right. It told me all along that you were just faking, pretending yet again, huh? How many times are you going to ride that see-saw?"

Ricky remains calm, he is not stirred at all by Bryant's words. "You are so lost in this world, Bryant. Someone like you would be totally crushed by this physical loss, but my legs, nor any other part of my body, define me. Everyday God blesses me, and the day I lost my legs was no different."

Michaels is stunned. He can't believe that Ricky remains undiscouraged, faithful; even with the severity of his body's condition.

"I love you, Bryant, but you need to leave. Get out, now!" Ricky orders, but 'Flight' doesn't budge.

"Don't just sit there, you heard him, Bryant, get out. I hope that I never see you again."

The love of his life delivers the death blow to their already decreased relationship. And what hurts him just as badly is, as his eyes water while staring into hers', he can see the 100% unwavering conviction in them. He's dead to her. His tears, all of their years together, mean nothing, and what's most frightening is that he sees no hope that this is ever going to change.

Without another word said, 'Flight' stands up, takes one final look at his loss, and steadies himself for the painful, humiliating trek to the opposite side of that door, and out of their lives'. As soon as he takes his first step towards that finale, all of Stacy's loving attention goes back to Ricky. She whispers, "Are you o.k., baby?"

That loving gesture charges all of the jealousy inside of Michaels' heart. His darkened mind begs him to take violent action, as his steps carry him closer and closer away from them. His anger says to him, "All she cares about is that cripple, he stole her from you."

Hate and jealousy mix to create insanity. Insanity pushes him to the brink, once he peeks back over his shoulder and witnesses Stacy lay another sweet kiss upon her love's lips.

Ricky asks her if she's alright, he caresses her stomach and she whispers back, "Don't worry, the baby and I are fine."

In a blink, Michaels turns into an out of control menace bent on destroying the person he blames for all of his sadness, the man who will share a bond of happiness with Stacy that she always denied him.

He doesn't afford them a chance to react. Michaels grabs Stacy by the back of her neck, pushes her out of the way, then, this troubled man attacks its main course. He locks his incredibly large and powerful hands around Ricky's throat, and squeezes with everything inside of him. Stacy scrambles to her feet, opens the door, and screams for help. Acting solely on adrenaline, she runs over and begins beating on Bryant's back, "Stop him, Jesus, he's going to kill him! Stop him!"

She digs her nails into the flesh of Michaels' enraged wrists, screaming as she slices his skin apart. She digs so deep and rips with such fury, two of her inch long nails break off inside; but he remains undeterred. He's too strong, too focused, too intent on erasing the man that he blames for taking everything from him. Satan eggs him on as Bryant shouts, "She wouldn't even know God if it wasn't for you!"

After what seemed liked minutes, but carried on for only more than a few seconds, two armed security personnel burst into the room. It takes six billy clubbed strikes to Michaels' forearms and shoulders to break his grip from his victim.

David Gimmer is in the mist of true joy, the kind of joy that a deep relationship with God can bring. David has left the darkness of the first forty plus years of his life behind him; Jesus took care of that. His savior has done for him, the same thing that he did for David's new friends, Stacy, Ricky, and Faith, whom he met through the church that he is now a member of.

Our Lord has brought understanding and peace to his life, no longer is he just a select hearer of the Word, he is a doer of the Word. Now, he is excited to learn about God, when before, he just went through the motions. He is finally living his life by faith.

David truly works for his community now and not just for his own selfish gains. He decided to keep the same old job, but it's a new man, with a new way of thinking, who runs it. Gone are all the flashy items that once filled his office, not because they are wrong; but because they are wrong for the new him.

You should have seen the surprise on Brandon Myers' face when David admitted to, then, vigorously and whole heartedly apologized for his racist talk and behavior. David confidently and proudly told Brandon about his transformation. Nowadays, these new best friends fellowship about the glorious things God has done for their lives', in and outside of the church they attend together.

David, "Brandon, I used to hate so deeply. I learned to justify and cover it up, but now I've allowed the Word of God to be the deciding factor in my life, and through His word, I understand that He wants me to love, totally and completely, without cause or reason, just as he does. That is what life is supposed to be about - loving everyone. I thank God that you are now my friend. I love you as my brother."

David's life has that glow that only others like him know about, but that does not totally eliminate the attacks on his flesh. The devil never quits. David battles lust and guilt. The enemy has chosen these to be his weapons of choice to his attempts to steal David's joy.

Infrequently, David speaks with Gwen, he tries to get her to open her heart, but she won't release the hate and anger that is subduing her life. David battles to forgive himself for Gwen's troubles, he knows it's up to her to change her life, but pieces of him want to wallow in guilt. So, being a man of real faith now, David prays and battles for his victory.

The room is dim. Candles provide only a slight bit of lighting. David and Faith are sitting side by side, alone, on the first row of the many belchers that comprise the seating inside their presently empty church.

David stares, but at nothing particular, he is deep inside his personal thoughts.

Faith beams with pride as she looks around and sees the grace of God in the rundown interior of their new makeshift church home.

Gone is the elaborate 10,000 seat arena that she formerly taught in, the government seized it. With much help from her spiritual family this building has been transformed to hold close to a thousand.

As time has passed, many of the faithful sin by allowing the fear of reprisal by the majority and their need to fit in to the mainstream to steer them away from coming to this, Anytown's last formal church, so instead, many of them have formed small groups, held at a group member's home, for their Bible studies and songs of praise to the Creator.

Nothing will steer Faith down their path; not the people that come by and shoot their bullets through the church's windows in the middle of the night, not the stores that no longer sell anything pro-God, nor the local government's decisions, which attempted to break the will of every remaining Christian in town by relegating them to this dilapidated, former office building, in the projects, that Faith, along with all of the other church members have roughly transformed into their house of worship.

None of these worldly factors matter to Faith, not when she sees all of the blessings and glory that has been born from this situation. She praises God for the magnificent beauty of this 'thriving rose' that has grown through the cracks of death in their barren world. Catholics, Protestants, Jews, Muslims, Christians, all religions are tolerated and respected in this church.

It's incredible what God's children can do when their backs' are pushed up against a wall. Time is actually taken to learn about different religions, so that they may understand others of varying faiths. Along this path, they learn to judge others by one factor only, a person's love of God. No, they don't all of a sudden agree with everything that is believed by another person's differing faith, but they all respect that person's right to worship the Lord in their own way. No one allows the stupidity of humanity's long, sad, and violent religious past to come between them and their fellow man. This church has broken the cycle.

Faith proudly thinks to herself. "Thank you, Father, look at how you have brought us all together. This is what you wanted all along, isn't it?"

Faith takes a break from her reflections to peek over at David; she's concerned about the unease seen on her friend's face.

"Sister Faith, may I say something to you from my heart?"

"Please do."

This humble and pleasant to the eye saved man tells his friend, "It seems that since I've handed my life over to the Lord, Satan has been after me harder than ever-"

"That's because he fears you now."

"My flesh has been steadily filling with desires that I know, even though I'm separated from my wife, are wrong. But they keep growing in strength."

"You are a true Christian, a true worshiper now, so greater is your strength in Christ than the strength of the world. You are stronger than your emotions."

"Thank you. I know that you're right. I still care a lot for Sasha, but this new woman seems like she'd be such a great woman for the right man to spend his life with?"

"David, I know that it is hard to see, right now...," she lightly taps on the top of his wedding ring, "but I believe God has already placed you with the right woman."

David slowly takes in her words, and innocently he informs, "I just have to keep trusting in God to direct my paths straight. I have to stop thinking about YOU in the ways that I have been lately."

Faith is speechless, but her mind screams, "Where did that come from?" He said it so casually, so nondescriptly. New feelings instantly blossom inside her.

Faith knows her body, she knows that she isn't a size 4. She's flattered that he sees her in this way, but she also knows that this is not appropriate.

David's handsome face turns towards hers'. Faith tries to keep them from doing so, but her shy eyes must flee the scene. "So… a… have you heard from Gwen lately?"

"She calls me every so often to let me know she is o.k., but she won't tell me where she has run away to. I worry so much about her. She tells me that she's fine, but there is still so much pain and anger in her voice."

"Does Sasha know where she's at?"

"She says she doesn't, but I can't be sure that she's telling me the truth."

"Just continue to pray for Gwen, pray that her eyes will open, that she will come back to you. Make sure that you have forgiven yourself, because God has forgiven you, just as He forgave my sins which may have destroyed my daughter."

"I will Sister, thank you…," Faith gives him a comforting squeeze on his knee, "have you had any luck with finding your daughter? What is her name again?"

"Her name is Sherry." Faith takes a loving look at her daughter through the scenes in her memories, "It's been so very long since I've seen her. When I do find her, Lord willing, she'll forgive me. I was such a horrible mother back then. Those drugs I was on stripped me of my decency. I just left her abandoned with predators like her father. The day Jesus turned my life around is the day I started looking for her, but I still haven't found her yet."

"So have you gotten close, any leads?"

"Well maybe, I may have caught a break yesterday. I found a shelter that she was staying at just outside of town, but that was like twelve or thirteen years ago. Through the grace of God, one of the ladies still works there after all of this time. She recognized Sherry from an old photo I always carry with me."

"Does she have any idea where she is now?"

"No, but she does remember a guy that came in to see her once. Sherry must have taken off with him, because after that day she never came back. I pray that she didn't get herself involved with some scumbag."

"So this lady at the shelter, she knows this guy?"

"Kind of, they went to Anytown University together. She said he was kind of a weirdo, back then, but that he was also a really bright man. What struck her as strange was, the day he came up to the shelter, he didn't recognize her, but when she told him she knew who he was, he acted really paranoid, like he couldn't wait to get out of there."

"So did you ask her his name?"

"Yeah, it was Edward something, all she could remember was his first name."

Anytown University… Edward? The wheels slowly begin to spin inside of David's head, "That's my brother's name and he went to school there."

Faith hasn't caught onto David's peaked curiosity yet. "That's not much to go on, that's a pretty common name to say the least."

"Did she have any other details about him?"

"No."

"How old do you think this lady is?"

"She's probably somewhere in her forties. Why?"

"Oh, nothing. I, I was just wondering." David tries not to get himself too worked up about these similarities, he knows the chances are low that what he is thinking is accurate, but it does make him want to investigate.

Faith walks over to what was one of the church's windows, but since it was shot out last week, all that's left is a small square hole with two by four boards covering the rest. Light provided by the moon and the street lamps shine through the small cracks, highlighting themselves on Faith's red and white skirt and blouse.

A fresh idea triggers instant energy inside of David, he pops up out of his seat. "Tomorrow morning we're going back down to that shelter. I've got a hunch."

Faith is befuddled as to why David is so curious about all of this.

They have no clue about the secrets that soon will be revealed to them.

Sticking out like a third trimester pregnant women during the swimsuit portion of the Miss America pageant sits Melvin's opulent truck. Curbside, he waits impatiently for tonight's girl-toy to emerge from her small inner-city duplex.

His face fills with blood, his pulsing veins raise his skin creating what looks like rivers and streams down his arms and neck. He can't even enjoy all of the stares and "wows" from the neighborhood's inhabitants as their eyes enjoy his vehicle, all he wants to do is stare at the front door that he can't wait to see open.

One chrome nine millimeter rest across his thighs, while its twin hides between the seats, their big brother, an Ak-47, sits camouflaged in an easily accessed specially rigged back seat compartment. All of this firepower helps to steady Melvin's nerve. He ain't sweating a lick. He loves this.

Melvin's entire happiness is built on the different adrenaline highs he is now afforded. He is cool, dangerous, sexy, rich, envied, loved, and hated, all at once. He has fully embraced all of the perilous aspects of his lifestyle. He envisions his first shoot-out often. In it, he kills many, and walks away a legend. He never dies, he always wins. He may take a grazing bullet across the shoulder, but he's never seriously injured. He told Stamp just a week ago, "I'm ready for one of these cats to try me."

He spots an old man approaching through his rear-view mirror. The touch of steel in his palm signals to him that he is now ready for whatever. His helps to calm his pulse.

The guy passes by, Melvin can tell by his clothing and jittery walk that he's probably a junkie. Melvin's anger reappears, his head returns to its swivel, his impatient thoughts return, "Her stupid ass needs to get out here. This better not be no muthafuckin' set-up."

"No, the hell this smoker ain't! Look at him, y'all!" Some young woman's less than afraid, but alarmed shouts moves Melvin's attention three houses up. The addict that just passed by has pried open a front porch window to someone's home and is now climbing in. Nine people, six young, one middle-aged, one old, the other who is him, witness this, and do nothing.

Melvin's passenger door opens, as his head is turned. "Damn Mel, don't point that gun at me, shit!"

"Girl, you surprised da shit outta me. Next time your dumbass better knock when you don't see me looking. It's about time you brought ya ass out da house. You about got left," he angrily exclaims to his slender, but voluptuous companion as she settles into her leather seat.

"O.k., I get the point, sorry." Off they go.

Three days later.

"Yup, I heard, dude kilt them people up in there. That's a trip." With a flippant tone, void of sorrow, Melvin responds to Dane, after he painfully mentions Anytown's latest murders, while they dine at their usual upscale restaurant.

"Killed dem for nothing." Miserably, Dane finishes saying just before he bites into his juicy steak.

Stamp's full attention is centered on his plate of jumbo shrimp. Melvin waits for his prime steak to return well-done, but super tender, like he asked for the first time. "Dog, I saw that smoker break into dat crib. I didn't know until this morning that he killed people tho'. I was just a couple of houses away picking up this trick I be screwin'."

Stamp, "The news said that those people had been dead for two, three days."

The angst on Dane's face is obvious, "And didn't nobody out there call da cops? People are so lost, dog."

Stamp. "So dey was lying then, 'cuz everyone that got interviewed on television said they didn't hear or see na'thin."

In a tone of achievement and coolness, Stamp and Melvin slap hands while Melvin proudly proclaims, "Anytown hoods don't be snitchin', baby. You know how we do!" Dane is agitated by their ignorance and their agreement in it.

Having quietly returned, Melvin's waitress is rudely commanded to wait until after he takes a bite, so that he may then command her to leave or take his ultra-expensive steak back again. "It's fine, you can go," she is rudely told.

Becoming stronger in his affirmation against their lifestyle, Dane blurts out, "And while we ain't snitchin', somebody else is dying because the killers know we won't tell nobody. That's part of why the hood is so jacked up now."

Stamp leans away in order to show his alarm, "Damn Oprah; what in the hell has gotten into you? The hood being jacked up has made you rich, nigga. You should be grateful."

Melvin has become so full of self-centeredness, "Amen Brother Stamp, yo, I didn't think about this before, but we do need to start snitchin' to da po'lease when a fiend does some shit like this. He took away some of our best customers, he fuckin' wit our money!" He doesn't get the extravagant laughter filled response he had hoped for.

Stamp, "That house had some smokers in it?"

"They identified them today. Three of the dead were smokers, I know. It was two dudes, da mother that lived there, and hey, I know that y'all know Zane, little young nigga. Dat fiend got him too."

Stamp, "I heard. Damn, he didn't have to shoot little dude too… Dane, are you alright."

He's not. Everything around him, of him, has slowed down. His body is stiff as a board. His eyes are open for looking, but his mind takes no note of what they see. Like a window being drenched in a pouring rain, tears flow heavily down his eyes. Dane's heart is breaking, he had only heard that some people got murdered, he had no idea that one of them was Zane.

Unconcerned about the obvious hurt on his friend's face Melvin continues on, "Little nigga went out like a G tho'. Peep this, da po-po said that shorty had ripped up money inside his fist when they opened his hand. He must have went out fightin' for his, I respect little dude for that, I feel 'em. He musta been like 'you gon have ta kill me if you want my money!" Melvin and Stamp slap hands in celebration of Zane's hood-honored feat.

"Oh God, please no…," Dane sniffs in his runny nose, "Oh God, I'm so sorry."

Melvin could care less about Dane's words, they bring about no sympathy. His focus is totally on the sight of his tears, and the weakness that he sees in them. "Are you serious, man. You gon sit here and cry like a little bitch in front of all these people, in front of ya boys?"

Dane tries to explain. "It's my fault. I gave Zane that money. I knew better, something told me not to do it, but I did it anyway."

Melvin looks upon his face with confusion and annoyance, "O.k. whatever, so that gives you reason to sit here and embarrass us, because you wanna be all sensitive, right now?"

Dane's flesh overtakes his spirit. His tears stop their flow as Melvin's callous words and challenging stare tempt him. "You better shut the fuck up about things you know na'thin about. If we weren't in this…"

Totally unnerved, unrelenting, Melvin 'fires' right back, with a cryptic message, "You don't know me like you think you do, Dane. Trust; you wouldn't want to start any problems with this… Just eat ya meal, bro."

I'm sorry, I have to do it. I know this isn't the proper format, but cut me some slack, I'm the author. I have to speak, this misunderstanding about God can go on no longer.

In this case, a young boy dies, or let's use for example some other innocent person's life that is taken prematurely by someone else; so many people want to criticize and question where is God, if there really is a God? If this world loved, believed, and followed as He told us we should, there would be none of this; not one senseless murder. Human disobedience deserves all of the blame.

We were forewarned as to how disobedience would bring death to us, but still we drive down the wrong side of the road, then blame God when we crash. These devilish times are the result of a slow deterioration through the generations towards our reliance on the Bible.

These last days are to the right of the equal sign, they're the sum of what we have built. THIS IS OUR FAULT! DON'T YOU DARE BLAME GOD! Our Father has never wanted us to live like this.

The cure is right there to ingest, but we keep swallowing the poison, and then wonder why we keep getting sick.

But new hope is about to be born.

Dane's knees press against his bedroom's hardwood floor, he reaches under his bed and pulls out the same Holy Bible he walked away from just days ago. His torso leans forward against his mattress. He opens the Bible to no particular page and places his sweaty forehead against it. He still does not fully trust all of the things Christians have said it can do, but his aching soul and the Holy Spirit now budding inside push him to give this thing a chance.

He doesn't want to live another day without Jesus as his savior and the protection of God's love. "This is for me and you, Zane. God, I'm asking you to bless me by giving me a piece of Zane's spirit, as I accept your spirit. Please Father, do this for me."

Deeply distraught, the devil desperately tries more tricks to stop Dane from speaking the words that hold the power to change his life. "How do you know he's really here? Your mind is just tricking you… You're a pimp, a player, baby; you can't be going around acting all goody goody. You wanna be broke like you was before? Just calm down, you still trippin' about Zane getting killed."

Dane, "Dear Heavenly Father, I accept the blood of your son, Jesus Christ, into my life. I accept the love, protection, and wisdom that he has for me…," Dane sits quietly, as if he's expecting something, then, "Oh! I almost forgot." Now that he has given his life to the Lord, Dane has released his first blessing, "I think that I still have that book."

His memory has been jogged in regards to the Bible Prayers book that one of his meaningless female conquests had brought for him over two years ago. Dane recalls how dumbfounded he was as he thought about why "some ho would bring some bulls*** like this to a playa like me. What in the hell made this girl give me this?"

Through his conscience, the Holy Spirit tells him the answer, "That book was handed to you for this very moment." Dane is just beginning to see that the Lord really does work in mysterious ways.

A firm decision has now been made in Dane's heart and mind. That decision brings along heaven's anointed angels and the Holy Spirit's guidance to support him in every facet of his life.

"My daughter and your brother are together? I can't believe it."

"Maybe not now, but at least they were," David's heart rapidly thumps as they resituate themselves inside of his car, which is curbside at the United Sisters Shelter in the heart of suburban downtown.

All it took was one quick glance at Ed's old college photo that David kept stored away, for the social worker to say, "Yup, that's him, that's Edward, I'm absolutely positive."

"Do you know how to get in touch with your brother or where he's at?"

"I have no clue. He went off on his own. Once Ed left home, he never kept in touch with me or our parents."

"He didn't go to their funeral?"

"No, he hated the both of them… and he hated me because I never stood up for him."

Faith defends her friend. "He can't blame you. You were just a kid yourself. There is nothing you could have done."

"I know, but…" David can't find the vocabulary to finish his solemn guilt as he starts the car and drives off.

"So what was your brother like? Was he a spiritual man?"

Excluding Mary, the sick existence for everyone inside of Ed's domain has been much smoother over these past months, ever since Ed switched up his tactics and loosened their reins a bit.

At Devin's request, his predatory father has eased up on the beatings that he imposes on Sherry. "Come on, Dad. It's no fun to nail her, and she's got bruises and cuts everywhere," he reasoned with him.

Although he still does not allow talking between anyone, without his presence, he does allow mother and son their 'time' together - four scheduled sessions a week. They just have to keep the door cracked open, so that he may listen from the other side. His fears need to be completely confident that they are not plotting anything against him.

Over the past week, Ed's health has suddenly started to deteriorate. It started out as simple flu-like symptoms and has progressed ever since. For almost a day now, he has been bed ridden, his strength totally sapped, his weight has diminished dramatically.

The family gathers around the edges of what may become his death bed. "Ed, talk to me, are we going to heaven now? Is this God's way of telling us he's coming to take us home?" Sherry intensely quizzes him as she dabs a cold towel over her husband's profusely sweating forehead.

He's turned pale white, his lips are bone-dry, his skin scaly. Even with all of this to worry about, the only thing on his twisted mind is keeping his secrets hidden. THE BASEMENT.

Mary states what should be obvious to her father. "We have to get you to a hospital, Daddy?"

"No, absolutely not, this is just some kind of infection. All I need are some antibiotics, I'll be fine."

"Maybe so, that is why we need to get you to the hospital." Sherry rightfully counters.

His weakened hand tries to grab onto her skinny, little arm to show her his force, just like always, but his grip is next to nothing, "I said no." Sherry takes note of the huge downward slide in his brute strength.

Devin recalls, "Dad, remember when I had gotten sick a couple of years ago? You went down into your basement and came back up with some medicine that made me better."

Wide eyed, Mary and Sherry glance at each other, the mere mention of that room has always been forbidden. They have never been allowed down there, they are scared to even think of it.

"Do you have anymore of that stuff, Daddy?" Mary asks.

He knows this is his only option, the situation is that dire. "I should have grabbed my box before I got this sick…," his twenty-twenty hindsight tells him. He knows that he has to let them in, someone has to go down those steps, "its pitch black down there. The medicine chest is right at the bottom of the stairs, she doesn't even have to really go into the room. NO! I can't do it, I have to do it! I have to!"

Sherry breaks up his frenzied thoughts. "Give me the keys, Ed. You don't have time to waste. You're dying!"

Ed slowly turns his head away from them. They wait in quiet anticipation for a response from him. "22, 34, 13, the keys are in a safe on the top shelf of Mary's closet."

Just as Sherry is about to get up to begin her mission, Ed successfully grabs her arm this time. "Look at me, woman." She does as he asks. He talks in the sternest voice that he can accomplish at the moment. "There are no lights as you walk down, you don't need any. When you get to the bottom of the stairs, you immediately turn to your right, there is a small closet there, don't bother concerning yourself with anything else. Reach up to the top shelf, the medicine chest is the only thing on it. Bring the entire box back to me, and Sherry…," he gives her the same stare that he's always given right before all of her beatings, "don't be snooping around, get back here fast."

She reassures Ed as she stands up. "O.k. Ed, I will. I'll do everything that you ask. I'll be right back."

Freedom; she's still within fifty feet of him, still inside the four walls that have been her entire life for the past thirteen years, but she feels it as she moves around the house unencumbered by his smothering presence. While getting the small set of keys out of the safe, Sherry's mind begins to open up and question. "Why for all of these years has he been so protective of that basement?"

She speed walks out of Mary's room, headed for the downstairs. She passes back by Ed's open door and glances in. Husband and wife make eye contact. That split second says a great deal to her, she sees the fear in his eyes. "Why is he so afraid? What in heaven's name could be down in that basement?"

God has released a blessing upon Sherry, which the evil in Ed now realizes. "I shouldn't have trusted her," he senses it through that one glance. His psyche can't handle his lack of control. He hears her running down the stairs, his mind scrambles; once again, just as his paranoia kicks in, the brilliance of his diabolical mind comes up with an idea that it doesn't have time to debate. "Mary, go to your room."

"Daddy, I'm scared, I-"

For the first time in Devin's life he feels a moment of physical tenderness from his father as Ed takes hold of his hand, while he simultaneously responds to Mary. To replace his lack of a stern voice, he makes a mean face to convey the seriousness of his words, "I mean it, Mary, now."

As she leaves, Ed begins, "Devin, my only son, you have to hurry down to the basement and stop your mother. She's going to destroy me if you don't."

"What are you talking about?"

"I don't have time to explain, but there are some things down there that she must not see."

"What is it, I don't understand? What could be down there that is so bad for you?"

"Stop questioning me, boy, and just go. Beat her brains in if you have to, your mother is turning against me, against God. I saw it in her eyes as she walked by. She's becoming just like all those people we read about in the newspaper, she is one of Satan's children. God will not allow us into heaven if you don't stop her."

As always, Ed knows just the right buttons that will activate his son's brainwashed mind. Devin's adrenaline and anger builds as he readies for his mission. He hops up, then, turns to charge out of the room. "Devin wait!"

"Yeah, Dad?"

"Don't forget the medicine chest."

With that, Devin runs off, his feet only land on every third step as he sprints down them, focused solely on doing whatever is necessary to fulfill his father's wishes and preserve his place in God's kingdom.

He yells, "Mom!," while darting through the family room on a beeline into the kitchen.

Hidden from his sight, posed against the wall, on the other side of the doorway that puts you inside of the kitchen is Sherry. She's to his left, Devin's attention is on the basement's door to his right, as he steps into the kitchen, he never sees it coming... WHAM!!

With a strength and confidence that she has never felt before in her life, Sherry slams the same large metal frying pan across the back of Devin's cranium that she has used to cook Ed's breakfast all of these years. The first strike disorients him, the next, knocks him to the floor.

She guessed right, she had a gut feeling that Ed would send him.

His sprawled out body slowly squirms and moans, Devin is harmless at the moment, but Sherry knows that she is not out of danger. "I gotta hurry."

She runs over to a drawer and pulls out a large roll of duct tape. She heavily binds her son's nearly lifeless hands and wrists. Devin begins to moan louder, just before she duct tapes his mouth shut. Sherry binds his feet together, then, drags him into the corner against two walls.

Ed heard the thud, but doesn't know that it was made by

his son's body hitting the floor. Ed's nerves muster up enough strength for him to yell semi-loudly. "Devin, is everything alright down there?"

Time is of the essence. Sherry's focus returns to that vault-like basement door that may hold the answers to the questions in her head. Her nerves rattle as she fumbles through getting each of the three keys in their proper locks.

There, she's done it; Ed's secret world is open. She hesitates for a moment, as if an invisible Ed is in front of her, ready to deliver a punch as soon as she takes that first step down into his private territory. She inhales deeply and exhales slowly to combat her anxiety.

Her path is pitch-black, just like Ed told her it would be. Sherry flicks the switch just to her right to light her passage down the stairs - no juice. Her search must begin through the dark.

Tip-toeing while gently holding onto the termite softened wood railing, she makes her way down. Sherry almost misses a step causing her to lose balance, her forehead taps into a dangling light bulb. She fumbles around for its switch, she pulls it; nothing. "You're o.k., I'm not going to stop, I'm not stopping."

Going against Ed's commandment gives her power over her life that she has never felt before. She reaches the bottom of the stairs, but this new woman does not stop as she was told. Sherry passes the closet and continues on into the rest of the room.

She walks through the 'black', one hand straight in the air, one out in front of herself, as she slowly moves about the room. She feels another string, her fingers tackle each other in a hurried attempt to pull it. Once on, the light illuminates an amazing story.

The large room is a shrine to a brilliant, accomplished scholar. Academic trophies and ribbons fill a tall glass chamber, plaques of young Ed's extensive scholastic achievements hang from every wall. Filling the spaces not taken up by his plaques, are newspaper clippings with headings like, 'Local senior receives ten thousand dollar scholarship to attend Anytown's top university... Grad

student is at the top of the list for prestigious national award...
Dr. Ed Wilson opens his own psychology office, specializing in
the mental health of abused children and battered women...
Owner and director, Dr. Ed Wilson, abruptly closes successful
practice, citing a higher calling.'

Sherry's brain is 'swimming', "Doctor... Ed was a doctor?"
She begins to search through the neatly arranged files on the
shelves above the only two pieces of furniture in the room; a desk
and chair.

She reads the name tabs on each file before she wildly flings
them to the floor. She stops, "Sherry Wilson," and gingerly opens
it up, curious, but afraid of what it may reveal.

"Devin! Sherry! Where are you, what are you doing down
there?" The control freak has no control, as he frets from
two floors above. The unknown is killing him, Ed has to do
something. It's just too quiet.

He drags his lifeless legs out of the bed and tries to stand
up, but they shake like jell-o, they will not hold any pressure, in
desperation, Ed allows his entire body to drop to the floor. Using
only arms and shoulders, he painfully drags his corpse-like frame
along the floor.

Sherry hears the thump that Ed's sickened body makes when
it hits the floor. "I don't have much time." Not having the luxury
of reading everything over, she scans through much of it.

The magazine sized file contains everything she could possibly
want to know about the past thirteen years of her life with her
captor. How and why Ed chose her, "I need a broken spirit, a
woman with low self esteem, one that can be easily dominated."

He wrote detailed notes, chronologically, about some of the
instances that he beat her and his diagnosis of the progressive
effects it was having on her. "I know she hates me. I can see it in
her eyes, she wants to leave, but she can't. She doesn't know how,
fear of the unknown always stops her."

He details some of the methodologies to his madness, "I
make her look at me when I beat her, so hopefully she has to

think about me as I do it. Sherry must also blink, no staring, this helps to prevent her mind from zoning out her plight… For my notes, periodically, I ask her questions about how she feels, what she's thinking… I keep her super skinny, so that her tiny frame can better feel the abuse, in addition, the smaller and hungrier I keep her, the less strength she'll have to defend herself."

His ego brags about the genius that it took to use the fear of God to his advantage, "Once I put the truth into her mind, that she must be saved through Jesus to enter heaven, I was then able, through constant repetition, to program MY truth into her empty head; that I am the gateway to the gateway."

Sherry is numb, there are no tears, no physical description that tells how she feels. Anger, resentment, disillusion, shame, and pain, she's being hit with so many emotions at once, that she can't respond to any of them.

A few pages down the line, Sherry is hit with information that brings her out of this 'vanilla' state, "It's for sure, all of the tests are back, the world is convinced that the Bible is fake, that God, and therefore, Jesus were all made up. Sherry and the kids must never know about this, then, I would lose all of the Bible's power to control her."

Her body quivers as it tightens, the tears rush out, the usual characteristics that overwhelm her right before she suffers another beating, surface again, but this feeling is different, the fear is missing, it's replaced by an avenging anger.

Ed's battered wife is homicidally mad. An entire life's worth of being pushed around, treated like used toilet paper, and lied to, fill her with strength, a resolve, she has never once felt in her life. And it feels damn good. She's finally ready to fight back.

A long rhythmic thumping that grows louder as it continues, brings a devilish smile to her face, "Ed is coming."

Without haste, this new woman strides over, and confidently, opens the closet. There is a blue light bulb hanging down directly in front of her, the light is meant to provide just enough lighting for the small space and nothing else. "He thought he had it all figured out, that I would be the same puppet that I've always been." She bathes in her newness.

Sherry grabs the square white medicine box, just as she was told, as she's about to close the door something catches her attention. Amidst some meaningless nick-knacks, a few shelves down, is a glass rectangular box with a .45 caliber pistol lying comfortably on velvet padding. Engraved on the outside of the box are the haunting words, 'time's up'.

Sherry snarls. "That's right, Ed, time is up."

"Devin… Sherry!" Battered, and bloodied after rolling his crippled torso down the stairs, Ed's shoulders resume dragging what's left of him towards the kitchen.

"Daddy, are you o.k.?" Mary comes out of her room, to the top of the stairs, to scream her frightened question.

"Go back to your room like I told you, I'm fine."

Ed's within a foot of entering the kitchen, when the basement door swings open towards him, blocking his view of what has come up on the other side. With one hand, he reaches up for the son that he hasn't yet seen lying tied up in the far corner, "Devin, you stopped her in time!"

The first thing he sees come from behind that open door are piles of his documents thrown into the air and softly floating down like a gentle snow. A strong, confident, and extremely pissed off woman with a gun inside of her hand then appears in the mist of the snow.

"If you're looking for Devin, he's over there."

His eyes follow where her gun gripping hand is pointed. He crawls into the kitchen to see his last hope, against the wall, tied up and semi-conscious. "Oh shit."

At gun point, Sherry orders her tormentor to climb himself up into one of the chairs surrounding the kitchen table. Instinctually, Ed crawls towards, then, grabs for his throne. Sherry delivers a powerful kick to his jaw that knocks him off to the side. "Find another one, this is my chair now."

Once his noodle-like body is able to prop itself up in the

next chair, she picks the box of medicine up that she had placed on the top step. Sherry brings it over and places it on the table in front of Ed. Like a drowning man reaching for a life raft, Ed goes for that box. Sherry grabs his waist, flips the gun around, then, pistol whips the 'daylights' out of that hand, sending her husband into a screaming, crying tirade. This ex-junkie has never been this high in her life!

Mrs. Wilson, then, duct tapes the hands of her prisoner behind his back, after which, she tapes his ankles together.

Sherry tauntingly, teasingly, wiggles her rump back into HER throne. "Damn, this chair feels good. Now I see why you liked it so much." She smiles as she leans in to pose a question to the man, who before God promised to always love and protect her. "Geez Ed, I wonder what could have gotten you so sick...," she whispers into his ear, "do you think that maybe it was all my body fluids I have been putting into each one of the meals I prepare for you, day after day after day?" Sherry power-laughs.

Completely serious and completely offended by her acts, with a scornful frown, Ed responses, "That's just sick, why would you do something like that. You don't play with people's food."

"No, but you can with their life, right?!"

Sherry's dreams have come true, she is living every battered woman's fantasy. It is she who has all of the power. She loves this, for the first time in her life she is the abuser, and she can hardly wait to make him feel the same terror and pain that has filled most of the moments of her life. With an aura of arrogance, the gun and her hand rest together on top of her open thigh. "Talk."

He looks down at the barrel, which is pointed directly at his stomach. "I guess I might as well tell you everything, you're going to kill me anyway, aren't you?"

"Yes Ed, slowly, I am. I'm going to savor every moment of your death, Mister God of the home. I know it all, Ed. I'm lucky that there isn't a God, because I don't think that he would forgive me for all the things I am going to do to you."

His dangling head snorts out a giggle causing drooling saliva to run down his chin. "You are such an idiot. You, these stupid kids, your entire life with me has been an experiment that will be marveled at by the rest of the world. You're just a guinea pig."

Sherry peeks over at Devin as he slowly regains consciousness and listens to his father's every word. "What do you mean we were an experiment... guinea pigs?"

"You were my study. As you now know, I am a brilliant psychologist. I've always been fascinated with people like you, people like myself. I wanted to document firsthand, in the flesh, what it would be like to distort the reality of an entire family, and see how long and damaging I could make and keep that reality alive. Everything I've done since I've met you has been calculated," Sherry hates for him to see it, but she can no longer hold back her fractured emotions, as she thinks of all of the years living with this animal has taken from her life.

"Oh, don't cry. The isolation, the systematic beatings I gave you, your total lack of a relationship with your children, which I must say I brilliantly honed and molded since their births', and the greatest of them all, God; your abuse was all for a higher purpose, a greater good. Religion is, or was, as you now well know, the pillar that upheld so much good in this world. What I wanted to do is see how much evil I could create from it. I wanted to see how long, how deeply, the fear of not reaching heaven could keep all of you under my control. Everything was going perfectly until the world found out that the Bible was all a lie...," he doesn't believe that, even in such a crisis, Ed is still thinking manipulative, "but I adjusted. My colleagues, the world, everyone will truly be amazed by the sacrifices we have made."

The rage inside of her won't sit there and listen to this egoistical maniac any longer. Sherry throws her chair aside, grabs him by the throat, and presses the gun into his right eye-socket.

This is one battered woman that finds out that these tough guys that beat them around aren't so tough when the table is turned. Ed commences to crying and begging for his life in his own crazy, unique way. "I'm just like you, Sherry, I was raped as a child also. Don't you see that I was making our worthless lives' meaningful? You were a useless junkie, now doctors from around the world can study what I've done to you and gain priceless psychological knowledge to help other people like us. I know that I've brutalized you all, but eventually, I was going to set you free, so society could monitor how your lives' would turn out. People would root for you as all of you tried to recover what you've lost. Sweetheart, please don't kill me!"

"So you set us up to be society's lab rats, for the rest of our lives'?"

"Yes, exactly! I know that it sounds kind of crazy, right now, but you have to look at the bigger picture here! After I'm gone, and you all are free, your challenge and society's will be to see if you and the kids can be rehabilitated. Could you be saved, could you all become productive people, or would the chains that I bound you in always hold? That's the question."

"So what was the gun for...," she presses the pistol farther into his eye, "times up, right?"

"So many times I thought about killing all of you, but that would have been pointless. The pistol was for me, it was the gift that I was going to give to you and our children. Oh Sherry, you and the children were going to be so happy. I was going to gather us together, as a family, in the family room, and allow the three of you to watch as I blew my head off. It was going to give you closure for everything that's been done to you all. Then the rest of your lives' could begin."

Sherry sees very clearly how manipulative Ed is, intuition immediately tells her that "closure" had nothing to do with his motives. "You sick fuck...," she twists the gun's barrel into his eye, as Ed screams, "you could care less about us. You were going to kill yourself, probably, as the final act to damage us forever. Even if it is you, we would never get over the trauma of seeing your brains all over that room."

Ed's cries morph into laughter. "For once in your stupid life, you're right. As a matter of fact, I was going to turn my back to you all, then shoot, so my bloody brains would land right in your lap, you stupid bitch!"

Sherry cocks her arm back to repeatedly slam the butt of the pistol into Ed's forehead until he dies. BOOM! They both freeze! It's out of their line of sight, but they know someone or something has burst through their home's front door. They can hear heavy breathing and footsteps closing in.

Sherry moves away from Ed, as she points the gun at the strange man that comes running around the corner and into the room. "Don't shoot him, David, thank God, please help me!" Ed is overcome with bliss at the sight of his forgotten brother and the woman right behind him.

"Honey, sweetie, put the gun down. It's o.k."

"Mom?" Faith and David move very slowly, very deliberately. Sherry barely recognizes her mother. Faith looks very different from the last time that she'd seen her.

"Thank God, you're here to save me, this woman has gone mad!"

"How did you find me, Mom?"

David answers for her. "I had a hunch. This is our grandparent's old house. No one had lived in it for years until you guys moved in. I had totally forgotten about it."

Sherry's shaking hand points the gun at David's head as her frenzied voice screams, "You're this animal's brother?!"

"Yes, I'm David Gimmer."

"You're lying, Ed's last name is Wilson."

"That's our mother's maiden name."

Faith steps in front of David. "It's o.k., honey. He's a good man, he won't hurt you."

Devin moans and squirms, once he realizes David and Faith have not noticed him. Ed seizes the opportunity for more manipulation. "Stop her, she's going to kill us. Look at what she's done to me and your poor grandson."

Sherry lunges at Ed, she jabs the open end of the pistol against his temple. "He's a liar. He's treated all of us like lab rats. He's turned our whole lives' into his personal experiment. I'm telling you the truth. He is a sick, sick bastard!"

Due to appearances, Faith and David are increasingly convinced that Ed is the victim here. Faith slowly goes over to begin unraveling the massive amount of tape that her daughter wrapped around Devin. Meanwhile, David tries to relax Sherry and the situation.

"Sherry, I know you don't know me, but through the grace of the Lord, your mother and I will do everything we can to help you, but you have to give us the gun." David extends his open hand towards her.

Untrusting, Sherry points the pistol at his hand. He quickly snatches his hand back to his body. "Stay away from me. There is no real God, no Bible, you're just trying to confuse me. It was all a fake, I saw it. Ed said so, I know about the tests!"

Faith. "It's all a lie, Sherry. The Bible and God are very much real, they always have been."

Ed, still confident through it all, throws out his 'ace'. "Don't believe anything she says, she's a liar. Devin will tell you the truth about everything, won't you, son?"

Devin's father gives him that "please, take my side" stare. The young man stands up, once Faith removes the last piece of tape.

Faith and David silently wait for the 'tiebreaker' to tell them who the truthful one is. First Sherry, then, Ed; their son glances into the eyes of each parent. He can see that each is desperate for him to tell their version of the story.

Devin points down at the huge mass of papers littered mainly by the basement's door. "You'll find everything you need to know right there."

David's eyes shoot down to the floor like he just realized he's standing on hot lava. With everything going on, he and Faith hadn't even noticed the mess of paper.

"I'll kill you for this, Devin. You hear me, I'll kill you!"

Finally something has gone right, when it could have gone

wrong, in Sherry's life. The joy from the weight that Devin has lifted from her tired shoulders breaks her down into a hysterical sob. "Thank you so much, Devin, thank you."

Faith walks across and embraces her long lost daughter, while doing so, she moves Sherry, a few steps farther away from the source of her torment.

Still frightened and timid, Mary has come down the stairs to join everyone. She's clutched to her teddy bear as she gingerly walks across the kitchen, never glancing once at the man who stole her childhood. She joins Faith at her mother's side.

The smile inside of Faith is bigger than the exterior one staring down at her granddaughter for the first time, "Is this my other precious grandbaby?"

Mary turns her beautiful 'baby blues' skyward, searching for acceptance in her mother's hazel eyes. Sherry does two things she was never allowed to do before, she smiles, and then, she embraces her daughter. "Mom, meet Mary."

"Hi sweetie."

Mary locks an arm around her mother's tiny thigh, she and the teddy bear wave to her grandma with her free hand. Her mother's warmth feels so new and so good to her touch.

Feeling Mary, basically for the first time ever, brings about a catalogue of horrible memories that went on in that house. Sherry's withered body collapses against her mother. Faith takes the gun out of her hand and places it on the countertop behind them. "I am so sorry for everything you have had to go through in your life. I was such a horrible mother to you...," Faith lifts Sherry's head off of her shoulder, then, looks her eye to eye, "but now I know God, and through your strength, my strength, and His almighty strength, we are going to make this one of the last unhappy days you ever have. I promise."

"God doesn't love me. I must not be good enough to love. You don't put someone you love through all of the things he has put me through."

"He does love you, sweetie, and I'm going to help you see the purpose and glory for your life."

As Faith and Sherry focus on Sherry, David focuses his attention on the well documented details of his brother's insanity.

Left alone, Devin's anger builds as he stares at the back of his father's head, "He has taken so much from us all."

Just out of reach, to his left, on the countertop, he spots something that, in his eyes, will help make everything much better.

Facing away from his sibling, David is horrified as he peruses the intricacies of Ed's devilishly calculated abuse of his family.

Ed can tell by his brother's body language that things are not looking good for him, but as always, he never gives up when his evil brilliance seems to be cornered. "David, I know things look really, really bad right now, but think of this like a war. People have to die for the greater good. As you'll read, that's what I was trying to do, something good. Do you know how many people will benefit from the unique viewpoint of abuse that I have provided? Do you realize how much can be learned through our sacrifice? Isn't that what serving God is all about, sacrificing?"

David doesn't have the stomach to look at him. "Edward, how could you? Your own family, you traded away the happy and goodness of their lives', so you could conduct a study?"

Offended by the negative tone of his statement, Ed 'schools' his older brother. "Yes, that's exactly what I did. And all of my research will be well rewarded when lives are changed all around the world. I sold my soul to God."

David. "That doesn't make sense. You didn't do this for God. He would never want you to do something like this."

"Look at how much I gave up to live this life. I could have had riches and a beautiful family, but that would not have helped the world. I gave up so much, so everyone can better understand how to help abused women and children. This was my calling. Because of my love for the world, I had to keep my own family buried. I was going to give them their life back, so they could begin their road to recover on the day I decided to go to heaven." The strength of the sickness coursing through Ed's body and mind returns, the corners of his mouth rise then fall rapidly as he fights back the pain.

Sherry screams. "If there is a heaven, you're never going there. You're going to rot in hell!"

"Oh, sorry my dear, that's never going to happen. You see, this entire time, all of these years, that I have enjoyed raping you...," as best he can, he smiles sweetly at Mary, "and raping you, cutie...," everyone's eyes turn away from him and his demonic justifications, they're disgusted by everything that he is, "I have always known the power of our almighty Father. I've never even thought about believing a word of that 'Bible Hoax' junk. Our Father - hallelujah! - and his love - amen! - have always been here, they never left me. And because of his undying, unwavering love for even those how are wife beating, wife raping, incest hungry monsters; as you all like to think of me, I'll still be forgiven as long as I take Christ as my Lord and Savior and repent for my sins. So guess what? Ed Wilson, Gimmer, monster, whatever you wanta call me WILL be in heaven. You know what, I'll do it now, Lord, I take Christ-"

Ed lets out a blood curdling scream which regains everyone's full attention.

He'll never get that chance for salvation, Devin makes sure of that. Having previously gained his weapon from a countertop knife rack, while everyone was occupied, from the side, Devin plunges, then, twists the same serrated knife that Ed stopped Sherry from ending her life with, into his heart. His life is over within seconds.

For the next few moments, bodies are as still as the air, until a gratified smirk blooms across Sherry's face.

Void of all feeling, Devin sits down on the floor Indian-style. He calmly and innocently asks, "So what do we do now?"

CHAPTER EIGHTEEN

From a street pharmacist point of view, business could not be going any better for Melvin. The cash is coming in faster than he can spend it. There are no law enforcement divisions of any kind breathing down he and the crew's necks, they're sure of this because Stamp has two well positioned 'eyes' supplementing their civil servant incomes by keeping them abreast of any and all new dangers.

Maybe it's the fear that others have of pressing their luck, maybe it's just not the time, or maybe it's how the team has strategically rearranged their men, whatever it is, that situation he, Stamp, and Dane had hoped would be a one time thing, has so far turned out to be just that. With all of the violence running rampant throughout inner city neighborhoods nationwide, somehow they manage to physically stay clear of it.

In the early evening, out in the parking lot of the local 'barberhoodshop' that serves as today's meeting ground for the cash exchange from one of the eight crackhouses that Melvin controls, a profusely sweating young man in a smoking, sputtering Cadillac Deville pulls up next to him. "What up Mel? Man, can you believe that it is only February? It's hot than a bitch out here, I hate to see what July and August is gon feel like."

Melvin glances over at a small section of grass separating the sidewalk and the street. "I know, everybody is trippin' off how this crazy weather done turned the grass bright red."

"Yup, one of them religious cats on the radio said that the grass is red because this is becoming hell on earth."

Junior's boss laughs, "Yeah whatever, that's what you get for listening to that crap...," Melvin eyeballs the vehicle his worker arrived in, "damn Junior, I said drive a car that will blend in with everyone else when we do this...," he frowns at the shaking, sputtering mess that his money paid for, while fanning the smoke from his eyes, "I know that there is a lot of garbage rollin' around town, but you went to the extreme, don't you think?"

Junior, whose car does not have a working air conditioner, pours an entire bottle of chilled water over his head. "Naw, this joints cool, it don't run as bad as it looks."

"Everything straight over at the trap?"

Junior looks around, then, hurriedly hands his boss a fully loaded duffel bag as he responses, "Yup... ain't no recession in our business, baby. With the economy going to shit, more and more people are turning to fiends eachday. Shit, I almost had to pack two bags... Aw snap, bruh, I almost forgot..."

"What?"

"I thought you told me your pops was dead... because if he is, there is some old, dirty ass crack fiend going around hallucinating that he's your father."

Melvin keeps his demeanor calm, but inside, it's a different story, "What are you talking about, who told you that?"

"He did, dude comes up to the spot three or four times a day, one of the fellas overheard him bragging to some other junkie about all this money his son, Melvin Jenkins, be making."

"Really... you call me immediately the next time you see this guy, and keep him there for me. Don't serve him na'thin, either. I'll be right over."

"Shit, you might as well come back to the trap with me right now, because he'll prob'ly be there. Dog, that crack has got its hooks into him real, real deep."

"Just call me."

Melvin peels off. Butterflies bump into one another as they fly around inside his stomach, his cell phone can't ring fast enough. Melvin hopes deeply that it is him; he's waited for this reunion for a long time. He may finally get to come face to face with the man that was supposed to play catch with him, teach him about the 'birds and the bees', take him fishing, the man whose job it was to make sure that he steers clear of a life like this. "Wow, please be him. We have so much to catch up on."

Junior was right, not even an hour goes by before Melvin gets the call.

From atop the rickety porch he nervously paces and twitches on, Dad smiles as he sees Melvin's face inside the shiny new Mercedes coupe parking in front of the house. "That must be my boy." He says with drugged up pride.

"So Mel really is your son, I figured that you were just having fiend dreams." Says Junior, as he dabs a wet washcloth across his forehead and passes the time waiting for Melvin's arrival by playing dominoes on the porch's edge with one of his co-hustlers.

Melvin comes from around the car dressed in urban wear's finest linens.

"Look at you… my son, walking up here clean as a whistle, got all that gold on, but ya shining like a diamond, baby." Dad animates with the best shuckin' and jivin' antics that a broken down, twenty plus years, drug addict can muster up.

Junior and his friend bust up laughing as they watch the show.

Son looks father over from head to toe. They're the same height; Melvin's body is more filled out, however. Through his nappy, long, sweat filled beard and despite his ball cap, feelings stir as Melvin sees their facial resemblance.

As he approaches, Me-ma's grandson can't believe this man is standing there, looking at him with such happiness on his face, like he's some proud father ready to hug his son after he's just been handed his college diploma.

Melvin forces the ends of his lips upward as best he can. "What's up man? So you're my father, huh?"

"It's me, baby!"

Dear old Dad reaches out for a hug. His stench, heightened by the heat, repulses Melvin, who bypasses his affection by turning the other way and giving orders to his employees. "Hey, I want y'all ta leave me and my pops alone for a while, is anybody else in the house?"

Junior speaks up, "Naw, but Reese and Kevin are outside in the back doing patrol."

"Tell them I want all of y'all to leave for a while. I'll call ya when it's time to come back."

"Alright bruh, hey… are you sure you're cool?" Junior quizzes as he senses an eerie vibe between Dad and Melvin.

"I couldn't be better…," Melvin looks at Junior with that smile, "everything is perfect."

The guys do as they are told and head around to the side of the house to inform the others.

"Come on in, Dad." Melvin warmly puts his hand on the shoulder of his father's tattered t-shirt, opens the screen door, and guides him inside the crack house.

The overwhelming smell of this long lost man sickens Melvin's stomach. They walk right past the two sofas and the small television that is propped up on top of a crate in the living room and head straight into the kitchen.

Melvin notices his father's mouth starting to salivate, on account of the kilo of powder cocaine on the counter next to the stove waiting to be processed.

Dad, "I'm so glad to see that you're doing so well for yourself, my boy. I know I haven't been there for you much-"

That last word wipes the grin off of Melvin's face, he fights the urge to yell aloud, "Much... what the hell are you talking about, you've never been there one day of my life for me!" They step out of the kitchen and into a bedroom that is empty except for a small, dirty mattress along the far wall, and a plastic crate next to the door.

"Son, I hope you know that I always kept you in my thoughts and prayers."

"Really, that's good, go ahead and have a seat, let's sit and catch up."

As Dad makes his way over to the bed, Melvin grabs the crate and makes it his stool, right in front of the room's only escape, which he closes behind him. "I just wanta thank you for coming back into my life, Dad...," he smiles that smile, "Now I can have some closure."

While Melvin digs through his pockets looking for something, Dad, with jitters, surveys the seclusion of the boarded up, isolated room. "Hey Mel, do you, I'm kind of embarrassed to ask you this, but-"

"Say no more, I already know what you want, Pops. I got you." From the pocket of his jeans, Melvin pulls out a zip-lock bag filled with rock cocaine.

Dad's face lights up, his jumpy legs express his demonic lust. "That's what I'm talkin' 'bout, dem young boys said they couldn't give me na'thin till you got here. I been waitin' on that."

Melvin raises the bag next to his face, and smiles, "You love this shit, don't you? So do I. It's a trip how this white bag has become the center of both our lives... We'll do some crazzzy ass thangs, because of this, won't we?"

Son walks over showcasing that smile. "I even got the pipe for ya, Dad. You're gonna love this, I got it especially for you. This coke is 99% pure, baby. Here, let me have the honor." He heats the pipe, which bubbles up the crack, as the smoker's anticipation grows.

"Thanks son."

Dad's boy leaves the crack-sack beside him, returns to his

crate across the room and, casually, leans back against the door as he watches Dad do the very act that took him away all those years ago.

Melvin waits until Dad is good and high, "So pops… where have you been my whole life?" He pauses for an answer, but can't wait, "Even through your filthy ass beard and dry cracked out skin, I can see myself. Tell me, Dad, how do you live in there, knowing that you abandoned your reflection?" It takes all of Melvin's might, to remain calm and appear neutral through each of those words.

Dad doesn't answer immediately, but after he exhales from another huge hit, "Mel, if I could take back one regret in my life, it would be leaving you, but hey, your grandmother took real good care of you for me. I prayed for that… Aw wow, you was right, this is some good shit!"

The smile is gone. Melvin leans forward, from across the room, he gazes right into Dad's bulging red, bugged out eyes. "Let me set the rules for you. One, I don't want to hear anything about any bullshit praying that your strung-out ass did on my behalf. And two, don't you ever mention my mom again."

Dad giggles. "I didn't say anything about your Mom, I said your grandma, boy."

Melvin's voice flies into a rage. "My Me-ma was my mom! You and that overdosed bitch wasn't never no parents to me!"

Dad is silent, fear pushes against his euphoria. He humbly responses, "Hey, your right, Melvin, I apologize. So, I'm just gonna go ahead and get out of here, I see that I'm beginning to upset you." Dad stands, puts the large bag of crack in his pocket, then, gingerly walks towards Melvin, fully expecting him to step aside and free him to leave.

Melvin has other plans, which he makes very clear. "Look at you… As scared as you are, you still made sure to tuck that sack away, didn't you? Let me chill out, my bad, Dad…," as his 'old man' gets to within a couple of steps, Melvin reaches behind his back, out comes a chrome nine millimeter gun that freezes Dad right where he stands, "I don't mean to scare you. My anger gets the best of me sometimes. So, go ahead back over there, pull that bag out of your pocket, and you can keep smoking while we talk some more."

Dad knows he's in deep trouble. To no avail, he tries to hide his blubbering on his way back to the mattress.

The smile is back. "Start smokin', I wanta see firsthand what is so good, that it could make you and my mom throw me away like trash. We'll sit here all night if it takes, but you're going to smoke up that whole bag."

Dad looks down at the large sack, he estimates that there must be at least ten rocks of pure crack inside. For the first time in twenty plus years, Dad looks at cocaine and wants no part of it. "I can't smoke all of this, I'll o.d."

"That's a chance I'm willing to take. I figure you both left me for dead, so it's only fitting that I return the favor to you, if you can't finish it. But if you do finish, you're free to go, but you better not ever come around here again. Or I'll kill you next time."

Tens of minutes pass. Dad has been chain smoking rock after rock. His eyes loosely flash from saucer sized to mere slivers. He and Melvin stare into their reflection.

"Do you know God has been watching you, Melvin…," Dad frowns, but at the same time giggles, "He knows that you have been a very bad boy."

"I guess you haven't heard you stupid junkie, there is no God, but if there was, He damn sure wouldn't choose you to be his voice to me."

"You just don't understand; I am the perfect person for God to pick. He's coming back, Melvin. If you look beyond your eyes, you'll see that?"

Melvin merely laughs at him. "You know, you are an awesome representative of just how much believing in God can do for a person. What, now God's down to having only crackheads believe him?"

"Melvin, he loves you. He's been trying to show you that."

"Man, I see why we have this whole neighborhood locked up, that smoke got you talkin' real silly. Go ahead, smoke some more." Melvin orders as he playfully waves the gun in the direction of his hostage's head.

"You had such a good life going for you. You were only poor financially, but your day was coming. You were so smart, so focused, but you let doubt and fears change your path, but God is inviting you back."

Son briefly reflects on his past life; his pride in the great grades he worked extremely hard for, how he used to aspire to be different and reach higher than the young men who are now his employees and adversaries, how he swore to himself that he would not end up in this dead end lifestyle, but here he sits.

Dad can no longer hold himself up. He falls over onto his side.

Melvin knows that time is running out for him to get everything off of his chest, "Die, I want to watch you die. You killed me, but you didn't get to see it…," he says each word with added emphasis, "but thank God I get to see your death."

Melvin thinks, "See if he has any i.d." He starts going through his defenseless father's pockets, "Don't move, keep smoking, junkie."

At first, he doesn't even notice it. Melvin speeds through every pocket his father has, he lays everything out on the wooden floor. He scans over the small heap, what he sees causes his eyes to bug out like it is he who is on crack. Shocked words explode out of Melvin's mouth, "What the hell is this? You killed him?"

Amongst the overused tissues, cigarettes, and empty zip-lock bags, are six ripped bills of money. Melvin's fanged teeth snarl at Dad, fire rages through his body. "You killed that kid, didn't you?"

Melvin could care less about the other three lives taken the day he witnessed that home being broken into, Melvin's focus is on what was done to Zane.

Frightened, "I didn't kill nobody, Melvin, I swear!"

His mind goes back to that day, what Melvin finds there startles him. "You walked right by me, didn't you?"

Dad is violently pulled up to his feet. Melvin didn't care at all about Zane's death before, but now it crushes him. The fact that the person he hates most in the world is the odds on suspect is just icing on the cake. "He was just a baby."

One punch onto the bridge of Dad's nose breaks it. The second shot across his jaw splatters blood onto the wall. "You did the same thing to him that you did to me!"

"Melvin, let me explain...," he folds up at the sight of Melvin's drawn back fist, "it was my partner. I came in the front side, he came in through the back window. He got what he could from the adults, he saw me fighting with the kid over the money, that's when he shot him. That's the truth, I'm not lying."

"No, that's too easy. You prob'ly switched the story around, you were the one who killed him."

"You're right, Melvin. I did play a role in his death, but so did you."

"I've never done anything to that kid."

Dad is no longer scared. "No, na'thin, you just sold his mother death, day after day. Everything that boy should have had in a mother was taken from him because of what you and your buddies sold to her. You profit off another person's addicts. My friend that killed Zane was just the result of the choices you have made."

The truth hurts. He puts the gun to his father's head with one hand, and with the other, forces the pipe back up to his lips. A part of Melvin wants to stop what he is doing, but that part is not in control. Melvin screams at his only living parent, "No more talking. Hold dis pipe, you better smoke it. You only have a couple of more, do it!"

Upon the completion of another huge rock, white foamy saliva oozes from the corners of the estranged biological's mouth as the man's intimate knowledge mystifies his son, "Remember when you looked at that picture of God's son? You felt Jesus, you were Him, but you chose-" Dad's words are cut off by the start of a violent seizure.

Dad falls on his side onto the mattress. "How do you know that? No one was there?"

Indifferent to his father's trauma, Melvin goes back at him for answers. He grabs and shakes Dad by the collar of his thrift store shirt, "How do you know that? Answer me!?"

"He tried to save you, son. He… loves-" the convulsions intensify, as Dad's breathing stops.

He lets go, Melvin's chest heaves deeply, but he weeps only for himself, as his father passes on. "How did he know, how'd he know what I've been through?"

ESPN just finished airing a wonderfully moving piece on him. His loyal fans send him supportive letters daily. His coaches and teammates visit every so often, they rave to the press about the calm they see in him. Days before his release, Mitch Law is quoted as saying, "It's hard to explain. There's just an undeniable glow, a peace he carries around now."

Three months ago, Bryant Michaels dreamt.

He's nervous. His feet stand on nothing. There is the brightest of bright lights all around him, yet somehow it does not blind him. He looks down for his body, it is not there. He searches for his hands, but he can't find them. All he has is the feeling of himself. Ricky appears next to him, though Bryant can not see him, "Are you ready, Bryant?"

"Ready for what?"

"It's your time… tell God why you should be allowed into his kingdom. Look out at Him, tell him about how you walked out your faith in his Word."

The Lord is before him, right there for him to see, but Bryant cannot force himself to look up into heaven. His thoughts search for reasons, excuses, but he is absent of clever ideas. Only the truth remains.

God speaks. "I tried so many times to convince you to come to me. I put the right people and situations around you, but you chose to rebuke them all. Why?"

Bryant turns to Ricky for help. He's trilled that he can now see his flesh. Instantly, Ricky's slightly defined fanged teeth lengthen by six inches and become death traps. Ricky's eyes redden and melt down his face, "Tell him, Bryant. Pretend now. I dare you!"

Bryant's shut eyelids burst apart! He is short of breath, his lungs can't gulp air quick enough. He rolls off of the bed, not caring about the impact he will suffer against the hard cement floor. All he wants is to be away from that bed, so he crawls to the far wall.

Inside his solitary box, safe now, his head begins to calm, but he continues to stare at that bed like he expects it to do something. His memory replays portions of the dream he's retained.

He deeply exhales as he shakes the tension from his arms. "Damn! That was a crazy ass dream. This place has got me trippin'. Keep it together, Bryant, keep it together, you're almost out of here."

Tabloid tidbits leak out of the prison walls, and o' how they have got people talking. According to anonymous sources, Bryant 'Flight' Michaels has been spotted reading the Bible quite often inside the walls that keep him.

'The Good Book' has become his constant companion during the ladder part of his cushy, six month, minimum security sentence on a plea bargained conviction of third degree assault charges.

Facing skyward, Bryant Michaels lays comfortably on his plush queen sized bed, inside his private cell, serving out the remaining minutes on the last day of his sentence by soaking in scriptures from the Word.

The sound of his twenty five inch television whispers down from its harnessed perch, caddie-cornered with the ceiling and two walls.

Bryant is so engrossed in his reading that he doesn't hear the breaking CNN report about the rising crisis between America and the entire Middle East.

"Bryant, Bryant, it's good to see you out. Are we to assume, judging by that Bible inside your hand, that you're a religious man now? Hey Bryant, after everything you've said about God, are you now one of those who still believes God is real? Will you please speak with us, Mr. Michaels?" Upon his release, 'Flight' Michaels is besieged by these types of questions from the hundreds of reporters waiting for him as he exits the prison's gate and walks towards his awaiting stretch Rolls Royce SUV.

Guarded from the media by his bodyguards and his legion of lawyers, Michaels says nothing, but his lead lawyer, without consultation with Bryant, just before his release issued a brief statement just outside of the prison's fifteen foot tall gate. "Mr. Michaels will hold a press conference sometime soon, but he will not be taking any questions today, but I will tell you that Mr. Michaels is an intelligent man, so he is not crazy. In my opinion, I'm sure that he does not still believe there's a God, come on, let's be real...," some in attendance giggle at the silliness of such a ludicrous thought, "now I'm sure he does enjoy reading about the values and morals that the Bible can bring to our lives', as do I. Hey, it may not be real, but it's still a heck of a good read. Thank you. No farther questions."

CHAPTER NINETEEN

He walks in alone. Except for his maid, all of his employees and acquaintances are gone, Bryant is alone. "Welcome home Mr. Michaels, I hope everything just how always you liked it." Migaila says through her limited command of the English language.

"Thank you Migaila, I'm sure it is. It's good to be back."

"May I take bag, its crazy this hot, hot weather Mr. Michaels, isn't it?" She follows him through the grand foyer as he heads towards his all-glass elevator.

"It's just some weird weather pattern, God willing, I'm sure it will cool down soon."

Migaila glances at him 'weirdly' due to his mention of God. Enthusiastically, yet pessimistically, she responds. "I don't know, hot, hot over whole world, and very dry. Its no rained in twenty days. The grass looks funny."

"Yeah, red is my favorite color."

"Mine too, oh, almost forget…, she reaches into the front pouch of her cleaning cape, "yesterday when here to work, this envelope was at the gates."

"Thank you, Migaila."

Bryant doesn't open the sealed envelope until he boards his

private elevator that will open directly into his bedroom. "It's from Stacy."

While unfolding the single sheet of notebook paper, he takes a deep breath to steady himself before reading the short, hand written paragraph.

"Dear Bryant, first of all, I want you to know that I have forgiven you, and so does Ricky. We happily do. We are both doing well, and so is the baby. He will be born in a few days just in case you care. The reason for this note is I have returned the entire fifteen million you gave to me in the divorce to your bank account. Thank you for your kindness. Myself and Ricky will always love you and pray for you...," her next words overwhelm him, "because we know that God's heart will beat inside of you."

Bryant can't believe their unconditional love for him, he lays face up on top of his bed's black silk sheets. To feel that unselfish, uncompromising love, from them, despite what he did to them both, is too much for him to calmly take in. He knows that if the shoe were on the other foot, he may not have forgiven Ricky are what he did; ever.

Bryant Michaels wants to feel love like that. He knows that their love is not a 'normal' love; it's a God kind of love.

It has been building, for the first time in his life, a true desire blossoms in his heart for what's beyond his eyes.

Fresh, unexpected movement startles him! Bryant hears mechanical noise coming from the slender box camouflaged into the foot of his bed. The slide door concealing his thirty two inch, one fourth inch wide television comes to life. "Folks if you would like to come to our church...," the volume rises right along with the screen.

"Did I hit the button?" It only takes a second for his eyes to locate the television's remote control. Migaila always puts it on top of the lampstand next to the bed. "There it is, way over there. So how did the television come on?" The God in him whispers the answer, "You already know."

He's blessed to watch a low budget television ad with Faith standing in front of an all-white background. "Come learn about the one and only living God in one of the few public churches that you still can. Don't continue to be fooled by a world that throws its creator away like garbage; get curious about the truth, because it will set you free!"

"That's the lady, I listened to that one day."

For the first time in his life, Bryant Michaels values that freedom. He wants to chase it! Finally, he has no ulterior motives; this isn't about Stacy, this isn't about money or fame. His spirit overpowers his flesh.

A new spirit is budding inside of his core, he can feel himself wanting more than this world can offer, and it does not scare him, he's not worried about what others will think, he does not worry about what he, himself, may think. His mind has made a firm decision.

He thinks about all of the knowledge and understanding he has gained from the Bible, he knows that it's time. "I'm so sorry, Father, for what I have done to you, what I have said. Before, I never took the time to get to know you. I pushed you aside so many times, when you did nothing but place people in my life to love me. I spit on your very name... and still you love me." Bryant's emotions overrun him. He has that indescribable peace that only accepting the Lord as the head of your life can provide.

Bryant didn't mean or plan for any of this to happen. His lawyer was accurate, he had plenty of time on his hands, so he decided what the heck, "I'll read the book that two of the most important people in my life tried for years to get me to read, just to see what all of the hoopla is about." He remembers when he first started reading it, how the tension was off his shoulders because he didn't go into reading the book with any expectations or pressure, "I'll just do it for fun, I got nothing else to do."

But what began to happen during that chance meeting has

lead up to this very moment, "I feel you taking root in me...," Bryant is so zoned into reality now, "God, you are real."

His spirit tells him to get as low as possible, without thought he rolls off of the bed and onto the floor. It is an honor for him to feel like he is at Jesus' feet, "Thank you for not abandoning me, Father. I don't know why you didn't, but you never left me. Thank you, Jesus. I accept you, and I love you. I can't do this without you!"

It is the middle of the night, while most of America is sleeping the night away, the leader of the free world is slumped on the sofa inside her dimly lit Oval Office, half awake and all of the way drunk. "I want them all dead. Those sons of a bitch gassed my troops. They think... because I'm a woman I won't do it." Thames takes another swig from her Vodka bottle, her alcoholic way of steadying her drunken thoughts and slurred speech.

"They just can't accept that it was a dream. O.k. then...," she pops up to vertical, "I'll wake them up, I'll erase them all. They want to test my strength; I'll sledgehammer the entire region, including Israel, those bastard traitors."

The same evening that Bryant goes home, President Thames delivers the most frightening address the world has ever heard. "Citizens of the United States and across the globe, today our enemies, who lately have been aided and abetted by Israel, have for the second straight day killed dozens of American and British troops by use of chemical warfare. Early this afternoon, I went before Congress and asked for their support for our possible use of nuclear weapons to end this evil massacre. An emergency vote was held, and overwhelmingly, myself and our troops were supported. So to our aggressors, I am issuing, in no uncertain terms, a warning to those who oppose our way of life. Our troops will press on, if anymore weapons of this sort are used against American and British military personnel again... like water, bombs will rain down upon your head."

Unrelenting, the fiery Israeli Prime Minister counters

President Thames' dire forecast. "First off, let me start by saying that Israel has never aided or abetted the war against America. However, if America were invaded, as our brother's soil has been, with a foreign army attempting to take over United States soil, the President would stop at nothing to run them out. So I say to my brothers here in Israel and abroad, be strong. This day has been prophesied, and that very day may be upon us."

As the chemical warfare continues, the proper equipment and bio-suits get to the troops, ending the growing death tally. Though this brings great comfort to those in Congress and to people worldwide, it is of little comfort to Thames.

The House and Senate hold long debates once the President goes before them and asks for permission to launch at a moments notice without their final o.k.

For the moment, China is the glue that holds the world together. China, the only superpower with the long range nuclear capabilities to reach mainland U.S.A, makes it clear that if the United States drops its bombs, "Then America will have destroyed itself as well."

With America's 'Star Wars' like nuclear defense shield still not anywhere close to being reliable, Thames doesn't take the chance that the Chinese aren't serious. She figures, "Our bombs would simply pass each other. What's the purpose of obliterating other nations if you are not going to be around to enjoy your work?"

The world waits anxiously each passing day, at times, they are optimistic a viable resolution will be reached, other days, they allow news reports to fill their thoughts with utter doom. Now that the situation has grown eminently dire, the citizens of America focus great attention to what's going on in Washington.

One week later, President Nicole Cecilia Thames is still buried in the stillness of her now daily drunken life. She knows that today could be the day she forever leaves her mark on the history of mankind. Thames, with a half-full glass in her left hand, doesn't notice her precious intoxicant trickling onto the Oval Office's plush carpeting, in response to her bouncing toes.

She stares out at the remaining beauty the orchards and different roses possess in the White House's wilting Rose Garden.

"We've got it, we've got it!" Chief of Staff, Jon Wilhelm shouts as he runs down the White House corridor towards the Oval Office. He burst through the double doors, inside the stench of liquor immediately announces its dominance.

Thames attempts to calmly and steadily walk back to her desk, now is not a good time for any tipsy stumbles that may alert Wilhelm to the fact that she is not in a good frame of mind. Her drunken body nails it perfectly.

Euphoric on the inside, but collected as mail on the outside, President Thames hopes that Wilhelm has exactly what she wants, "Do we have them?"

"We do."

"You've found the third launch site?"

"The third one is the closest. We'll have over a hundred fighter jets in place ready to give their life to disable all of China's facilities and destroy anything that comes into the sky. We know all of the sites the Chinese can launch from, our men can be there and ready in a few days. We'll knock them all down while they're still over Chinese land and water."

The most devilish smile that could ever come to a person's face befalls hers'. "You're sure of this?"

"Yes, absolutely." Jon shows her the classified specifics on the laptop computer he's brought in. "See there? Look at how everything will time out if Congress allows us to do it in the next few days."

"Terrific."

"Madam President, we still need more time to get our troops out of the region."

"We've scaled back our forces, greatly, over the last couple of months."

Jon can't believe how coldly her words come out, he chooses to make a stand for America's sons and daughters. "So are you saying to hell with the several thousand soldiers left over there?"

Thames does not immediately answer with words, she allows her silent stare to shout her answer to him. "If we move our troops that will tip the Chinese off to what we are doing… Now I need you to leave me alone."

As Wilhelm's chattering knees exit the room, America's top elected official goes back to staring out at the God-made flowers in the garden. She repeats over and over to herself, "This is the right thing to do for America. The world will be a better place if we don't have to deal with this problem anymore. They can do all of the protesting that they want, I know what's best for everybody. Of course, people are going to be upset at first, but over time they will see the good that I've done for the world." Her words try desperately to convince the pit of her stomach to believe them.

It hasn't been but one month since the most terrible chapter of Sherry's terrible life has ended. Her mind has a long way to go, but it is already beginning to climb out of its battered shell. Her mother slash pastor ministers to her constantly, building the bond that they never had.

They often go and sit in Faith's prayer room, just the three of them: Faith, Sherry, and the gospel. "Just as our Father did with me, Sherry, our Father has allowed you to go through extreme trials and tribulations, so when you come out of it, like you are doing now, you will be at your strongest to accept and appreciate the massive amount of blessings that you will receive. I'm not sure what His plans are exactly for you, but I know that he has great things in store. Put your complete faith and trust in him, and he will show you the way to healing everything that was done against you."

Sherry does just what her mother suggests, but Satan battles her every step of her way. He does what he always does, the only thing he can do, he targets her self-esteem, her self-worth, he tries to put doubts and fears into her head, but it's not working. She doesn't listen to the lies preached in this new world that she is reacclimating herself to. She puts the Lord's armor on and it protects her. Our Father stays on her mind night and day, he loves her deeply.

Victimized survivors like her hold a special place within Him.

Sherry's mind drifts, at times, curious about the carnal side of this new world. Satan tries to plant seeds that maybe this world does hold the answers for her to get over her deeply troubled past. "Just try some crystal again, remember how good it used to make you feel, it'll make you forget all about Ed, just do a little bit, you won't get hooked again." Every time she thinks about drifting, God pulls her in closer. The Holy Spirit brings wisdom to her, "The devil is trying to do the same things to you that Ed did. They both kept you in bondage… They both distort my words and fill your head with things that aren't true… They both want to destroy your life, if you listen to Satan, than Ed wins."

That revelation motives her daily, "No way will I ever let that happen again."

Slowly, Sherry's rebuilding all of her broken family bonds through the power of her newly released Christianity. "Who redeems your life from the pit and crowns you with love and compassion," she doesn't just read scriptures in the Bible, she Re-READS those scriptures, and she meditates on them until they beat in her heart. Sherry won't stop until she reaches God's promise of 'life in abundance, to the full, until it overflows'.

The power of love is the greatest and strongest power that God has given us. That is no more evident than today when Bryant 'Flight' Michaels boldly stands in front of a room full of reporters and cameras and steps up to the podium inside of the media room at his team's practice facilities.

"Greetings everyone, thank you all for coming today, the words that I, wholeheartedly, will speak to the world today, are different than what I would have said a few days ago. First off, I would like to express my great remorse to Ricky Walters for the violent, despicable act that I committed against him. Ricky, I hope that you are watching (yes, he and Stacy are watching from their home) me speak these words; my heart has truly changed due in part to the love borne out of the friendship that you always gave to me. You and your beautiful wife tried over and over again to show me what's truly lasting in this world, instead of what is temporary, but I wouldn't listen because I was too afraid to change and too settled in my bad beliefs. I see now that God was working through the two of you for my behalf.

"I, Bryant Michaels, announce to the world, for all eyes to see, and all ears to hear, that there has been a change in my heart, in my soul, and in my mind…," Bryant's voice slows to emphasize each word, "I accept, I believe, and I have confident faith, in the very God that I once believed didn't exist, that I may have helped others to believe didn't exist." A hushed awe comes over those in attendance, the mouths' of the reporters salivate, they came expecting to hear just another athlete's boring get out of jail speech, but they are getting so much more.

"Ricky, my friend, I am so happy for you and Stacy, God has given you each a great blessing; each other. The two of you are under God's covenant, so I know your relationship will always be full of love. Congratulations on your marriage and the impending birth of your beautiful child, Stacy. I wish you, Ricky, and your child, all of the happiness God has in store for each of you. Stacy Stunning; you are truly someone special."

Both she and Ricky are moved by Bryant's words, they are so proud of him. They can tell that his heart is behind his words, not his ego or some other motive. Stacy's voice crackles, "Ricky, this isn't like before. Bryant truly accepts God. I can feel it, he has faith!"

Bryant wipes his eyes, before continuing, "Part of the path that I walked that's lead me to my salvation, I owe to your loving relationship with me. The two of you have been a rare commodity in my life, you were true friends, when all the rest of them were just my cheering section. Ricky, you once told me that 'the only thing I'm missing in life is letting go of me, so that I could trust in

Him', I have finally for the first time in my life done that. And I must thank God for accepting my repentance and my sorrow for the shameful, blasphemous path that I lead myself down. And for all of you who were in anyway influenced by my decisions, continue to be influenced now, as I return for the every first time into the loving will of our Father. He still loves each of you, and He wants you back. God loves you."

Through the flesh of a lost soul, a powerful demon enters the room.

"In jail, I began to casually read the Bible, and I soon began to understand what this life is all about, and even though I continued to fight the truth, God continued to fight for me. He told me to guard myself against these disbelieving times that we're living in right now."

Tears begin to form in Bryant's eyes, "We just don't see it, do we? This is about slavery. The slavery that this world has us bound in because we choose it over faith in God. So many people are so deeply trapped in it that they'll never believe any differently until it is too late. The Lord warned us that these evil days would come, that people would believe more in their 'sight' than their faith in Him. To believe in this world is death, to have faith in God is life. Well today, and forever more; I choose life! Thank you, Jesus."

"Shut your fucking mouth, you're a liar!" Inspired and 'pushed' by the angels of hell, Tom Bracken, from the third row leaps over and between his colleagues, hell bent on stopping the power coming out of Bryant's mouth. Satan knows the impact that Bryant's faith could have on the world.

Chaos and bedlam break out! Tom tackles Bryant, just before he is tackled by others. He and Tom are face to face, eye to eye. Bryant sees the open gates of hell in his eyes.

Tom, "This won't work, Bryant. He has them!" Five have sprung to Bryant's aid, but Tom is not his fifty-one-year-old self, there is an extra power teeming through him. He flings them off just enough to lift up his shirt and grab the knife concealed in its waist high sleeve. Gripped by ten strong fingers, Tom cocks the blade behind his head, "He has them!," which enables him to get all of his 220 pounds behind his strike.

Bryant yells the one word that gives him the single minded steadiness needed to execute the perfect catch of Tom's two powerful wrists, "Jesus!"

Two policemen finally get through, they snatch the man off of Bryant, he's thrown face first onto the ground and handcuffed. The room is totally abuzz as Tom Bracken is hauled off to jail.

The Holy Spirit instructs, "Don't give them time to think…," Bryant hops to his feet, shakes himself off quickly, and reestablishes his command at the podium, as if little has just occurred, "as I was saying, before I was rudely interrupted, if we walk in love, then we will have life… and the killings, and the hate, and the general meanness that plagues our world will decrease; all because we got back to putting God first…," like Faith's sermon, Bryant ends with what will become the unofficial rallying cry for Christians worldwide, "God is real, and He is here, right now!"

—————— CHAPTER TWENTY ——————

Did you know that only God creates love that will last forever?

The young lady that Dane once thought nothing of, that he disrespected like all of the others, the one that bought him that prayer book; well just yesterday, as fate would have it, they re-met outside a local convenience store.

When he spoke to her, she was totally prepared to be cordial, then, send him on his arrogant way, but when he spoke this time around there was a difference. Gone was his bravado, all of his fowl-talk, he spoke so respectfully, so humbly, that once they left that convenience store to go for a walk around an old abandoned athletic track behind one of the project's elementary schools, and he began to speak of his journey and his life falling in line with the Word of God; she didn't stand a chance. She was completely smitten by him.

How blessed is Dane? Now that he has given himself to the Throne, God gives him his first of an abundance of blessings. His blessing has come in the form of his future wife and mother of his children. *Ask any Christian and I bet they could tell you about the "welcome to the club" huge blessing that God gave them soon after or right after they gave their life to him.*

Drug profits brought Dane a measure of happiness, even if

only for a season, but now he is beginning to experience joy, and joy lasts forever. Our Father has so much more in store for Dane.

Suspended from the league for the entire season, Bryant Michaels has been crisscrossing the country for a week doing all of the public relations and endorsement work that God would have him to do.

His staff has been pleading with him to slow down, if even for a little bit, but he can't. "God has been talking to me, so strongly, he's told me that I have much work to do, and I need to do it quickly."

By jet, having just arrived back in town, Bryant goes straight to his next speaking engagement, his third today. It is down at a local elementary school in the downtrodden 'Melvin' side of Anytown, mere blocks away from the church that he now attends with the Walters family, David (who holds no grudge or idolatry towards him), Dane and his girlfriend, and Sherry's family. Bryant is there to talk to a school full of endangered youngsters.

He isn't allowed to say all that he wants to say, because, of course, talking about God is demonized in the nation's public school system. But none the less, he still manages to slip God's message into his motivational speech, at the half-court circle of the school's gym floor, to children at Martin Luther King Elementary, concerning ways they can uplift their community and stop the scourge of violence and drugs. "Always continue to read, never stop, because there is a book out there that gives you history's greatest lessons about love, forgiveness, and always trying to do the right thing, this one book if taken into your heart can change and rearrange everything in our city. I would say its name, but I don't want to get in trouble."

Just as he is beginning to wrap up what's turned out to be a passionate dialogue with the children about their concerns and fears, "BANG!" One side-shot travels completely through one knee, then, lodges in the cartilage of his other. In front of an entire auditorium full of beautiful black and Hispanic children, Michaels crumbles to the hardwood.

Masked gunmen have entered through each of the gym's three exit doors. Panicked, the frightened children scramble to nowhere.

One of the assailants shouts, "Shut up… shut up and sit down, now!" Shots fired into the ceiling help the children do as they're told.

Rendered a paraplegic, Michaels drags his legs behind him as he crawls towards the kids, thinking only of protecting them as he moves.

The other terrorists guard the doors as the person who shot 'Flight' stalks towards his victim with a powerful pistol down by his side. The perpetrator stops Michaels' slow, bloody crawl across the polished floor, when he steps on the back of one of Bryant's shattered knees.

"Stop your screaming and look at me." Michaels notices it's a female voice speaking, he rolls over flat onto his back.

She rips off her mask. Michaels' traumatized mind takes notice of her youthfulness. "I'm sorry, I'm sorry, please don't hurt these kids. What do you want from me?"

She leans in close to him. "You probably think that I want your money, don't you. You don't know me, but this is the face of the family you destroyed. And now, it has come back to destroy you."

"I haven't destroyed anyone!"

"Remember Sasha? She was one of your whores awhile back. Allow me a brief synopsis. She had a beautiful life, a loving husband, and a great daughter. That was until you came along and took our happiness away."

It's Gwen. David is spared from witnessing what is left of the daughter that he loves. Her hair has been cut to where it is almost bald, a swastika tattoo is inked into the flesh on her right cheek, with the word hate branded through the middle of it. She points her handgun at his face. Reflex causes Michaels to uselessly put his hand up to stop the bullet that he fears is coming. "I'm so sorry; I apologize to you, your father, and Sasha."

With an ice cold glare, Gwen notifies him. "It's too late for apologies."

"Your father misses you so much. He told me."

"How do you know my father?"

"David is a very good friend of mine, we go to church together."

"You go to church together. He's forgiven you after what you did to his family? Now I'm going to enjoy killing you that much more."

Gwen turns her attention to the children, "Hello boys and girls, guess what? We're going to play a game, but it's not really a game, it's your life. I know most of you have studied slavery in your history books. Well, from now on, until the day you die, you're going to have firsthand knowledge of the struggle your ancestors went through."

One of her fellow gunmen can't contain his enthusiasm any longer, he shouts slurs and fires shots into the ceiling. "Power to the almighty, pure America, pure America!" Gwen and the others join in and chant their rallying cry.

"Time to die, 'Flight'." Bryant gives up and accepts the fate that she has for him. His mind prays to the Lord to grant him admission into the kingdom of God.

Shooting first, a squadron of Anytown's finest burst through the doors, killing Gwen's gunmen instantly, "Put your hands up, now!" Gwen stands facing them, with Bryant on the floor, between her feet. Her hands are down at her sides, the gun casually dangles, in line with Bryant's chest.

She calmly informs the officers, "I can't do that... I just can't." The officers scream their demands at her again.

The enemy of life speaks to her, "Kill him, Gwen, your life is over anyway, don't let him live when you're going to die. Do it!"

Three shots ring out. Sadly, the first shot is from Gwen's weapon, the next two go through her forehead and neck.

She drops beside her victim. Bryant clutches his deeply heaving chest, as Gwen's dead eyes involuntarily stare into his as she gurgles on her own blood. With one hand over his own, he places his other over Gwen's heart, and with the love of God, Bryant Michaels speaks his last words, "Thank you, Father, for saving me. On our Judgment Day, I will ask forgiveness for the both of us." Gwen's gags stop, as does Bryant's heaving chest.

As the students are being hurried out of the building, the school's principal is questioned by two officers, "I have no idea how they could have gotten into our school so easily. Because of all of the violence out in the world, we just recently got our outer doors bulletproofed. We always, and I mean always, keep them locked, but they just walked right in. Where in the heck was our off-duty officer, he's always here? I haven't seen him since all of this began."

Alarm and suspicions grow within the police force.

Minutes after the shooting, six avenues away, Melvin has just arrived back at the apartment he still maintains with Dane. "What's up boy?"

"Hey, how ya doin', Mel?" Dane's eyes never peek up from the Bible he is reading, as he lies on the sofa.

With a snarl attached to his face, Melvin glares at Dane as he walks into the kitchen to retrieve a cold drink from the refrigerator. "Why you keep spendin' yo time readin' that bullshit lately? It's screwing you up from focusing on what's important, dog. You ain't even wearin' ya gold no more, you don't holla at the ladies, and we startin' ta get low on product. You call ya boys ta get that next shipment in yet? I only got ten keys left, so we gon need it in a few days."

Dane closes the Bible, then, sits up from his slouched position on the sofa. "I need to talk to you and Stamp about all of that."

Melvin detects the seriousness in his employer's voice, panicked, he comes running out of the kitchen, back into the living room. "What happened, don't tell me our Miami connect got locked, did they?"

"No, it's not like that…" Melvin breathes a sigh of relief, "It's not about them, it's about us."

"What's the problem now." He says with an annoyed tone.

"I'd rather wait until Stamp gets here to-"

"Naw nigga, tell me now."

"O.k. then, simply put, I can't do this anymore."

"What, can't do what anymore?"

Dane leans back, confident in his position. "I can't poison our people or ourselves any longer. I've changed, Melvin. Don't you see, can't you feel the evil in this world, how in spite of the heat outside, this world is getting colder? So many people are headed towards hell, and I don't want to go with them. And I don't want you to go either."

Melvin carelessly laughs as he flops down on the other sofa. "You need to quit reading that book. You're letting it fill your head with fear and doubt about what's real."

"That's not-"

"Yeah, it is. You gettin' scared, like everyone else, 'cuz you think our crazy ass President really is going to push the button?"

"It's not that, either. It's me, I know that the Bible is the truth. I know this is gonna sound kinda funny to you, but I can physically feel God's spirit."

Melvin screams, "Come on, man, don't start this shit. I don't need this right now!"

"I've been blessed so much, I can feel Jesus walking with me, Mel, if you'd think about it, dog. You know that he's real too."

Those words bring Melvin back to his father's supernatural knowledge, angered, he jumps up right into Dane's face, "What the hell is that supposed to mean?"

"I'm just saying, you used to go to church, I'm sure that you felt his presence back then."

Denial, couples with anger, to help Melvin block out any revelations that speak against the choices he's made. "So what you gon' do Dane? You gon' live off the hope that you're right, you gonna go back to havin' na'thin, being broke cuz you sittin' around waitin' on his ass?"

"I actually believed that I would be giving up so much more than I would get, if I gave my life to Jesus, but I was wrong, I've gained everything. All I've been able to hear lately is God's voice in my conscience saying, I want you back. I want you back."

Melvin despises it, but tears well up in his eyes, no matter how hard he fights. Melvin lies, "well God has never told me anything, so miss me wit that one."

"Melvin please, you know that I'm telling you the truth."

"Hey, you can quit with the tryin' to convert me act."

"That's exactly what you need to do, because something big is about to happen."

Scared to death of the answer, Mr. Toughguy tries to be nonchalant with his question, "What, so you're really scared that Jesus to about to come back?"

"Look at our world, Melvin. Look at all the crime, I ain't even talking about the murder rate, look at our crimes against each other for money, because we don't care about one another like we should. Think about what we'll do to each other for greed, how we're all scared of each other now, how much superficial crap we give our attention to. Look at how people have turned their back to God, this isn't some coincidence, it's just like the Bible says the last days will be. This is a real thing, and so is God."

"Man, people been talkin' that last days nonsense forever."

"So what, who knows how long the last days will last? You better be ready when they end, because this might be it. It seems our President is determined to make sure of that."

"Man, she ain't gon do na'thin."

"You can't be sure of that. Let's say she does, and China fires their bombs at us, are you absolutely positive that the choices you've made are the right ones, because once it's over, there is no going back. I'd hate for you to stand before God on Judgment Day knowing that you put your eggs in the wrong basket."

The devil speaks to Melvin, "He's just trying to scare you."

Melvin, "You know what, you're a grown man. You do what you do, if you want to backpedal from kingpin back to Joe Nobody, that's fine. Stamp and I will work out how we'll take your spot...," his darkened mind contemplates ways to deal with Stamp, and nothing is out of reason, "All you gotta do is take a trip with us down to Florida, we do a meet and greet with ya people, you tell them the situation, give us a great referral...," Melvin dusts off his hands, "and you're done, free to do and believe whatever you want. Everyone goes away happy."

"I can't do that."

Those words freeze not just Melvin's body, but also his heart. Silence fills the air. His eyes stare into Dane's, as he calmly speaks his eyes don't flinch. "Whoo boy...," Melvin walks over and has a seat right next to him, he calmly states, "I guess we got a mu'fucking problem on our hands, huh?"

The air between the two turns from chilly to awkward.

"Remember back a couple of years ago at that basketball game I took you too?"

"Yeah, I remember that. Ya boy, 'Flight' went off dat night...," he looks right at Dane, "he was killin' 'em."

"Yeah he was, but remember when I was talking about getting paid now and that you should not worry about God."

"Yeah, and you were right. Thank you."

"No, I was wrong and I've asked God to forgive me, just as I'm asking you. That is why I can't-"

Melvin leans closer in to him for a better listen. "A... you can't what again?" He asks while discreetly dropping his right hand to his side to shorten his reach.

"I won't do it. We're not going down there, and I'm not going to connect you to them. I love you too much to..."

Not more than a second later, Dane is facing the end of his earthly life. His eyes stare down the long, dark barrel of a black semi-automatic pistol.

"Don't make me kill you...," Melvin forcefully orders, "give me the numbers, right now! I ain't debatin' this shit wit you, bitch. You got the numbers somewhere in here, I will find them without you, if I have to, so you got until the end of my voice to start talkin'.'"

In total confidence, Dane speaks with ease, "God left himself in all of us. Melvin, you are good, I don't care what you think about yourself, how gangsta you have gotten, God's good is inside of you. There is no way that you will shoot me."

He can't believe that Dane is this calm. "You are fuckin' crazy, bruh. I'll shoot you."

"I'm not crazy. I know that God is inside his room, and all my angels surround me. They're not going to let you do anything to me."

It's so quick, it makes him question whether he really saw it, but he knows that he did. There was like five of them. They had no white wings with matching white gowns, no faces, but he knows that they were there right beside Dane.

"Mel, think about how you used to be, before all of this Bible Hoax stuff, all of the dreams you had of getting out of here, making a better life for yourself. Now, all you care about is money, what happened to doing enough, so you could go legit and get your cousins back?"

Melvin wants to take the rage he has for himself, for not following through on his plans, out on Dane; but he can't. He can think of punching, kicking, and shooting him, but divine forces hold him back. "Kill him... do not touch him," opposing forces speak their opinion in his mind.

He drops the gun and sits back down on the couch. He fights it with denials, but Melvin knows that he and Dane aren't the only ones in that room. "Just give me the numbers, Dane, and I won't ever bother you again, please."

"No Melvin, your life doesn't have to be like this, God can give you back everything that you allowed to be taken. He still loves you."

"If there is a God, he couldn't love me after all of the things I have done."

The Lord's supernatural powers intervene again and speak

through Dane, "He does love you, Mel, you just haven't noticed how hard he has been trying to make you see that. You felt Jesus, you knew He was real, why do you keep walking away?"

Dane can't believe what he just said, he asks himself, "How do I know that?"

'Lightening' striking twice is more than Melvin's fragile psyche can handle. "Are you Jesus, are you him?!"

The front door burst open, Stamp comes running in with his gun drawn, "Hey man, there's some crazy shit goin' on outside. I keep on hearing gunshots."

Melvin's tormented face looks across at Stamp, then, shrivels into a lake of emotion. "How do they know, Stamp? Who keeps telling them about me?"

"How do they know what? Who? What are you talking about?"

Dane, "I don't know how I know. I just know, Mel."

"How do they know?" Melvin stands up, that single question continually rewinds in his brain, so much so that everything else is blocked out.

Dane tries to stop Melvin from leaving the apartment, but Stamp steps in and stops him. "Yo, let him go. He looks like he needs some time to be by himself."

Stamp isn't so innocent either; he's had thoughts of his own hostile takeover, just like Melvin. He is fully aware of the horrors going on outside.

Throughout the hallways, terrified neighbors, young and old, screaming and crying, run by Melvin. He takes no notice of them.

Just a moment too late, Stamp's conscience gets the better of him, at the doorway, he shouts at Melvin, though he can not see him. "Mel, don't go out there. People are going crazy... Mel!?"

He is so deep within himself, Melvin can't tune in the random screaming, or the gunfire, that is coming from outside, as he limply trudges along down the cement chipped stairs that draw him nearer to the building's exit.

Melvin is having serious doubts about the basket he chose to place his 'faith eggs' in. "What my dad, Dane, and Faith all said… that day in Me-ma's room, was there a purpose to it all?"

Bang, bang, bang! Immediately, upon his exit from the building, a masked man with an automatic machine gun busting off from the back of a speeding pickup, snaps him back into the moment. He runs back inside for cover from the gunshots and towards God to cover his soul.

With a hurried voice, Melvin speaks to God, "Why did I choose this world? God, please save me, I'm sorry, I don't want to die!"

Clarity fills his thoughts, as he races back up the steps to the apartment, "Dear God, you gave me so many clues, you tried to tell me so many times, in so many ways, my whole life you've done that. I need you and accept you, Savior. I repent for my sins, Father. I'm leaving my will, and accepting yours', right now!" In that instant, all of the things Melvin has come to care so much about over the last couple of years suddenly mean nothing.

Pop, pop… pop, pop, pop! Two seconds, five shots, five executions.

Everyone alive runs, trampling, crawling over each other as they flee towards the front of the church as four masked gunmen rush in from the back. The two hundred and some captives realize there is nowhere to escape the small, single exit church as they all bunch up together.

One of the gunmen shouts, "Calm down, everyone, calm down!" After repeating that command several more times until everyone is compliant, he calls out, "We kindly ask for all foreigners, which means, Mexicans, Blacks, Jews, Muslims, gays, all none pure Caucasians, please step over to this sidewall. Where you will be set free and released."

"He said released," fear and panic erases clear thinking as spirits lift for those who fit this category. Feet move swiftly, believing that they will be allowed to go home.

David takes notice of the commonality between those who have been shot. He hears distant whispers that turn his attention to his right, "Damn it, she's one of us, I didn't mean to shoot her. She jumped in front of him," one killer says to another.

He is talking about the woman, whose violently twitching body lies at his feet. This body lies partially on top of a teenage Hispanic appearing male; from his angle, David can only partially see their faces, but he sees enough to know that he has lost two loved ones'.

"Oh dear God…," David struggles to keep his stricken heart from enticing his mouth to cry out, "it's Carlos and Faith."

Faith Jylin Tillman is gone. Blurry eyed, David looks around at everyone's faces', in search of Brandon's, they find him. David's heart breaks as he watches, from across the room, Brandon's sorrowed eyes stare down at his son.

Sherry, who had lost sight of her mother during the stampede, sees her now, as does Mary.

If Faith had it to do all over again, she wouldn't want to leave this earth any other way. Her last act, her last movement, the last thing that she will be remembered for on this earth will be what she lived the last twelve years of her life doing; acting out of love for others. The last grain has emptied into the bottom of her life's hourglass. The race God set before her, and Bryant Michaels, has been fulfilled in full.

Her earthly life is the blueprint for all life on earth to follow; she went from living to do such wrong, to accepting God, and dying with only love for others in her heart. Do not cry for her; it is her time to move on to a new chapter in her life; this temporary life is over for her, the next time her eyes open she will see the glory of everlasting glory and joy.

No, don't go, it's a trap." To no avail, David quietly tries to discourage a young woman close to him not to move over with the others; but Stacy Stunning won't listen.

Even in this most horrific of moments, her elegance, the internal calm and beauty that has always been her strength, will not be weakened. Stacy takes hold of Ricky's hand and softly gazes into the eyes of the man she loves. They don't need to speak it, they both know exactly what is about to happen.

From his wheelchair, Ricky is eye level with his wife's third trimester stomach. Through softly spoken words he tells his unborn child goodbye. A smile rises to Stacy's lips, "Don't worry, honey, we'll be just fine. God loves us."

Suddenly, a bronze skinned man panics, he barrels out from the back of the pack, running straight towards those who bind him. The only thing that his desperate mind sees is that exit door behind his attackers. Two shots through his heart and face ends his quest early. The fate of the room's minorities suddenly becomes clear to them.

Stacy steps forward and speaks up for the entire group, "Will you please give us one minute to pray."

The terrorists laugh, their leader speaks for their group, "Pray about what, to what?"

"So that we can pray to the God that is in this room with us... at this very moment."

Every Christian hears her words, but only one is blessed with a revelation about it.

"No bitch, we don't have time for your nonsense...," he looks through the groups to make sure they're divided out, "do we have everyone gathered now? Good, let's begin."

Stacy's heart 'skips' a beat, when she sees the strength and love of her husband's actions. "If they are to die, then I will gladly die with them." Ricky wheels himself over in front of the minority group.

"If you want to die with these disgusting people... fine."

David coldly stares the lead gunmen right in the eyes, "Then I will die, too, unlike you, I'll only be dead for a second."

Sherry, "You must kill me also..."

The sweetest voice of all steps forward with a total confidence in her words. Mary, "If you are going to kill my mommy and my grandmommy, then you will have to kill me, too. I am a

Christian just like them, and we're not running from you evil meanies anymore."

Sherry takes hold of her hand, she's proud and panicked all at once, "No Mary, thank you, I love you, but stay over here," she tries to walk away from her, but Mary stays with her step for step, "No mommy, you just started being my mom. I want to go to heaven with you and grandma."

In all, eighteen of the forty nine 'pure whites' inside of God's temple, with fleshy apprehension, but an even stronger love and brotherhood for their fellow man, acquired through their faith and belief, position themselves to lay down their life for their brothers and sisters through Christ.

The lead gunman tries to soothe the dread and angst in the thirty one persons left alone, "Don't be alarmed white America, I know this seems horrible, and cruel, but in a short time, you will come to realize our world is much better without the cancers these races bring. Power to the new, almighty, pure America! Say it with us." Ruled by fear, they all reluctantly shout the chant along with their captors, as these agents of hell steady themselves and position their weapons for slaughter.

Those who face this firing squad have made their decision, or been forced into it, and they have conceded their fate. They believe that it is their destiny, that God has called them home. They mumble prayers and think final thoughts about their life and their loved ones; but one of God's creations stands tall against such defeat. One of God's children was divinely reminded, through Stacy, about the absolute, unending power that his Lord, by promises of their shared covenant with Jesus, has given to him. The Holy Spirit within his soul moves him to call upon that power, so that no weapon formed against him will prosper.

Brandon Myers, confidently, in perfect faith, steps to the forefront with an unwavering announcement, "There will be no more dying today, I declare with the authority given to me, through the blood of Jesus Christ, that there will be no dying today!" Those words reverberate off of the walls and ears of everyone who hears them.

Out of the corner of his eye, Brandon spots a smile. It belongs to his son, who though badly injured has coyly been playing dead beneath Faith.

Farther encouraged by the son he thought he had lost, Brandon powerfully repeats his decree.

The lead gunman looks at his cohorts and laughs, as they enjoy themselves, he points to one, "Would you please do me the honor of blowing his head off."

"Thank you. I would love to... What the hell!" His firearm jams; it will not do what his human hands command it.

Heaven's angels have heard Brandon's declaration. They answer one man's faith, one man's power to speak over one hundred deaths out of existence, because as promised by the Bible, spoken from the very mouth of Jesus Christ, and closely quoted by Brandon Myers as he watches their guns jam, "I have been given the keys to the kingdom of heaven, that whatever I bind on earth will be bound in heaven...," as the men uselessly 'click' their weapons of mass destruction like little cap guns, his mouth salivates, spit flies after his words, his powerful, deep voice rises to a shout, "the mountain will move today! The mountain will move today!"

Brandon stares each man down. They cower, not to the sight of him, but to the power and glory that they see surrounding him.

There is not a shadow of doubt in Brandon's faith that today, he will be going home with his wife and son, and being cornered by enough weaponry to start a small army is not going to change that! There was but one chance, one option, to prevent a massacre, and Brandon's deep belief, and his knowledge of his authority given by God's Word, helped him to take full advantage of it.

The thunderous announcement of police sirens suddenly hits everyone's ears. The sound of tires screeching to a halt just outside of the building gives relief or brings panic; depending on who you are.

One of the men, "Run! Hurry up, let's get out of here!"

The assailants are all shot dead along the sidewalk's pavement outside of the building.

Inside, there is no tremendous celebration; no one champions Brandon by throwing him on their shoulders to parade him around the room. These Christians know that they are still breathing, not because of what was done by Brandon, but because of what was done through him and Stacy. Everyone falls to their knees and gives thanksgiving to their savior of today, yesterday, and forever more.

─── CHAPTER TWENTY ONE ───

And so it begins. The largest, most coordinated and secretive, grassland coup in American history, simultaneously, spreads with schizophrenic precision across every major inner city this country encamps.

The hatred within man has reached its boiling point. Even as they hear of their comrades being wounded, killed, or arrested, the male and female members of White America Coalition press on for days before they are totally neutralized.

America's pulse races as chaos surrounds them from every direction. The public is stunned by the singular focus of the government's extremely violent crackdown of these separatists. No questions are asked, dropping their weapons and raising their hands in the air means nothing, their surrender or capture means that person took a bullet in the head.

The men and women within the coalition didn't get what they desired, which was to return America to its shameful, oppressive era of slavery and one race domination.

They did not succeed, but yet Satan smiles, for inside of the faithless; he has yet again heightened fears and hatred along racial and cultural lines. He uses what's happening on the political front concerning the world's apocalyptic fears and this murderous coup to push America once again to the edge of total chaos.

Just days earlier, as the first shots by those involved in the takeover are fired; seated in front of a secret panel that unfolds from the north wall in the Oval Office, President Thames stares at a framed photo of her greatly missed husband and daughter. For the past hour, she's been daydreaming about their missed opportunities for fun and joys, "Oh Sidney, Cherie, I wish that you were still with me, to help me through this time."

Nicole's 'dreamscenes' flip to a conversation that she and her husband would be having from atop their bed after sharing in some of the greatest lovemaking they have ever made. She remembers him as such a kind man, Nicole is sure that at this very moment he would be trying to talk her out of doing this. She delights in thinking about how firm she would stand against his wishes, the power she would feel against his passionate feelings and wants, "I have to do this, Sidney, I can't allow them to embarrass or push us around any longer."

The necessary codes are encrypted, the key is in place, the go ahead has been given, all that remains is a simple twist to the left. Civilization and the fulfillment of man's worldly prophecy rest in her hands.

The Word of God enters her free willing mind. Thames thinks about some scriptures she knows from the Bible, "Love thy neighbor... be slow to anger... trust God, lean not on your own understanding," but instead of embracing them as God would have it, she thinks as she would have it.

She giggles, "It's funny how crazy life has turned out to be, it turns out that I have to be God, and do what is best for America and the rest of the good people on this planet."

Jon Wilhelm burst through the doors just as Thames places her fingers on the key and takes a deep breath. "Mrs. President, you have to see this!"

He sprints up to her with a small television monitor in his hands. "You have to do something. There is a large band of white supremacists that have gone into the cities and begun shooting people at random. Our field Intel says that the goal of their mission is to incite a national race riot to purify America or return it to the days of slavery…," Jon didn't notice before, but now he does, he sees that the President's hand is on that key, "we have to wait and do this later, you have to take care of this matter now, before it gets even more out of hand!"

President Thames solemnly responds as she watches the footage of the evil sweeping across the country, "That's what we have our different levels of law enforcement for, they'll handle it. Time's up, Jon… It has to be now!"

"But, this is going on nationwide, this isn't isolated, it's…"

Thames roars, "Are the warplanes ready!"

Wilhelm reluctantly answers his commander. "Yes, they're just waiting for your command; they could be in place in just a few hours."

"Spectacular. Give them the word. Leave me alone, I need to think."

Thames refocuses as she places her hand back onto the key. "If there ever was a God… let him be with us now."

Satan. "Do it."

Five hours later, Thames flips the key left.

Those who have turned their back to the Lord, those who have but act as though they haven't, Christians who say that God is always on their mind and in their heart but rarely ever is, people from all walks of religions that truly walk their faith in the teachings of the Lord, it doesn't matter where they are at spiritually, starting today; God takes their minds' off of everything but him. He gets all that he ever wanted. The entire world is about to know or knowingly deny that 'God so loved the world'.

Just as the remaining hold-outs of the 'White America' takeover are taken down, the time has come for everyone to know, beyond a shadow of a doubt, that God is real, and He is here right now! The soon to be crowned highest rated program ever in television history begins to tell the story.

"Hello America, this is Stan Bather, on America's number one station for breaking news…," the nation immediately sees Stan's uncomfortable disposition as he robots through his job with sorrowful eyes, "there is an incredible report coming out from the Gaza strip, Jerusalem to be exact, that the Bible Hoax scroll, which so many people have come to accept as true, was nothing but a hoax itself." Heart stopping panic sets in across the world as this news breaks.

"For this report, we take you to Lucy Goldstein outside of the world renowned Historical Sciences of Christian Faith building in Jerusalem."

"Thank you, Stan. Right now, inside of this building behind me, the world's best archeological scientists, some of which are the same scientists who conducted Israel's testing of the writing found by John Richards, are looking at a newly discovered writing that dispels the validity of the 'Bible Hoax' writing. An Israeli dig team, almost four days ago to the minute, found a new scroll written specifically to all of mankind.

"In just over three hours, we are told, in what is sure to be a stunning, deeply resounding press conference held by the Israeli Prime Minister; he says that he will tell the world exactly what is written on that scroll."

The deafening sounds of picture snapping cameras fills the air as the Jewish Prime Minister steps to the podium. "Just tens of feet away from where the first manuscript was found, days ago, our great country's scientists unearthed another message written to mankind. Tests have concluded that it dates back to the exact same time-period as the Bible Hoax scroll. It says-" The hearts of billions beat in their throats'.

"Brethren, why won't you trust His love, but trust evidence that speaks against Him? He still loves you wholly, why do you only give a part of you or none at all? Why did you allow the enemies of faith to fool you away from God's love, when he has entered your mind and showed you that he is here?" The Prime Minister pauses to bring the message to its crescendo, "and lastly, it reads, 'Who will become wiser after is, their ultimate test of faith?'"

The same four countries that gave the world its definitive answer on the first writing are allowed to test this new finding. When their testing is complete, all will admit to the same level of authenticity that they did on the first one.

Complete clarity comes to the minds' of all true worshipers. The Lord puts into their thoughts what he will now have them to do. God sends them out to disperse his message loud and clear.

"This was never real?" Panic, shame, fear, and condemnation, fill the hearts' and minds' of the faithless. They fear that they have chosen wrong. The faithless assume that God has or will damn them all to hell, conspiracy theories and inaccurate conclusions abound, as the same hysteria when the 'Bible Hoax' was first confirmed reignites, "What if this was our Judgment Day? We were tested, our fate was decided when we chose against God. I think those damn Americans knew this was all a lie from the very beginning, I should have never trusted everything they say. I'm going to hell, God will never love me again after what I've done. Why didn't I give my life to him when I had the chance, now it's too late." They think of everything except for the right answer.

They don't understand what this was all about, as is their nature, they assume the worst. Now that their arrogance is gone, their pride is no more, they see their level of nonbelief for what it is. The fear of God is back! He knew that it would be, that is why, days before, he graced the world with a miracle that only one person on earth will ever know of.

Whispered thoughts energize her panic, "What happened... Where did they go?"

Another whisper answers, "I am here."

President Nicole Thames can't take her eyes off of the four

dimensional radar screen in front of her, "They were moving, flying… now they're gone. They've just disappeared."

Jon enters her office. She looks at him with angst, but his mannerisms are not how she expects them to be during such a grave crisis. Her frightened, searching eyes observe his calm, ordinary walk. "Call the Naval commanders; ask them if they are seeing what I'm seeing. The bombs have disappeared off of my screen. It's like they've vanished."

"What are you talking about, the bombs are still on our ships. Nothing has been fired, you know that. They're still primed and ready to launch the moment this situation that's going on around the country ends."

"What?"

"Madam President, you definitely made the right decision to delay the launch, but our forces are still on high alert and can be in place within hours, if anything changes… Nicole, why are you looking at me like you don't understand what I am saying?"

She's known Jon Wilhelm for years and years, so she can tell when he's in one of his playful moods; and this isn't one of them. Her thoughts, "He believes every word that he is saying."

She asks, "So I never launched the missiles?"

He glares at her with a befuddled stare. "Nicole, are you o.k.? You decided that you were going to, but remember, we talked it through and decided that it would be best to wait. We have more pressing matters to handle right now."

With her head hung low, under her breath, she speaks to herself, "This can't be happening, I know that I twisted that key…," she looks over at it, the key is still in its vertical position as if it has never been touched, "just hours ago he was in this office. I told him to leave, I twisted the key. I know I did… I think so."

Her head rises, her eyes stare into Jon's chest, "So no one knows anything about what happened?"

"What do you mean? There is nothing to know. We haven't done anything."

"Jon, I need to be alone, right now."

Jon has a confused stare, "Are you sure, would you like for me to call your doctor?"

"No, I just need some time to clear my head."

"O.K... Oh, as we speak, your speech addressing the country's crisis is being prepared. We need to move quickly, do you think you'll feel up to it, in say an hour?"

"Yes, I'm sure I will."

As Jon walks out, the Holy Spirit returns and reveals the simple answer, "This is another chance."

Thames' can feel His supernatural presence inside of the room with her and it does not come not in condemnation, but in love. Ashamed, her first thought tells her to make a run for her bottle. Her second thought tells her that the running needs to stop. Her spirit informs her that she has a power much greater than what vodka has to offer.

Her heart wilts as she thinks about the personal decisions she has made that have lead her to this moment. Her broken soul leads her into a kneeling position, so that her heart and mouth can return back to prayer.

Thames humbly begs God for forgiveness, she's willing to do anything to be close to him again. The faults within her character, that have lead her here, are revealed to her. She makes a firm, unwavering decision to right the wrongs inside of her. "Through you, great Father, I will wipe my slate clean and give myself another chance, only because you have given me another chance. And this time, I will not walk away from you and your guidance, because I truly, for the first time in my life, have belief and trust in you. I know this was you! Glory be your name, I dedicate my life to serving you, Savior. I will lead this country like no leader ever has before, because you have given me a second chance. I will serve this country the way that you, not me, nor anyone else who is not of our like-mind, would have me to serve it. Thank you for another chance, God. Amen."

Rays of sunshine creep over humanity's horizon, our Lord

sends David and Brandon out immediately to be a blessing to others. From the pavement of Brandon's upper middle class cul-de-sac, they speak to a large group of his surrounding neighbors, many of whom will then go out and minister what they've learned to their family and friends.

Just like He will do through thousands of faithful followers, God's desires are spoken through Brandon's and David's earthly voices. Brandon starts it off, "When you love God, his Word will dictate your path, that's all God wants is for us to have a consistent love for him, like he does for us. That's what got us in trouble in the first place, because we had come to trust in what this physical world has to say, instead of having faith in Him."

A youngster from the middle of the crowd shouts, "Are you sure that because we didn't have faith and we dropped him from our lives, that we'll have another chance to reach heaven? I think that we're already dead."

The crowd waits with baited breath for their answer, David steps up to speak, "No, we all are very much alive, this is the beginning of a new chance for us, through him. We've been totally exposed now, that's our blessing. Now we can stop hiding behind this world and really see where our heads' are spiritual, and not make the same mistakes ever again."

Someone screams out through a rattled voice, "He doesn't love us anymore, He can't after what we've done!"

Brandon, "God can and he does love you, love is the only thing that he knows how to do! This was meant to make all of us see that playtime is over, that all of our pretense and excuses are finished, that we can no longer choose this world over him. Look at the chaos the world has lead us into. All God has ever wanted was to show us glory, to bring blessings to our lives', but he can't until we become the faith trusting people that we were supposed to be all along."

David blurts out a divine revelation to the people, "Tonight, throughout the world, our Father will show each of us that he has always been here."

That night, as He's done with Melvin, Bryant, and David, God, through their memories, God shows earth's men and women all of the different times in their life that he tried to get their attention. They see that those things which they called coincidences or luck, those things that passed so easily by their conscience, was him showing them the right way through life's events. Most come to realize and appreciate all of the different moments that God tried to convince them of his loving presence in their life. Before, so many discarded these precious moments, but no more.

The faithless begin to build a foundation with the Lord, as he gives them revelations about their spiritual shortcomings. Across the world, billions truly accept what they have to do, I'm not talking about a decision based on the emotions of the moment, they gain lasting acceptance. This whole ordeal, this back and forth with the very core of what and who they are, has shaken the binders off of how the masses see their flesh, this physical world, the devil's tricks, and their COMMITMENT to their spiritual faith.

Their denials are gone. Their procrastination exits. Society no longer feels awkward, embarrassed, or ashamed for loving the only living God. Just as they played follow the leader, as the world lead them astray, now earth's citizens flock to be like those who walk the Christian walk.

Most of society chooses life! They bury their pride, their thoughts and ideas on how best to manage their life, they finally, completely trust everything that the Bible says to them. They repent for their sins and begin a new walk. No longer are their good deeds absent of faith, now their faith leads to good deeds. Here and abroad, God's loved ones decide to take the long way around to meet all of their desired successes, and when they do, God shows them a quicker way to reach their desired goals. He showers them, collectively and individually, with small miracles in their daily life just to show them how much he loves who they have become.

You all will be happy to know that Sasha is not one of the few who will remain so lost within the world's lies and deceptions that she can not open her eyes and heart to see the truth sitting out before her. She is a new woman through Christ, her materialism, arrogance, and various other wrong ways of thinking can now only be seen through her life's rear-view mirror. Sasha gets herself in order before returning to the husband that she is now free to love properly, as God would have her to love.

The listeners finally, truly do believe, setting the stage for their generation to teach future generations. Their ultimate test of faith was put before them, and largely they failed. But because of God's one-track mindset towards loving his creations, he didn't quit on them, he allowed them to unmask their selfishness, disbelief, mistrust, and excuses, for themselves, so that it laid before them and they could no longer deny its existence, or his.

Through man's own freewill, and the grace of their Father, they no longer need to witness His physical form for absolute confirmation of his existence; they see him vividly through their eyes of faith.

In just a few short weeks, the world begins to see huge changes. The media watches much more carefully the images that it projects out to its watchers and listeners. Only in positive ways does race figure into people's decision-making. It's cool for them to respect their bodies now, because honoring God's wishes is cool. As fathers return to the home to teach Christian family values to their children, the plague of wayward youth and the crimes they commit plummets. Led by President Thames, leaders of nations figure out ways to trade in their violent clashes, in exchange, for peaceful and lasting resolutions. People all across the globe crave the overflowing benefits that come with loving God. They honor God by honoring his Word; in return, he honors them with abundance in all they desire.

Don't believe for another second that their new world cannot be our new world, that this is not realistic. Every one of these abundant blessings can be ours', we just have to put ourselves, our faith, in position to receive them. If we'll choose God's ways over our own, the Lord is OBLIGATED to rain his PROMISED prosperity upon us, so why do we continue to choose the world's poverty?

Man has come home; weary from his battles. He lays his head down onto his Father's lap, thanks him, then, closes his eyes. He now rests unworried, assured that he is where success is truly found. Man's trust and hopes are in the Lord... until.

Ask yourself, is it going to take such extreme measures to get many of us out of our disobedience and disbelief and into following his will and direction?

In these, the last days, God wants to show us that these don't have to be the last days. If we turn to Him, completely, He will end our doubts, then, we will change the wrongs of this world, instead of accepting them. He is not going to do it for us. Our generation doesn't have to be the generation that fulfills the Bible's prophecies concerning these perilous days.

We have to make a change, because there is no future in us staying the same.

Our Father is alive, and He is here right now!

GOD BLESS US ALL.